OTHERS

Also by James Herbert

The Rats
The Fog
The Survivor
Fluke
The Spear
The Dark
Lair
The Jonah
Shrine
Domain
Moon
The Magic Cottage
Sepulchre
Haunted
Creed
Portent
The Ghosts of Sleath
'48

Graphic Novels

The City
(Illustrated by Ian Miller)

Non-fiction

By Horror Haunted
(Edited by Stephen Jones)

James Herbert's Dark Places
(Photographs by Paul Barkshire)

JAMES HERBERT

OTHERS

MACMILLAN

First published 1999 by Macmillan

an imprint of Macmillan Publishers Ltd
25 Eccleston Place, London SW1W 9NF
Basingstoke and Oxford

Associated companies throughout the world

ISBN 0 333 76117 0 (Hardback)
ISBN 0 333 76136 7 (Trade paperback)

Copyright © James Herbert 1999

3 5 7 9 8 6 4 2

A CIP catalogue record for this book is available from
the British Library.

Typeset by SetSystems Ltd, Saffron Walden, Essex
Printed and bound in Great Britain by
Mackays of Chatham plc, Chatham, Kent

Only in this world can there be no perfection.

His is the House of Pain.
His is the Hand that makes.
His is the Hand that wounds.
His is the Hand that heals.

H. G. Wells,
The Island of Doctor Moreau

1

My redemption began in Hell.

It was a day like any other – except there are no days in that singular (in both senses of the words) place. No minutes, no hours, weeks, or years. No seconds either. There is no time in Hell, you see. There just *is*. That's the hell of it.

There I ruminated under the faintest light from above, nameless, Godless, with no sense of humour at all – I existed as a wretched and self-sorry soul, all reflection and no projection – contemplating the base, wasted life I'd once lived. Regrets? Too many to mention, but occasion enough to remember them all. Credits? Not enough to dwell upon. No, the balance was tilted in the worst direction and at the most extreme angle. Legions in this (literally) God-forsaken place still couldn't figure out what they'd done wrong – or, more accurately, why it was deemed so damned offensive – while others understood only too well. The former would come to know eventually, but in the meantime, theirs was a different kind of torment. As I pondered my own iniquities, a light suddenly brightened a corner of my dark 'cell'.

Two of them appeared, tall and seraphic, their radiance pushing back the shadows around me, guarding themselves against contamination from this murky realm I inhabited (interesting how the ancient artists intuitively had got it right when they depicted bright auras enveloping the holy spirits on their sojourns into the infectious world of mankind) and I was blinded until they wished their dimmers to a more comfortable level. Both wore annoyingly benevolent smiles.

1

'Good day to you,' one of them said as though time had relevance.

I nodded back, wary and too surprised by their visit to appreciate the break in the routine.

'We hope we didn't disturb you,' greeted the other one, neither sarcasm nor irony in his manner.

'Glad of the company,' I returned, all nervous humility and dread.

The first entity, essence – *angel* if you like – sensed my fear. 'Don't be alarmed. We're here to comfort, not chastise.'

Chastise? Nobody had chastised me since I'd arrived. The torment was too subtle and yes, too *drastic*, for that.

'Not more punishment, then?' I asked half-pleadingly.

'Oh, we wouldn't say that,' replied the second, and they both glanced at each other.

'Something punishing perhaps, but not really punishment,' said the first.

I groaned. 'Something worse than this?'

'Not worse. I told you we're here to comfort you. No, this is something infinitely better.'

He smiled down at me and I took in a countenance so serene, so pure, that tears blurred my vision.

'A chance,' he announced before straightening again.

My thoughts, as well as my emotions, raced. A chance? A chance for what? To leave this place? To attain a new level? A chance to escape the perpetual misery of an existence without hope? What did he – *it* – mean?

He knew my thoughts. 'All of those things,' he said, beckoning me to rise so that I wouldn't have to gaze up at him any more. 'But more importantly, an opportunity to make amends.'

Instead of rising I knelt before them both. 'Anything,' I said. 'I'll do anything.'

'I wonder,' was his response.

'It would be a harsh test.' The second one gently loosened my grip on his robe. 'And it's more probable that you'll fail. If that is the outcome, then there really is no hope for you.'

'I don't understand.' I looked from one to the other.

No 1 took me by the elbow and drew me up. 'We have a tradition on the, er, uppermost level.'

'The Good Place?'

He gave a slight bow.

'Heaven?'

His smile twitched. 'If you like.'

'Anything,' I pleaded. 'Just tell me what you want me to do.' I admit, I was weeping floods by now. You had to know what Hell is like.

'Calm yourself,' he soothed. 'Stay your tears and listen.'

Angel 2 started to explain. 'Every half-millennium we are allowed to choose a few souls for . . .'

'We call it the Five Hundred Year Plenary Indulgence . . .' No 1 interrupted helpfully.

'. . . whereby all grievous and venal sins of the chosen souls are forgiven, their spirits become untainted once more. As they were before Earthly birth. They are able . . .'

'. . . eventually . . .'

'. . . to enter the Kingdom and at last find their peace.'

It was too much for me. I sank to my knees again, disturbing the vapours that swirled low to the floor of my cubette. 'You've chosen me . . .' I burbled as my hands again caught the hems of their gowns.

I heard a throat clearing, a sound of disapproval, and immediately let go, afraid of irritating these wise and wonderful creatures. I remained doubled over though, my nose disappearing into the mists.

'You and one or two others,' Angel 2 corrected.

'Thank you, oh thank – '

No 1 cut me short. 'In your lifetime you were thoroughly wicked and your punishment here is richly deserved.'

'I know, I kn– ' It was my own sobs, like sharp hiccups, that interrupted the self-mortification.

No 1 had paused. 'Yes, yes, it's never too late for tears, but please save them for after we've gone,' he admonished, a little impatiently I thought, given the stress I was under.

Well, wailing, gnashing of teeth and the beating of breasts was the norm in this place, but I guess it could be upsetting – or just plain tedious – for visitors. I snuffled into my hand and choked back further lamentation. If they didn't want woe, then woe there wouldn't be. A few snivelling whimpers maybe, just to show I was truly contrite, but nothing distracting. Besides, I was desperate to hear what was on offer.

'You were blessed with so many gifts for your test-time on Earth, yet you squandered them all, used them for your own self-gratification.'

'Yes, I know, I know,' I agreed with a barely-repressed sniffle.

'You were guilty of hedonism . . .'

'Yes.'

'. . . sensualism . . .'

'Yes.'

'. . . eudaemonism . . .'

'Er . . .'

'. . . and you used your charm, your wit and your exceptional presence to cheat and humble those around you. Duplicity and betrayal was your canon, to lie and abuse was your doctrine. You debased the worthy and downtrod the already downtrodden.'

'Well, I . . .'

Angel 2 added his own condemnation. 'A libertine and a roué.'

'Both a philanderer and a gigolo.'

'Indeed, a rake of the lowest order.' No 2 didn't want to be outdone.

'You were a great star in a celluloid firmament. A moving star . . .'

'Uh, mov*ie* star, actually,' I corrected.

'. . . in the place they call Holy Wood.'

I felt it unwise to correct him again; no point in ruffling his feathers (just an expression – they don't really have wings. They don't really have bodies or voices either, but let's not get pedantic).

'Women adored you, men admired you.'

'Until they got to know you,' No 2 added darkly. 'The people worshipped your debonair image; to them you were a devil-may-care sophisticate, whose bluff exterior secreted a caring and sensitive core. Or so they thought. The public only knew you for the black and white image you portrayed.'

And they *hadn't* come to chastise me?

'But most wickedly of all, you caused premature death and suicide. You caused despair and yes, even insanity to the ones who loved you most and who forgave your amorality and hardness of heart.'

I offered no excuses. I had once before, at my Judgement, and they'd got me nowhere. This time I kept my mouth shut.

From their thunderous countenances I thought they'd changed their minds about giving me a second chance, but it was Angel 2 who threw some light into the shade: 'However, you did have some – *not many mind* – redeeming qualities.'

I kept my lips clamped tight, even though a small, tingling excitement was beginning to lift my spirit once more.

'And it was those few – very few – redeeming qualities,' he went on, ' that gave us cause to review your case. It seems you were not altogether a *bad* person, although there are those among us who disagree about that. In fact it was the Final Arbiter – you know *Who* I mean by that – who made the decision to allow you another chance. You might just save your own soul if . . .' and he made it sound like a big *IF* '. . . you are willing to take up the challenge.' His raised hand halted further gibberings from me. 'True repentance is not so easy, you know. Hell isn't necessarily just here, it can be found in other places, and if you go back . . .'

'Go back?' My body snapped up so suddenly that you

5

might have heard my spine crack – *if* I'd had a spine and *if* I'd had a body. 'You mean . . .'

They nodded as one and there was an odd sadness to their demeanour. 'It's a most serious thing,' No 1 said mournfully and No 2 repeated just as mournfully, 'A most serious thing.'

'For if you fail, you will be lost to us forever, you will never be allowed another opportunity to save your soul. Your damnation will truly be eternal . . .'

'And even worse than this,' his partner added.

I gulped. 'Worse?'

'Oh, much worse. Infinitely worse. Perdurably worse.' Angel 2 was shaking his head in pity. 'So think carefully before you agree to a new life and the harsh reveille it will bring.'

'I . . . I won't go back as myself?'

'There has only been one Resurrection – two if you count Lazarus, and eventually he had to give up his body again. Besides, you left your Earthly vessel almost fifty – in human-kind terms – years ago. You'd create quite a stir if you turned up in it once more.'

Fifty years? It could have been fifty thousand for all I knew.

'You'll find that your old world has changed considerably since you left it, and part of your atonement will be the loss of the privileges and gifts you once had, so we urge you again to think carefully before you decide.'

It took me all of two timeless seconds to make up my mind. But I chose my words with more care than I'd made the decision. 'Let me make amends,' I begged. 'Please give me the chance of a new Judgement.'

The Angels continued to regard me pityingly. 'There will be conditions,' No 1 said.

'Just tell me what I have to do.'

'One of those conditions is that you won't know.'

'But how can I – '

'You will choose what is right. Or perhaps you will choose what is wrong. It will be entirely up to you.'

And so saying they left me. Just wafted away so that I stared into darkness and shadows once more. Then I lowered my head and wailed.

All this, of course, metaphorically speaking.

2

She began hesitantly, her gaze never leaving mine, even as she drew a long dark cigarette from a pearl and silver case. She tapped the filtered end unnecessarily against the metal, an old-fashioned gesture that made me smile – inwardly. Shelly – she had already impressed on me there was no 'e' before the 'y' – Ripstone looked anywhere between thirty-five and forty, one of those not pretty but handsome women who had time and money to keep their figures trim and their skin soft. Only a faint regiment of fine lines marching across her upper lip and spreading from the outer corners of sad, mascaraed eyes spoilt the illusion, but that was only on close inspection – and I'd been inspecting her closely from the moment she'd walked into my office to sit in the chair facing my desk. Bottle-blonde hair – ash-blonde, I suppose you'd call it – the tips, curling beneath her chin, struggling to meet below the jawline as if to hide those other wrinkles, those mean, tell-tale give-the-game-away neck furrows that were the bane of maturing women. Her neat grey suit was Escada, or a fair copy of, and her high-heels Italian (I was good at that kind of thing), but her voice, whose vowels became more flattened and her mid-word *t*s more absent as our meeting progressed, was ill-disguised estuary (I figured southside Thames, maybe Gravesend or Dartford, no further east than that – accents were another thing I was good at). Shelly Ripstone exuded new money, both in apparel and voice – even her scent was Poison – and I had no hang-up with that. In fact, I kind of liked it: it made her more human,

8

more vulnerable, someone with whom I could empathize. Let's face it, we all try to be more than we are and there's no harm in that.

She took a thin Dunhill lighter from her purse and lit the cigarette. 'D'you mind?' she said as an afterthought.

I shook my head. 'Go ahead.'

'Would you . . . ?' She lifted the pearl and silver case from the purse again and offered it towards me, another hint at her origins (the wealthy middle classes rarely shared their straights with strangers).

I shook my head again and she seemed fascinated by the awkwardness of the movement. Mint-flavoured smoke drifted across the desk at me.

'Can I ask who recommended my agency?' I enquired to interrupt the apparent attraction.

She was suddenly aware she shouldn't be staring like that. 'Oh. Etta Kaesbach. She said you were the best.'

I uttered a short 'ah' of understanding. Good old Etta. Etta Kaesbach was a first-rate solicitor who'd passed a lot of work my way over the years. In fact, she was the one who'd helped me most when I first set up business as an enquiry agent. She had great heart and a contrary streak that dared anyone to challenge her recommendation. It was embarrassing for me sometimes, embarrassing for the undecided prospective client too, but usually their surprise worked in my favour – nobody liked to appear discriminatory in these PC days – and once they'd realized how pro I was, there was no problem.

'Is Ms – ' I hated the *Ms*, but it was expected ' – Kaesbach your lawyer?' I asked.

'No. But her senior partner was once my late husband's.' She blew a stream of blue smoke which dispersed half-way across my desktop. 'Gerald died five months ago. Heart attack. His heart had never been strong. It was over very quickly.' She offered the last bit of information as if it were a blessing, and perhaps it was. Still the memory was fresh enough to upset her: her eyes lost focus for a moment, moisture softening their hue. And for some reason her face reddened, as if embarrassment played a part too.

'Would you like some coffee, Mrs Ripstone?' I wanted to give her time to regain her composure. 'Tea?'

'No. No, thank you. I'm fine.'

'Okay . . .' That was fine by me also. It would have been nice to impress clients by using the intercom on my desk and asking my secretary to bring us refreshments, only I didn't have an intercom and I didn't have a secretary. Sometimes Henry would shift himself to bring me a hot drink or a fruitjuice, depending on whether it was one of his health-drive weeks, or, when young Philo was around, I could yell through the open doorway for him to get busy with a brew, but neither option was very ritzy, and to do it myself was even less so. I opened a notepad on my desk and reached for a felt-tip.

'If you could just outline what this is about and I can ask questions as we go,' I said, Pentel poised.

She straightened her shoulders, which by now had become hunched. 'Well, I told you my husband, Gerald Ripstone, died five months ago,' she began, and I jotted down the name and the month he'd passed away.

'You'd been married how long . . . ?'

'Oh, sixteen years, I think. Yes, it would've been sixteen years this August.' She exhaled more smoke and watched the cloud for a few seconds. 'He was a good man, my Gerald. He could be pretty ruthless in business – he exported refrigeration units, you know, cold storage containers – but generally he was good to me. I was his secretary before we were married.'

'Were either of you married before?' The question was just out of curiosity, not relevant to anything as far as I knew at this stage; I like to get a full picture, that's all.

She eyed me sharply. 'I wasn't. But yes, Gerald was, and yes, he did leave his first wife for me.' She dared a judgement, but I had no problem with it. Why should I? 'He was a good man, Mr Dismas, a little – ' little was the kind of word where her *t*s went AWOL '– bit hard on me sometimes, but only when I'd done or said something stupid, especially when we were in company. Gerald never liked to feel foolish or embarrassed, especially if I was the one showing him up. He was a very proud man. A very . . . a very rigid man and, I suppose, old-fashioned in some ways.'

'Children? D'you have any?' Again I asked for no particular reason, just a way of getting her to open up, but the question stopped her dead. She glanced away and it was a relief to escape her carelessly veiled gaze at last.

'No,' she replied after a pause. 'No kids. Gerald always thought it was me; y'know, that I was to blame. But it wasn't me. I was sure of that, although I never let him know.'

'You had tests?'

'Didn't need to.'

I sensed we were finally getting to the point of her visit. (Yep, I'm good at that kind of thing too.)

'It's the reason I'm here, Mr Dismas,' she confirmed.

Ah, I thought. 'I see,' I said.

Now she looked directly into my one good eye. Oddly she didn't proceed; she had to be prompted yet again.

'You do have a child, then,' I ventured.

She looked at the tip of her cigarette held in her lap and I pushed the ashtray across the desk towards her. She tapped ash into it, a hurried, jerky gesture.

'I think so,' she said quietly.

She thought so . . . 'I don't understand, Mrs Ripstone.'

'Could we . . . could we have the office door closed?' she asked.

'Of course.' I lumbered round the desk, my limp not too bad at that time of day; it'd grow worse as the day wore on, depending on how tired I got. As I was closing the door Henry looked up from his desk and raised his eyebrows; I gave a small shrug. Clients were entitled to all the confidentiality they demanded, and then some; that was the first rule in the private investigation business. Henry's balding head was already bowed over his accounts again before the door clicked shut.

'Okay, Mrs Ripstone, we can't be overheard,' I assured her as I returned to my seat. 'This is strictly between you and me, although other members of my team will have to be brought in if I decide to take your case and if the subsequent investigation requires extra hands. Even then, any personal information will always be kept in a locked briefcase carried only by myself, or it will never leave the precincts of these offices.' I indicated a row of four grey filing cabinets to my left. 'While on the premises, your file will be kept under lock and key as a matter of routine. If particularly sensitive, that file can be locked away in our multi-cylinder, combination-lock Stratford Clarendon safe which, incidentally, is bolted to the floor.' I pointed to the big metal box against the wall behind her. 'And only myself and my first assistant know the combination.'

If she was impressed, she didn't show it; I think her thoughts were too inward to pay attention to my blatherings. She needed another deep drag on the cigarette before she could proceed. A blue haze was beginning to fill the room, but that was okay – I enjoyed smoky atmospheres.

'I had a baby two years before I met Gerald and I was single. A son. My name was Teasdale then. Shelly Teasdale.' She blurted it out, as if it had to be said in a rush because she still felt some guilt, some shame even. 'He never knew . . . I never told Gerald about the birth,' she added. 'I didn't think it was necessary.'

I nodded sagely; it seemed the right thing for me to do.

'But now I want to find my baby,' she said, leaning forward on the desk.

'Well, hardly a baby any more. You said eighteen years ago . . . ?'

'He's a young man now, I know that. But I only knew him as a baby.'

'And you've had no contact with him since? Look, I have to be frank with you here. The only people who can help you find your son are the authorities who arranged the adoption or for the boy to be taken into care, whichever the case. Barnardo's would be your best bet, although there are special agencies that deal with this sort of thing. Even then, it would be up to the boy if he wanted to see you. Eighteen years is a long time to be disowned by your own . . .' I didn't have the heart to finish; the poor woman was distressed enough.

She was clutching the cigarette in both hands and shaking her head, slowly, deliberately, as if she didn't want to hear. Her eyes were liquid as she said: 'You don't understand. They told me he was dead. There was something wrong with the baby at birth. He didn't survive.'

'I'm afraid you're right – I don't understand. If the baby died, why would you – ?'

'Because they lied. My baby didn't die. They said he was born with too many abnormalities to live long. They told me he was dead within minutes of the birth.'

'You must have seen it . . . him . . . for yourself.'

'No. It was a difficult birth, I'd been in labour for more than twenty-four hours. I was exhausted, only half-conscious when he finally arrived. They took him from me immediately, but I heard him, I heard his cries. They were . . . different, somehow, but I definitely heard them. They were very strong.'

I tried to be gentle. 'That may be so,' I said softly, 'but that doesn't mean the child didn't die soon afterwards. Did you see him again?'

'I told you, I didn't see him at all.' The tears were beginning to spill over and ruin her mascara line.

I hoped she took my small groan for a sigh as I sat back

in my chair – not a very comfortable position for me, incidentally. 'I'm sorry, I still don't get it. Why would they tell you the baby was dead if that wasn't so? It doesn't make sense. What kind of hospital was it anyway?'

'An ordinary National Health hospital in Dartford. The Dartford General.'

'Well, there you are, there wouldn't be anything sinister going on in an NHS place, nor any other type of hospital for that matter. I wonder . . . uh, there's no easy way of saying this. I wonder if the death of your husband hasn't left you overwrought? You've lost a loved one unexpectedly and tragically and I assume you're alone, so maybe now you're reaching for another possibility, one that tells you that the son you had all those years ago and thought was dead might still be alive. You're full of grief, remorse, and dare I say, guilt? Guilt that you never told Mr Ripstone, you kept it a secret for eighteen years, and guilt that you might have abandoned your only child.'

She stabbed the cigarette into the ashtray, her fingers trembling. 'I'm not a neurotic widow, Mr Dismas, despite what you might think. You don't know the full story yet.'

She took a small handkerchief with lace edges from her purse and dabbed at her eyes, now smudging the running mascara. The tears ceased though, and her voice became steady again as she looked me directly in the eye (I think she was getting used to me now that the initial shock had passed). 'Do you believe in clairvoyancy, Mr Dismas?' she said.

I groaned again, inwardly this time, already guessing where this was headed. I had enough problems dealing with reality without bringing hokum into my life. I didn't want to upset her any more, though, so I replied: 'I've heard a few interesting stories about such things over the years. Let's face it, Brighton has more than its fair share of fortune tellers and psychics, not to mention New Age and alternative medicine practitioners.' (And not to mention private enquiry agencies, which was why I wasn't keen to lose a prospective client, no matter how off-the-wall they might be; competition was too fierce for that.)

'Then you do believe certain people have psychic powers?' she pressed on.

'Telepathy, a sixth sense, that kind of thing?' I shrugged noncommittally. 'It's a possibility, but I wouldn't know for sure.'

'But if I told you that when Gerald died I consulted a clairvoyant, you wouldn't laugh at me and think me stupid.'

'Of course not. Nothing unusual about that kind of thing these days. In fact, I've heard some of these people – clairvoyants, mediums, psychics, whatever you'd care to call them – can bring a lot of comfort to the bereaved. The one or two I know around town seem harmless enough.'

'They can do more than just comfort. Some of them can heal the sick just by thought or touch.'

She was a believer all right.

'You mean faith-healing? Well, I'm not too sure about – '

'Don't dismiss it so easily.'

Tetchy about it too. 'Many of them can look into a person's future as well as their past. Some can know your thoughts just by looking at you and without your saying a word.'

Yeah, and some can con you into parting with cash by providing all manner of useless information. 'Can I take it, then, that you've consulted such a person, Mrs Ripstone?'

'Gerald's death left me in a bad way,' she replied by way of answer or an excuse, I wasn't sure which. 'I missed him so much and his death came so quickly and so horribly. He was an awkward man sometimes and he had his black moods. But he cared for me. I *know* he really cared for me, despite some of the things he said, the things he did . . .' Her tiny handkerchief had become a scrunched-up ball in her fist. A large, diamond-cluster ring on one of her fingers caught the light from the window behind me. 'I'm still not over it, Mr Dismas. His death, I mean.'

'It can take a while,' I commiserated, 'maybe a couple of years to get over the loss of a loved one, and even then you're not really over it. You just learn to cope.'

'You've been through it too?' She seemed almost hopeful.

'Uh, no. No, it's only what I hear.'

'Oh.' She wiped the dampness from her cheeks, then squared her shoulders as if determined to get a grip on herself. 'It was so hard to accept that Gerald was gone at first. I think I went a little bit crazy with grief. I locked myself away, saw no one, talked to no one, wouldn't even answer the telephone for a while. And then a feeling came over me – I don't know how to describe it. I just woke one day and felt there was something I could do about my loss, that if there really was something called the "soul", as the Church tells us, then perhaps I could contact Gerald again. I didn't have to be entirely on my own.'

Uh-oh, I thought.

'I hadn't really believed in spiritualism before, you know, contacting the dead? But at the same time, I'd never *dis*believed in it. I just hadn't given it much thought. D'you understand?'

'Sure,' I answered. 'Most people don't like to think about death until it comes close in some way or other. So that was when you decided to approach a medium?'

'Not at first. It wasn't a sudden urge, anything like that. It just come on gradually, a sort of feeling I should contact Gerald. And I wanted to find a good clairvoyant, a genuine one, not one of them phonies.' Estuary kept breaking out despite her efforts to contain it. 'Lucky for – *luckily* for me, one of my friends knew of someone who didn't live too far away.'

'You wouldn't have to look far in Brighton.'

'Well, this one lived in Kemp Town.'

(Kemp Town is an adjunct of Brighton, although it likes to keep a separate identity.)

'Her name's Louise Broomfield,' Shelly Ripstone continued. 'You've heard of her?'

I shook my head.

'She's quite well-known. In those sort of circles, I mean.'

'You went to see her.' I tried not to let my impatience show.

'I got her phone number and I rang. Apparently she doesn't just see anybody, she has to talk to them first. She knew I was distressed right away.'

There's a surprise, I thought.

'And she could feel there was something to tell me. She knew just by our conversation on the telephone.'

A light tap on the door just then. It opened a little way and Philo, my youngest employee, and Sam Spade wannabe albeit a brown one, poked his head round.

'Sorry to interrupt,' he said cheerfully, his short black hair glistening with gel. 'You wanted to know about the writ this morning.'

I used Philo a lot for process serving, especially if there might be some running after the recipient to do (and as process serving took up half the agency's business, on some days there was a *lot* of running to do).

'Any problems?' I asked, looking past Shelly Ripstone. The particular debt dodger Philo had had to confront was more slippery than most – I'd had dealings with this character before – but the kid had to learn some time, and the hard way was often the best.

'Well, he pretended to be his own brother, but I recognized him from the Polaroid you gave me. He wouldn't touch the papers, so I dropped them at his feet in the hallway, then did a fade.'

'You're sure you got the right man?'

'Definite.'

I gave him a lop-sided grin. 'Okay, make out your notes

17

for the affidavit right now so you don't forget the details. Then Henry's got a trace for you to work on, only telephone stuff, but it might be complicated. I'll catch up with you later.'

He took a last look at the back of Shelly Ripstone, appraised her ash-blonde hair, raised his eyebrows a couple of times at me, then disappeared from the doorway. The door closed quietly behind him.

I apologized for the interruption before prompting my prospective client once more. 'You went to see this, er, Louise . . .'

'Broomfield,' she finished for me and I wrote the name down on the pad.

'Okay.' I waited for her to continue.

'She was wonderful. And she's a faith healer too. There was something about her, a sort of . . .' she searched for the appropriate word '. . . a *goodness*, a sort of . . .' she struggled for another description.

'Compassion?' I suggested.

'Yes, that's it. I sensed it as soon as she opened the front door. You know she hugged me right there on the doorstep, before either one of us had said a word. That broke me.' Tears were brimming again at the memory and she swiftly dabbed at her eyes with the soggy hanky. 'I'm sorry. I'm an emotional person.' She sniffed a couple of times as evidence.

'It's all right. Take your time.'

A snuffle to end the sniffs, then she regained control. 'Louise took me into a room at the back of the house, a bright little room, walls and ceiling painted pale blue. I felt at peace as soon as I entered it.'

With most prospective clients you learned to cut to the chase pretty fast, getting to the facts without too much embellishment. Some, though, I'd learned to let tell their story in their own way, guiding them with the odd soft prod here and there. Shelly Ripstone fell into the latter category; she'd get to it at her own speed.

'What was she like, this medium?' Medium or clairvoyant,

it made little difference to me. What I think I wanted to know at this point was whether or not Louise Broomfield was genuine, and any information about her might help me decide. I would naturally distrust anyone who adorned themselves with pendants or crucifixes and dressed in black as symbols of office. That was showbiz, artifacts of illusion, and not for the serious-minded. There were quite a few hucksters around town and, I had to admit, some of them I liked; in general, though, I had an aversion to robes and regalia of any kind, especially when they were to do with the Church.

'Louise is very ordinary. More like a kindly counsellor than a clairvoyant. She makes you feel . . . well, good inside. She understood what I was going through right away and she let me have a good cry before asking me anything.'

'You told her about the death of your husband?'

'She already knew.'

I didn't push her. It would have been easy enough to conclude Shelly Ripstone was grieving, inevitably for someone she'd recently lost. Guessing it was for her late husband would have been easy enough by minimum probing.

'So she contacted Gerald for you?'

The question from me was genuine enough, despite an in-built cynicism towards anyone who claimed they could communicate with 'the other side'. Even if I didn't believe it, it was evident that this woman across the desk did.

'No. She contacted my son.'

'But you said you thought your son was still alive.'

'It's how I now *know* he is. I'd always had that feeling my baby hadn't died. Intuition, a mother's instinct – I don't know what it was, but it was always there, always with me. And Louise said I'd been right to believe it all this time.'

'I thought clairvoyants could only communicate with spirits, not with the living.'

'Like lots of people, you're mistaken. Louise can pick up the thoughts of people who might even be thousands of miles away. Living people, I mean. She can heal just by thinking of a sick person who could be on the other side of the world. She can "see" the auras of people she talks to. She told me she had communicated with a little boy who'd been in a coma for two years and who still showed no signs of recovering. Sometimes she can tell if a person is going to die soon, even if that person doesn't know they're sick. Her mind reached my son, through me, just by my being there. She picked up his presence.'

Shelly Ripstone leaned close across the desk, her anguish overriding her nerves of me. Her eyes were pleading, regarding me purely as someone who could help her and not as some misshapen thing to be pitied, or repulsed by. 'Louise fainted away in front of me, Mr Dismas. Whatever it was she sensed, whatever it was she saw in her mind, it caused her to collapse. And when she came round she wouldn't – couldn't – speak of it. She just kept telling me over and over again that I had to find my son before it was too late. That if I didn't, something terrible – *something awful* – was going to happen. And it would happen very soon.'

3

It was at least another half-hour before I finally showed Shelly Ripstone out. Earlier, her loud weeping had brought Henry to the door, enquiring if he could be of any assistance, his real motive just plain nosiness, and I'd shooed him away. In private again, I rose from my desk and patted the distressed woman's shoulder (was that the slightest shudder I felt run through her, or just a sob-spasm?) and offered her my own dry handkerchief. She took it gratefully and eventually stifled the tears.

I think it was sympathy rather than the fee I'd charge that made me agree to take on her case. Truth is, I thought an investigation wouldn't amount to much anyway, that the search for her lost son would be a wild goose chase – hospitals just didn't lie about newly-born babies, even if there was no supporting father involved. I explained this to Shelly Ripstone, *née* Shelly Teasdale, but she insisted my personal view wasn't important as long as I did my job properly. Fair enough, I told her, and promised that all the agency's professional skills would be put into force to resolve the matter one way or the other; it was her money, so it was her shout. A little cynical, I know, but it cheered her up considerably.

We talked some more, with me taking notes and my new client still snuffling as she supplied the details: address at the time of her pregnancy all those years back, the address of the Dartford General Hospital where she'd given birth (together with some unfortunate news concerning that particular place), Louise Broomfield's contact address and phone number. We also agreed on my fee and expenses. When she left she was in better shape, although not much better: those smudged eyes were still anxious and her fist clenched the borrowed handkerchief as if to wring it dry. Nevertheless, there was a glimmer of hope in those eyes when I promised to call her the moment I had anything to report.

On the way downstairs to the ground floor she had to edge past the large frame of Ida Lampton, my third and last employee, who was ascending the creaky staircase with heavy breaths and even heavier steps. Standing at the office door I watched Ida turn her head and stare after our attractive client as she descended the next flight of stairs; no chance, I thought, and Ida looked up to catch me grinning. She smiled back and shrugged her meaty shoulders, then came all the way up, bringing her plastic bags full of light shopping with her, for all the world looking like a favourite maiden aunt returning from her morning's shop. It was a great guise, especially for someone hired as store detective for the week.

I stepped aside to let her through, then closed the door marked Dismas Investigations behind us. When I turned, three sets of interested eyes were focused on me.

So. I'm Nick (Nicholas) Dismas and I run the Dismas Investigations agency, a two-room office with leaning walls and crooked door frames a couple of floors above a charity shop a few doors along from Brighton's Theatre Royal. In the heart of the seaside town, we're close to the train station, shops, seafront, and more importantly, a crush of solicitors' offices, from which we get most of our business. Note it's an investigations agency, not a detective agency: we don't 'detect' anything – that's for the big boys, who have more contacts, generally richer clients (in particular, companies and financial institutions) and who earn a whole lot more from a higher scale of fees than we humble investigators. Also – unlike us – they quite often get involved in criminal cases. The one thing we do have in common, though, is that neither party has any real power or authority: we're ordinary citizens with no official status whatsoever.

The private investigator's job generally involves process serving (handling writs and summonses and the like), tracing (tracking down certain people who had decided to go 'missing', usually because of financial or domestic difficulties), status and credit reports, accident and insurance enquiries, repossessions, debt collecting, surveillance (which includes anything from watching individuals or premises, to joining a company as an employee in order to catch out pilferers or industrial spies, to following errant husbands or wives). Mostly mundane, even boring, work that requires patience, care and an eye for detail. A sense of humour sometimes helps, too.

Henry Solomon was the agency bookkeeper and administrator, who occasionally took on fieldwork. He was tall, hook-nosed, bespectacled (in fact, he was one of those types whose glasses seemed to be built into their heads – you couldn't imagine the face without the attachment), balding, with a midriff bulge that mocked his overall leanness. He dressed neatly and conservatively, although when the mood took him he sported colourful braces and socks, or a flashy bow-tie, sometimes – when the mood *really* took him – all three. Henry was mad on old movies (in fact he looked a bit like the dead actor Henry Fonda) and ballroom dancing (watching, not partaking of) and lived with his elderly mother in the Kemp Town. He enjoyed a gin and tonic, although never to excess, and loved to try and catch me out on movie trivia. His downside was that he hated blacks, Asians, the French and Chinese, and socialists; to be honest, he was the only Jewish Nazi I'd ever met. His sense of humour was waspish-acerbic, but his basic nature – *despite* those imperfections mentioned – was benign (folks are complicated, right?).

Ida Lampton, the big woman who'd just climbed the stairs and who looked like that maiden aunt with her short greying hair and plump face, was my main asset. Equally good at serving summonses and injunctions or repossessing unpaid-for goods, she also made a great store detective, especially when dressed as she was that day in light summer frock and cardigan, with sensible brogues for walking. Six-foot one, big-boned and broad of girth (more than fifteen but less than seventeen stone was her last admission regarding weight), Ida could play the heavy – in trousers, neck scarf and reefer jacket you could be forgiven for taking her for a man – or the sweetheart (useful for debt counselling and collecting). In the latter guise she could be pleasantly persuasive, in the former she was goddamn intimidating.

I'd first clapped eye on Ida in a Brighton gay club called the Greased Zipper (no subtlety there, then), where she was serving behind the well-packed bar and I was searching for a runaway youth who was known to frequent such haunts, despite his tender age. His parents, my clients, were frantic and only too willing to accept his burgeoning lifestyle if only he would return to the nest, and I was showing his photograph around to either uninterested or excitable, mock-eager male clubbers, some of whom snatched the picture to show their giggling clique. As in any other city or big town club, straight or gay, there are many variations in type among members – the quiet, the flamboyant, the drunks, the troublemakers, the hard men and women – and in this particular one (I'd done the rounds that night) a combination of the last two types, all leathers and glory moustaches and naked arms (and that was just the women – joke), had decided I was an affront to their delicate (despite their muscles and blue jaws) sensitivities. If they'd stuck to verbals everything would have been okay – I could always handle that – but they'd become physical, shoving me around, giving me no chance to back off either with wit or reason before things turned any nastier.

Now I'm no pushover, despite my problems, but before I could retaliate, aware I'd come off worse and not giving a damn anyway, lovely big Ida stepped in. Five minutes before she'd given the photo I carried time and attention, even though she was mobbed at the bar, genuinely sorry she wasn't able to provide me with a lead on the missing kid (she was only too aware of the predators that stalked the streets here for fresh, inexperienced meat), and now she'd noticed the trouble I was in. A swift knee into one bully-boy's leathered crotch and a sharp big-boned elbow into another's powdered nose settled the matter quickly enough (I learned later that Ida was also engaged as club bouncer as well as barmaid). One of the boy-bitches had screamed blue hell and Ida grabbed my arm to steer me towards the door. Outside I'd jabbered my gratitude and given her my card in case she happened to see the youth I was searching for. Two days later she'd called in with a sighting of the runaway selling copies of the *Big Issue* outside a Virgin record store, which led to my taking his parents directly to him (the record store had become his regular pitch). After contact he was their problem, but I had become interested in Ida herself. That she could take care of herself there was no doubt; that she had many contacts all over town soon became evident. I offered her a job with the firm and, after she'd consulted her live-in partner of twenty years, a sweet, gentle woman who taught pre-school infants in a small village eight miles outside Brighton and to whom I was soon introduced over a Little Harvester Sunday lunch, Ida agreed to give it a try. That was six years ago and she'd been with me ever since.

Young Philo Churchill was the newcomer to the agency, the sometimes hopeless but ever-enthusiastic novice. It's usually a mistake to take on young apprentices in this game – in fact, most agencies won't touch them – because once they've learned everything from you, every trick in the book, every procedure to be followed, often making themselves a pain-in-the-butt in the process by asking too many questions and fouling up too many times, they strike out on their own, setting up their own agency and taking some of your clients with them, promising a cheaper deal and more (ha!) care. But what the hell, Philo had left school at seventeen with seven GCSEs and two A levels and had vainly been searching for work for two-and-a-half years before turning up on my doorstep. Yep, I felt sorry for him. A little ashamed too, because I knew the fact that he was black – a light brown tone actually – hadn't helped him in the job market. Besides, I needed an extra hand – the workload was good at that time – and he was willing to accept low wages. Almost twenty, he was a good-looking kid whose grandparents had arrived in Southampton shortly after the Second World War, when the country was in desperate need of young, manual labourers. They'd done their bit, and so had their offspring son, who eventually had married a Greek girl; now Philo, English bred and born – as English as his surname might suggest, in fact – wanted to do his bit, if only that residual prejudice, rump of a sorry past but still rampant in certain low quarters, would so allow. Philo hadn't sought work to prove himself worthy as an Englishman; no, he'd never suffered from that foolish kind of race-paranoia. He simply wanted to work because that was the normal thing to do. Besides, he was ambitious.

Philo dressed smartly, despite his meagre earnings, and he looked good. Even Henry was impressed by his keenness, and working together, Henry, Ida and Philo, well, they made a good team.

So that just leaves me, Nicholas Dismas.

I was found, thirty-two years ago, among the dustbins behind a nuns' convent in a poorer part of London. Found by the convent's caretaker/handyman when he took out the trash early one cold winter's morning. God knows what he thought of the misshapen little gnome lying there among the bins, barely a few hours old and not even wrapped in a blanket but swaddled in yesterday's newspaper, although without doubt it must have given him one hell of a shock. Perhaps he even crossed himself, while muttering a prayer and wondering what demon had had the temerity to leave its hideous spawn on holy ground.

I was born a monster, you see.

I'm not shamed by the term, nor embarrassed. Saddened, of course. Made desperately bloody miserable by it. But that's the way it goes. It's what I am in most people's terms.

Doctors told me in later life that my physical condition was probably due to *birth trauma*. I'm not diseased at all, there was never any sign of spina bifida or any form of deficiency: I was just born malformed. And as I grew older, the deformities augmented, became more defined and ever more distorted. The infant monster ripened into a grotesque.

My forehead overlapped my eyes, a Neanderthal protuberance that frightened children and dogs; my jaw grew more pointed, my mouth more leering, lips more twisted. The curve of my spine increased and veered to the right so that my shoulder was huge, the blade amalgamating with the hump of my back. I crouched further and further forward until crooked was my normal walking, sitting, resting stance, and my right leg was slightly – oh thank *You* God, only *slightly* – withered, so that I walked with a hobbling lurch. Even my chest was disfigured, breastbone and upper ribs on one side overlapping their neighbours, and hair spread down my back to form a tail between my buttocks, one that I kept shorn regularly, a DIY job because I'd have hated for anyone else to see my naked body.

Would the hair on my head were that thick, but no, His torment – did I *thank* God a moment ago, albeit ironically? – was far too comprehensive to allow such favour; it hung in loose drab strands over my scalp and forehead, the bushiness of my eyebrows mocking its very sparsity. My ears, too large even for this large cranium, looked as though they'd been chewed by a couple of unfriendly Rottweilers.

But there was nothing wrong with my brain, no lumps or dents in the bone had damaged its fibres; no, only bitterness bent my thoughts. My nose was flattened, but its shape was no worse than the nose of an incompetent pugilist's, and my hearing, despite the gnarled receivers, was keen, as was the vision in my one grey/brown-speckled eye (its twin, the left one, was useless, mutilated in an incident which occurred in my younger years). I wasn't tall, but was by no means a dwarf; somewhat below average height, I suppose, which was hardly surprising considering how crooked I was. So on the plus side, I was smart, could see and hear comparatively well, had an acute sense of smell, and my arms and left leg were exceptionally strong (nature compensates, right? Hah!). Despite these small compensations, it was difficult for me to believe that life was God's precious gift. In fact, was my wretched body an indictment of His will? Did He issue some of us with faulty meat-machines on purpose? Or was it a mistake, an oversight? Or truly deliberate, all part of His Master Plan? Who knows? I only knew my *mistake* – if *mistake* it was – was worse than most, not as bad as some. I hardly felt grateful for that.

In the early years I used to wonder about my mother, mostly as I lay in my narrow cot at night in the dormitory of the boys' home they – the authorities – had sent me to. Was she like me, a hunchbacked monstrosity, or was it my unknown father who bore the mark? Perhaps they were both like me. You know, it takes one to love another? Maybe they'd been freaks in some age-old circus show, the kind that would be banned for being politically incorrect these days (and how I agreed with that!). I didn't often think of *him*, though. I don't know why; he just wasn't part of the reverie. My thoughts were nearly always of her alone.

In my fantasies, my mother was a princess, or the beautiful daughter of some wealthy lord, and it was they, the King and

Queen, or the lord, who had forced her to give up the child who had been born with such hideous deformity. The shame for such grand people would have been too much to contemplate. So I'd been stolen away while she was sleeping, or perhaps dragged from her outstretched arms, her pleas, her tearful protests, ignored; and then I'd been lost somewhere, given to the captain of the guard or, more probably, the lowly groundsman to take me away to some faraway place to be left there with nothing to identify my august status. But someday she would defy all those around her and she would search and eventually find me. Then she would claim me for her own and we'd never be separated again. The tears of pleasure and misery those romanticisms would bring me.

As I grew older, such fancies dimmed to be replaced by the thought that my mother had had no one to help her in her desperate straits, that the unwanted pregnancy was the last straw in circumstances of abject poverty, and she had been forced to leave me on the nuns' back doorstep, knowing they would not reject me, that I would be cared for if not by the nuns, then by the State, until I became a man.

And as I grew older still and unhappiness had moulded (and even mouldered) my psyche, that fantasy too, had faded. My mother had been shamed and repelled by the variant she had given birth to – perhaps she had even sensed my awfulness while I was still in her belly – and had dumped me as soon as the umbilical cord had been cut. She neither cared for me, nor was she curious about me: the search had never been undertaken and I was never to be claimed.

I believed all this until other visions started coming to me, uncertain revelations mixed with night-time dreams that made me wonder if the bitter discontent I had felt all these years, the resentment, the loneliness that only my kind could ever know, was finally leading to madness. Then again, they might only have been due to the drugs.

*

Philo was the first to speak: 'So what was *her* trip?'

'You'd think she would've invested in bawl-proof mascara,' Henry added in his waspish manner. 'All Coco and no class.'

'Poison, actually,' I corrected.

'Hmn, with a nose like yours it's a wonder you can tell.'

I could take that kind of remark from Henry – unless it was on a bad day, that is.

Ida flopped her bulky frame into our one and only guest's chair and exhaled a rasping breath. She crossed her ankle over her knee and eased off a shoe. She rubbed her toes. 'Who did her wrong? Is the lady after revenge or recompense, Dis?'

'Nothing like that. Shelly Ripstone is a grieving widow.'

Henry peered winsomely through his spectacles as if interested in the woman's status, that she just *might* be the one for him. We all knew that was pretence though, but we were never quite sure if Henry knew we knew. 'Of course, she is reasonably attractive, despite her kitschy style.'

Ida shot me a secretive glance, then let her eyeballs swivel towards heaven.

'What is it then?' said Philo, sitting on the corner of Henry's desk. Henry frowned and moved his accounts books further away from the black youngster's butt. 'Problems with the will? Dodgy relatives turning up for a share?'

'A trace,' I informed them all. 'A baby son she hasn't seen for eighteen years.' The answer was met by a collective groan.

'I thought we never took on a trace for anyone missing more than ten years,' Ida grumbled.

She was right: that kind of contact rarely earned out – too many phone calls, too many document searches, too many blind alleys; and often the client's reluctance to pay the bill when we came up with zilch. To make matters worse as far as this particular assignment was concerned, we didn't even have a photograph – let alone a description – of what the mark once looked like (and even if we had, what use would a picture of a baby be?).

Now I broke the *really* good news. 'Our biggest stumbling block is that her son may not be alive anyway.'

'Yes, I'd say that was a definite snag to finding him for his poor dear mum.' Henry, as caustic as ever. 'Dead people rarely turn up again, do they?'

Ida removed her other shoe and wriggled the toes on that foot. 'In fact, that should make it easier. There would be a record of his death somewhere.'

'There is,' I said. 'Or, there was. The hospital where the baby was born. Problem is when Mrs Ripstone – her name was Shelly Teasdale when she had the baby, by the way – tried to track down those records herself, she discovered the hospital no longer exists. It burnt down ten years ago and all the records, along with several patients and medical staff, went up with it.'

Henry slid his fingers beneath the glasses and massaged his closed eyes. 'Er, you're losing me here. Did – does – the mother know her son is dead or what?'

'She was informed of the baby's death minutes, maybe only seconds, after it was born.'

Now he was shaking his head wearily. 'Then why on earth has she come to us?'

The reason sounded even more crazy when I heard myself telling them.

4

Before heading home that evening to my basement flat on the other side of Brighton, I made a little detour. I'd taken an instruction the previous week from a building society for a house repossession and had gone along with a court bailiff, who was the only one with the legal authority to repo the particular property, and I'd stood by while he went about his business. Fortunately, the occupants who'd reneged on their £90,000 loan from the Halifax had already skipped, so there was no problem with eviction. Less fortunate though, for the creditor that is, those same people had trashed the house before leaving.

Now I know it's easy to feel sorry for anyone turned out of their home, but the truth of it is it generally *isn't* their home. They've borrowed the money, a large amount at that, and refused – yes, *refused*, in this case – to pay it back. So the home wasn't rightfully theirs in the first place. The building society had done its best with the debtor, a guy in his early forties who, it was later discovered, had a habit of running one business after another into liquidation, every time setting up again a few months later under a different company name. When he'd approached the Halifax, his current business had looked pretty healthy – on paper, at least – so the building society had no problem with advancing him the loan. It wasn't long before his business went belly-up, though. Almost a year of letters, phone calls and personal visits by the building society people failed to produce a satisfactory resolution – our debtor always promised to pay the next month's mortgage and somehow make up the rest over a period of time; but he never did. And as I'd been sent round to see him a couple of times, more as a counsellor than a debt collector, I knew he never would. He was a fly-by-night builder who had a record (I eventually discovered) of letting down clients with shoddy workmanship, overcharging and, more often than not, beginning a job and not completing it. There were genuine villains around town that I respected more than this joker, and my advice to the creditor had been to claim the property before the debt rose any higher. As it turned out, the errant builder was smarter than all of us – he disappeared within a week of my last visit.

So this one I wasn't sorry for at all. And when I'd arrived with the bailiff, whose duty it was to force entry if necessary, I even hated the bastard. Not only had he and presumably his wife and two strapping teenage sons wrecked the inside of the house – skirting boards and door frames were ripped off, light fixtures, sockets, even the fuse box, torn from the walls and ceilings, toilet bowls and sinks smashed – but they'd also smeared the walls with special graffiti. Special? Oh yes, because this moron and his retard family had had a fine old time leaving messages especially for me.

On this particular evening I could have sent one of the others – Henry or Ida – to check out the house, but frankly I hadn't wanted them to see the ugly and obscene drawings with which the clan from hell had daubed the battered walls. More shame than embarrassment, I think. Embarrassment about my physical irregularities was something I'd managed to get over a long time ago; shame, though, was something different, and a little harder to shake off. Those spray-can daubings had been bad enough, because they were grotesque cartoons, warped but so badly executed they were almost abstruse; but one of the family, one of the boys, I think (I'd hate to think it could be the woman) had an undoubted talent for art, and I don't mean of the primitive kind. The draughtsman of the brood had used a brush and gloss paint (so much harder to remove or coat over) and his depiction of my misshapen body was exaggerated only enough to emphasize but not to distort. It's lurid accuracy was what made it so humiliating.

Just why the artist had decided to paint me naked and why he should depict my genitals so enormous and mangled (the one *big* overstatement he'd allowed himself), I had no idea, except to surmise that the obliquity of the imagination can far exceed any aberration of the physical. And exactly why he'd depicted me copulating with something that might just have been a pig (talented though he was, farmyard animals were not his forte) God alone knew.

No, I'd been shamed before the bailiff and his crew and I had no desire to be shamed further before my own colleagues and friends. I wanted to spare them that.

After the bailiff and his men had left I'd turned off the house's water supply by the stopcock – water had been flowing down the stairs from the bathroom for at least two days, I figured – before emptying the hot tank by running water from the tap into the kitchen's metal sink (the only sink that hadn't been smashed). After that, I'd switched off the electricity from the broken main fuse box, then turned off the gas by the tap on the meter's main feed out (I suppose I should have been grateful that these lunatics hadn't tampered with that or left the gas stove turned on). Any telephones that had been there were gone, so I used my mobile to ring a local handyman I hired regularly to change doorlocks, board up windows, and carry out any other jobs that would make the property more secure; personally, I had no argument with squatters, but building societies, banks and landlords in general detested them, so it was part of my brief to keep them out. Lastly, I'd taken an inventory of anything inside the house that might be worth selling on, so that the creditor could at least recoup something towards the damage caused. Unfortunately, nothing of much value had been left behind.

That evening – it was a Monday – I'd returned to the empty, vandalized house to check everything was still in order and that my handyman had done his job properly. It's location was in the rougher part of Kemp Town, the building itself set in a terrace of similar type properties down a narrow turning, and I let myself in with the shiny new key. Because of the boarded windows it was dark inside, like winter dusk, and there was the mouldy stench of damp everywhere.

Any of the undamaged furniture that had been left behind had been removed by the bailiff's men, and my steps along the gloomy hallway had that echoey resonance peculiar to empty buildings. There was enough natural light seeping through the small, dusty, arched window over the front door, as well as from the unboarded landing window above, for me to see my way, but still I took out the pencil-thin torch I always carried in my jacket pocket and switched on its beam. First I ventured into the front parlour, checking the window boards, making sure they were secure enough. My workmen had done an excellent job as usual, only a narrow shaft of light shining through the middle join. Next I examined the kitchen, trying the dry taps even though the stopcock was off. My report to the building society would state that I'd visited the reclaimed property a second time to make sure everything was in order, all services shut down, the house itself impregnable to the casual intruder. The cost of alarms and stronger defences was prohibitive to the creditor, who had already lost enough on their unwise loan, and my report would say that the precautions now taken were satisfactory. It was when I was checking the bolts on the back door that I heard the noise from upstairs.

It had sounded like something breaking.

I swore under my breath. Surely nobody had forced entry so soon. The squatters' grapevine in Brighton was finely tuned – they even had their own advice bureau – but I'd considered this place a reasonably hard nut to crack.

The sound again, sharp, tight, over-loud in the empty building. Outside a seagull gave out a startled shriek as though it, too, had been alarmed by the sudden noise.

I left the kitchen and shone the slim torch beam up the hallway stairs, treading cautiously as I went, for some reason wary of my own footsteps. Stupid, I told myself silently. I wasn't the intruder.

'Okay,' I hollered up the stairs. 'Who's there and what the hell are you doing on private property?'

That should be enough to send them scurrying for the nearest window, I figured. Obviously the trespasser or trespassers had found their way in from a garden window at the back of the premises, a window I'd thought not worth boarding. I paused at the foot of the stairs, waiting for more sounds, hopefully of running feet. Nothing stirred, though.

I'd have to investigate. I'd have to go up there. Probably it was only neighbourhood kids up to mischief, aware that the property was vacant. Even more likely, it was an animal of some kind, maybe a cat on the prowl, or mice searching for food. Could even be rats. I shuddered.

'All right, I'm coming up,' I called out reluctantly, wanting to give whoever or whatever the chance to make a getaway. I didn't want trouble – my fee didn't warrant it.

I began to climb, the damp stair-carpet spongy beneath my feet. Mildew had already begun to set in and the smell was unpleasant. Come on, make a break for it, I said to myself, a voiceless plea to the intruder above, and the dusty stair-rail was shaky under my grip (in their rage, the vengeful builder and his tribe had obviously tried to loosen it).

Half-way up and the noise came again, only this time even louder, almost like the sharp report of a pistol being discharged. It brought me to a halt.

Dust motes swirled in the beam of light from the torch as I aimed it at the landing ahead. Did I really want this? Did I *need* it? Much better to retrace my steps and leave the house entirely. Inform the police of the break-in and let them get on with it. Like I said, I wasn't paid enough to put myself in danger. Unfortunately, if nothing else, I'm a pro. Part of my contract with the Halifax was to make the building secure, so it was my responsibility to keep the place free of intruders. Although right then I tried to resist the idea, I knew I had a duty towards my client. God damn it, why hadn't I gone straight home from the office?

The thought suddenly occurred to me that perhaps the debtor himself had returned to reclaim something he'd forgotten during his moonlight flit. I prayed that was not the case. He'd already unleashed his wrath on the building itself and I didn't want what was left over taken out on me. The graffiti had been enough to deal with.

Then I thought, what the fuck, and headed on upwards again, working up a steam of anger as I went. Yes, I hoped it was the bastard builder and I hoped his sicko son was with him, because I had something to tell him about his particular artistic gift, a whole lot to say about his mean-minded, bigoted, self-fucking-expression in gloss paint. I stamped the stairs, squelching liquid from the carpet with my heavy footfalls, and pulled at the fragile banister rail, causing it to rock to and fro.

Where are you? I called out in my mind only. *Don't mess with me*, I warned, still in my mind. *Don't be fooled by my appearance, I can handle myself all right.* Ah, the power – the self-deception! – of anger.

I rounded the bend in the stairs, reached the landing, looked this way and that, craning the whole of my upper body in that awkward movement of mine.

'Come on you bastards!' I shouted aloud this time, invigorated (or fooled) by my own temper. *'You want trouble, you've got it!'* All bravado, of course, but it had carried me through before under similar circumstances; a bit of bluster could sometimes save you a whole lot of hassle.

But the landing was empty. The evening sun shone through the grimy window at the far end, reflecting off the wall over the stairs with its word-graffiti, the Neanderthals' imagination obviously having run out of ideas for illustrations by the time they'd reached the upper level. Even so, the scrawled letters were equally obscene.

There were three open doorways along the landing, one behind me, the other two on my left. The cracking sound exploded again and I almost hopped into the air.

It had been even louder than before and seemed to come from the middle room. I stayed a moment or two, trying to analyse the sound. It was brittle, acute, a sound that cleaved the still, damp air, now more like the crack of a whip than a pistol shot. I made for the open doorway.

And stopped at its entrance, shocked rigid by what I saw across the darkened room.

Then, as the large cracked mirror on the wall opposite fragmented into a thousand more pieces, I stumbled backwards, terrified and aghast by what I'd seen in its fractured reflection, the hideous images, the grotesques mouthing silent screams, curious oddities whose malformed limbs seemed to claw at the glass from the other side. And I screamed myself and heard the sound, the *only* sound in that terrible tenebrous twilight. And I backed away from the room as I screamed, moving fast, my bent spine breaking the frail banister behind me, so that I plunged into the stairwell below, thudding against the sodden carpet, rolling down, over and over, head over hump, until I reached the bottom.

I wasn't knocked unconscious, but I was dazed, my one good eye deliberately closed again after observing the hallway revolving around me. The pain of landing had hit me instantly and as I lay there it gathered force rather than subsided.

I whimpered first, and then I moaned. Oh dear Lord, that fucking hurt.

I sucked in a large draught of musky air, then resumed moaning, for a short time the shock of the fall outweighing the fright I'd received inside the upstairs room. But quickly the fright claimed the upper hand and I began pushing myself along the hallway towards the front door. I didn't get far though: the dizziness and gathering pain soon brought me short. Hunched there, on knees and elbows, I drew in more breaths and closed my eye once more.

The worst of the pain eventually passed, along with the giddiness, and I managed to lift my oversized head a little.

What the hell was that up there?

I blinked, blinked again.

What the hell had I seen in that mirror?

My panic began to ease as I considered the question. Unfortunately, my heart still thumped too hard and too quickly, my hands and arms continued to tremble against the carpet. Shapes, horrible, disgusting shapes – that's what I'd seen. It was almost as if the room itself had been alive with monsters that could only be seen as reflections in the broken mirror. A long shudder ran through me, seeming to start with my head and shoulders and coursing right down to the soles of my feet. It couldn't be. The room had been empty. I would have heard those things before I'd even entered the room if they had truly been there. No, something had triggered my imagination. Maybe my *own* distorted reflections, multiplied by the fractured glass, were the images that gaped at me across the darkened room. Or maybe it was just another acid flashback, a lingering chemical imbalance among the complex neurons of my brain. Lord knows, it wouldn't be the first time.

Not entirely convinced by either solution, I mentally began to explore my limbs and body, wondering if anything had become broken or detached in the fall. I breathed more easily when everything appeared to be intact; well, as intact as it ever could be. I pushed myself back against the wall and rested there awhile.

I let a minute pass by, then another, knowing what I had to do if only for peace of mind. I had to go back up there and take a second look. No rush though. I had all the time in the world.

I hesitated at the top of the stairs. I really didn't want to go inside that room again. There was no percentage, no incentive. No gain. Not really part of the job description. Except I had to; for my own satisfaction.

I'd suffered flashbacks before, a result of too much Eighties acid, but they'd never been as nightmarish as this. And the last one had been well over a year ago and had involved hundreds of thousands of dancing legs, a black and white Busby Berkeley extravaganza of torso-less limbs and sparkling sequins, a Grand Guignol musical of severed parts danced to a full Latin-rhythm orchestra. Where that peculiarly horrid fantasy was dredged from, I'd no idea – probably from watching too many Thirties musicals on TV while tripped out on A – but it had been patently unreal, easy to cope with, unlike this latest vision – *hallucination*? No, there had been something all too real about those mutants in the mirror.

I inspected the broken landing rail before moving on, a delaying tactic, I guess. I must have hit it with some force to smash right through, even though the mounting had been weakened by the last tenant. That was going to be added to my damage report, just another item the absent builder would have to pay for when the building society finally caught up with him. Time-wasting over, my gaze drifted towards the open doorway.

It was so dark in there because, as the middle room, it was windowless, only light from the landing window seeping into the open doorway. I edged closer, unwillingly, treading carefully while not exactly creeping. This time I peered round the door very slowly.

The mirror on the dingy wall opposite had broken into myriad pieces, yet still held together like a great big jigsaw of silvered glass. And it was my own image I saw reflected there, my own fearsome self mirrored a thousand times or more, my imperfections multiplied; and even though I could not understand why the glass had shattered at my approach, I now realized that it had been my own hideousness, viewed in a new and awesome way, which had shocked me so.

I stood transfixed, watching myself in this jagged confederation of plagiarized horrors, this horrendous coalition of likenesses, and after a while I began to weep.

5

I got back to my flat late, having lingered in a bar on the way. Not one of my regular haunts – too many friends and acquaintances would have wanted to gab, even buy me a drink or two, and I had a need to be alone with my own thoughts, my own personal misery. After five Bushmills Malt and three Buds, I'd left, stepping out into the warm night and turning towards the seafront, the salt-breeze almost clearing the fug from my head, which was something I hadn't wanted. I needed that alcohol haze between myself and my demons, needed it to restrain them, lest their grip clung too tight, held me in terror till dawn. They had come knocking before, more than once, possessing me through the night, mesmerizing, haunting me; and with daylight, I had never understood why.

Hobbling along the coast road, I listened to the voices of people, youngsters in the main, rising from the open areas outside clubs and cafés along the lower promenade. For years the arches between the town's two piers had lain neglected and derelict until a bright local councillor had worked his butt off attracting investors to a scheme by which the area would be revamped. Now it had metamorphosed into a lively boulevard of clubs, bars, cafés and craft shops, where locals and tourists mingled on mild evenings and the younger ones, too many of them high on Special K or GHB, raved to their particular caste of Jungle or Techno, Nu Energy or Drum 'n' Bass, Trance or Speed, Hip Hop or Big Beat, Waltz or Foxtrot (just kidding). Ironically, it was both what I needed and didn't need at that moment: the noise, the shrieks, and the babble of life was good, and, together with the bright lights, told me that life was incessant and encompassing; and that, in itself, let me know how alone I was. An outsider. Always had been, always would be.

In that lachrymose mood, I moved on, eventually reaching the steps to my basement flat. My home was situated in one of the seaside town's broad, sweeping crescents, a hilly green park at its centre, the main thoroughfare and the sea itself bounding the open end. It was a terrific location, most of the tall, white Regency properties – some in better condition than others – nowadays split up into flats or grand apartments, the residents a mixture of rent-paying youngsters and high-earning owners. Vehicles lined both sides of the horseshoe road, many of them double-parked, but still the vista from the apex of the curve was breathtaking, day or night. Descending the stone stairway to my front door, I drunkenly scratched the wood around the keyhole with the key's tip before inserting it. I pushed my way in, flicking the lightswitch quickly as I hurried down the short hallway to the bathroom where I kept part of my stash. My hands shook like a regular druggy's – which, take my word for it, I wasn't, not really – as I reached inside the bathroom cabinet and scrabbled with the lid of the Elastoplast tin. Somehow I managed not to spill the contents as the lid came off.

Inside, instead of plasters, were my ready-mades (Sunday afternoons was generally reserved for rolling enough joints to get me through the week), comprising of two varieties, some rolled in brown cigarette skins (papers), the others in white. The Skunk – in this case Kali Mist, named after the Hindu goddess of destruction – was for when I was really strung out, and the other, white-skinned, was more gentle, a good Jamaican sinsemilla. Tonight I chose the brown.

Lighting up, I went through to the small furniture-crowded sitting-room and poured myself another Highland Malt, this one a Dalmore, before drawing the curtains of the barred windows a little and flopping on to a cushion-strewn sofa. Anticipation as the smoke burned its way down my throat was almost as pleasant as the mellowness that I knew would quickly follow. No rush involved, just an easy sinking into a better place, and while waiting for the mood change the drug and alcohol hopefully would bring about, I surveyed my surrounds, something I often did when my emotions were low, my perspective hopeless. Two small versions of magnificent sculptures stood at each end of the sideboard, Rodin's *Eternal Spring*, a dark bronze whose male and female figures were wonderfully natural on one side, and Epstein's *Genesis*, an anti-naturalistic carving of a pregnant woman, an elongated hand stretched across her swollen belly, a piece that was the very antithesis of its opposite neighbour but no less beautiful. Adorning the wall over the room's mean little fireplace was a wood-framed print of Agnolo Bronzino's *Eleonora da Toledo and Her Son*, the mother serene in her beauty, the young boy placid in his innocence, and on the mantelshelf below was a miniature copy of Hepworth's *Mother and Child*, an abstract carving in marble, all fluid lines and pierced stone (make what you will of my choice, its romanticism, the obvious underlying yearning – I only knew that they took my mind on journeys). I sipped whisky between the drags.

Sleep, helped along by a couple of Motivals before I turned in, was uneventful that night. Rather than fall into another dimension where everything was troubled and plausible only in the dream state (which was my usual sleep pattern), I drifted off into oblivion instead, cares and worries excluded, fantasies barred. Even my hangover next day was tolerable, and although I suffered a few hurts and bruises from the tumble I'd taken, there seemed to be no real harm done (thank you squidgy stair-carpet).

I wet-shaved in front of the bathroom mirror, used to the

ugliness that stared back at me; used to it, yes, but never willingly accepting that countenance, still disturbed and saddened by it, even after all these years. An everyday ritual like shaving was still a routine torture. Once, when I was on heavy stuff like Ice – crystal meth – another face would sometimes regard me from beyond the glass, one that watched me with two good eyes and whose features were regular, though too blurred for recognition. That ill-defined but handsome countenance had hinted at something too evasive to remember properly, too vague to focus upon, yet still filled me with a strange, elusive regret. Regret *and* guilt. At one time those emotions had become so overwhelming I'd turned away from hallucinatory substances completely – what good was a high whose sidekick was profound but unaccountable remorse? Maybe a shrink would have some answers, albeit predictable ones: cut out the bad stuff, think positive, drugs altered and eventually deteriorated your mind state. You take the drugs to escape your own reality, but in the comedowns the reality only becomes more depressing, and the stronger the substance, the harsher the aftermath. Well, I'd already cut out the heavy stuff, because it scared me too much, and I didn't need a shrink to tell me so. In fact, Acid, Charlie and Amphets had been easy to dump, and I'd never used H anyway – heroin was too addictive for someone like me who constantly sought escape. My main gig nowadays was Skunk and booze. Hell, I'd spit in your eye if you even offered me E. Sure, I knew it was considered smart to be part of that scene, but I also knew that those poor suckers were the losers in the long run (and that was their problem – it took time to find out). No diatribe here, no preaching; just the hard facts.

Naturally, more than one psychologist – not psychiatrist; nobody's ever thought me crazy – had tried to get me on their metaphorical couch, assuming I had to have some kind – *any* kind – of inner turmoil because of my 'impaired' physique; and maybe I had – *of course I bloody had* – but I'd never felt the need, or even the urge, to discuss it with the medical profession – or anyone else, for that matter. My mind was my own territory. Let doctors prescribe medicines and pain-killers for the afflictions my physique brought me, but my thoughts were private, they belonged to me alone. Tormented I might be, but it was my own personal torment, invisible to outsiders, unlike my deformities, which were on show for all the world to see. Besides, I had the constant and irrevocable feeling that no shrink would ever understand, let alone resolve, the reason for my lifelong disquiet, this unease that was always with me and which grew more ponderous as the years went by. They'd assumed my troubled mind was due to my dysfunctional form, and I knew – don't ask me how I knew, I just *did* – the issue was far more complex than that.

Self-discovery had never been an indulgence of mine. That earlier time of fierce drug-taking had always had two clear purposes: pleasure and escape. With both there came a 'lifting', a supposed ascent on to a higher plane where creative thought is enhanced and where you feel at one with all around you, at one with the essence of life itself. Huh! Try it enough and you'll discover it's a false concept; that, rather than being a great mind-expanding experience, it's ultimately a closing down of avenues of reason, an occlusion of actuality, and so a limiting of the thought process. At the time you may think you're on the road to perception, to Nirvana even, but in truth you're travelling blind alleys (although instead of heading towards a dead end, you're on the way to cerebral dissipation). Am I sure? Sure I'm sure. Just look around at all the deadheads left over from the sixties, the mental cadavers of the drugs revolution, those once creative musicians and artists and writers, and even businessmen and financiers, their powers of creativity long since withered, their drive stultified, not through passing years but through damaged brain cells and enfeebled resolve. You know who I mean, those dried-up facsimiles of their former selves, their talent mere echoes. Many – of those who survived, that is – are rarely heard from, they seem to exist in some intellective timewarp, while the bleatings from those still in the public eye tend to be an embarrassment.

Anyway, for me the comedowns that followed the highs were too disenchanting to bear and the pursuit itself too ineffectual, meaningless and self-deceiving, to desire. Besides all this, the cost was too great, both to pocket and body (let alone the mind).

These days, I stuck mainly to cannabis and booze for no other reason than to dull my own wretchedness.

I retraced last night's route to the office, on the way passing by the bar I'd swilled in last night, not even giving its locked door a second glance, and stopping to breakfast at one of those archway café's along the boulevard. The sun was already working up to a steady blast, the slight sea breeze cooling the few holiday-makers who were about so early. The sea itself was a fresh blue, dark on the horizon, white caps breaking easily along the shoreline; one or two sunbathers were already stretched out on towels on the pebbled beach, but these were probably office workers or hotel staff, catching the early morning heat before commencing duties for the day. Watching sky-weaving seagulls as I sipped lip-burning coffee at an outside table, I felt a calmness come upon me. I wasn't at peace with myself – I'd never known what that was like – but at least the trauma of the previous night had settled, and the illusion in the broken mirror had become precisely that to my rational mind: an *illusion* caused by fragmented glass and embellished by the darkness of that windowless room. Why had it shattered completely at my approach? Easy. The former occupier had already smashed it and my footfalls had caused the final meltdown. I refused to consider the fact that I'd witnessed an *explosion* of glass – that just wasn't part of my rationale on that warm civilized morning.

A craft-shop owner gave me a wave as she opened her

shutters, the young waiter who'd served me breakfast loitered for a friendly chat. As I climbed the steep ramp to the
upper road, another acquaintance hailed me from the doorway of the Old Ship hotel. I returned a brisk salute and went
on my way.

Looking as I did, I was more noticeable than most around
town, and hence had become part of its scenery, a familiar
figure to the locals; and that was no bad thing in my line of
work, because it made me well enough known to gain
people's confidence and so much easier for me to pursue
enquiries. A lot of these people were eager to talk to me,
either out of some guilt-ridden pity (there for the grace of
God, and all that . . .), or because they were ashamed of the
repugnance I aroused in them and felt noble when they were
able to hide it. Maybe I'm being a little over-cynical here, but
I can only explain the vibes I got from them. Some – a
certain few – were unabashed at how I looked, and I received
genuine warmth from them, while others – there's always
the opposite extreme to anything – never even tried to
conceal their loathing of me. All in all, though, I was generally accepted and only the tourists and out-of-towners tended
to give me the hard, or at best, discreet, stare. Kids were
always a problem, but then I'd learned to accept that.

Cutting through the Lanes, a pedestrian area of narrow
turnings and alleyways filled with antique, jewellery and gift
shops, I crossed a broad thoroughfare and turned off into
the road that led past the old Regency theatre and the Royal
Pavilion's park opposite. The theatre's display boards adver-
tised an 'all-new *Rocky Horror Show!*', not quite my taste in
live performance, but the kind of thing that brought in the
holiday-makers and locals (especially the kids and weirdos)
in droves; next week might be a Gilbert and Sullivan, or a
murder mystery, or even a ballet. Variety, in the broad sense,
is what kept the place going. My mood considerably brightened by the sunshine and 'hail goodfellows' along the way, I
climbed the creaky stairs to the agency.

'Okay,' greeted Henry, who always seemed to beat me into the office, no matter how early I arrived, from his desk. 'In which movie did Cary Grant say his male co-star resembled Ralph Bellamy and who was that co-star?'

I groaned at the regular ritual, not quite ready for it so soon in the day. Nevertheless the answer came to me before I'd even reached my office door.

'Easy,' I told him with a smug grin. '*His Girl Friday*, and the co-star *was* Ralph Bellamy.'

Henry wasn't pleased. He went back to his paperwork, grumbling darkly under his breath.

I went around my own desk and studied the day's agenda, which I usually scheduled in a large diary before leaving the office the previous night. Ida would have gone straight to store duty and Philo, when he arrived in about half-an-hour's time, breathless and over-heated from his dash from the bus stop and ascent of the stairs, would be busy for most of the day with an assignment that meant catching the train to London. I wanted him to pay a call on the General Registrar Office, where there should be a record of baby Ripstone/Teasdale's birth, as temporary as that condition might have been.

As I hit the first cigarette of the day I thought of the baby's mother, Shelly Ripstone, and wondered why she was so positive her son was still alive. Just on the word of a possibly fake clairvoyant? Didn't make sense. And something else that didn't make sense was why I shared the same intuition.

6

I was on my second repo of the day when I got the call from Philo on my mobile.

The first of the two vehicle repossessions had been for a BMW, which unfortunately was parked in the driveway of an upmarket residence situated in a plusher part of Brighton's suburbia. The car's owner – or non-owner, because he hadn't kept up his payments – was one of those flash businessmen who knew all the answers, someone who did well by living on his wits and running up debts. He was aware of his rights and was only too pleased to inform me of them when I rang his doorbell and showed him the letter of authorization from the credit company that empowered me to take the BMW away. With a self-satisfied grin he'd snatched the letter from me and torn it to pieces (that was okay, I had three photocopies, two of them in my briefcase). Standing on his doorstep, he towered over me, yet still he stretched himself to full height (I could see him pivoting on the balls of his feet) in an effort to intimidate me even more. I got that kind of thing all the time: people either patronized me, letting me know my deformities meant nothing at all to them, that I was just one of the chaps, or they got nasty and made the most of what they considered my shortcomings. Either way, it made no difference to me: I was there to do a job, that's all there was to it.

This debtor had been expecting my call, no doubt forewarned by a prior visit from the finance company's own man, and his only surprise was my appearance itself. He hadn't bothered to lie by telling me the cheque was in the post, or that the lender and he had come to some agreement about the unpaid sums only an hour or so before I'd arrived; no, he didn't bother because he knew that legally I couldn't touch the BMW while it was on private property, i.e. his own driveway. If I tried to repossess, I'd be guilty of taking and driving away without consent, and the police held a dim view of auto theft, whatever the circumstances. However, in such cases there is an answer as far as the poor old repossessor who, after all, is only trying to do his job, is concerned: you turned the tables, reversed the situation. I stuck a copy of the authorization letter under the windscreen wiper and informed the defaulter, who remained on the doorstep, hands in pockets, grin mouldering into a scowl, that the vehicle had been officially repossessed by the finance company and that if he took it out on the public highway (my address was as formal as this) it would constitute an arrestable offence because he was no longer the legal owner. The police would be informed and if he were to be stopped by them, he, himself, would be charged with taking away and driving without the owner's consent.

That ruse hadn't pleased him one bit, but I knew as he slammed his front door on me that by the time I returned next day he would have seen sense and given in to the inevitable. He might throw the keys at me, but at least I'd be able to drive the BMW away.

My second 'bust' that day was a lot easier. The car was a Golf GTi and I had expected some trouble: you can usually tell by the vehicle the kind of person the driver is likely to be and a sports model invariably meant 'aggressive'. So I was delighted that the GTi was parked in the roadway and even more delighted that when I knocked on the debtor's front door, there was nobody in. Pushing the authorization letter through the letterbox, I went back to the car and opened the driver's door with the Slim Jim (a thin metal strip that slides down easily between the window glass and rubber sealing strip, its hook contacting the doorhandle locking pin and opening it by a sharp pull) I always carried on such occasions. Once inside, it was almost as easy, although it took a little longer, to hot wire the ignition and drive off. It was as I was pulling away from the kerb that Philo's call came through on my mobile.

'Dismas,' I said.

'Dis?'

'Philo?'

'Yeah. Just left the Family Record Centre. At the GRO?'

'Yes, I know, Philo.' I pictured him outside the registrar office, mobile phone, compliments of the agency, clamped against his ear to cut out the sound of busy London traffic. 'I'm in a repo at the moment, so give me a couple of seconds to get round the corner.'

I didn't want the debtor returning to find me driving away the vehicle he still considered his own. Like I say, GTi drivers often mean trouble and I could do without that today. Parking around the corner and tucking nicely between a Metro and a Volvo estate, I retrieved my mobile from the passenger seat.

'Still there, Philo? Good.' I took a look around the street before switching off the car's engine. 'So what's the story?'

'That's just it, Dis. There isn't one. No birth or death certificate for the Ripstone – sorry, the Teasdale – baby was ever issued as far as they can tell at the registrar office.'

'That's impossible. Our client had the child and it was delivered at the Dartford General.'

'Well, you know the place burned down.'

'Sure but that was some years later.'

'Yeah, but the point is that the records can't be checked at the point of source if there was an error or oversight at this end. That's what they've just told me.'

'There's another GRO in Southport; we can check with them.'

'Uh-uh. Already did. They did it here for me. No record of the baby there either.'

I sat in silence for a moment, trying to make sense of it all. Was Shelly Ripstone *née* Teasdale lying? But why should she, what was there to gain? Could she be deluding herself, imagining she'd given birth all those years ago? No, she was overwrought at the loss of her husband, but she didn't seem crazy or hysterical. I wondered if the clairvoyant, this Louise Broomfield, had planted the thought in Shelly's troubled mind. Some kind of auto-suggestion. What would be the point of that, though? I shook my head in mild frustration: I had no answers.

'Dis?'

'Sorry, Philo, just thinking.'

'What d'you want me to do?'

'Get yourself off to the Search Room at Companies House. It isn't far from where you are now.'

In the investigation business you always tried to kill two or three birds with one stone to justify the expense of long excursions; it was important to cover the expense in time and travel for the agency. In this case, one of the national banks' local branches in Hove had asked me to look into the commercial background of a prospective client who was seeking a substantial loan for a new business venture and the bank had a feeling that other branches and different brand banks had been approached by the same man before for similar type loans, but under different company names. They were aware that money had been lost on those deals and didn't want the same to happen to them. Reluctant to turn away a future and apparently well-heeled client, they were, nonetheless, proceeding with extreme caution. Hence my agency's assignment.

'Sure thing,' Philo came back at me. 'I've got the details. Anything else while I'm up here?'

'Can't think of anything. Just get the train back as soon as you've finished – no loitering around the fleshpots. Keep away from Soho. I need to work on a report for the bank tonight, if poss.' I didn't, but neither did I want my apprentice roaming the big city on my time.

'Right, Boss. Catch you later.'

The line went dead and I switched off the mobile. Because of my hump, my face was only inches away from the steering wheel and I leaned even further forward, resting my forehead against the warm, hard plastic for a moment or two. What the hell was Shelly Ripstone playing at? Why waste my time and her money? I straightened again – that is, I straightened as much as possible – and lit a cigarette. I could end the assignment there and then, call her with my apologies and close the case. But something – I didn't know what: instinct, intuition, I had no idea – prevented me from doing so. It was an odd reaction at the time, but it makes sense to me now.

The first thing I had to do before making any final decision, I told myself, was to find out more about Shelly Ripstone herself. And there was one particular person who could help me with that.

I tapped numbers into the mobile.

Early that evening we met at Brown's, one of the seaside town's trendy eateries, where the waiters and waitresses were hip and friendly. Etta was a few minutes late and stood briefly by the door, searching the tables for me. I gave her a wave and she returned a smile.

Etta Kaesbach was slim, almost skinny, with long brown hair and intelligent eyes. I'd always be grateful to her for helping me set up business in the first place, giving me the chance to do work for her firm of solicitors after I'd bombarded her with letters, mailshots and phone calls. She'd been the first solicitor – and it was from this profession that most private investigations agencies got their work – to provide me with the opportunity of proving my worth, not, she once told me when we'd got to know each other better, because of my obvious disabilities, but because of my over-whelming enthusiasm (yes, I had been over-anxiously keen in those early days, eager for the work, desperate to show I could do a difficult job as well, if not better, than the best of my particular trade).

She sat opposite me at the round table, her face a little flushed from her obvious dash from her office to meet me. Etta's hair was held back from her forehead by a child's hairgrip, not a slide, and her hazel eyes were encircled by round, wireframed spectacles, somewhat like ancient National Health specs, but which were Armani and probably cost well over two hundred quid. Perched on her fine, straight nose, they actually softened the intelligence of her face rather than enhanced it, and the absence of lipstick on lips that were already a pretty shade of pink, as well as nicely defined, combined with the neat-but-dated hairstyle, gave her a fresh attractiveness that was easy on the eye (literally in my case). She wore a deep-brown soft velvet jacket over a flowing maroon skirt, the collar of her beige shirt/blouse overlapping the jacket lapels. Etta was in her mid-thirties, although she looked ten years younger, had one disastrous marriage behind her – it had only lasted eighteen months, due mainly, she admitted, to dedication to her own career (although I knew there was more to it than that; she'd chosen a real bastard for a partner) – and had suffered poor on-and-off relationships since. As far as I knew, there was no man in her life at the moment and, I have to own up, I'd often dreamt of playing a larger part in her life myself, but had never had the nerve, nor the encouragement from her, to make a move in that direction. I was too scared of spoiling things between us. And too afraid of rejection.

A young girl in white shirt and black leggings was at the table before Etta had placed her briefcase by her chair.

'Hi,' greeted the waitress, all sleeked-back hair and stunning smile. 'What can I get you?'

'Just coffee, regular.' Etta smiled back, then glanced at my brandy glass. 'One of those might be useful too.'

'You'll need to order some food if you want alcohol,' I said, indicating the remaining half of my chicken salad sandwich, brown bread, no mayonnaise.

'That's okay,' said the waitress obligingly. 'We'll count yours as the meal. Unless you'd like something to eat?' She raised her eyebrows at Etta.

'No thanks. Coffee and a brandy will be fine.' Etta smiled back, then returned her attention to me as the waitress left us.

'Busy day?' I enquired.

Etta rolled her eyes. 'Like all others. You switching from whisky these days?'

'Needed something a little more substantial.' I sipped the brandy to show how necessary it really was.

'Having problems, Dis?' It wasn't an idle question; those hazel eyes were full of concern.

'Uh, no, nothing drastic.' The episode last night with the broken mirror wasn't one I cared to relate.

'Nothing to do with the new client I sent you, I hope.' She pulled a wisp of hair away from her mouth.

'Shelly Ripstone? Uh-uh, she's fine. But I did want to talk to you about her.'

'So I gathered from your phone call. Oh Lord, I hope I haven't sent you trouble. I thought it might be an easy one for you, a straightforward trace.'

'And so it should have been,' I reassured her. 'Thanks again, by the way.' I meant for the continuing work and she acknowledged with a shrug.

'You're the one who's helping me out, Dis. I'd hate to refer a good client to the wrong agency.'

I gave Etta my lop-sided grin. 'So long as you know it's always appreciated.'

'Are you getting sentimental in your old age, Dis?' She

was smiling too, but she watched me keenly, a little puzzled I suppose.

'God forbid,' I joked. 'You'd only take advantage.' I was suddenly embarrassed by the sexual connotation of that remark – like as *if* – and I quickly moved on. 'I only wondered if you could tell me more about Shelly Ripstone.'

Etta gave me a surprised look as the waitress arrived back at our table with her coffee and brandy. I quickly drained my own glass and tipped it towards the girl. 'Sorry, I should've asked a minute ago.'

'No problem.' No strain at all in the waitress's smile. 'Back in a moment.'

I put the empty glass down and returned Etta's gaze. 'S'okay, Mrs Ripstone isn't being difficult. I'd just like to know some more about her background. We drew a blank on tracing her baby at the first hurdle and I wondered how badly she'd take it.'

'I see.' I could tell Etta didn't quite believe what I'd said, but she seemed prepared to indulge me. 'What did Mrs Ripstone tell you when she came to your office?'

'She was distraught, missing her late husband. I gathered she was afraid of being left alone in the world and the thought of finding her long lost son seemed to provide her with some comfort. I told her a trace on the child wouldn't be easy after all these years, but she didn't want to hear it. I guess getting her son back might have compensated for the loss of her husband in some way, so I was sympathetic.'

Etta gave a small shake of her head before sipping the coffee and it was my turn to be surprised, this time by her cynical smile. A fresh brandy was placed before me and I nodded a thanks to the waitress as she retrieved my dead glass. Picking up the new brandy, I held it towards my companion and Etta lifted her own glass. We clinked them together, a minor ritual I always believed in when I was with a friend.

'She didn't tell me it all, did she?' I said, and Etta was hesitant.

'Oh, what the hell, she is a mutual client, so I think it's okay to share a confidence with you. But it *is* in confidence, right?'

'Hey, it's me you're talking to. When have I ever broken a confidence?'

'Yes, I know, you're a pro. And in this case, I think it might be useful for you to hear the whole story. It won't help you find the missing child – if there *is* one – but you'll at least understand why it's so important to Shelly Ripstone.'

'So it isn't just because she's a lonely widow.'

'Well, that might be part of it, but there's also a much more material side to the whole thing.'

Becoming more interested, I leaned forward on the table.

'Did she tell you how her husband died?' Etta asked.

I raised my eyebrows, not an easy thing for me to do. 'She said he'd had a heart attack.'

'She didn't explain the circumstances?'

I shook my head slowly, wondering.

'No, I suppose there's no reason why she should have.' Etta put down the brandy and sipped coffee again. Whirling ceiling fans sent down cool, welcoming breezes. 'It was downright embarrassing for her, in fact.'

'Come on, Etta, get to it.'

'Gerald Ripstone had a heart attack while he and his wife were, uh, well you know, Dis . . .'

'While they were making love?' I grinned again. 'Not good for her, maybe, but not a bad way for him to go.'

'He shouldn't have been at it at all, his doctor had warned him to take things easy.'

'I thought the heart attack was a one-off, the first and fatal one.'

'She told you that? No, Gerald had been suffering from a heart condition for some time. He really should have been more careful. At least, he shouldn't have used Viagra, especially combined with the drugs he was on.'

'Well, I guess it's natural enough for a man to want his own wife, no matter how debilitated he is. And his wife is an attractive woman.'

'That's as maybe. I'm more inclined to think that Shelly persuaded him to use the pill. As for Gerald, he was desperate for a son and heir. Needed someone to leave his business to, someone who'd carry on his name. Incidentally, you won't know the worst part about that night. The embarrassing part, that is.'

Now I was intrigued and moved even further across the table towards Etta, my back so bent I must have resembled a turtle.

'I'm not sure I should tell you about this, mutual client or not.' She looked down into her coffee cup, just a little flustered.

'You can't stop there, Etta. What'll it take to bribe you?'

She sighed. 'You won't let it go anyway, will you?'

I shook my head. 'You know you want to tell me.'

She smiled, revealing small, even teeth. 'Yes, I do, you bastard.' She took a nip of brandy, grimaced, and chased the taste away with coffee. 'Okay. You've heard of couples becoming locked together during intercourse?'

My turn to grin again. 'I've witnessed dogs in that awkward state, but I always thought it was a myth as far as we humans were concerned.'

'No, it isn't, actually. It's not common, but it happens – ask any experienced doctor. Sometimes a woman might panic for some reason or other while copulating and then becomes incapable of relaxing her legs, which become locked tight.'

A young mother on the next table feeding a toddler chocolate ice-cream from a glass dish glanced over. The little boy, sporting a brown moustache and beard, smacked his lips impatiently until he caught his mother's attention once more.

Etta lowered her voice. 'The abdominal muscles become locked too, as well as the muscles around the vagina.'

'Nice,' I commented.

'Not really. The man's working part is gripped so tightly he just can't break free, no matter how he tries. And I think the blood concentration in the penis because of the Viagra Gerald was using might have made things even more difficult. Personally, I think he took more than one pill and was locked in tight as a result.'

'Pretty humiliating when you have to call in the fire brigade.'

'No, it requires hospital treatment.' Etta's face was quite serious. 'The woman, and maybe the man too by that time, has to be given a muscle relaxant so they can be separated.'

I made an 'ouch' sound.

'It can quite often happen if the male partner has a heart attack while ... well, while on the job. The sexual act itself raises the blood pressure, which is dangerous for anyone with a heart condition, and the woman's fright when she realizes her lover is dying on top of her is enough to send the relevant muscles into spasms.'

I needed a cigarette, but Etta wasn't a smoker and I'd chosen the non-smoking area of the restaurant in deference to her. Instead, I drained my second brandy.

'Surely the Ripstones would have been aware that the strain might be too much for Gerald,' I said.

'You'd have thought so, wouldn't you? Perhaps Shelly wanted her husband even more than he wanted her that night.'

'And he couldn't resist.'

'Or she made it impossible for him to resist.'

'She wouldn't have – ' I began to protest.

'Shelly wanted his child too. She had a special reason to.'

'If she thought she might lose her husband at any time, I suppose it's understandable. A child might compensate – '

Again, Etta interrupted. 'Without an heir, she stood to lose half Gerald's fortune.'

I pulled back a little, one good eye staring at my companion. 'You want to explain that for me?'

'When the Ripstones were first married, Gerald made a will through our firm leaving everything – his wealth, the business – to his wife and any children they subsequently might have.'

'Only they didn't get to have any kids.'

'Correct. And they were never likely to. Not together, at any rate.'

I looked askance.

'Gerald Ripstone was sterile. He consulted a specialist after a few years of marriage and no offspring, and discovered he was incapable of siring an heir. He kept it to himself, never told his wife.'

'Wait. How d'you know all this?'

'Eventually, Gerald confided in his lawyer, the senior partner of my firm, who'd become a good personal friend over the years. Howard Benson, my boss, gave me the information when I queried a specific clause in Gerald Ripstone's will, the part dealing with inheritance.'

'But why wouldn't he tell his own wife? From the way she blubbered in my office she must have thought the world of him. Surely the fact that he was firing blanks wouldn't have mattered to her?'

Etta shrugged. 'Who knows why? Pride? Embarrassment? The way you've just expressed it shows how the male of the species views that kind of thing. You know what men are like, Dis.'

Well no, I didn't, not in that respect, anyway. Sexual prowess or high fertility having never been an area of contemplation for me.

'The point is,' Etta went on, 'Shelly was never aware that she couldn't have a child by her husband. But here's the weird thing: Gerald loved her so much and cared about the continuance of his business enough for him not to worry by whom she had a child so long as there was someone around to take care of both after he was gone. Unfortunately, he didn't have enough confidence in his wife's business acumen or her ability to survive without him.'

'I can't decide if the guy was eccentric or admirable.'

'Probably a bit of both. If you ask me it was his way of dealing with his own guilt and self-imposed shame.'

People are complex, right? Lord knows, I've dealt with enough oddballs, both professionally and personally, to be aware of how complicated we mortals are.

'Okay,' I admitted. 'Curious, but it makes some kind of psychological sense. It was his way of compensating for something he deemed his fault. What I don't understand though, is why they didn't adopt?'

'I think it was because he wanted the child to be part of one of them. If it couldn't come from his loins, then at least it would be from Shelly's womb. However, I do know they were finally looking into the matter of adoption – Gerald dearly wanted a boy – just before he died. They left it too late.'

Her coffee was almost gone and I asked if she'd like another. She declined and twirled the brandy glass around by its stem. She took a sip before placing it back on the table.

'In his will,' Etta said, 'Gerald gave his blessing to any new partner that Shelly might find. All part of his guilt trip, I suppose, and his obsession for the continuation of his business, which he seemed to regard as his own epitaph.'

'But even if she had a child soon, a baby couldn't run a business. It doesn't make sense.'

'That's why everything has been put into a trust for now.'

'What? The money *and* the business?'

'Yep.'

'The trustee . . . ?'

'The bank that helped Gerald set up business in the first place. The one that likes to say yes unless you're asking for overdraft facilities. He'd always maintained a good working relationship with that particular bank.'

'I can see how Shelly would be just a little upset with that arrangement. It's treating her like a child herself.'

'She was more than a little upset. She yelled blue murder when the terms of the will were read out to her.'

'So the trustee looks after the business until the child is old enough to take over.'

'And if it's a boy, all the better.'

I let it all sink in, drawing back from the table and staring into space. The waiters and waitresses had gathered in a clique by the bar, occasionally breaking into laughter at a shared joke. The toddler at the next table grizzled for more ice-cream, while his mother wiped the mess from his face with a napkin. The restaurant's glass door opened and a couple of wide-eyed tourists wandered through, looking around as if not knowing what to do next; one of the waiters quickly joined them and showed the way to an empty table. A gabble of Dutch or German drifted our way.

'So that's why she's so keen to find her missing son,' I murmured at last.

'Shelly? I would think so, although I've tried to convince her she'll be well taken care of without the worry of dealing with a business she doesn't understand. She seems to have got it into her head that she'd be better off by being independent of the bank, and in a way, I can see her point. Why should she have to be accountable for every penny she spends and every business decision she makes to some faceless wonders at head office?'

'Wait a minute.' A new thought had struck me. 'This clairvoyant thing. You knew about it, didn't you?'

Etta nodded. 'Yes, Shelly was very excited. That's why

she wanted the name of a reputable private investigation agency.'

'But did she visit Louise Broomfield seeking some kind of consolation for the loss of her husband, or has she always suspected her baby had lived and wanted help in finding him?'

'What does it matter?'

'I'm just wondering if the clairvoyant picked up Shelly's desperation, somehow tuned into the *thought* of a missing child. Isn't that how this kind of thing works, by extrasensory perception? Maybe Shelly just passed the idea on to this other woman.'

'Dis, as I said: what does it matter? Your work is done as far as this case is concerned. When you rang me earlier today you said there was no record of the baby's birth, let alone its death. Submit your fee and forget about it.'

I wished it could be that simple. Unfortunately, something was nagging at me, something I couldn't get a handle on. Some creepy little voice way back in the deeper recesses of my mind was telling me I was more involved that I dared to imagine.

7

'James Stewart.'

'You got it wrong this time. It was Gary Cooper.'

Henry shook his head vehemently. 'No. I'm telling you it was James Stewart.'

'You're thinking of *Mr Smith Goes to Washington*, not *Mr Deeds Goes to Town*. *Deeds* was made in '36 and *Smith* in '39, same year as *Destry Rides Again*.'

That gave Henry cause for pause, but not for long. 'Henry Fonda was *Smith Goes to Washington*.'

'No, you dope. Fonda was *Young Mr Lincoln*.'

'Okay, okay. So who played *The Thin Man*?' My account-ant's eyes narrowed behind his thin glasses and he grinned with expected triumph.

'William Powell, of course.'

'No! *That* was James Stewart!' He banged the desk with the flat of his hand, triumph complete as far as he was concerned.

'Sorry, Henry, but James Stewart was in *After the Thin Man*, made two years later, and he was the villain; William Powell was still playing the thin guy, Nick Charles, and Myrna Loy was his partner, Nora. His dog was called Asta, by the way, played by Asta the dog.' I tried not to gloat.

Henry's mouth was open, his jaw loose. He quickly regath-ered his wits though. 'Answer me this one, then. What Roger Corman B movie did Jack Nicholson star in?'

'Ah, you know I don't have a clue about modern movies,' I returned disgustedly.

'Modern? *Modern?* This was Sixties stuff, my friend.'

'Yeah well, anything made after the Forties escapes me. I prefer the really old ones.'

'God, anyone would think you were ancient.'

'I just like the black and white style. Films had class in those days. Men and women dressed right and sex was suggested and all the sexier for it, and there was no profanity then. Didn't need it: the story was everything.'

'It was the Edgar Allan Poe one, wasn't it?'

We both turned to look at Ida, who was sitting in the visitors' chair, stirring her mug of tea with a plastic spoon.

'What?' I said.

'Directed by Roger Corman, starring Jack Nicholson. He was a soldier or something. Bit part. You know – the horror film, *The Pit and the Pendulum.*'

'Oh don't you start!' Henry was gritting his teeth, his fists clenched. 'It was *The Raven. The* bloody *Raven*, okay?'

'Yes, but Nicholson was in the other one, too,' Ida offered helpfully.

'No he bloody wasn't!' Henry always got wound up over movies; he considered himself the oracle as far as the silver screen was concerned.

I'm not sure if Philo was deliberately winding Henry up, but he chipped in with a grin: 'No, Jack Nicholson was in *Fall of the House of Usher*. That was the one he had a small part in.'

'He didn't! *He didn't!* He didn't come anywhere near it!'

That was it as far as the rest of us were concerned. Ida broke into a fit of giggling first, closely followed by Philo. I was just chuckling. Henry gripped the edge of his desk, glaring at all of us, not quite sure yet if the tease was deliberate. Watching Henry, usually so calm and rational, even during his racial diatribes, lose his rag over something so trivial was always fun.

He gave up in disgust, his only way out. 'All right, we've all got plenty to do today, so why don't we just get on?'

I put my empty coffee mug down beside the plastic kettle, which resided on top of a filing cabinet (it was Philo's job to do the washing up in the small loo just off the main office), then lumbered towards Henry's desk. It would have been awkward for me to sit on its corner, so I leaned back against it instead, arms folded over my misshapen chest.

'Ida, you've got a status report for our old client, the Ownback Catalogue company. They need to know if there's any chance of getting their money from a customer who's suddenly gone sour on them. Henry has the details.'

Our accountant and administrator, still miffed, handed a typewritten brief from the catalogue company to Ida, who took it and began noting the details.

'Check with the receiver's office if the debtor is bankrupt and the County Court Office to find out if there's any outstanding judgements against him,' Henry instructed her.

'I *have* done this sort of thing before, Henry,' Ida reminded him, still scanning the two-page letter.

'You'll need to pay the debtor a visit on this one,' I advised, only because I wanted the option followed up. 'If he's uncooperative, talk to his neighbours – and let him know you're prepared to do that; he might just want to save himself the embarrassment.'

'Want me to pad out the report?'

'Shouldn't have to. By the time you've checked on what car or cars he runs, his personal possessions, whether he's paying rent or mortgage on his home, if he works full-time or is he on the dole, you'll have enough to fill a couple of pages.' It's a common practice in this business to make sure the client feels they're getting value for money, even on – no, *especially* on – a negative result like a non-trace.

I shifted attention to Philo, who had one foot on the desk he shared with Ida and was polishing his already glossy black shoe with a duster. 'Henry has an accident report for you, Beau Brummell.'

'Stewart Granger and Elizabeth Taylor,' Henry chipped in,

anxious to regain his authority as movie-buff of the century.
'Peter Ustinov played the Prince of Wales. Or was it Robert
Morley . . . ?' He appeared deeply worried at this fresh
uncertainty.

'Yeah, yeah,' I growled. 'Playtime's over, Henry. As you
said, we've got a busy day.'

Philo's brown eyes, meanwhile, had lit up. Accident
reports were tedious to do, but for a novice, it was a step up.
This was the first one I'd allowed him to carry out on his
own.

'It's an NOF, of course.' Henry's mind was back on the
job, but there was a certain coolness in his voice that let our
apprentice know he wasn't yet forgiven for his part in the
tease. 'No Obvious Fault,' he added, just in case the acronym
wasn't clear to Philo (Henry loved acronyms – they lent him
authority). 'It's cheaper for the insurance company to use us
to investigate the RTA – "Road Traffic Accident" – than loss
adjusters, and it's cheaper for us to use *you*.' The last
emphasis was unnecessary, but Henry was never one to
forgive easily. 'You're to meet our client's driver at the scene
of the accident, so take the standard interview sheet with
you – that way you won't forget to ask the right questions,
will you?'

'What else will you need, Philo?' I quickly asked, more to
smooth over Henry's sarcasm than to test the kid.

'Camera, surveyor's tape measure, and pen and pad for
sketches,' Philo answered immediately.

'SLR camera *and* the Polaroid, dummy,' Henry corrected.
'You never know, the SLR shots might not come out.'

It was a valid reminder, despite the sneer that went with
it. I'd taken scene-of-accident photographs myself with no
film in the main camera, and high street developing was
always a risk. 'Three sketches at least, and let me see the
report before you send it off to the client. In fact, let me
sign it.'

Still pleased about the assignment, Philo nodded, a smile brightening his good-looking face.

'Report the facts only,' Henry warned, 'not your opinion, or the driver's version of what happened.'

'Gotcha.' Philo was already reaching into a low cupboard for the cameras and film.

'What're your plans for the day, Dis?' Ida enquired as she pulled on a light summer jacket and took an umbrella – it was raining outside – from the coat stand.

'Couple of debt negotiations this morning.' I held a Credit Consumer's Licence, categories D and E, which allowed me officially to come up with ways a debtor might solve their financial problems. Usually it was simply to suggest they pay off a little at a time on a regular basis, or at least by laying down a lump sum towards the whole amount. Sometimes there was a more complicated process to go through, the main object being to keep the whole thing away from the courts, which was always expensive and time-consuming for all parties, including myself as far as time was concerned. I preferred counselling these people, many of them in debt through no real fault of their own – a sudden loss of earnings, a death in the family – to demanding they pay up, and category D allowed for debt adjusting as well as advising, while E was what actually empowered me to collect payment if at all possible. These jobs frequently took time and patience, but if the agency handled enough of them through the year, they were quite lucrative. Sometimes it bothered me, this chasing people for money, even though I knew that many debtors were either crooks or irresponsible, and if they fell into neither of these categories, then better to deal with me than the bailiff. Ultimately, I was there to help, not to threaten or take things away.

'And what about our Mrs Ripstone?' Was there just a hint of malicious glee behind Henry's smile? 'Are you going to keep the poor woman hanging on?'

James Herbert

'No, Henry.' I turned to face him. 'I'm going to ring her right now and tell her there's nothing more we can do. Unless you'd like to tell her for me?'

He shook his head slowly and deliberately. 'That's what being the boss is all about,' he said.

'Thanks for reminding me.'

I went into my office and, still oddly uneasy with my decision, I picked up the phone.

8

It was around 10.30 that night that I stepped outside the pub in a side street near the seafront, the steady drizzle that had marred the day over with for the moment, but the streets still shiny damp. The noise from the saloon bar behind me died with the closing of the door and I took in great lungfuls of almost pure sea air, exhaling long and hard to rid my lungs of the residue cigarette fumes they'd been collecting over the past couple of hours. I felt only a little better now, the irritating sense of dissatisfaction that had been dogging me for most of the day dulled by booze and company. A burst of laughter behind me was raucous enough to pass through the thick wood and glass of the pub door and I was pretty sure it wasn't at my expense: I knew nearly all the regulars, who were mainly of the – how shall I put it? – of the 'exotic' variety; young and not so young gay men, pensioned-off chorus boys of untold age but with fabulous stories to tell, cultured antique dealers who'd had other careers in their prime, but who now saw this last profession as a means of genteel employment for themselves and their (invariably younger) partners. There were shammers and schemers, duckers and divers, women who love women, the lonely and the disparate. A good bunch. And whenever I entered that bar I was greeted with friendly calls rather than odd stares.

The air may have been moist, but it was warm; warm and scented with the aroma of sea and salt. As I began to walk towards the front, depression settled over me like a well-worn cloak, and even the bright promenade lights at the end of the long, narrow street failed to offer any cheer. Moving along the glistening pavement I wondered why this mood of – what? I couldn't focus on it. Inadequacy, perhaps? – had pursued me all day. Since I'd first opened my eye that morning, in fact. Since my conclusion that there really was nothing more I could do for Shelly Ripstone.

When I'd rung her earlier, she'd pleaded with me to stay on the case, even phoned me back seconds after I'd broken off the call. She'd offered to double my fee if only I would agree to continue the search for her lost son, and nothing I said would convince her that it would be pointless, that the child – and now I was beginning to doubt there ever was a child – had died only minutes or seconds after being born. Doctors didn't lie. The authorities might, but then why should they in such a case?

Shelly had become more distressed. Didn't I understand that a mother intuitively, *instinctively*, knew these things? And besides, the clairvoyant, Louise Broomfield, also had no doubts that her son was still alive. The evidence – or lack of it – said otherwise, I told her, but that had made her more aggressive. Pleadings became insults. But fine, I'd had plenty of those in my time. Firmly, and quite politely, I said my goodbyes and replaced the receiver.

This time she didn't ring back.

I could, of course, have mentioned the fact that she had not been entirely open with me, that maybe – well, quite likely – her motivation had more to do with her late husband's money than maternal love. But that would have been rude of me. And unnecessary.

Even so, this night I reviewed the case in my mind as I shuffled on towards the sea, yet still I could make no sense of her claim. Even if Shelly Ripstone *née* Teasdale had given birth eighteen years ago and the hospital had been razed to the ground some time afterwards, the baby's short existence would still have been noted by the General Registrar Office. But it seemed nothing at all had been documented, neither at the London office nor the one at Southport, where all such records were kept after the closedown of Somerset House in the capital. Also, in adult tracing the method is relatively simple, even if the disappearance is intentional (I rule out murder and dismemberment here); credit card purchases, the electoral roll, National Insurance number, bank statements, car registration, friends and associates – all conspire to track down an absconder; but when there is no life history, when there isn't even any evidence that the subject of the trace was ever born in the first place except for the word of a bereaved widow of dubious (although understandable) motivation and possibly of distracted mind, then finding that person is next to impossible.

There was *nothing* I could do. I'd only waste time and the client's money, and I'd never been into that kind of scam. No, I'd made the right decision. The assignment was a dodo, a dead duck. The agency had done all it could. So what was nagging at me? Why couldn't I let it go?

'Spare some change, chief?'

I'd almost passed by the figure huddled in a doorway before his voice, both plaintive and cheerful at the same time, brought me to a halt. I peered closer, searching for a face among the darkness and rags, but only when the headlights of a car crawling down the narrow street lit us both up did I find one. Wide, friendly eyes looked up at me and I realized the beggar was a kid, somewhere between seventeen and twenty, with spiky hair and a ring through his nose and grime on his skin that looked more than a week old. The sleeves of his ragged jumper were pulled over his hands, even though there was no coolness to the night, and his well-worn boots were metal-tipped and too hardy for the season.

'Just for a bit of food, like,' he said, working for whatever I was prepared to give him. He seemed uncomfortable under my scrutiny, perhaps with my features. What he couldn't appreciate, though, was that I was only doing my job. Even half-drunk, I did what I always did when I came upon vagrants or beggars (not necessarily the same thing): I gave them the once-over – all of us at the agency did – trying to catch any resemblance to photographs on our files, old images of persons gone astray, missing youths, absent husbands, absconded wives, even mothers or fathers who'd decided normal society wasn't all it was cracked up to be. You never knew when you might strike it lucky.

He became uncertain, having had a good look at me as the glare from the headlights had peaked before moving on. He appeared very uncomfortable now that we were in the shadows again. He drew up his boots and curled up in the doorway, his body seeming to shrink.

'It's okay,' I said quietly – soothingly, I hoped. 'When did you last eat?' It was important for me to know.

He didn't answer straight away. His neck craned from the untidy bundle of clothes, and he looked around the doorway's corners, up and down the street, as if searching out other company. This was a lonely little side road though.

'This morning,' he answered at last, his face featureless in the gloom. He cleared his throat, a nervous rasp.

I sighed and rummaged through my pockets, finding only a pound coin and a few odd pence. 'Fuckit,' I grumbled to myself and reached inside my jacket for my wallet. Pulling out a ten-pound note, I sensed a fresh, a more trusting, alertness about the boy.

'Promise me you'll get yourself something to eat, okay?' I thrust the note towards him and he accepted it with both hands.

'Bloodyell,' he said in a low breath. 'Thanks, man. I mean, really – thanks.'

'Sure.' I stepped away from him. 'Remember: food. Right?'

I could just make out the nodding of his head before I turned away, already wondering if he'd stick to the handout's condition, or if he'd head straight for his regular supplier.

A tenner wouldn't buy him much, so maybe he'd just drink it away. I let it go: I could only make the offer – the rest was up to him. I'd learned a long time ago it was all you could do.

As I neared the seafront there was more activity. Tourists strolled arm in arm along the broad pavements that edged the wide King's Road, many of them still in shorts and T-shirts, despite the earlier drizzle and the lateness of the hour, all of this – the people, the coast road, the edge of the beach below the promenade railings – lit up by street lamps and festive lights, lights from hotels, restaurants, the big cinema and theatre complex, lights from traffic rushing by as if late for curfew. And noise came from all directions, the jabber of crowds and their laughter, and muted music from bars and clubs, the conversations of diners drifting from open doorways.

I stepped over a puddled gutter that rainbowed oil or spilt petrol in its waters, and waited anxiously for a break in the traffic, a chance to cross the broad expanse of road at my own lively but slow speed. The gay lights of the Palace Pier stretched out into the blackness, their mirror image on the sea below dancing with every wave that rushed to shore. The pier resembled an ocean liner in celebratory mood.

Taking my chance, I made it to the centre of the road, then waited for a gap in the opposite lane's flow. Faces stared out at me from passing cars, one or two vehicles even slowing down so that their occupants could take a more leisurely look, and I saw myself with their eyes, a ridiculous stunted shape, bent as if cowering in the roadway, a clown of a figure whose mask was not funny in transient headlights, its shadows too severe, mien too crooked, the body too unseemly. Laughter passed me by as I waited; someone even took the trouble to wind down a passenger window and call out to me, call out something I didn't quite hear and did not want to hear. I seized the moment to hobble the rest of the way, my bad leg dragging across tarmac as it does when I'm tired or inebriated, my left arm waving in the air ahead for balance. I arrived safely but a little dead in heart.

A group, a horde, of language students – Brighton is always full of language students – paused to allow me through, the hush in their voices as I avoided touching any of them making their alien whispers easy to comprehend. I lowered my head even more, ashamed, vulnerable – naked under their gaze – not even my alcohol haze dimming the ocular assault, and I kept moving until I reached the ornate rail overlooking the lower promenade and beach. There I leaned, my chest pressed against hard metal, my only eye watching the blackness of the sea's horizon, a barely visible dark against dark, and I concentrated on that alone so that self-pity would not overwhelm me. My breath came in short heaves and my hands clenched the rail tightly until my thoughts, my feelings, began to settle; not calm – I didn't feel calm at all – but to quieten down, become absorbed into me so that my hands on that rail no longer trembled, so that my gasps steadied, my breathing became deeper, more even. With the quietening, there soon came the question: why had I panicked so quickly, so easily? Ridicule was something I'd borne for as long as I could remember and pity for the same length of time, but I'd learned to cope; hadn't accepted, could never accept either insult, but I'd learned to endure. So why this abrupt overpowering fright? Why had my mental equilibrium, that hard-earned stability gained only after a lifetime of abuse and sniggers and curious glances if not downright ogling and well-meaning but so often *de*meaning patronization, why had it so swiftly deserted me? Had I only kidded myself that I'd adapted to all those jibes and kindnesses? Well no, because I knew I'd only ever placed a barrier between myself and the prejudices and good intentions of others. I suppose my surprise tonight was that the shield was gossamer-thin instead of cast-iron thick. Even the whisky and beer I'd consumed that night had failed to dull the senses, to thicken that self-preserving defence even more.

An urge to be nearer the sea overcame me (because the sea was clean and as far away from people as I could get?) and I lurched from the railings, heading towards the ramp that led to the boulevard below. I was aware that my shambling walk was exaggerated by weariness – and yes, no excuses, by alcohol too – the limp now a parody of my normal gait, my hump even more rounded. Crouched and shuffling, I hastened down towards the beach, momentum increased by the slope's angle.

The ramp was wide enough for wheelchairs and delivery vans alike, but not user-friendly for hunchbacks of awkward stride, and I steered myself to one side so that I could slide my hand along its rail, steadying myself, occasionally gripping to control the descent. Near the bottom, customers were overflowing from the Zap club, milling around its door, spilling out on to the level boulevard. Getting in my way.

Now I deliberately kept my head bowed, my one eye watching other people's feet as the noise from the club's open door became horrendous, the chatter of voices around me intimidating. I could tell by the shifting of legs that some of the crowd were anxious not to become an obstacle in my way; others failed to notice me though, only becoming aware when I tried desperately, solicitously, to nudge by without giving offence. A girl's shriek was followed by laughter, a male's derision followed by embarrassed shushes.

At last I was through, but as I raised my head to see the way ahead I was confronted by the customers of the Cuba Bar, a large section of its patronage seated at tables arranged in an open area outside the bar itself. I slunk around them, regretting my impulse to reach the seashore, aware that not only did people *en masse* stare harder but that they felt anonymous enough to voice their humour or shock. Several of them pointed me out, and one or two shouted comments, and only when my feet crunched pebbles did I stop running.

I sneaked away from the bright lights towards sweet covering darkness, away from mocking sounds and cries of pity, making my way diagonally across the beach so that I'd also be moving closer to home in my sea quest. Noise behind me became a general hum of voices and music, the stony shore grew dimmer with every shuffling pace, and I'd almost reached my tidal sanctuary when I heard the insult that was the worst of all, the one I dreaded because it was never the end of it, it was always the precursor to further torment.

'Oi, fuckin Quasimodo!'

They were sitting around in a circle on the stones, unnoticed in my rush, difficult to see in their mainly dark attire. They drank from cans of beer but the smell that drifted across our neutral ground was pure weed; their spliffs glowed in the gloom, bright one moment, a dull amber the next, each burning dot thick with Jamaican promise. I ignored the call, hurrying on, my feet sliding on the little pebble hills that spoiled any rhythm I could build, but something large and hard struck the hump of my back. The stone clunked on to the beach and I went on.

'The bells, the bells!' someone behind me wailed to much snickering.

I stopped, hung my head, closed my eye for a moment, then turned to face them.

I was between the group and the boulevard, between it and the broad stretch of light from the roadway above, so that as they collectively stood, some moving sluggishly as though heavy with dope and booze, one, the nearest to me, rising almost sprightly, fired by youth's arrogance, I could see their shapes in the muted illumination, could take in their leathers and amulets, their spiked collars, their freaked hair and high, laced boots. They were an unlovely bunch.

I could just make out the peppy one's leering grin, no mercy in that expression.

'Going swimming, Quozzie? Only swim at night, do yer?'

The others enjoyed the taunt, adding their own drolleries.

'Didn't know the freak show was in town.' 'What yer do for sex, date a spazzie?' 'Didn't know abortions could walk about.' You know, remarks of that ilk, and others that were plain degenerate. Every one seemed to inspire the next, and the gang had great fun.

'Oh shit,' I said quietly to myself, then turned away and began moving again, not rushing, just taking it steady, not wanting them to see how much I was shaking. Shaking with rage, with fear, with impotence.

A beer can hit me this time, half full so that liquid spilt into my hair, ran down the back of my neck.

'Hey, we're talkin to you, 'umpback!'

I didn't reply. I kept going.

Footsteps crunching after me.

Knowing I couldn't outrun them, I whirled around and it must have been my expression that stopped them dead, shadows formed by the dim light probably deepening my scowl, maybe even making me look fearsome.

'Listen to me,' I said, allowing anger to override my nervousness. 'I'm not bothering you, so just leave me alone. Okay?'

But the sprightly one, the arrogant one, the one I assumed was the leader, swaggered towards me, features screwed up into a grimace that was as ugly as mine.

'You got it wrong, Quozzie. You are botherin us.'

Another step closer allowed me to see a face so full of loathing and bigotry that it surely must have poisoned this one's soul; it came in waves, a silent rant against everything this zealot thought of as abnormal and not up to the perceived order of things. Although my gaze never left those venomous eyes, I was aware that the others were outflanking me so that soon I was surrounded. I took a step back; my main tormentor took a step forward.

I sensed no euphoria among them, no laid-back pleasantry that the fat Jamaicans and drink should have induced, and I began to suspect they had all been on something harder earlier that evening, maybe Ice, which was the drug of the moment in Brighton around that time, a street methamphetamine, pure crystal shit that gave a big rush that ultimately and invariably fucked up the brain with its worsening withdrawals. Sometimes the tweakers freaked out with meth psychosis and hallucinations, and that was never a time to be around them.

I consoled myself with the thought that this merry little band of junkheads could just as easily be on GHB, or Liquid Ecstasy, both popular drugs around the clubs, whose comedowns sometimes could be scary as well; then again, they could be on the nutter stuff, Special K. Whichever, I figured their smoking mixed with booze was their way of making the descent easy on themselves. Only it didn't seem to be working: aggression was bristling from this mob.

'Look,' I said placatingly, hoping the tremble in my voice wasn't too noticeable, 'what d'you want from me? D'you want money? I've got money. I can give you some.' I reached for my wallet, an action replay of a short time earlier when I'd willingly offered charity to the beggar. I wasn't proud of myself at that moment, but if that was what it took to get me off the hook, then so be it.

'Yeah, we want money.'

Eyes looked greedily at the notes in my hand. 'But we don't want some, we want all of it.'

My wallet, as well as the notes, was snatched away and when I reacted, reflexively reaching out to grab it back (cash was one thing, credit cards and driving licence was another) something whacked against my head. I think it must have been another, even larger, stone from the beach, because I heard it crack as it struck my temple, and it hit me so hard I fell to my knees.

My brain went numb for a second or two and I brought both hands up to the wound, rocking there on the beach on my knees. I remember crying out, pleading with them to stop it there and then, not to let it go further, that I was hurt enough, but then they were on me, kicking, punching, pounding me until everything became a blur – everything except the pain – and I was tumbling, tumbling forward and curling into a foetus position, a frightened, confused, malformed thing scrunched up as small as I could make myself, there to be pummelled and humbled because I was an oddity, because I was an oddity with money, because I was an oddity with money who wouldn't fight back.

I don't know how long it went on for – a thousand years, two minutes? In its way, it was a lifetime – but I heard them calling me names, snarling their hatred, screeching their bile, and I absorbed it, let the pain and the name-calling sink into my system, so that soon my body and my mind had swallowed it whole, and then I allowed it – blows and words – to deaden me. That was the only way I could make it tolerable.

And when it was finally over and the five leather and amulet clad girls had walked off, I cursed them under my breath and prayed that one day the sickness inside each and every one of them would cause them to suffer the way I had suffered that night.

It began to spit with rain again.

9

The wet stone steps to my basement flat were treacherous in my condition, mainly because my vision was still bleary with tears of self-pity and humiliation and my limbs were stiff, the joints almost locked; each movement, each lumbering step, took willpower, each draw of breath took an effort. Both body and mind were in a wretched state.

Practically falling against the front door, I dug inside my trouser pocket for the key and then, for the second time in two days, scraped its point over the paintwork to locate the hole. Once inside, I fell back against the closed door and blubbered there in the darkness. I was hurt, but by now I knew it wasn't badly, and although I'd lost the cash, the girl-gang had contemptuously tossed the wallet back at me; it had struck my head, then lay open on the pebbles beside me. They hadn't been interested in the credit cards, just the money for their next fix. No, I wasn't crying because of the physical pain they caused me, nor the loss of hard-earned cash; I wept because of the dagger thrusts of their derision, their unconscionable and conscienceless verbal assault. And I cried because of their gender and their youth – two at least could have been no more than fourteen or fifteen years old. I had been broken by a team of young girls and it wasn't their blows that had weakened me, left me foetal on the beach, absorbing every punch from their fists, every slap from their hands, every kick from their high-laced boots; no, it was the viciousness of their barbs that had struck so deep, words so vile and uncompromising that it seemed as if my muscles and my mind had atrophied, had become useless and limp. It was their disgust that had defeated me.

'Oh God, why, why?' I heard myself mumble between sobs. And when I asked again, it came as a shout, a *demand* for an answer, and the question was full of loathing for myself and the Supreme Being who had created me, for I was not questioning the attack on me that night, not challenging the violence dealt to my miserable twisted body, but asking why I had been born this way, why had He created me as a monster to be reviled or pitied but never to be accepted as a normal human. How did He justify such cruelly protracted torment, a lifetime's punishment which would only end when my lungs gasped no more breaths and my heart lost its beat? I *needed* to know. I *had* to know. Yet even as I raged, implored, I was aware there would be, could be, no response, because no matter how often I'd asked – how often I'd *begged* – the question in the past, never, never, never even in my deepest despair – and this was one such moment – had an answer been given.

And eventually, as I crouched there and the last tears flushed from the undamaged ducts of my one good eye, I berated myself for believing there *was* a God to give any such rhyme or reason. Nothing – No Thing – no Heavenly Creature, no Ruler of Heaven and Earth, no Divine Deity, no Almighty, no Omnipresence, no Allah, Elohim, Yahweh, or Jehovah, would ever devise such a hellish torture. Maybe a Devil could, but surely no God?

Finally, miserably, I dragged myself up from the floor and lumbered along the short hallway to the kitchen, where I flicked on the light-switch and knelt before a low cupboard. Opening it, my hand scrabbled around behind the tins of baked beans and pineapple chunks and all the other easy-cook packages sad, single people keep stored for instant sustenance, until I felt what I was searching for: a medium-sized square-shaped, coffee jar. I pulled it out and held it to my chest while I wiped the dampness from my face with the sleeve of my jacket.

This was my special stash, used only on specific occasions; not for celebrations, nor social gatherings, but for when I needed it most – like tonight. I used it infrequently, because it was highly addictive and I couldn't afford to become highly addicted. Snow. Coke. C. Charlie. Cocaine. A cheap commodity nowadays compared to some other drugs, but still prohibitive for the likes of me. Beneficial though, at certain times. The quick rush would take me through to the other side of this trauma, the sense of wellbeing would overwhelm all else. I'd become a man again.

I took the jar through to the bathroom, unscrewed the lid and placed both on the glass shelf in front of the mirror, all routine and carried out in semi-darkness. Only then did I pull the string that operated the bare light-bulb over my head.

Dipping my fingers into the coarse coffee grains I drew out a tightly sealed plastic bag, inside which was another tightly sealed plastic bag. I unsealed the first, extracted the second, opened it and carefully poured a portion of the white powder on to a clear area of the glass shelf, my right hand trembling so badly I had to steady it with my left. I took a razor blade from the medicine cabinet beside the wall mirror and left it next to the little white hill of euphoria, of instant Nirvana, of deceptive redress, while I returned to the kitchen to get a straw. A dozen of them stood in a long plastic tumbler on a high shelf and I had to stand on tip-toe to reach them. I pulled out one and snipped it in half with scissors from a cupboard drawer before hobbling back to the bathroom.

My hand still shaking, I used the razor blade to make thin uneven lines of the coke, then bent forward with the brightly striped straw stuck half-way up my nose. I sucked up white bliss like an anteater snorting lines of ants, working my way along the short rows, thumb against the clear nostril, until only a scattering of fine dust remained. The high hit me almost immediately, a rush that was like nothing else on this earth for quick, appeasing pleasure and I jerked upright (as upright as my body would allow), still inhaling as I did so, my good eye closing as the exultation flooded my brain and a lightness swept through me.

I let out a long sigh and removed the straw, my other hand gripping the edge of the sink, the trembling already beginning to calm itself as my whole being relaxed into a wonderfully silky warmth. Pain still throbbed, but it was accommodated, harboured within a better sensation. I moaned aloud and went with the flow, my chest swelling as my misery detached itself from my psyche and floated to another place, still in reach but sequestered for the moment. The rapture swept through me and I accepted it gratefully, my poor misshapen head rocking back, my lips split into a grin of joy, my eyelids closed so that a few more tears were squeezed between them.

But when I lowered my head and opened my eye again another's face was staring out at me from the bathroom mirror.

I staggered, just a step backwards, my gaze never shifting from the figure that stood watching me from the realm beyond the glass.

I knew that face. I knew those strong, handsome features, the deep, brown eyes framed by heavy, almost feminine, lashes, the classic and very masculine shape of the nose, the lips so defined and sensual in their half-smile, the jutting, cleft chin, so rugged in its appeal, softened only slightly by that carnal mouth. Somehow I recognized the smoothed-back black hair, sleek and glossy in the mirrored light, and the heavy eyebrows, beautifully shaped over those watchful, amused eyes.

I knew this person.

Those broad shoulders, with their relaxed strength, underlying tension beneath a studied looseness, was familiar to me. I knew this man clad in shiny-lapelled tuxedo and black tie, was aware of the raw, even coarse, nature that the fine apparel disguised.

And from the expression in those roguish yet brooding eyes, I was aware that this person also knew me.

I think I swooned from shock just then, or else the room itself spun around me, and it was only the strange, extraneous sound of the doorbell that stopped me from passing out completely.

10

Whoever it was at the front door wouldn't go away. There was I, holding on to the bathroom sink, now with both hands, my eye shut again – I didn't want to see that handsome image in front of me any more – and my body still swaying, my legs enfeebled, while that persistent bellringer kept their finger against the button, releasing the pressure every now and again before starting all over, the shrill sound travelling down the short hallway and driving me crazy with its insistence.

'Go 'way,' I mumbled, not sure myself if I were talking to the visitor outside or the phantom in the mirror. '*Go away!*' I hissed, and then I opened my eye, very slowly, afraid of what I might see again.

Even as I did so, a vague recollection of having observed or perceived that handsome countenance in the past came to me, vague, peripheral glimpses that were always reflections, never the real thing, nebulous visions that vanished before they could be fastened on. Now relief – oddly tainted by disappointment – shuddered through me as my own unsightly features gawped back from the mirror.

I scrutinized my reflection, wondering at the hallucination of a moment before, silently asking myself what the hell was it with me and mirrors these days? Had the sudden rush of cocaine triggered the illusion? But I wasn't doped up yesterday when I stood in front of that cracked mirror in the repossessed house. The sound of the doorbell startled me again.

The bell, the bell. *The bells, the bells.* I shivered at the thought of those girl-gang jibes, my misery returning like a great grey cloud of chemical poison. Where was the heady coke glow, where had it gone? I was stone-cold sober, yet the traces of white dust were still on the glass shelf before me, evidence of what I'd sniffed only a few moments ago.

Knocking now. The person at the front door had given up the bell and was now rapping wood. And calling to me, calling my name. A woman's voice, soft but loud enough to reach me in the bathroom. I swore and screwed up my face even more. I had to open the door. Whoever it was outside was not going away.

Sluggishly I wiped powder residue from the shelf with my hand, then returned the rest of the stash in the clear plastic bag to the coffee grains, pushing down hard, burying it beneath them. Yanking the light cord so the bathroom was in darkness once more, I went to the kitchen and put the coffee jar on the working surface next to the sink. Then I drew in three long breaths, steadied myself, and limped down the hall to the front door.

She was small, smaller then me, and her face, illuminated by the light behind me, was round and concerned. Somehow I knew who she was even before she spoke.

'I'm Louise Broomfield.'

I wondered why she was swaying, gently rocking backwards and forwards, then I realized it was me who was in motion. I held on to the door and squared my feet against the hall carpet.

'Are you all right, Mr Dismas?'

She reached out a hand, but quickly withdrew it when I flinched away. The clairvoyant had been squinting at me because the light at my back obviously threw me into gloomy silhouette, but now her eyes widened as she got a closer look.

'My God . . .' she said in a whisper.

At the time I thought her reaction was due to my appearance together with the general dishevelment and marks the beating had left; later I was to discover it was because of something else entirely.

It was a few seconds before she had recovered enough to say: 'May I come in, Mr Dismas? It's important that I talk to you.'

'Uh, no. I don't think so. It's kind of late and I've had a heavy day.' Any irony wasn't intended: I just wanted to be left in peace to lick my wounds, brood over the mental hurts, consider reflections in mirrors. My voice sounded slurred to me and I wondered if she thought I was drunk; I decided I didn't care.

'Please,' she said urgently, the flat of her hand against the closing door. 'It really is very important.'

I hesitated, unable to make up my mind. I wasn't usually ill-mannered towards sweet-looking old ladies (although often they could be rude to me), but I really wasn't in the mood to discuss missing children and dishonest clients. I suppose it was her wide-eyed earnestness that persuaded me; either that or it was just plain too difficult to shut the door in her face, no matter how awful I felt right then.

'Okay, just . . . just say what you've got to say, then leave me alone.'

'Won't you invite me in? A few minutes of your time, that's all I need.'

Reluctantly – very reluctantly – and aware I was in no state to offer resistance, I stood aside so that the clairvoyant could come through.

She seized the opportunity, her feet across the threshold before I could change my mind, and she watched me all the way, her eyes never dropping from mine.

'Room on the right,' I instructed her and ran my hands over my face as she disappeared into the sitting-room. Closing the door, my shoulder brushed against the wall for support as I followed her down the hall. I paused in the doorway to switch on the sitting-room light and I lingered there awhile, appraising this little, rotund woman who'd invaded my space; the appraisal was reciprocal. She continued to gawk at me, and I was certain now that it wasn't because of my poor condition; I was used to stares, and hers was different – somehow it had more depth to it. Louise Broomfield had thoughts about me well beyond what she could plainly see.

'It had to be you,' she said quietly.

'Nice song,' I replied sourly, still wondering what had happened to the coke euphoria. 'I could sing a few bars, if you'd like.'

There was no smile, but she didn't appear to be offended. 'You must think I'm a little bit batty,' she said. 'It's the usual response.'

I could have told her all about usual responses, but I didn't. Instead I said: 'Look, I'm not feeling too good right at this moment, so can we make it short. There's nothing more I can do for Shelly Ripstone and I'm surprised she persuaded you to visit me.'

Concern glimmered in her eyes again. 'Oh no, Shelly didn't ask me to see you. She told me your enquiries had come to nothing, but she had no idea I would come to see you personally. No, that was entirely my own idea, Mr Dismas.'

She had a soft, reassuring voice, one that went with the kindness in her face. Louise Broomfield's hair was grey-white and she sported the kind of hairdo ladies of a certain age – sixty and over – seemed to wear like military helmets: neat, pulled away from the face, stiff-permed. Her dress was pale blue, her full breasts resting on a full tummy, and her shoes were a sensible brown brogue (not unlike the kind Ida usually wore), her stockings those thick sort that concealed varicose veins. A light, pink raincoat, open down the front, hung well below the dress and in her hand she carried a stubby, closed umbrella, tiny droplets of water sparkling from it like sequins. Studded through her earlobes were discreet shiny earrings that twinkled like faraway stars whenever she moved her head. She looked powdered and smelled scented, although her lipstick barely tinted her lips, and her eyes were a pallid green.

'How did you find my home address?' I didn't really care – she was here anyway – but I suppose I was stalling for time, trying to pull myself together.

'You gave your home number to Shelly when you agreed to take the case, so the address was easy to get from Directory.' Her hand stretched towards me again; she seemed to be a reach-out kind of lady. 'You've been hurt, Mr Dismas. There's blood on your face and shirt. Shouldn't you call a doctor or go to casualty?'

I was suddenly conscious of the wetness beneath my ear and under my chin, and when I touched my skin my fingers came away sticky with blood. From the throbbing pain just below the closed hole where my other eye used to be, I knew there'd be a swelling by morning. 'No, I'm all right. Just a disagreement with some ... with some people on my way home. No real damage done.'

'Are you sure? At least let me clean it up for you.'

Clean it up? Maybe wash away the humiliation at the same time? Could she get rid of the degradation while she was at it? I didn't think so.

'Mrs Broomfield, I'm tired. And yes, I'm hurting quite a bit too. I want to lie down and rest if that's okay with you. I'm trying – believe me, I'm *trying* – not to be rude, but I want you to say what you have to say, and then leave. D'you get me?'

'Of course, I understand. Why don't you sit yourself down and let me make you a cup of tea? It'll perk you up.'

Perk me up? *Perk me up?* God save me from the kind and caring. She means well, I told myself, she doesn't realize she's a bloody nuisance, she doesn't know how close to the edge I am. Resignedly, I went over to the battered sofa and sank into its soft cushions. 'No tea,' I said to her, defiant to the last. 'A brandy might help, though. A large one.'

'I think you've drunk enough alcohol this evening, Mr Dismas.' There was no mistaking the accusation in those pale green eyes; I got the feeling she knew I'd taken something else besides a few whiskies and beers, but was choosing not to mention it. 'How about some coffee? Yes, that would be more appropriate in the circumstances. It won't take a jiffy.'

She was out the door before I could stop her. Oh hell, I thought to myself, let her get on with it. It'll give me more time to get my act together. The clairvoyant was back before I'd even had the chance to light a cigarette, bringing a dampened bathroom towel with her.

'Here, wipe the blood away with this, then hold the towel against your ear for a while.' Wordlessly, I took the wet cloth from her. 'Oh dear, I think you're going to have quite a bruised cheek. Use the end of the towel to press against it; it might help reduce the swelling.'

I did as I was told and she disappeared again. My thoughts went back to the mirror and the image I'd seen therein; I was surprised to find the shock had lessened. Maybe the coke's feel-good factor was finally kicking in again and I was mellowing out enough at least to accommodate the bizarre bathroom episode. I heard the cluttering of crockery from the other room.

'*Christ* – ' I shot off the sofa, moving as fast as my shaky legs would carry me. 'Not that one!' I shouted when I reached the kitchen.

But it was too late. The spoon was already scooping into the jar and I could see the top of the powder-filled plastic bag emerging from the coffee grains. The clairvoyant had spotted it too and I could tell by her expression she knew exactly what was inside the package.

'Not that coffee,' I said lamely, opening a cupboard door above a work surface and reaching in.

'I'm so sorry,' she apologized, quickly screwing the lid back on the jar she held in her hand.

I took it from her, handing over the legit coffee jar as I did so, both embarrassed and angry at being found out. 'It helps sometimes,' I growled defensively.

'It's none of my business, Mr Dismas.' She busied herself filling the kettle with water.

'You can't understand what it's like for me,' I said quietly, some of that anger cooling.

'I think I might have an idea.'

'No. No you don't. You have to live it to know.'

She pushed the plug into the kettle and switched it on. 'I have an imagination.'

I gave a snort of derision. 'You can imagine what it's like to be trapped inside a shell so hideous it makes you ashamed to walk the streets? What it's like to be pointed out as if you're some kind of freak? You know the kind of physical pain a twisted body gives you? The fear of losing sight in your only good eye? The refusal of your own body to do what comes so naturally to other people? You know all that, you can imagine it?' My short laugh was full of rancour and she had the decency to lower her gaze. 'You have *no* idea,' I told her.

'I'm sor –'

'Don't keep apologizing! It's not your fault, *you* didn't do this to me. Just don't patronize me. And okay, so I take a little stuff now and again. It helps get me through. For a little while I can escape who – *what* – I am. The feeling doesn't last long, but it helps me get by. Can you understand that? It makes me feel fine, and sometimes it takes me somewhere else, some place where I can see, I can sense, other things, better things.'

'No, Mr Dismas.' My anger didn't intimidate her. 'Drugs

never really work that way. They close down your sensibilities so that reality can't interfere with your delusions. It might be pleasant, it might make you feel better, at peace with the world, but it isn't the truth.'

'*Well, who the fuck needs the truth!*'

She took a step backwards, suddenly afraid of my rage, and I was immediately contrite. I hadn't meant to scare her, it was just frustration, self-pity, resentment – you name it.

The kettle bubbled steam and switched itself off. Something was thumping hard inside my head.

'You ought to go,' I said more quietly, although no more calmly. 'I'm bad company tonight.'

The clairvoyant managed a weak smile. 'You've taken more than just a beating. Please go and sit down and let me bring you a cup of coffee. Would you like something for your headache?'

I looked at her sideways. 'How did you know I had a headache?'

She laughed and there was no fear in the sound. 'After all you've been through tonight, why *wouldn't* you have one?'

I returned to the sofa in the sitting-room, puzzled, mystified, by this little old lady. My head hurt like hell and my body was a mass of aches and pains. The swelling below my absent eye provided its own special torment. But although I'd taken a lot of kicking, a lot of bruising, the worst thing going on was in my mind: the memory of that charming face in the mirror. Yesterday monsters, tonight perfection. From the grotesque to the sublime. Visions through a glass darkly.

'Here we are.' Louise Broomfield bustled in like a squat Angela Lansbury, Disney's Mrs Potts to my Beast, and carefully placed the mug of coffee on the small table next to the sofa, shifting aside one of the heavy art volumes I kept close at hand for easy browsing (the lives and works of the masters is another one of my 'things'; I guess I used wonderful images as an escape route when reality was on overload) to make room. 'It's very hot, so don't scald yourself. Now, let's see about that headache of yours.'

Before I could protest, she was behind the sofa, the palms and fingers of her hands slipping round to encircle my temples. I had to resist jerking my head away; nobody had ever touched me like this before. Almost immediately I felt a heat spreading from her hands into my temples and forehead, a warm, white, invasive seeping which, once the mild shock had passed, became a gentle soothing. Miraculously – or so it seemed to me – I felt the tension leaving my body, the throbbing pain inside my head diminishing to a dull, inconsequential ache until that too, melted away. All this happened within a minute or two and I was astounded; only a good grade hit had worked on me that fast before.

'It's . . . it's gone,' I said unbelievingly.

'I know,' the clairvoyant replied.

'How . . . ?'

'I absorbed the pain myself. Took it from you, then simply threw it away.'

I had noticed, or sensed, the flicking movements of her hands, preceded by the soft stroking of my temples and forehead; it was as if she were shedding water from her fingers.

'That's – '

'Nonsense? Yes, I know that too. Works though, doesn't it?'

I couldn't deny it and I wondered how well the treatment would work on a regular hangover. A fortune could be made if it could be packaged and marketed.

'Drink your coffee now.' She came round and sat next to me and I could feel her gaze as I picked up the mug. 'I didn't know if you took sugar, so I left it. Too much sugar isn't good for you anyway.'

'The coffee's fine.' It hurt my lips to drink and I realized I had taken more than a slap or punch in the mouth; somebody had put the boot in.

'Can I help you, Mr Dismas?'

She had put the question quietly and I stared at her, not sure of its meaning.

'I thought it was the other way round,' I said at last, turning away from her and continuing to sip the coffee. 'I thought you needed my help.'

'Shelly – Mrs Ripstone – does. She needs your help badly.'

'Yeah, right,' I scoffed, remembering Gerald Ripstone's will.

'Why the cynicism?'

I explained the complications over the inheritance and the clairvoyant expressed surprise. 'Shelly didn't tell me that.'

'Well, you're a clairvoyant, aren't you? You should've known.'

She laughed. 'I'm afraid it doesn't work that way. I only wish it did – I'd have a much clearer picture of things.' She joined her hands together on her lap and I shifted position on the sofa to observe her better. Underlying the sweet aroma of her perfume was a hint of lavender water and I noticed that beneath its thin layer of powder, her skin had a translucent quality, a waxy thinness that belied her years; bluish veins were just visible at her temples and her broad forehead was unusually smooth. It was the lines from her eyes and the corners of her mouth that bore witness to her true age, and the chin that was supported by another more fleshy swelling underneath which gave her matronly appeal. Those pale eyes were quizzical at the moment, but they held a deep compassion within them as well as a kind of knowing, an ability to see beyond the superficial. It seemed that her gaze might reach my soul.

'Tell me something,' I said, still taking in this weird/ordinary little woman beside me. 'Which of you was the first to mention Shelly Ripstone's missing son: you or her?'

'Shelly told me about the birth of her child soon after arriving at my home. She said she couldn't live with the loss of both her husband and her baby.'

'So she put the thought of the missing baby into your head?'

'No, she confirmed it, Mr Dismas – '

'Call me Nick. Or Dis – everyone calls me Dis.'

She gave a brief smile, a nod of her head. 'Sometimes we clairvoyants need some affirmation, even guidance. It can help clear our minds of extraneous matters, provide a focal point for our perceptions.'

'Sure. So she did instigate the idea of a missing son.'

'I understand your scepticism, but I believe her desire to see me was inspired by a force that we on this Earth will never quite understand. Just as I believe a hidden but no less forceful motivation led her to choose you out of all the many private investigators in this town.'

'That's ridiculous. My agency was recommended by her own solicitor, someone I've carried out a lot of work for over the years.'

'Synchronicity, Mr – Dis. You know what synchronicity is, don't you?'

'I've got a rough idea. It's when two unplanned things come together for a specific purpose.'

'Well . . . close. It's a meaningful coincidence in time of two or more similar, or even identical, events that aren't necessarily related.'

'I think I prefer my version: it's easier to make sense of.'

'Fine. It'll do. You see, I believe you were always meant to carry out this investigation.'

That knocked me back a little. I was still trembling slightly from the beating I'd taken and the shock of the vision in the mirror. I was also still wondering what had happened to the cocaine hit.

'I know it's difficult when you're a non-believer,' the clairvoyant said hurriedly, no doubt worried by the doubtful look I was giving her, 'but I'd like you to trust me.'

Trust her? Why the hell should I trust a stranger who

believed she could talk to the dead? 'D'you mind if I smoke?' was all I could find to say.

She shook her head, so I reached into my jacket for a pack and lit up. The clairvoyant frowned but made no comment as smoke drifted over her.

After two slow draws, I said: 'Can you give me one good reason why I *should* trust you?'

'Because I know more about you than you think,' she responded immediately.

It was my turn to be amused, albeit represented by a very crooked, maybe even sardonic, smile. 'You know nothing about me. We've never met before and as far as I'm aware I'm not in *Who's Who.*'

'You weren't born with one eye. You lost it when you were a young boy, didn't you?'

I looked at her sharply. 'How could you know about that?' Unconsciously, and a little melodramatically, my hand had gone to the sealed, red-rimmed socket where my left eye used to be. Embarrassed, I let my fingertips fall away.

'A few minutes ago, when I touched your head, I sensed something horrible had happened to you many years ago. An accident of some kind – no, worse than an accident. It was done deliberately, wasn't it? The shock of it is still present in your aura.' She touched my shoulder as she asked the question: 'You understand what your aura is, don't you?'

She waited until I'd given a nod of my head.

Truth was, I didn't know much about so-called auras except what I'd read in various magazines and newspaper articles. Apparently a person's body radiates a kind of energy field that can be 'picked up' by certain people – psychics, clairvoyants, and the like. They generally describe it as a halo of light, usually multi-coloured, that shimmers around people, or even animals, and that your state of health or mind can be diagnosed by its glow. I'd also heard that nowadays there's a technique by which it can be photo-graphed.

'Well, yours is very odd,' she informed me.

Yes, wouldn't you know it, I thought. Odd body, odd aura. Seemed natural that the two would go together.

'It's very weak, Mr Dis – '

'Just Dis,' I insisted.

' – I sensed it even before I came in. It's somehow depleted.'

'Could be I'm just unwell. A beating tends to leave me below par.' Not to mention a shock or two. I held up a finger when she started to speak. 'And anyway, I'm not sure how this aura thing works, but if it's some kind of reflection of someone's inner self, then one belonging to a one-eyed semi-crippled hunchback is bound to be somewhat off-colour, you know?'

'You said it yourself: "Inner self". There's nothing to say that your inner self should reflect your outer self.'

'Inner self, outer self – who the hell cares which it is? I'm not happy inside, can you believe that?' I was growing annoyed again; why was this woman wasting my time like this? 'Being . . .' I indicated my own body '. . . this way doesn't make me happy. In fact, it pisses me off.'

'Please don't be angry.'

'Angry? Why shouldn't I be? My mother, whoever *she* was, gave birth to a monster. Me. I'm that monster. I was so grotesque she abandoned me when I was only a few hours old. Left me among the dustbins at the back of a nun's convent, not caring if I froze to death, or some urban fox had me for breakfast. And maybe that would have been the best thing for me – a few minutes of pain, or a quick death from hypothermia, that would have been a kinder fate. Instead, the convent's caretaker found me and took me inside. His name was Nick – Nicholas – so that became my name too. And the surname – know why the nuns called me that?'

I carried on before she could speak.

'I learned about the name years later when I went back to the convent, when I was trying to trace my origins, trying to

99

find out if they had any idea of who left me there in the cold. And one of them told me about my name, first about the caretaker Nick, then why they'd chosen Dismas as a surname. She told me quite eagerly, as though the knowledge somehow would help me in my future life. She said Dismas was one of the two criminals crucified alongside Christ, the Good Thief, the one who repented before he died and was promised paradise because of it. I was so ugly, you see, those nuns thought I was being punished for some terrible thing I would do later in life. You get that? Not for some past sin in another life, because nuns don't believe in reincarnation, but for some crime yet to be committed. So they prayed for my soul every day I was with them and long after I'd left. Not for me, the person, the poor thing they'd found among their garbage, but for my invisible *soul*. They hoped I'd repent before I even sinned and Dismas was their way of wishing me luck!'

I was breathing heavily by now, the bitterness of years beginning to spill out.

'Living as a freak of nature was bad enough, but it had to get worse. At least when I was young I could see with both eyes, but it seemed that was too good for me, I wasn't suffering enough.'

'How did you lose your eye, Dis?' Her voice was soft, encouraging, as though she were urging me to shed some of that bitterness through the words. 'Someone hurt you, didn't they? Tell me how it happened.'

'I was put in a home for boys, not a bad place in some ways. You were fed, looked after: You couldn't ask for much more, not for love and affection, at any rate. When I was eleven years old, one of the male carers tried to make me do something I didn't want to do. A big, puffy man with slobbery lips and squinty eyes, someone who should never have been left in charge of pigs, let alone young boys. He was a pervert who wanted sex with a freak.'

I shivered at the memory. I could still see him now,

towering over me, his pants down, his lips and member drooling slime.

'I resisted. I hated this man, and I feared him more than anything else in my young life. I hated his foul breath, his scratchy chin, the blackheads that covered his fat nose, and I was terrified when he nuzzled his face against my cheek and tried to reach inside my clothes. I fought against his advances and I think he was surprised by my strength, strength he couldn't understand was from fear and disgust. And the scissors I picked up were meant for his throat, but instead, in the struggle, they stabbed my own eye. While he ran off yelling there'd been an accident, I was left screaming on the ground, the scissors still in my eye socket.'

The cigarette was half burnt down and I flicked ash on to the floor, not caring where it landed, not worrying if it scorched the carpet. Louise Broomfield brushed it away with her fingers.

'Others came, adults, other kids, but no one could pull those scissors out. They were stuck there, embedded, and I was kicking too much for anyone to get a firm hold. They took me to hospital like that, the scissors sticking out like some weird attachment to my head, the blood from the wound soaking me through.'

The clairvoyant closed her own eyes for a moment, either out of pity for me, or to picture the scene, who knows which?

'And he got away with it. That big, perverted slob was never charged, never arrested.' The words came in a rush, gathering pace until I was almost spitting them out. 'No, they didn't believe him when he said it was an accident, because they knew what he was like, they'd always known he was a pervert, but they didn't want it made public, and now the worst had happened, he'd nearly killed a disabled boy in his care, they didn't want the facts to get out, didn't want more investigations because they might uncover other, secret things that had gone on inside that place and they'd all lose their jobs. So they kept it quiet, bided their time before taking action against the perve. Nobody would believe the freak-boy anyway, because Christ-in-Hell, who in their right mind would molest such an ugly piece of shit? Besides the boy was so delirious with pain and shock he couldn't speak anyway, and when he was on the mend, when what was left of his mutilated eye was removed, they would speak quietly to him, confuse him so that even he wouldn't remember the truth of it all. *Convince him it was all his own fault.*'

Spittle moistened my lips, my hands shook with old hatreds; the clairvoyant sat quietly.

'And later I paid for defending myself. Even when the confusion went away and I remembered exactly how it had happened, nobody would listen. I was just a disturbed child, a kid with too many hang-ups who was traumatized by the loss of an eye. No one listened, and the truth is, no one cared. Freaks like me, too hideous even to kiss, to hold, to cuddle, we never had real understanding. Pity maybe, and sometimes sympathy, but nobody in that place really cared enough to hear me.'

I was finally running down, exhausted before I started on this trip down nightmare alley, now racked out completely. My voice had lowered and the words were more measured. 'Every day I wake and I live with this . . .' I indicated my own body again, the crooked shell I'd been forced to inhabit, no choice required or given '. . . and I take the taunts and the stares, the jokes and the abuse, and I learn to accommodate it, even though inside it shames me, and tonight I get the hell kicked out of me by a group of girls, most of them pretty under the junk they wore and the shit they smeared their faces with – and *you* wonder why my fucking aura is not up to strength!'

And get this – this is just how pitiful I'd become that night – I began to weep again, silently though, no blubbering this time, the tears oozing from my good eye to slip down my cheek and well along the jawline.

'I'm so sorry,' I heard Louise Broomfield say before

feeling her hand rest over mine. 'Please forgive me, Dis, I didn't mean to be so insensitive.'

The insensitive sensitive. If my misery hadn't been so enormous I might have smiled at that. Instead I pulled my hand away and snuffled against the knuckle.

'Okay,' I murmured. Not, 'It's okay,' because it wasn't; just okay, leave it there. I revived the half-dead cigarette in my other hand with a long draw and its glow wavered in my trembling fingers. My tears dried and surprisingly, I felt a little better, as though the emotional release had somehow lightened my load, or at least shifted it so that it was less uncomfortable. The mood wouldn't last, I knew that, but it was a reprieve, short though it might be. I blew my nose and stuffed the crumpled handkerchief back into my trouser pocket.

'Can we talk some more?' The clairvoyant was cautious. 'Would that be all right?'

'I'm tired,' I told her, and it was no exaggeration. I could have added that I'd emptied out, there was nothing left in me that night. Events will do that to you.

'A few more minutes.' She was pleading, not insisting.

'One more minute. Then please . . . leave.' I could have cursed again, but I just didn't have it in me.

'I've shown you I have the gift . . .'

'Sorry, lady, but you haven't proved a thing to me.'

'I took your pain away.'

'The headache . . . ?'

'Your pain. You were badly hurt when I first arrived: are you in physical pain now?'

I blinked. My mind probed my body, my fingers touched my bruised ribs; I looked at my hands, examined the marks and grazes where they'd been trodden on; I thought of my battered head and hump. I blinked again, turned to the clairvoyant, the healer.

'It won't last, the pain will come back,' she said apologetically. 'But right now you're not feeling any discomfort, are you? Perhaps some stiffness, and I'm sure you're quite numb in places; but there isn't enough pain to cause distress, is there?'

'How . . . ?' It was never going to be a fully completed question, but the situation at least required an attempt.

'I explained before. I took the pain from you and discarded it. It will probably return the moment your scepticism overwhelms the idea it could really happen. Only surprise is preventing that from occurring right now.'

She'd got that right: disbelief was already setting in and the first twinges were already starting.

'I've been very disturbed since Shelly Ripstone first came to see me,' the clairvoyant said without wasting a second more of her minute. 'I could tell she was deeply troubled the moment I opened my door to her and I sensed it wasn't just because she'd recently lost her husband.'

'How could you tell?' I really was curious to know.

'I'd been prepared beforehand.'

I suppose I regarded her quizzically.

'I had been hearing strange voices for a few days, jumbled voices, confused, distraught. I could make little sense of them until Shelly came to my home. They had first begun when she rang me to book an appointment, and once she was there with me, they became clearer, one of them more distinct than the others. This voice was that of a young man who told me he was Shelly Teasdale's son. Shelly only confirmed what I suddenly knew.'

I couldn't stop myself from interrupting – all this was getting too silly. 'Wait a minute. You're telling me you actually heard a voice telling you this? A voice from out of nowhere?' I didn't bother to hide my incredulity.

'It isn't quite like that. They aren't voices as such. In fact I only hear voices when those talking to me are dead.'

I brought her to a halt with a raised hand; I needed time to let all this sink in.

Louise Broomfield sighed. 'I'm sorry it's so difficult to

accept, but there it is, this is what happens when I'm contacted by outside entities. I can't explain why the deceased appear to have proper voices and others communicate with thoughts and visions.'

'Then why did you tell me you *heard* the voice of Shelly Teasdale's son along with these other voices.'

'To make it less confusing for you. It isn't important, Dis; messages have their own way of reaching me. In this case I was sent thoughts and images. The main one, the one who claimed to be Shelly's son, said there were others with him, but it was all so distorted. In my mind I could see vague shapes, figures that appeared to be in pain, or in great anguish, I'm not sure which. I had the feeling that they were trapped somewhere. I saw walls without windows, and doors, lots of doors with strong locks. And everywhere was so dark; these people were just shapes moving in darkness.'

Perspiration beaded her forehead and she dabbed it away with a tiny handkerchief that smelled of lavender. She fixed me with those pale green eyes.

'I saw you, Dis. Amongst all those contorted images I saw you.'

'What? You've never met me before tonight.'

'Yours was the clearest image of all, although it didn't make sense to me at the time. It was only later when Shelly had hired you that it took on any significance.'

'She told you the private investigator handling her case was a hunchback and then it all made sense to you. Yeah, it had to be me you saw in those visions.'

'They revealed to me that this particular person had also lost an eye in an accident when he was a boy. When I came here I was still in doubt, but as soon as I touched your forehead I knew you were the one. It came to me as surely as if you had told me yourself. That's why I'm begging you to help Shelly find her son, Dis. That's the key to all this; finding him will lead us to them all.'

'Even if there was some sense to this, how do you propose I find the boy? There is no record of Shelly Teasdale's son ever being born, let alone having died, and the hospital where she claims to have given birth burned down years ago. The trail – if there ever was one – is stone cold dead.'

'I can only tell you you've got to try.' The clairvoyant's eyes searched my face as though she might find some sympathy there. She seemed desperate when she added: 'I think they're counting on you. I think they know you're the only one who *can* help them.'

'Why? Why me?'

She shook her head slowly, almost as confused as I was. 'I . . . I can't see that. It just isn't clear to me. But I know I'm right, Dis, I can *feel* the truth of what I'm telling you.'

'Okay, okay. Let's just say you are right. I'm not saying I'm going along with this, but just for a moment, let's say your feeling is correct. How do I go about finding Shelly Teasdale's lost son – assuming he really is alive?'

'Why should Shelly pretend she had a baby all that time ago?'

'Let's not get into that right now. I can only say I've dealt with crazy people before. But if it is all true, how can I find him if there's no record of him ever having existed? I'm an investigator, not a magician.'

'Because the voices, the visions, have provided us with a clue.'

That startled me. 'You didn't tell me.'

'You never gave me the chance.'

'So tell me now. What kind of clue?' Yes, I was full of scepticism right then, and when Louise Broomfield revealed exactly what that clue was, I nearly threw my hands in the air in exasperation.

'Sometimes we see things in dreams that appear to make no sense at all,' she proceeded with hardly any embarrassment, 'until later you realize they were there to represent something important to you. It might be something very ordinary, mundane even, or it might be something that's highly significant.'

She fumbled with the tiny, lavender-scented handkerchief, twisting it in her fingers while I waited impatiently.

'I saw wings,' she said. 'Hundreds upon hundreds of wings. They were of all colours and they flapped madly, as if agitated or frightened, and they made a terrible, thunderous roar. It was as if . . . as if they were trapped too.'

And as she spoke, I saw those wings in my mind. The odd thing was, my own image was among them. I saw myself in the midst of thousands of fluttering wings.

Only I did not hear their flurry: I heard their screams.

11

For the second night I fell into a dreamless sleep, which was not only unusual given the events of that evening, but extraordinary, because I'd always suffered – and I mean *suffered* – from full-Technicolor, Dolby sound, Senserama dreams and nightmares since I could remember. You'd have thought that the past two nights would have made things worse.

As it was, I slept soundly and awoke around 8.45am, which was pretty late for me. I felt a little hungover and my limbs were stiff, but apart from that and a few bruises (the worst was the discoloured swelling below the absent eye) I was fine. I think mentally I had absorbed the bad things – the humiliation, the fear, and the self-pity – while I slumbered. I was instantly awake and just as quickly out of bed, heading for the bathroom; only when I was in mid-flow did thoughts of the previous night steal into my consciousness. I pondered them long after concluding my daybreak liability, finally flushing the loo and returning to my bed where, pyjama-clad (I rarely slept naked), I reflected further, oblivious to cold feet and parched throat.

What the hell was going on in my life? Beggars, beaches, bitches and batty old ladies – the images spun round my mind like a carousel filled with harpies. And then there were the hallucinations to contend with, the monsters in mirrors, the face that stared back at me in the bathroom. What did *they* mean?

When my feet eventually became too cold – even in

summer it took a while for my basement flat to warm up in the mornings – and my throat too parched to bear, I wandered into the kitchen and made a brew. A cup of tea rather than coffee, a couple of paracetamols for the general pain, which had nothing to do with the beating I'd taken, and my head began to settle so that I could think more clearly. Taking the mug of tea and collecting my cigarettes on the way, I went into the sitting-room.

After my third cigarette and second mug of tea I reached for the phone and made three calls.

The Ripstones' residence was one of those big but not quite grand homes set back from the broad road that runs from the top of the South Downs, through Brighton's suburbia and down to the sea itself. The area up there is quiet and expensive, just a little dull, and in winter the wind tears up from the English Channel to rattle windows and worry rooftops. Apart from the quietness – if you liked quietness, that is – the other advantage was that within minutes you could be in the centre of a town large enough to be a city, with all the amenities that come with it, or, moving in the opposite direction and in even less time, you could be among the meadows and valley woodlands of the Downs themselves. From the tops of the rises you could see as far as the hills around London itself, although on this particular day, because there was still too much moisture left in the air after yesterday's showers, this now warmed by the morning sun, mists ran across the valley floors, veiling green pastures and wooded areas, and the distance was lost in white haze. I'd taken a slight detour before arriving at Shelly Ripstone's place, driving to a favourite spot on the Downs that overlooked a huge rent in the hills known as Devil's Dyke, and I'd sat a while in my car, windows down so that the breeze could waft through. I'd watched the shifting mists below as they rolled lazily across the landscape, sunshine catching open patches, turning green pastures to shimmering gold, but my thoughts were of my own life and the apprehension that had suddenly filled me even before I had made the phone calls. In my heart, if not in my head, was the feeling of something momentous about to happen to me, something as inexplicable as it was certain, an eerie sense of impending ... what? I had no idea. But with it there also came a feeling of excitement, which was just as unaccountable.

Sitting there in my car, the soft wind up there breezing through my lank hair, I tried to analyse the sensation, tried to understand its cause, but answers came there none. There was only confusion – and wonder. Yes, a deep, disturbing wonder. And it scared the hell out of me.

I drove from the parking area and headed towards Shelly Ripstone's place, doing my best to calm this inner turmoil by concentrating on the road. The pragmatist in me would not allow those vague yet potent thoughts to hold sway: I was a PI doing a job, at that moment employed to help a grieving widow find her missing son, real or imaginary, and there were procedures to follow, rules of the game that would keep me on line and eliminate fanciful notions that might only get in the way.

But if it really was as straightforward as that, I wondered, why had I asked the clairvoyant to meet me at my client's address?

Within four minutes I was driving through a set of open double gates to park in the semi-circular, paved drive. By then I was composed, those irrational thoughts tucked away in some dim corner of my psyche, perhaps to be taken out and examined at leisure later on, for now my innate professionalism fully in charge. Climbing from my car – a nondescript Ford Fiesta, beige in colour, elderly in years, its only special feature a hidden isolation switch wired in series with the coil so that with the switch in the 'off' position, no one other than me could start the engine. It prevented the car from being stolen and while on surveillance I could always claim my vehicle had broken down (neither the pushiest policeman, nor the best mechanic could get it to move once it was in that mode) – I took a moment to look up at the house. Two storeyed, white painted, red-tiled roof, I guessed it had been built around the 1920s, with extensions added and picture windows replacing former, more traditional windows over the years, the whole building much larger than originally planned. It was a wealthy man's – or in this case, a wealthy widow's – abode, but by no means a palace. Gerald Ripstone had lived well, but I guessed he'd never been part of the jet-set.

A small blue Renault was parked in front of the mock-pillared porch (one of the later additions, I surmised) and I wondered if it belonged to Louise Broomfield. The clairvoyant had left her number with me the previous night, and after first speaking to my client, I'd rung her to say perhaps I'd changed my mind about the case and would she meet me here? My third call had been to Henry at the office, letting him know my plans for the morning.

Lumbering awkwardly up the porch's two steps, I rang the doorbell and waited. It took a couple of seconds for the door to swing open and for Shelly Ripstone to smile out at me. Along with bright make-up she wore a look of expectancy on her face, and she was dressed in loose-fitting black slacks, gold and black sandals on her manicured feet, and a tight pale yellow sweater which seemed to be moulded over her ample breasts. Her ash-blonde hair was held back from her cheeks by a black velvet bow at the nape of her neck and, although her eyes initially betrayed the slightest revulsion at what stood before her, they swiftly recovered again and lit up in welcome.

'Thank you, Mr Dismas,' she said in a breathless, Marilyn Monroe way. 'I'm so glad you changed your mind.'

'I'm not sure that I have yet,' I said, stepping inside the hall as she made way for me. 'It depends on what information you can give me today.'

Her frown, I think, was a reaction to the bruises and cuts on my face, particularly the swelling below my missing eye, rather than my reservations.

'Are you all right, Mr Dismas?' she asked, her voice full of concern or curiosity, I couldn't be sure which. 'Your poor face . . .'

'Kind of spoils my looks, doesn't it?'

She didn't catch the irony: not a flicker of a smile. 'Oh, you poor dear,' she said.

I dismissed it with: 'It's okay, really. No pain – not much, anyway. It's not as bad as it looks. Is Mrs Broomfield here?'

She was and she was waiting to greet me in a room just off the hall itself, a lounge area that boasted an awful russet-red wall-to-wall carpet, broken by a white shag-pile rug in front of a York stone fireplace and two mammoth pink settees that faced each other across a wide glass-and-chrome coffee table. Hanging over the polished teak mantelpiece was a picture of Shelly and a middle-aged man, presumably her late husband, Gerald; it was one of those photographic portraits, varnished and stippled to look like an oil painting. Although cunning lighting and obvious retouching had conspired to bring out Gerald's finer characteristics, nothing could disguise the plumpness of his face and the plumpness of his nose and the plumpness of the flesh below his chin; nor could his hair be made to look other than sparse and his paunch other than portly; nevertheless, there was a cleverness in his eyes, an alertness to his expression, that told you he had been nobody's fool. Standing close behind and over him, as if he had been sitting for the portrait, Shelly looked harder than she did in real life and oddly proprietary, as if she were the dominant partner, as if she were in charge of Gerald and not the other way round, which hardly related to the impression she had given in my office. Maybe it had been a trick of the flashlight, an erroneous image caught in that split second; the camera mostly lied, I told myself.

Louise Broomfield was dressed in the same clothes as the night before, although minus the pink raincoat, and as she rose from one of the settees a warm smile spread across her chubby face.

'I'm so pleased you changed your mind, Mr Dismas,' she said as a greeting.

'Dis,' I reminded her. 'Call me Dis. Even my enemies call me Dis.'

I took her proffered hand and was taken aback by her sudden change of expression. Her body swayed slightly and I felt resentment rising at what I mistakenly thought was her unguarded aversion to the contact. I'd assumed she had grown used to my looks the night before, but I guess broad daylight brought out the worst in me. I suppose I couldn't be blamed for taking her reaction the wrong way and my irritation soon broke surface.

'I'm not sure I've changed my mind,' I said brusquely, letting go of her hand. 'I still think this is a wild goose chase.'

The clairvoyant was about to reply when Shelly, who had followed me into the room, spoke up. 'It isn't, Mr Dismas,' she insisted. 'Why can't you just believe me?'

I turned to her. 'Because I deal in facts, not fancies.'

It was as if I'd slapped her face and Louise Broomfield quickly interjected. 'Yet you're here today, so you must feel there is some truth in what Shelly has told you.'

'Right now I don't know what I feel,' I replied. 'Last night you convinced me to give it another shot, but in the cold light of day . . .' I regarded her meaningfully '. . . I'm not sure if I'm wasting my time.'

'This meeting was your idea.'

'I like to think I'm a pro, as well as a businessman. I don't like disappointing my clients and I don't like turning away a good fee.' I didn't mention the wilder notions that had entered the equation. 'I'll explore all avenues to complete an assignment successfully, as long as there are avenues to be explored.'

'Why don't we all sit down and have a nice cup of tea,' said Shelly placatingly – or was it desperately? 'Then you can ask me anything you think might help.'

'That would be sensible,' agreed the clairvoyant. 'And thank you for being so frank, Dis.' The puzzlement in her eyes told me she couldn't quite understand my irritation.

'No tea for me,' I said a little huffily, because I'd expected something more of Louise Broomfield; she was supposed to be a *sensitive*, after all.

'Coffee then. I've got some already made.'

Shelly Ripstone disappeared before I could decline further. I only wanted to get this over with as quickly as possible, my mood rapidly changed since I'd arrived. I guess I was annoyed at myself for allowing Louise Broomfield to persuade me that I really could help the widow. But then I realized the clairvoyant's influence had been minimal – I, myself, had resolved to see it through only that morning; in fact, I'd awoken with the conviction that I *had* to see it through.

'Are you feeling any better today?'

I wasn't sure to what Louise was referring: my physical or my mental state. Perhaps she was only making polite conversation in Shelly's absence.

'I'm okay,' I replied curtly, still misunderstanding her reaction to me a few moments earlier.

She was giving me that weird look again, a kind of scrutiny that was searching beyond the physical, and at last I began to realize her reaction wasn't one of abhorrence.

'Have you ever had any kind of spiritual experience, Dis?' she asked out of the blue.

Surprised again, I couldn't at first think of a reply. Then, stalling, I said: 'What d'you mean exactly?'

'Have you ever had an out-of-body experience, have you ever seen a ghost, heard voices in your head?'

'You must be kidding.'

'No. No, I'm not.'

I was beginning to feel uncomfortable under her inspection. I remembered – how could I forget? – the visions in the mirrors.

'I don't think I have,' I told her. 'No, I'm sure I haven't.' Hallucinations didn't count. 'What makes you ask?'

'There's something about you . . .' she shook her head and at last dropped her gaze.

We were interrupted by Shelly returning with a tray of tea, coffee, and even chocolate biscuits. 'Coffee was made just before you arrived, so it's still fresh.' She smiled at me and I could see the hope there in her eyes. I told myself that maybe her late husband's money wasn't the important thing, that maybe she really did want her son back for himself. (Of course, if the birth *was* in her own imagination, then maybe her smile was that of a crazy woman.) 'I know you only drink tea, Louise, so I've made you a pot all to yourself. Shall I be mum?'

I smiled at the irony of her last words, wondering if it was a deep-felt but subconscious plea. I watched as she poured tea, then coffee for herself and me, the perfume she wore today – Chanel No 19, I suspected – almost as powerful as the coffee aroma. She kept up a barrage of noise-speak about the changeable weather, how difficult it was to find good housekeepers, the price of lemons and other nonsense I couldn't be bothered to take in, all of it a verbal discharge of her own nervousness. I waited for a break in the flow.

'Mrs Ripstone . . .'

'Shelly, please.'

'Shelly, can you remember the names of any of the doctors or nurses who attended you in maternity?'

Her still-pretty face took on a blank expression, then frowned in concentration.

'The midwife, maybe?' I suggested helpfully, hopefully.

'It was such a long time ago.' She closed her eyes and

115

after a lengthy pause, began to say slowly, 'Doctor . . . Doctor . . . Rhanji . . . Rhamsi . . . Rham . . . ? Oh, I don't know. Was it Djani? He was Asian, I know that. A young man, very nice hands, I seem to remember, long fingers, almost feminine.'

'It's okay, I can probably check with NHS records. Anyone else you can think of, perhaps not on the medical staff?' I wanted an independent witness, someone who was around at the time and who knew Shelly had been pregnant and had had the child, someone over whom the medics had no influence. Because if the baby really had 'disappeared' then the medical authorities, for whatever reason, would want the matter kept quiet.

Shelly was slowly shaking her head, her eyes open once more. I sipped coffee and waited. The clairvoyant drank her tea.

'There was someone . . .' Shelly said after a while, the memory dredged up as if from a deep well. 'I think he was another doctor, although he didn't wear a white coat, or anything like that. Very . . . very distinguished looking. Like an actor, you know? I remember thinking that at the time. But I can't place him, I think I only saw him twice. He never even spoke, although he did examine me. No, I don't think I was even told his name.'

I put the coffee cup on the glass table and took out a notepad and pen. Quickly I scribbled down the selection of names she'd applied to the Asian obstetrician under the heading of Royal General Hospital, Dartford. 'Try to think, will you?' I urged. 'Just try to give me some more names. I mean, who else did you have conversations with?'

'I was an unmarried mother in a ward full of happily married mothers. None of them were very much bothered about me.'

The 'good old days', I mused. How things have changed.

'Well, what about your own relatives? They must have visited you.'

'I left home at fifteen, Mr Dismas. I haven't seen my

parents, or brothers and sister, since. For all I know, and for all I care, my mother and father could be dead.'

Groaning inwardly, I lowered the pad. At this rate I couldn't find corroboration that she had even been pregnant, let alone lost a baby. Louise Broomfield, following our exchange attentively, placed her teacup and saucer on the table close to my coffee cup. The spoon in the saucer rattled against china.

'Look,' I persisted. 'How about the midwife? You must have had plenty of contact with her.'

The spoon in the saucer clinked against the empty cup again and I saw the clairvoyant look down at it.

'Of course, yes.' Shelly had brightened a little. 'She was very kind to me. In fact, she was the one who delivered the baby, because the young doctor was out of the delivery room at the time.'

'The midwife actually made the delivery?'

'That's what midwives are for, Mr Dismas. But she needed help at the end. That's why she sent for the other doctor, the older one.'

'Why would she do that?'

'Because I was having trouble with the birth, I suppose.'

'No, I mean why didn't she call for the normal doctor?'

'I've no idea. I think the other one was more senior, or a specialist or something.'

Now Louise Broomfield's empty cup rattled along with the teaspoon in the saucer and I assumed a heavy lorry passing by on the main road outside the house had caused a vibration.

'You're sure you can't remember his name, this senior doctor?' I said.

A firm shake of the head. 'I told you, I didn't even know it then. I never saw him again after my little boy was born.'

'But he was there at the birth.'

'I already said.'

I pondered on this a moment. 'Okay, tell me more about

the midwife. You say she was kind to you and you had lots of long chats. Surely you can recall her name?'

Shelly made a grumbling-groaning sound, frustrated by her poor memory. 'I remember she had a foreign accent. She was German or something.'

'You think she was German?'

'I'm not sure. Probably.'

'Think of her name.'

'I'm trying to,' she complained. 'Why would that help anyway?'

'Because if I can trace the midwife she might verify your story.'

'You don't believe me?' She sounded mortified.

I changed tack. 'She could validate the birth when I asked for a search of the records.'

The clairvoyant interrupted. 'Surely the midwife will have brought hundreds, perhaps even thousands of babies into the world. Why should she remember Shelly giving birth, especially all that time ago?'

'You got me there. But it's all we've got.' I noticed Louise looked very pale. 'If I can find the woman and show her a photograph of Mrs Ripstone, then maybe, just maybe, she'll remember her stay at the hospital. With luck she might also remember what happened to the baby. Are you okay, Louise?'

The clairvoyant looked momentarily surprised. 'Why do you ask?'

'You've suddenly lost colour.'

Her hand went to her cheek as if she might feel the draining of blood. The teaspoon inexplicably slipped over the edge of the saucer and we all glanced at it, and then at each other.

Louise's eyelids drooped and she closed them completely. 'I can hear them,' she announced quietly.

I sighed and shrugged dismissively; I wasn't into that kind

of thing and was more interested in discovering the identity of Shelly Ripstone *née* Teasdale's midwife.

'You said she wasn't English, possibly that she was German, so did she have a foreign-sounding name?'

Shelly screwed her face up again in concentration. 'I don't . . . wait . . . it's there, I can . . . No, it's gone. I almost had it.'

My head cocked to one side as I listened, not to the widow, but to something distant, something like whispers from another room. I looked around and saw nothing unusual. I glanced towards the empty doorway leading into the hall, glimpsed parts of a dining table and chairs in the room opposite, a corner of an etched mirror, probably Venetian or facsimile of.

'They're here,' the clairvoyant said in a soft breath.

'Who's here?' Shelly was alarmed. She craned her neck, trying to see into the hall. 'I can't see anyone.'

'Can't you hear the noise?' I asked her.

Bewildered, she returned my stare. 'I can't hear anything.'

But I could, and so could Louise Broomfield. Whispers, slowly increasing in volume, a jumble of agitated murmurings, and they were not from another room: these sounds were there among us. My coffee cup, along with Shelly's and Louise's teacup, began to vibrate on the glass table and the portrait of the widow and her late husband above the mantelpiece began to tilt. Suddenly the teacup, with saucer, slid across the coffee table and fell to the floor, dregs of tea and tealeaves spotting the russet carpet.

The whispering became ever louder, the sounds swirling around the room as if borne by some fierce gale.

The clairvoyant reached across to grab my hand. 'You can hear them too.' It was a statement rather than a question.

'The voices? Yes, I can hear the voices.' I snatched my hand away – her touch had been too cold. 'Who are they? *What* are they? What do they want from us?' I think my voice cracked a little.

'I don't know,' she replied. 'I can't understand what they're trying to say. They're so frightened, too frightened to make sense.'

'*They're* frightened? They're scaring the hell out of me.'

I looked around the room, this way and that, trying to locate the source. But the voices were ever-moving, never settling, not even becoming united. The long drapes at the windows were fluttering, fresh flowers on a side table were trembling in their vase.

'Christ, make them go away, Louise,' I appealed. 'Isn't that what you do? Don't you control this sort of thing?' I was perplexed, curious, and fearful all at the same time.

'I can't. It would be wrong to make them. They're trying so hard . . . so hard . . . to tell me . . . No. It's you they want to tell, not me. Please listen to them, Dis.'

Tiny sugar grains hopped and danced in their little China bowl. My coffee cup glided towards me over the glass, coming to rest precariously on the table's chrome lip.

'*What's happening?*' Shelly was sitting bolt upright, clutching the arms of her chair, her hands like claws over the ends. '*What's moving everything? Please make it stop, Louise.*'

It was then that the voices seemed to find entry into my own head and they began their circling in my mind, the confused cacophony almost overwhelming, the excited whisperings and mutterings becoming thunderous. I clapped my hands to my head and shook myself, trying to rid my mind of the demons, afraid they would drive me mad with their incessant babbling, but instead, I sank into them, became a captive inside my own head, joining with their mutterings as though I were part of them, that their anguish was also mine. I leapt to my feet, fingers pressed tight against my temples, and was aware that the clairvoyant was reaching up to me, trying to calm me; but the voices inside drowned her words, and she seemed a long way away from me, beyond assisting.

I rocked on my heels, afraid for my sanity, the intrusion becoming too much to bear. I called out, not a word, just a sound, anything to counteract that inner noise, but it made no difference, the voices continued their tirade.

Louise was on her feet and Shelly had pushed herself further back in her seat as if trying to get as far away from me as possible, the horror on her face frightening me even more. I twisted my body as though that might help loosen the voices from their fierce grip, but still they persisted, tormenting me with their harangue. Louise held on to me and I saw her lips moving, but couldn't hear her words, didn't *want* to hear her words, because she was to blame for all this: innocent, even matronly, though she appeared, she was the catalyst, she was the one drawing these strange forces to me. I knew it, I could feel it! She had evoked those terrible sounds of wings that had haunted us the previous night, whatever sensory powers she really did possess had induced or provoked the phenomenon! But then I remembered the reflections in the mirrors. On neither occasion had Louise Broomfield been present. Christ, I hadn't even known her!

It was the thought of those mirrors that sent me fleeing from the room and across the hall into the dining-room beyond.

On the wall opposite the door, mounted above a polished, walnut sideboard containing silver-framed photographs, candlesticks and a full fruit bowl, was the Venetian-styled mirror whose edge I had glimpsed from the lounge earlier. Fake or not, it was a magnificent piece with carved, bevelled edges, the tall oval centre framed by etched flower motifs and topped by an ornate mosaic floral design. Standing across the room from it, the long, walnut dining table between, I saw my own unpleasant image reflected in the glass.

But even as I watched, a new sound was rising not just inside my head but in the room itself. It came like approaching thunder, growing louder and louder, a low rumbling that began to drown the urgent whispered voices. Before my eyes, my reflection began to fade and in its place there appeared thousands of small fluttering creatures, birds of all kinds that flew against the glass as though trapped in the dimension on the other side. Their wings beat against the clear barrier, creating the noise: there were no screeches, no chirps, only the thrashing of those agitated feathered wings and the shifting of air.

I felt the presence of the clairvoyant and Shelly Ripstone, who had followed me into the room, felt them beside me, looking at my face and not at the mirror. Only then did they follow my gaze and look, themselves, into the chaos inside the glass.

Yet when I glanced away to see their faces, perhaps seeking assurance that I was not hallucinating, was not going insane, I realized they did not see the same as I in the mirror, for their expressions held no surprise, no wonder, but merely puzzlement. I faced the mirror again and saw that the images were fading, gradually vanishing, the noise – the flurry of wings, the turbulent air, the voices – abating.

In a few moments, the room was quiet again, and in the mirror was only the reflection of Louise, Shelly and myself.

But as Shelly Ripstone stared at herself, she was speaking, her voice almost distant as though she spoke only to herself and perhaps unconsciously.

'I remember now,' she said. 'I remember the midwife's name.'

She seemed to snap out of her distracted mood. She turned to us.

'It was Vogel. The midwife's name was Helda – no, *Hildegarde* – Vogel. God, it's clear as day now. Hildegarde Vogel.'

12

Like most big town centres nowadays, getting to a specific place in Dartford had been screwed up royally by its one-way traffic system and I was forced to use a car park some distance away from where I wanted to be. Walking long stretches was always a problem for me and after the beating I'd taken on the beach the previous night, the bruising and stiffness in my limbs didn't help much. It even hurt when I breathed too deeply, although I didn't believe I'd fractured ribs – one particular kick I'd taken while I was down had merely left its mark, a deep purple and yellow contusion over my left rib cage. The afternoon was hot too, which had a draining effect on my energy as I walked.

Grumbling to myself all the way, I eventually reached my destination, the road where the Dartford General had once stood. It was a broad, busy thoroughfare with metal railings on either side to prevent idiots, children and dogs from running out into the traffic. On the spot where apparently the hospital in which Shelly Ripstone/Teasdale claimed to have given birth had stood was a massive, granite and glass office block, an insurance company's name and logo over the main doors. I lingered outside awhile, leaning against the pavement rail, catching my breath and resting my legs, inspecting the territory at the same time.

On this side of the main road were mainly other offices, these broken up by a couple of estate agents, a betting shop and a bank, all of which looked comparatively new – at least built within the last ten years, that is. On the opposite side of the road, though, I saw what I had hoped to find. It was a longshot, but all I had.

That morning, my client had been quite certain of the midwife's name. Hildegarde Vogel, a little, thin woman, not at all robust as you might expect one of her profession to be. And very kind. Shelly had impressed that on me: she recalled that Hildegarde had been very kind to her.

Both Louise Broomfield and the widow had been shaken by the mysterious storm that had erupted inside the Ripstone house, and further worried by my actions during it. Why had I fled to the dining-room to gawp into an ordinary if fancy mirror on the wall there? I told them both of the tiny birds I had seen trapped inside the glass and although Shelly had stared at me as if I were mad, the clairvoyant had merely nodded her head, not in comprehension, but in belief. The message was becoming stronger, she informed me. Somehow it would eventually make sense to us.

Shelly Ripstone was pouring herself a large gin and tonic when I left the house, while the clairvoyant tried to assure her that all would be well, that while the phenomenon might be unusual, there was no evil intent to it. I wondered how she could be so sure.

When I got back to the office, I had spent some time on the phone, checking out the midwife's identity with the NHS, and after being transferred from one office to another, finally learned that yes, there had been someone on the Dartford General's staff who went by that name. The records said she had been transfered from the Prince Albert Hospital in Hackney, in fact, their records did not go back beyond ten years, so she was only just on their list. Did I know that the Dartford General had burnt down? Ms Vogel certainly wasn't on the NHS list any more, so if she had left the service there would be no record of her current address. Great. Another dead-end.

However, there are certain processes you can go through to trace an adult missing person: checking the electoral roll of the area where the person was last known to have resided is one, scouring through the local telephone directories is another. Or you can use specialist computer tracing companies, which are linked into data bases all over the country. Unfortunately, their services are very expensive. Speaking for myself, I liked to use the method that had rarely let me down: local enquiries, visiting the missing person's old neighbourhood and asking around. It's surprising what you can dig up by personal contact, which is why I found myself in Dartford on that hot summer's afternoon.

I had to walk further along the road to reach a break in the pavement barrier where a pedestrian crossing would get me over the lively main road, my limp quite pronounced by now. I hobbled across, feeling the glares of drivers forced to stop – not their impatience, but their curiosity – then retraced my steps to a spot almost opposite the insurance block. The shop I sought out was a tobacconist/newsagent/confectioner and although it had obviously been modernized some time within the last decade, I was hoping the shop itself had been around for a lot longer. A lottery ticket sign was on the window and through the plate-glass I could see magazine displays and stacked shelves full of sweets and chocolate. Just the kind of place that would be frequented by staff and visitors alike from the hospital that had once stood opposite, particularly if there had been no railings to prevent easy access.

There were few customers inside: a couple of little kids by the ice-cream treasure trove, an elderly man with a stick browsing the magazine shelves. The kids, a boy of seven or eight years old, a girl a year or so younger, regarded me with large, solemn, dark and beautiful eyes, and the boy slyly nudged the girl. She nudged him back, a little harder, so that he tottered.

'Shabir! Farida! Behave yourselves or go into the back room.'

The youth who had admonished them had the same

exquisite looks, but was considerably older, somewhere in his late teens. He stood behind the counter at the far end of the shop and his eyes revealed nothing as he watched my approach.

'Can I 'elp you, sir?' His accent was a peculiar mix of Hindi and Estuary.

'Uh, yes, you might be able to.'

The boy giggled.

'Shabir!' The youth said sternly and the two kids wandered off towards the shop's entrance.

I showed the young shopkeeper my calling card – it meant nothing in itself, but many people assumed (mistakenly) that it carried some authority.

'I'm from the Dismas Investigations agency and I'm trying to locate someone who used to work in the hospital over the road there . . .' I indicated with a thumb '. . . before it burnt down.'

'Oh, I'm very sorry, but I don't think – '

'There's a chance she used to shop here.'

'I know nothing of any 'ospital.'

'It was destroyed about ten years ago.'

'We – ' spoken as '*Ve*' ' – were not here then. But wait – '

'*Vait*' ' – a moment. Perhaps my father . . .'

He called through the open doorway behind him. 'Father, I have someone here who is enquiring about an 'ospital.'

I heard the stirring from the room beyond and a middle-aged man appeared, a copy of the *Sun* newspaper in his hand, a curved yellow pipe with a large foul-smelling bowl drooping from his lips. What little hair he had stretched over his brown scalp was a contrasting mixture of black and white; his whiskers and the hair at the back of his neck were more abundant, bushy even, the white amongst it more dominant. Despite the heat of the day, he wore a threadbare green cardigan over a collarless shirt, and weary-looking slippers peered from beneath the folds of his baggy trouser legs.

He regarded me without expression before removing the pipe with his free hand and saying: 'Yis, there used to be a hospital.' No southern-sprawl accent here, although his English appeared to be good. 'But that was –' again, the *v*as '– long time ago, before we came here.'

Bugger, I thought. 'I don't suppose anyone who *used* to work there still comes in?' I ventured without much hope.

'Oh no, I do not think so. Why do you want such a person?' *Vy do you vont such a person?*

'Just making enquiries for a client. No problems involved, but it is important that we contact this person or anyone who knew her.' I thought quickly as father and son watched me, neither one saying a word. 'How long have you been running this place?' I asked.

'My father has owned the shop for eight years,' replied the youth.

'Nine years,' the older man corrected. 'You were ten years old, Rajiv, and the little ones had not even been born yet.'

'Ah,' said the son.

I rested a hand on the counter between us and shifted my weight to my good leg. 'So the people you took over from would have been here at the time of the fire and presumably for some time before.'

'The man and his good lady-wife owned the shop for many, many years. I am told the business was passed on from generation to generation, but the couple had no children of their own to keep it in the family.'

My heart sank a little. 'They were elderly?'

'They were of near retirement age and the closing of the hospital affected custom considerably. I think they had had enough of life's hard toil so they were very pleased to sell to me at a good price.' He was watching me shrewdly, sucking on the pipe between replies. Scented smoke drifted my way.

'D'you know if they're still alive?' I asked hopefully.

'That I do not know, sir. We kept in touch for a while – they advised me on supplies and stock requirements, that sort of thing – but I have not spoken to Mr and Mrs Vilkins for many years now. So my answer is that I do not know if they are still among the living.'

'But you still have their next address?'

'Oh yis, I believe so. It would be in the book.' He turned to his son. 'Rajiv, go and fetch my big red address book to me. Hurry for the gentleman – you'll find it in the cupboard under the television set.'

He gave a little bow in my direction as his son disappeared into the back room. Then he took the pipe from his mouth and gave me a benevolent smile.

'Thank you, Mr . . . ?' I said gratefully.

'Dahib Sahab is my name and I am most pleased to be of assistance.' Without any embarrassment, he studied my crooked form as if wondering how it could possibly function. Then he nodded as if satisfied that he had figured it all out. 'Very unlucky this time, no?' he said to me.

'What?'

He pointed the stem of his pipe at me and was about to say more when his son returned carrying a battered red-covered book, many of its pages loose and threatening to spill on to the floor. The shopkeeper took the address book and opened it out on the counter.

'Let us see,' he murmured to himself as he leafed through. I noticed that the little girl had wandered back down the shop and was leaning against the counter, her wonderful dark eyes peeping up at me. I did my best to give her a friendly smile and was relieved when she smiled back, not at all afraid.

'Vilkins, Vilkin . . .' the father was muttering as his stubby finger slid down the pages. 'Ah yis. George and Emma Vilkins.' He turned the book around so that I could see the name and address he was pointing at.

'Wilkins,' I said.

'Yis, Vilkins,' he agreed.

'May I write it down? The address and phone number?'

'Please.' *Pliz.*

I took out the small notepad I always carried with me and jotted down the information I needed. 'Ramble Avenue,' I said as I scribbled. 'Is that far from here?'

'Not very.' It was the son who spoke, his eyes slightly suspicious, as they had been throughout the exchange. 'On the other side of the motorway, going towards Swanscombe.'

'Great,' I said, studying my note. 'And you say you haven't spoken to Mr and Mrs Vilk . . . Wilkins . . . for some time?'

The shopkeeper shook his head mournfully, as though the lapse made him sad. 'I did not like to bother Mr Vilkins too much in his retirement. In any case, the business is not difficult, so there was no need.'

The girl, Farida, was touching my arm as if to feel if I were real. I gave her another smile, which she returned again, continuing to run her fingers along the sleeve of my jacket.

'Uh, thank you very much,' I said to the shopkeeper and his son. 'You've been very helpful.'

The older man accorded me another small nod of his head, but the son merely walked away and began tidying newspapers further along the counter. I turned to leave, then glanced around at the shopkeeper again.

'What did you mean when you said I was unlucky this time?' I asked him.

For a few moments he said nothing. Then, his gaze going beyond me, focusing on something in the middle-distance, he replied: 'If you do not know yourself, my friend, then it is not for me to say.'

Gathering up his ragged, loose-leaved address book, he retired to the backroom.

The sun was hard on me as I traipsed back to the car park, its harsh rays pounding my head without respite. I peeked longingly into the open doorways of pubs that I passed, but bravely resisted the urge to drop in for a cold beer and shade every time. In my line of work, it presented a bad image to make enquiries with alcohol on your breath.

I was still puzzled by the Asian shopkeeper's last remark, wondering what was behind it, precisely what was he getting at? He had said it so sagely and with such inscrutability, as though he were the Keeper of Hidden Knowledge and I was the poor sap who didn't have a clue. I remembered that the Hindu religion subscribed to reincarnation, so maybe that was what he was getting at: I'd come back this time in a less than lovely form. Shit, what nonsense! What would have been the point in that? Yes, I really was clueless.

When I finally got to my car I collapsed on to the front seat, leaving the door open wide to get rid of the build-up of heat inside. Giving myself a minute or so to get my breath back and to rest my aching legs, I struggled out of my jacket and threw it on to the passenger seat, first taking my cellphone from a pocket. I wiped my face with my shirtsleeve before tapping out the Wilkinses' phone number with my thumb.

There was no reply, but at least the line was still in service. I sat and pondered awhile, enjoying the comfort of the car. Okay, I was down in this neck of the woods so I might as well drive to the Wilkinses' last known address; even if they had moved away, or passed on in the terminal sense, the neighbours would be able to tell me either way. Stretching over to the back seat I picked up the Greater London Street Atlas I always kept in the car – it covered all the streets in the suburbs as well as the city itself and was invaluable in my line of work – and consulted the index before flicking through the pages to find the area I wanted. Ramble Avenue wasn't far away, a couple of miles at most. I closed the car door, flicked the isolation switch (yes, even in a car park I still took precautions, out of habit, I suppose) and started the engine, turning the cooler on to full blast.

It didn't take long to locate the tree-lined road and I

slowed the Ford as I drove along it, noting the house numbers on the gates of small, tidy front gardens. The homes were mostly bungalows, ideal for people of a certain age for whom climbing the stairs was an unnecessary grind. I drew up to the kerb when I saw the one I was looking for and, as I wound up the window, leaving a narrow gap at the top for air to circulate, a face appeared over the hedge of the garden across the pavement. The face belonged to an elderly man wearing a checked flat-cap, his creases and wrinkles deepening as he eyed me through horn-rimmed bifocals.

'Mr George Wilkins?' I called out, winding the window down again.

'Who wants to know?' came the reply.

'Nick Dismas,' I told him, satisfied that this was the person I'd come in search of. I pushed open the car door. 'I'm with Dismas Investigations.'

I reached back inside for my jacket and slipped it on before approaching the gate (whatever the weather, I always felt more comfortable fully clothed, something to do with concealment, I suppose). He watched me without saying a word.

'May I come in?' I asked, pausing at the entrance to his God's little half-acre.

'Depends,' he responded noncommittally.

The tiny lawns on either side of the stone path leading up to the bungalow's front door were parched and brownish, despite yesterday's showers, but the flowerbeds that edged them were well-maintained and full of begonias, petunias and geraniums, their reds and oranges slightly past their best, the recent hot weather having sapped their vibrancy.

'Ain't been usin the 'osepipe, if that's what yer've come about,' the old boy insisted gruffly.

I rested my hand on top of the gate. 'Didn't know there was a hosepipe ban in force.'

'There's always one down 'ere, every bleedin summer. Always been the same, ever since water was privatized.'

'Profits before services,' I agreed amiably.

'Bleedin right.' He eyed me up and down again and moved closer to the gate on his side.

He was a spry little guy, the paunch beneath his faded NEVER MIND THE BOLLOCKS T-shirt (I hadn't seen one of those in many a year) belying the thinness of his arms and exposed lower legs. He wore scuffed sneakers (imitation Nikes), no socks, and long shorts (below his knees) and I was mildly disappointed that he'd chosen an old-fashioned flat-cap rather than a back-to-front baseball cap to cover his silver hair (which protruded enough to top large stick-out ears). Dirty green pads covered his knees and in his hand he held a short hoe.

'So what d'you want?' he asked suspiciously.

I showed him my card and he squinted at it through the lower half of his bifocals. 'You are Mr Wilkins, aren't you? You once owned the newsagents' and confectionery shop opposite what used to be Dartford General?'

'That was a long time ago.' He pointed at the bruised swelling above my cheek. 'Get that bein nosy, did yer?'

'Walked into a door,' I lied.

'Oh yeah?'

I don't think he cared one way or the other.

'So what you after? I been retired years since.'

'Yes, I know. But you and your wife ran the shop for quite a number of years, didn't you?'

'Too bloody long. Weren't a bad business, though. Emma liked it, God bless her.'

'Emma's your wife?'

'She was. Dead now. Passed on six years ago.' He shook his head as though still mourning his loss. 'Never had much of a retirement, shoulda sold up long before we did. You gotta get the most out of yer life, son, all work's no good to no one. You want some lemonade?'

Maybe the mention of his late wife had softened him now.

He suddenly seemed pleased to have company, someone to chat to for a while, and that was fine by me.

'I'd love some, Mr Wilkins. It's a little too hot today, isn't it?'

'Never complain about that, son – it's a bloody long cold winter.' He lifted the latch and opened the gate. 'Come on through. You can sit on the doorstep while I fetch us both a nice drink.'

I followed him up the path and waited as he placed the short-handled hoe against the step.

'Take a pew and get rid of your jacket – you'll roast in this heat.'

I did as I was told and the old boy disappeared into the house. I lowered myself awkwardly on to the scrubbed stone doorstep and draped the coat over my knees. Squinting around with my good eye, I took in this little piece of suburbia heaven, the neatly-kept dwellings, the immaculate miniature front gardens, all under a vast, clear blue sky. It held an ambience far removed from the drama and aberrations of my last couple of nights in Brighton, the eerie whisperings of only that morning, the very normalcy surrounding me, although probably boring to some, offering a pleasant kind of comfort.

'There y'are, boy, get that down yer neck.'

Wilkins was back with two still-bubbling glasses of lemonade in his gnarled old hands, one of which he gave to me. I shuffled my bottom along the step but, instead of sitting next to me, he reached back inside the door and dragged out a foldaway canvas chair. Wrestling it open with one hand and one leg, he placed it on the pathway in front of me and sank into it. His grimy kneepads stared me in the face, the thin legs beneath them bristling generously with white hair.

'Your very good health,' he said tilting his glass and taking a long, glugging swallow.

I sipped more moderately, although I relished the cool taste as much as my companion apparently did.

'Ah,' he sighed, wiping his mouth with the back of his hand. 'Nothing better than a nice cold lemonade after a couple of hours' gardening. Beats all the booze, or tea and coffee. Now then, Mr . . . what's your name again, son?'

'Dismas.'

'Mr Dismas. The good thief, eh? Yer don't look too dishonest.'

At another time I'd have wondered what he thought I did look like, but at that moment I was too surprised he had caught the religious connotation to my name. Not many people did.

'Now then, Mr Dismas, what's this all about? Why d'yer want to know about the old shop? Yer not from the VAT, are yer? Finally caught up with me, eh?' He chortled to himself, fully aware that I was from no government department.

I grinned back at him. 'Nothing like that. As I said, I'm from an enquiry agency and I'm trying to trace someone who worked at the Dartford General eighteen years ago.'

He studied me seriously, pinching his grizzled chin with thumb and index finger. 'Eighteen years, yer say? We had a lot of them doctors and nurses comin in buyin their fags and newspapers and all that. Lot of 'ospital visitors used to pop in for sweets and chocolates for sick relatives and friends, too. No shop in the 'ospital itself, yer see, not like nowadays. Oh yeah, we had a good turnover in them days. Even had my boy workin for us full-time. Afore he went off into the music business, that is. He loved all that punk – we had him late, yer see, so regular rock 'n' roll, which we could've stood, wasn't good enough for him. No, he had to go potty with all them earrings and face studs and things.' His eyes rolled behind the glasses. 'The rows we had.'

As he shook his head I caught the connection with the Sex Pistols T-shirt. Anxious to get back on track, I prompted him: 'So would you remember any of your customers?'

134

'Don't see much of him any more. Lives in Newcastle. Come down for his mum's funeral, that was the last time.' His attention was still a long way off.

'You must have got to know some of them quite well, didn't you?'

'What's that? Oh yeah, sorry, son. Driftin, yer see? Comes to us all.' He took another swig of lemonade and smacked his lips. 'Yeah, we were busy, but we did make friends with a lot of 'em. Blowed if I can remember their names, though.'

'The person I'm looking for was a midwife. She went by the name of Hylda Vogel. A foreign lady, German.'

'Why didn't you say? *Hildegarde* Vogel, not Hylda,' he corrected.

'You remember her?'

My eye must have lit up, because he gave me a broad, pleased grin.

'We were good pals of Hildegarde's. My old girl and her used to go to the pictures together. Lovely little woman, very kind, very generous. Mind you, she might've been a midwife, but she looked like a strong fart would knock her flat. Tough as old boots, though, really; couldna' done the work otherwise. Very good to kids, she was, always buyin the little mites in the wards sweets and comics. Spent a lot of her 'ardearned wages on that.'

He was silent for a while and I didn't press him. He gazed over my shoulder, eyes distant, as though recalling his old friend.

I waited an appropriate time before asking hopefully: 'D'you happen to know where she lives currently?'

'I don't even know if she's still alive, son.' He took off his cap and wiped perspiration from his forehead with it.

My heart sinking, I said, 'You lost contact with her?'

'Oh, we stayed friends long after we retired. Hildegarde was always poppin round to see my Emma until she took ill.'

'Until your wife became ill?'

'No, son, it was Hildegarde who took ill first. She was

never the same after the 'ospital caught fire and they was all left out of work. Most of the staff either moved away or got took on by other local 'ospitals, but Hildegarde decided to call it a day. Some of the kiddies died in the fire, yer see? Down to the smoke, not the fire itself. If y'ask me, I think that done her in a bit. Loved the kids, didn't she? Anyhows, she was past retirin age, so it was no bad thing in that respect: she'd worked long and hard enough. She was terrible upset at the time, though. Loved her job, she did.'

'She moved away from the area?'

'Had to in the end. Stayed hereabouts for a while, but when her health got too bad, they took her into an old people's home. She was gettin on a bit, y'know.'

'This home – is it local?'

He shook his head gravely. 'No. That's the pity of it. Meant Emma couldn't visit her as often as she'd have liked. Somewhere on the other side of London, near Windsor I think it was. Never went there meself – don't like them places – and my old lady only managed a coupla times. Too fur, y'see? And anyway, accordin to Emma, it was a bit snooty and they didn't seem to like too many visitors. Hard place to get to, enall. When Emma became poorly she couldn't travel that fur any more.'

'So you really don't know if Hildegarde Vogel is still alive?'

'Told yer, didn't I? I suppose I shoulda tried to keep in touch meself, but after Emma went ... well, I didn't have much heart for anythin. Kept meself to meself, got on with the gardenin in spring and summer, played indoor bowls down the club in winter, and looked after me canaries all year round.' He nodded towards the front door just to let me know where he kept his pet birds. 'Mind you,' he went on, 'I shouldn't be surprised if the old girl was still around. Had bags of energy, did Sparrer, even when she retired. Always flappin around!'

'But you still have the address of the home, don't you?' I was leaning towards him, my elbows resting on the jacket over my knees, knuckles almost touching his dirty green kneepads.

'Got it somewhere, phone number enall. Emma always used to ring her after she packed up visitin.'

'Would you mind finding it for me?'

He lounged back in the seat, the almost empty lemonade glass resting in both hands on his lap. 'What's this all about, Mr Dismas? What d'yer want with Hildegarde? I don't want to be causin her any trouble if she is alive and kickin.'

'Oh no, no,' I assured him. 'There's no trouble at all. She might just have some information that's important for a client of mine. I promise you, I won't bother her in any way.'

'What sort of information?'

'I'm afraid I can't tell you. Client confidentiality.'

He weighed me up, undecided.

'It really would be helpful,' I said.

He appeared to make up his mind – maybe he thought I could do with any small break life would give me.

Placing the glass on the stone path, he hauled himself out of the canvas chair and went into the house. 'I'll do my best to find it, son,' I heard him say as he disappeared out of sight.

It was a good ten minutes before he returned and I was pleased to see he carried a scrap of paper in his hand. I stood and on the doorstep he towered over me; NEVER MIND THE BOLLOCKS was at eye level.

Holding up the piece of paper, he fixed me with his gaze. 'I'm trustin yer not to pester Sparrer too much, mind.'

'I promise. No pressure whatsoever.' I held out a hand for the address.

With one last moment of reservation, he gave it to me.

I examined the scrawled writing, then looked back at the old man. 'Tell me something,' I said.

'Go on.'

'Why did you call her Sparrer?'

'Spar*row*, son. Like the bird. Sparrer. She was always

137

flappin her arms around when she was excited or busy. Just like scrawny little wings. Went with her name, too. That's why I started callin her that.'

'I don't get it.'

'I spent some time in Germany just after the war, picked up some of the lingo. A bit of National Service wouldn't do some of the yobboes 'angin around the street corners and muggin' old ladies nowadays any 'arm, either. Soon straighten that lot out. Would've done my own boy a bit of good too.'

'I still don't understand. Why Sparrow?'

'Because of her name, Vogel. Don't you know what it means in German?'

'I don't know *any* German.'

'Means "bird". Vogel's German for bird.'

I suddenly had an image of hundreds – thousands – of flapping wings beating at the glass of a mirror.

'That's what she was like, yer see? A little bird with flappin wings. A little sparrer.'

13

I was still in a mild daze as I closed the car door behind me. Old man Wilkins had gone back inside his house for his 'usual afternoon's kip', leaving me to find my own way out of the gate. I sat and stared out the Ford's dusty windscreen.

Wings . . . birds . . . Sparrow . . . Vogel – what the hell was that all about?

Merely a coincidence? Or was I truly being sent some kind of message through the clairvoyant and mirrors? Before I had left Shelly Ripstone's home earlier that morning, Louise had claimed it was the disturbances that had jogged the widow's memory, helped her think of the old midwife's name. Even though neither Louise nor Shelly had witnessed the phenomena in the dining-room mirror, those thousands of tiny wings, they had both heard the sounds before the whisperings in the lounge. Although more subliminal than the vision itself, had the effect been the same? It still begged the question why I had been the only one to 'see' the wings, but Louise had suggested that the full power of the communication was directed at me and that she, herself, was only some kind of conduit for it.

I gripped the hot plastic steering-wheel in both hands and watched as a small bird – a sparrow, no less – landed on the car bonnet. It eyed me with beady detachment, cocking its head to one side and issuing a throaty little chirrup. If I had been more fanciful, I might have assumed its arrival was of some special significance: but I wasn't – as yet – that far down the road. No, it was just a sparrow taking a breather.

As if in agreement – although, in truth, displaying no such interest – it chirruped again and flew off.

Better to be like that bird, I told myself. Okay, things that I didn't understand were happening and, it seemed, with increasing frequency. And the clairvoyant insisted I was a key player in all this. So go with it. You don't *have* to understand, just let it roll. Maybe then the answers will find their way through. The feeling I'd had up on the Downs that morning, that something momentous, perhaps even portentous, was about to happen? Well, everybody got that same kind of feeling at least once in a lifetime, and it didn't necessarily signify anything, it was only chemicals in the brain overloading or mixing in the wrong way. No big deal. Not necessarily so, anyway. The thing of it is, there's nothing you can do except ride it. Go along with it and see what happens. Feel a little better? No, not at all.

Resignedly, as if my own free will was no longer playing a part, I reached for my mobile and tapped numbers, glancing at the scrap of paper old Mr Wilkins had given me.

The number rang at least eight times before: 'PERFECT REST, how can I help you?'

It was a woman's voice, more brisk and efficient than the time it had taken to pick up the phone might have suggested. It was also totally cold.

'Ah, yeah, um, I wanted to visit one of your residents today, if that's possible.' I had deliberately chosen not to enquire if Hildegarde Vogel was still living – I didn't want to appear to be a stranger to her if she was, because some of these residential care places could sometimes be fussy about visitors and private enquiry agents in particular.

'We do usually require at least twenty-four hours' notice for visits,' came the curt reply. 'Whom did you wish to see?'

'Uh, Hildegarde Vogel. She's been with you for several years.'

'Of course she has.'

I breathed a quiet sigh of relief. So the midwife was still around.

'Unfortunately,' the voice on the other end continued, 'Ms Vogel is quite unwell at the moment.'

'Yes, I know,' I improvised. 'That's why I wanted to come and see her.'

'Are you a relative?' Same cold tone.

'Not exactly. I knew her some time ago and I've only just learned of her illness. I'm a friend.' If the ex-midwife was poorly, all the more reason for the care home to be reluctant to allow a 'snooper' to bother their charge.

'Oh, just a friend? That's a pity. Ms Vogel doesn't appear to have any relatives – at least, not in England.'

I wondered just how ill the old lady was. 'Well, I am a kind of *special* friend. I know she'd be very pleased to see me, so can I come along?'

'I'm afraid I can't say. Let me put you through to someone who might be able to make that decision.'

Before I could say another word I heard distant clicks down the line. Within seconds, another voice came on.

'Hello. I understand from our receptionist you wish to see one of our residents?'

This new voice also belonged to a woman, but oh, the difference. It was soft, almost gentle, with none of the aloofness of the first speaker.

'Yes,' I replied. 'I'm an acquaintance of Hildegarde Vogel.'

'I'm afraid she's very ill these days.'

That voice. My response might seem ridiculous, I know, but over the years as a PI I'd learned to tell a lot from disembodied voices at the other end of telephones. This woman – girl? She sounded quite young – had a sweetness of tone that threatened to turn my natural, in-built cynicism to mush.

'Is she getting worse?' I had to keep my mind on the job in hand.

'I'm afraid there *is* no cure for emphysema, Mr . . . ?'

'Nick – Nicholas – Dismas.'

'. . . Mr Dismas. And of course, she is very elderly. We can only keep her as comfortable as possible and protect her from infection. Then, of course, there is the other problem we have to deal with.'

I guess I was too distracted by the sound of her lovely voice to pay full attention to what she was actually saying, so I failed to follow up this last remark. It was probably just as well though – I didn't want to appear too ignorant of the old lady's condition.

'You say you're an acquaintance? Our receptionist informed me you were a friend.'

I had to think fast. 'Yes, I am a friend. A special one. Hildegarde delivered me into the world.' I tried to put some lightness into my own voice. 'You know, when she was a midwife? That was a long time ago, of course.' I gave a little laugh. 'Too long, in fact. The years have gone by so fast.' Why did I feel so guilty deceiving this woman? 'She always kept in touch and was very kind to me when I was growing up. Haven't seen Hildegarde for a long, long time though.' Despite the guilt, how easily the lies came.

'How did you find out Hildegarde was here?' She didn't sound suspicious, only interested.

'A mutual friend, George Wilkins. His late wife used to visit Hildegarde at PERFECT REST.'

'Yes, I remember her. I think we can make an exception with you, Mr Dismas. You're obviously very anxious about Hildegarde. But we will have to see how she is when you arrive, so I can make no promises. Are you sure you want to make the journey? I'd hate you to waste your time.'

It'd be worth it just to put a face to your beautiful voice, I thought. 'No, that's fine,' I said. 'I'll take the chance.'

With a sweet goodbye, she rang off.

*

I had checked the road atlas before setting off on the long hike around the M25, feeling both apprehensive and strangely drawn. To break the tedium of the drive I hummed bars of old songs – Twenties and Thirties stuff, the sophisticated, romantic ones that came out of that era – but I was constantly distracted by the memory of her voice. I chastised myself for not having got her name, irritated that I didn't even know her position at the home – nurse, supervisor, carer, administrator? I tried to put a face to those sweet, almost soothing, tones, an overall image of her, visualizing an elegant yet soft-featured girl/woman, graceful in movement and manner as the voice suggested. I was sure she was beautiful and, as such, way out of my reach. *What the hell was I thinking of?* I'd had one brief conversation with this person and I was already thinking in terms of a relationship. Was that how desperate my fantasies had become? And anyway, she didn't have to be beautiful to be out of my reach – she could be ugly and still be beyond me. When *was* your last love affair, Dismas? Oh, never? Yes, that's right, you've never had someone fall in love with you, have you? So quit dreaming and just do your job. Be who and what you are, that way you won't get hurt. Not too much, anyway. All right, not as much as you would be by entertaining notions of romance.

Angry at myself, I took my own advice and rang the office, a diversion that might just get me back on track. Henry, as ever, was heavily involved in paperwork, but took time to inform me that Ida was at that moment swearing affidavits on papers she had successfully served, while he, himself, was writing a 'letter of appointment' to some scallywag who was never at home (or pretended not to be) whenever legal documents had to be served on him. If he failed to answer the door or was 'out' next time, despite the appointment having been made through the letterbox, then the matter would go to court anyway. Philo had nothing special to do, so Henry had set him the chore of cleaning the insides of the office windows (which, apparently, our apprentice was none too happy about). Henry wanted the okay from me to contact a computer data agency for information on a particularly elusive debtor whose personal and business affairs appeared to be uncommonly complicated and I expressed doubts about the expense of doing so.

'Well, it's the client who pays, Dis,' was his unconcerned reply, 'and I honestly believe it's the only way we're going to get this joker.'

'Get the client's agreement first, then.'

'Will do. Hey, I've got a good one for you. Who played the bombshell in the 1933 film *Bombshell*?'

'Come on, Henry, you can do better than that. Jean Harlow.'

'Right, right. It was based on a true story about a movie star who was abused by her studio and family. So who was the real star it was based on?'

'Clara Bow, Henry. Clara Bow.'

I heard a curse from the other end – he had expected me to say Jean Harlow – so just to cheer him up, I added: 'Did you know she once slept with the entire USC Trojans football team?'

'Clara Bow did?' His voice had brightened.

'Yup.'

'How do you *know* these things?'

'Just love the old movies.'

'Yeah, but that's not the kind of thing you find in old movie mags.'

'Well, I picked it up somewhere.'

'Sometimes I suspect you make up half these little tidbits. Hard for us to know, isn't it?'

'Just trust me.'

'Wish I could, Dis. But I know how despicable you can be.'

We both laughed and I said, 'Okay, gotta go. I think I've got a date with a beautiful lady.' Briefly I told him of the new lead in tracing Shelly Ripstone's 'alleged' missing son and of my destination that afternoon.

Henry wished me good luck. 'But I'm not sure all this is worth it, Dis,' he said. 'We're spending a lot of time and effort on something that might turn out to be a wild goose chase.'

'Like you say, Henry, it's the client who pays the bill. I'm going to hang up now before the patrol cops stop me for using the mobile while driving. I'll call back later, let you know how I got on with old Sparrow Vogel.'

'Who? Did you say "Sparrow"?'

'I'll explain later. So long.'

It would have been too complicated and would have sounded too foolish to explain to Henry about wings and birds and German names over the phone. Then again, it was going to sound just as foolish face to face.

PERFECT REST wasn't an easy place to find. According to the map book, it appeared to lie directly under the flight path to Heathrow airport, just a few miles away, which was surprising as it was supposed to be a *rest* home. I'd come off the great circular motorway around London at Exit 13, then driven along B roads towards Windsor, passing vast half-empty water reservoirs along the way, until I reached a long, winding main road that had many inconspicuous lanes along its length. In fact, so unnoticeable were some of these that I had to turn back and drive more slowly to locate the one I was looking for.

A sign of some kind giving a clue to the home's where-abouts would have been helpful, but there was none. Aware that the River Thames, on whose north bank PERFECT REST was situated, was nearby I began trying each lane one by one, heading in the general direction of the river. Most of the properties I passed looked pretty expensive, and the area itself, with fields and woodlands lending a rural setting, would have been an estate agent's dream had not the constant drone of aircraft disturbed the natural peace and quiet. After a while, though, the sound of those engines high overhead became almost subliminal and I realized that was how the locals here must cope: the noise was no more than a background hum if you paid it no mind. Only when Concorde flew over did the noise become an intrusion, one that lasted minutes after the hook-nosed jet was out of sight.

I came across no pedestrians along these lanes and, although tempted to knock at one of the houses to ask directions, I decided against it: it was sometimes a shock for people to find me unforewarned on their doorstep, an embarrassment I tried to avoid whenever I could. I'd try one more lane at least before I took that risk.

Fortunately, I had at last found the right one. It was a long, narrow lane of hardened mud, with a few twists and turns and mostly fields and hedges on either side. It was difficult to believe it might lead to the kind of establishment I was looking for, but I knew PERFECT REST had to be somewhere in the area, so I persisted. I passed very few houses and these were mainly gathered near the lane's beginning, although I did eventually come to one that appeared deserted, its lower windows boarded up, front door heavily padlocked. The further I travelled down the winding lane, the more I had the feeling of being miles from anywhere, of venturing into a remote part of the countryside, even though I was aware that the city itself was no more than thirty or forty minutes away. Even the steady stream of air traffic high above failed to convince me I wasn't in some distant hinterland.

Soon, however, and just when I was considering turning back, I spied rooftops and chimney stacks rising above the trees ahead. Judging from what I could see, it was a large, tall building, at least three storeys high, its roof and gables topped with aged, red slates, a multitude of television aerials attached to the chimneys. Relieved, I drove on and soon came to a wide entrance, its large iron gates closed. The sign on one of the stone pillars on either side of the entrance was discreet and in faded gold script on a deep brown background declared:

PERFECT REST

Residential & Nursing
Home for the Elderly

Dir: Leonard K. Wisbeech, MD, FRCS, FRCOG, FRCP, DCH

I'd had to press a button and speak into an intercom mounted below the sign on the pillar to get someone to open the gates for me, and as I drove through I noted my surroundings, a mental exercise I invariably performed in my role of private investigator. In this case it wasn't necessary, it wouldn't answer any questions, but it was a habit that was hard to break. The lawns on either side of the lengthy driveway were scorched brown by the summer's sun, the grass itself cut too short for middle season, and flowerbeds strived to cheer the approach to the house, although their colours had passed their best and were not varied enough anyway to raise the spirits. To my left, almost by the gate itself, was another drive, this one overshadowed by trees so that it looked more like a tunnel than a roadway. I gave it scarce attention, for the home itself loomed up soon after I was through the entrance, a big white building, beyond it the great wide River Thames, swift-flowing and muddy-brown. Across the water and through the trees there, I glimpsed fast-moving traffic, and I assumed this was the main Windsor road that I'd noticed in the map book. The broad river formed a natural moat, the trees on the opposite bank a partial screen that afforded the home all the privacy and peacefulness it could desire as well as a barrier against a busy world that had little time for the elderly; on this side, the long twisting lane through fields and woodland provided another buffer against the outside intrusion, and I wondered if this was the purpose of PERFECT REST's location. It certainly seemed to be the perfect half-way-house towards oblivion.

The building had projecting wings on either side, hence the gables, and was, as I'd guessed, comprised of three storeys, the windows on the ground floor high and elegantly framed. The white stonework was cracked in places and a fresh coat of paint would not have been amiss, yet it was still a grand structure and it was easy to imagine its former glory. At one time, perhaps in another century, it had obviously belonged to a wealthy landowner or nobleman, a private mansion house now given over to commerce, and it occurred to me that present residency in such a place would come expensive, too expensive, I would have thought, for an ex-NHS midwife. Maybe she had a rich family back there in Germany, relatives who could afford to pay for her care here. But then why wouldn't they take her home again, so that she could be close to them? And George Wilkins hadn't mentioned any rich relatives. I shrugged my shoulders. What did it matter? The case I was working on concerned a missing baby, not the financial affairs of an ailing elderly ex-midwife.

I pulled up outside the main entrance, an incongruously modern addition to the original structure with its plate-glass doors and side windows, framed in mahogany, seemingly 'stuck on' to the main building itself as if the architect or builder had no concept of architectural harmony. A gentle wheelchair ramp led up to the doorway and inside potted plants brushed against the glass on either side. Craning my neck to get a better view I saw that beyond this conservatory-type vestibule was a long, wide hallway stretching towards the back of the building, a screened receptionist's desk positioned a little way along its length.

Climbing awkwardly from the car, I made my way up the ramp and pushed open one side of the clear doors. A head popped up from behind the white panel screen and I felt myself scrutinized as I hobbled towards the desk. The pale cream walls were hung with wonderfully reproduced gilt-framed prints, the glorious works of Ingres, Reynolds, Renoir, Cassatt, all depicting beautiful women, perhaps chosen to cheer the home's elderly residents (although I would have thought such reminders of youthful loveliness might depress the more age-sensitive among them). A particular favourite of mine, although scorned by many present-day élitist critics for its elegance and ideality (which made it, of course, too 'populist' for them), caught my eye: it was Alma-Tadema's painting of women bathers in a Pompeiian bathhouse, and it wasn't just the incredible feel for texture and surfaces that got to me – no, it was also the understanding the artist had for the human form, its grace, its vulnerability. Its perfection.

Even though my pocket would only allow me to indulge my love of art through galleries and artbooks (even my reproductions were minimal), art stirred the imagination – my God, it *allowed* the imagination! – in a way that reality rarely does. Through art I could yearn without bitterness, fantasize beyond restraint, the picture itself was the dream and my own mind the observer, the visionary; my thoughts could go anywhere without hindrance from truth. The brushstrokes here proclaimed the natural symmetry between the figures and their environment, shape and substance extolling a harmony that would always elude me because of my own *dis*symmetry (unless, of course, I were to stand amidst clamour and distortion); yet rather than be reminded of my flaws, I was persuaded to become part of this fabulous insight (those piss-poor critics might label it 'visual fallacy') and this kind of *escape* never ceased to please me. I had paused in front of the print, momentarily captured by its delicate power, and the receptionist's voice rudely reclaimed me.

'Can I help you, sir?'

Her screened desk was positioned on the other side of a junction, narrower corridors leading off from the main

hallway, left and right, and I crossed over to it, avoiding
a white-haired, crook-backed gentleman in pyjamas and
dressing-gown and supported by a Zimmer frame shuffling
by as I did so. I noticed a Titian print on the wall to the
receptionist's left, the print depicting a naked woman reclin-
ing while a dark figure seated before her showered her with
gold dust. Again, the nude's form was beautifully defined,
the colours rich and adding to the sexual lustre.

'My name's Dismas. I rang earlier – about visiting Hildegarde Vogel?' Resting my elbows on the screen's shelf, I
watched her smile adjust to my closeness. It withered slowly.
A visitors' book lay open by my left arm and I noticed there
were very few sign-ins for that particular day. Only one, in
fact.

'Sorry, your name again . . . ?'

Her smile was almost rictus by now. The name-tag pinned
to her cream buttoned-to-the-neck blouse declared her to be
'Hazel'.

'Nicholas Dismas.'

The receptionist was plump and on the other side of forty,
the circles of her mottled-blue-framed spectacles almost
usurping her face, so big and statement-intended were they.
She tapped my name into a computer hidden beneath the
screen's shelf, stopped to consult her wristwatch, then continued tapping. Bare details registered, she returned her
attention to me.

'You spoke to Ms Bell, didn't you?'

'I'm not sure. I spoke to *someone* about Hildegarde.' My
use of the ex-midwife's Christian name might indicate
familiarity.

'Yes, I put you through to Constance. Just one moment,
I'll see if I can contact her for you.'

'I only need to see Hildegarde Vogel,' I insisted.

Her voice became frosty. 'Just one moment . . .' She
picked up the receiver of a grey telephone next to her
computer and with an imperious gesture of her other hand

she indicated a row of brown-fabric armchairs against a wall back towards the entrance vestibule, a low, blond-wood magazine table in front of them. 'If you'll just sign the visitors' book, then take a seat . . .'

Picking up the pen that was attached by a thin ball-chain to a black base fixed to the shelf, I scribbled my name, but where it said 'Address or company', I put in the agency address without its title. At this delicate stage I wanted neither to reveal my profession, nor to give away my flat's location (I was always reluctant to divulge my home address in case anyone with a grudge decided to pay me a visit at home – some debtors or errant members of the public I'd had dealings with seemed to regard me as their personal persecutor). That was why I carried two calling cards with me, one with both addresses (for clients only), the other with only the agency's (for witnesses, informants, debtors, anyone who had no real cause to contact me at home). I replaced the pen and as I retreated to the visitors' chairs by the vestibule I heard the receptionist tapping again, this time digits on the telephone base. As I sank into a seat, my eye immediately going to the two prints opposite, the Cassatt and the Ingres (the latter another exquisite female nude), I heard her say: 'Constance? I have a Mr Dismas here to see Hildegarde Vogel. You said you'd want to have a word first? Right. I'll ask him to wait.' She replaced the receiver and once more those owlish eyes regarded me over the top of the screen. 'Ms Bell will be along shortly,' she informed me before lowering her head again so that all I saw was a grey-streaked bush apparently resting on the shelf.

Constance Bell, I mused. A nice name to go with the beautiful voice I had heard over my mobile. My expectations rose.

An ambivalent odour of staleness and sterility pervaded the air, my nasal passages, with their keen sense of smell, irritated by the mixture. Distant noises came to me – a clank of metal, the squeaky wheels of a trolley, a soft crash somewhere, followed by a muted burst of laughter – none harsh enough to disturb the general serenity of the place. The elderly man who had crossed my path minutes before escorted his Zimmer frame back across the reception area again, looking neither left nor right, or even ahead, his attention exclusively concentrated on the marble floor two feet in front of him. His breath seemed to rattle as it escaped his lungs. I heard the almost entirely invisible receptionist shuffling papers on her desk, then all became still and quiet again.

Ignoring the back-dated yet still gleamingly new-looking copies of *Punch, House & Garden, Tatler* and the like spread over the squat table before me, I studied the paintings on the wall opposite once more, wondering at the choice for such a place as PERFECT REST.

The sound of footsteps approaching along one of the corridors, a clatter on marble that oddly was without a regular rhythm, drew me from my musing, and I looked towards the open area where the hallways met. The person was still out of my sight as the receptionist, her position allowing a good view of all approaches, glanced up and said, 'Hello, Constance,' before nodding in my direction.

The footsteps grew louder and I straightened my body as much as I was able (not much, unfortunately), surprised by my own growing expectancy. The sound of her lovely voice, heard only over the phone, was still fresh in my mind.

Oh my God, I said silently as Constance Bell came into view.

14

Her face was beautiful. Her face was perfect. With those deep brown, liquid eyes, that slightly tilted nose and chin so softly drawn, her face was exquisite. Her medium-brown hair was pulled back from her face revealing the elegant curves of her cheeks and neck, and her gentle smile was as perfect as a smile could be.

But Constance Bell's body was like mine. Only in some ways it was worse.

It was twisted and small – not dwarfish by any means, but little (had it been normal, it would have been described as *petite*). Her body had been deformed by spina bifida, her limbs twisted, her spine misshapen by the *sac* it carried, her walk, assisted by metal elbow-crutches, ungainly. But even so she was beautiful and I wanted to weep for her.

She hesitated when she saw me, her clumsy steps faltering for a moment; her expression – her so-sweet expression – was a mixture of surprise, curiosity, and something more, something I could not define. It was as though a veil were drawn across her innermost thoughts, the hint of darkness around her eyes the subtle manifestation of sleepless nights, a secret kept. Still, her smile did not vanish completely.

'Mr Dismas?' She had quickly recovered her composure and was walking towards me again.

'Yes . . .' My response was almost as hesitant as her own initial reaction.

'I'm Constance Bell. I'm a care-supervisor at PERFECT REST.' She held out a small, delicate hand, the crutch on that

153

side perfectly balanced by her elbow, and I felt a shiver run through me, not one of aversion – God forbid that *I* should feel such an emotion – but a kind of *frisson* that seemed to run between us. I'm perhaps ashamed that I also took pleasure in being able to look *down* into a woman's eyes, an all too infrequent occasion for one of my stature.

'I spoke to you earlier . . .' I said for the sake of saying something. 'On the phone.'

The fullness of her smile returned and again I was lost in her beauty. 'Of course,' she replied and it occurred to me that she might misinterpret my unease. I rushed my words.

'Uh, Hildegarde Vogel. I asked you if it would be all right. To see her, I mean. I'm a friend . . . I know her. Used to know her.'

'Yes, I checked on Hildegarde after your call.' Her eyes were serious, searching mine, looking for . . . ? Looking for what? Dishonesty, subterfuge? No, I didn't think so: her gaze was too sincere, too gentle. Perhaps she was just wondering how I'd acquired the bruises and swelling on my face. 'It's one of her relatively good days,' she went on, 'so I'm sure she'll be pleased to see you, even if she doesn't recognize you at first. I'm afraid it will have to be a brief visit though – Hildegarde tires very quickly.'

Her voice was as alluring as it had been over the phone, a voice that matched her face but held no alliance with the irregularities of her body. I let its sound sink into me, just as I allowed her gaze to search mine.

I pulled myself together, remembering something Constance Bell had hinted at during our telephone conversation. 'You said Hildegarde had another problem as well as emphysema . . . ?'

'You weren't aware? Mr Wilkins didn't mention it?'

I shook my head and hoped those penetrating eyes wouldn't detect my guile.

'Well, I suppose it has been a few years since Mrs Wilkins'

last visit, and Hildegarde's decline into senile dementia has been more rapid recently.'

'Senile dementia?' I could feel my hopes sinking.

'I'm afraid so. Hildegarde rarely even remembers her own name now, although recently she's been referring to herself as "Sparrow".'

'That was her nickname.'

'I know. We learned that even before she arrived here.'

It was something else I let go for the moment, this time distracted by the closeness to Constance Bell herself. I remained unsettled by the sight of her, my inner thoughts in a strangely pleasant turmoil, my emotions turning cart-wheels. I'd never been quite so captivated by anyone in this way before. She wore a pale blue, short-sleeved tunic with lapels, a buttoned front and a plastic name tag above her left breast, the home's nursing uniform, I guessed, which had obviously been tailored to her awkward shape. I noticed that her hair was tied into a neat little tail at the back, unusual for a girl who appeared to be in her mid-twenties, but all the more beguiling for it.

'Now if you'll come along with me, we'll see how she is,' the cause of my distraction was saying. 'I can't let you stay too long though, Mr Dismas – Hildegarde is very frail these days and, as I said, tires easily. I'm afraid conversation with her might be difficult because of her deteriorated mental condition anyway – unfortunately brain atrophy isn't some-thing that can be reversed. Just lately we've found her wandering the corridors late at night as if searching for someone. When we question her she can never remember who.'

Constance Bell led me past the reception desk towards a broad staircase further along the hallway and I realized, as Hazel, the frosty receptionist, twisted in her chair to watch, we must have made an odd sight, both of us hobbling along, in some ways twinned by our appearance. I noticed more superbly reproduced prints of old masterpieces adorning the walls on the way, but these were subtly changed. They still portrayed beautiful women – a Klimt to my right, a Mucha to my left – but they were more stylized, less realistic, impressions of beauty rather than exact representations, and they were both incorporated into symbolic or swirling designs. There was also another aspect to them that might have been considered out of place in an old people's home: both bore suggestions of eroticism. As we drew nearer to the staircase and further into the innards of the home itself, the artwork appeared to take on yet another aspect. These reproductions were by the likes of Cézanne and Munch, the themes as before, but now ill-drawn, as if the artist cared little for the qualities of the physical form but chose to describe them – in my view, at least – in more exaggerated and sinister terms. Perhaps the fault lay with me; perhaps because of my own physical distortions I idealized the perceived perfection too much and felt only disdain for its corruption. Foolish, maybe, philistine to some, no doubt; but there it was. Possibly a shrink could convince me to lighten up, not to take these things so personally.

Now my thoughts centred on Constance Bell once more. How did she cope with her disability? I wondered. My heart suddenly ached for her and not *just* out of pity. It was cruel enough to be born such as I, ugly both in features and shape, for at least it was a *corporate* image, a bitter unification; but this woman bore the extra torment of having the face of an angel shackled to an impaired body. Perhaps this was the inner turmoil I thought I had recognized in her earlier, the dealing with the dichotomy of her own identity. All these reflections of mine were fleeting as most thoughts are, and soon we had reached the broad stairway.

The care-supervisor, this lovely creature Constance Bell, turned to me. 'Are the stairs all right? We could take the lift if you'd prefer, although it's only one flight.' One of her hands rested on the post of the thick, oak stair-rail.

'No problem.' I gave her a smile, more concerned for her than myself: I didn't need crutches to get about on.

'We like to keep the lift free for our more elderly and infirm residents. And those in wheelchairs, of course. Besides, the exercise is good for me.'

I wondered if she simply refused to give in to her condition.

'How long have you worked at PERFECT REST?' I asked as we began to climb. I was curious about this extraordinary woman, wanting to ask much, much more.

She smiled. 'Oh my goodness, for more years than I can remember. Dr Wisbeech brought me here when I was a teenager.'

Another print mounted over the stairway caught my eye. I couldn't be sure, but I thought it was a Modigliani, a portrait of a girl's face, the shapes distorted, elongated, yet the expression revealing grace and vulnerability.

'You said Hildegarde was the midwife who delivered you into the world,' Constance said, a slight breathlessness to her voice now that we were half-way up the stairs. She used her crutches expertly, but I sensed the climb was harder for her than she pretended. She added, with a hint of playfulness: 'I bet you gave her a shock.'

I almost missed a step and she laughed, the sound as pleasing as her voice.

'I'm sorry.' She was smiling again, enjoying the tease. 'You just looked so . . . well, so concerned with yourself.'

'Is that how I come across?'

'To me you do.'

My turn to smile. And to apologize. 'Some days it just gets you down, y'know?'

'Oh, I know, Mr Dismas, believe me, I know. Try to remember there are others even worse off.'

'You think so?' I meant it lightly, but in a flash her humour was gone.

'I know so,' she said.

We began the next flight of stairs and until we reached the landing there was no more communication between us. I'd observed the stark cleanliness of the place before, the freshly painted pale cream walls, polished woodwork and doors, the crystal chandelier hanging over the main hall; now I noticed the change in smell, from chemicals and senility to the mixture of boiled cabbages, decay, disinfectant, the general malodour of such places, when the old mingled with the old-sick. I supposed nothing on earth could ever truly disguise the resident scent, not even in the grandest of old folks' homes.

Two ladies of late years and dressed in nightwear shambled past us, supporting each other, their heads close as if sharing a secret. They broke their journey to look back at us, their imperious expressions rather spoilt by their obvious curiosity. To them I guess the care-supervisor and I were the odd couple exemplified.

Constance greeted them with that wonderful smile. 'Good afternoon, ladies. Hildegarde has a visitor today, isn't that nice?'

One of the ladies sniffed, while the other muttered something I couldn't quite catch. But at least they each faked a quick smile before turning and shuffling on their way.

'I'm not sure they even know who Hildegarde is,' Constance confided to me in a low voice.

'It's got to cost quite a bit to be a guest in this place,' I commented as we began walking again.

'It is quite expensive,' she replied, 'particularly as PERFECT REST is completely privately run without any funds at all from the government or local council.'

'I hadn't realized Hildegarde Vogel was wealthy,' I said, bemused.

'She isn't,' Constance replied.

'Then how – ?'

'Hildegarde is a special case.'

Before I could follow up this new piece of information, we

were interrupted by someone leaving a room – from the glimpse I caught, it appeared to be an office of some kind – we had drawn level with. She was a tall woman, five-nine at least, and her build, while not hefty exactly, was substantial. She looked as if she had more than average female strength and knew how to use it. Her red hair was a little faded, as though it had lost much of its original vibrancy, and it was curled back over her ears in sensible fashion. I guessed her to be in her early forties. The uniform she wore was similar to the care-supervisor's, except a wide black belt drew in her waist and the long sleeves ended in white cuffs. Her eyes were small and puffy, and they seemed to regard me with suspicion.

She shifted her attention to Constance, a question in her cool expression.

'Rachel, this is Mr Dismas,' the care-supervisor responded quickly. 'He's here to see Hildegarde Vogel.'

The look I now received from this tall woman could have frozen chili. 'On whose authority?' she demanded, continuing to look down on me.

Constance was flustered. 'Hildegarde is much better today – I was sure it would be all right.'

'You should have checked with me first,' came the rebuke. 'You know Hildegarde becomes very confused.'

I thought it was about time that I spoke. 'I've come a long way and I'd really like to see her.' Not if she's *that* confused though, I thought to myself. How would I get answers from someone who didn't know what day it was?

Her piggy eyes glared and her fleshy throat appeared to quiver, but just as she was about to speak the door behind her opened again. A big bruiser of a man clutching a document of some kind stepped out to join us. His uniform was obviously the male equivalent of the supervisor's: pale blue, short sleeves (revealing well-muscled, hairy arms), but reaching just below the waist and with a buttoned Nehru-type collar; he wore joggers rather than trousers, the same shade of pale-blue as the tunic, and casual, white Nikes rather than formal shoes. His dark hair was cut short, brushed forward, speckles of white adding texture, and I imagined he modelled himself on *ER*'s George Clooney, although he looked more like Stallone – Stallone gone wrong, if you can imagine *that*; even his chin was heavily shadowed as if he'd neglected to shave that morning (although he was probably the type who had to shave twice a day). A hooked nose and a curled-lipped mouth completed the presentation. Oh, and the sorry smell of Blue Strata.

'Rachel,' he began, 'they want us to confirm the order for – ' He broke off when he saw me. He glanced at the tall woman, his eyebrows raised.

'A visitor for Hildegarde Vogel,' he was told curtly.

His eyes came back to me. 'That's not a good idea, is it?' he said. 'Has Dr Wisbeech been informed?'

I was becoming a little annoyed at people staring at me while speaking to someone else.

'I only want to spend a couple of minutes with her just to, y'know, just to let her know someone out there cares,' I said, appealing to the tall woman.

'I doubt she'll even know you,' was her chilly response.

The man – orderly, nurse, I didn't know what he was – nodded in agreement. 'Some days she doesn't even remember who I am and I've dealt with her for nearly ten years.'

He may have been around six-foot-two, but I didn't like the way he said 'dealt with her'. What was wrong with 'cared' or 'helped'? 'I think she'd like to see a friendly face,' I said, not caring what they made of that remark. 'And I gather she doesn't get many visitors.'

'None at all, actually,' Constance chimed in helpfully.

'So I might just cheer her up a little bit. And besides, for my own personal satisfaction I'd like to thank her for all she did for me years ago, even if she can't remember me.' I said all this in a firm, no-nonsense voice that sometimes worked for me. By then, I'd realized that Hildegarde's senility might, in fact, run in my favour – when she failed to recognize me it would be blamed on her condition.

'All right,' said the woman called Rachel, irritation on her face and in her tone. 'Dr Wisbeech is away today but, Constance, you'll have to let him know of Mr Dismas' visit this evening when he returns. And next time I'd like you to check with me first.'

'Of course,' Constance agreed meekly. 'It was such short notice and I know how busy you are . . .' She let her words trail away.

Without further comment, although disapproval was still evident in her body language, the heavy-set woman turned on her heels and marched off down the hallway, the big guy following, holding the paper he clutched towards her. 'I need your signature and then it can be faxed through,' we heard him say before they disappeared from sight round a corner.

'Nice lady,' I remarked as their footsteps faded.

'Rachel Fletcher. She's both senior nurse and chief administrator.'

'I can see why she's busy then.'

'I hope you won't be too disappointed if Hildegarde doesn't remember you,' my companion said, moving on towards the same turn in the hallway that the senior nurse and orderly had taken.

I'm counting on it, I thought to myself, although hoping her memory wouldn't be completely wiped: I needed the ex-midwife to tell me about Shelly Ripstone's long-lost baby. I groaned inwardly, realizing how slim the chances were.

'Tell me something,' I said. 'With senile dementia, does the victim forget everything?'

'Good gracious, no.'

Good gracious? I loved it. I hadn't heard that kind of exclamation in many a year. A curse or blasphemy usually did the job nowadays.

'The victim might be unable to think clearly or understand complex ideas, and they will forget people's names, even the

names of relatives or close friends. They might also forget
recent events, even what they had for breakfast, but some
can remember what happened in the distant past as if it were
yesterday. They could tell you what they did fifty years ago,
yet be unable to tell you what they did that morning. It's one
of the mysteries of the illness.'

By now we had reached the corridor leading off from the
main hallway and we turned into it. It must have run along
the centre of the building, for there were doors on either
side, some open, others shut. I heard the muted rumbling of
a large aircraft passing overhead.

'Isn't it a bit noisy for your patients?' I asked as we went
on. 'You know, with the airport so near?'

That coaxed a smile again. 'Most of our *guests*,' she
corrected, 'are hard of hearing anyway, and the windows
here are double-glazed, so the noise doesn't bother them
much. Sometimes the vibration might, especially when a
plane is too low or Concorde is passing over, but it isn't often
and you soon get used to it.'

'It's in an odd location, though. It was pretty hard to find.'

'Dr Wisbeech likes it that way – it's more private for our
residents. Besides, the house belonged to the Wisbeech
family long before the doctor turned it into a nursing home
for the elderly. He completely renovated the place to make it
suitable.'

'He must have come from a wealthy family.'

A plump, blue-uniformed figure appeared from a doorway
further along the corridor and gave Constance a wave. Her
hands occupied with the crutches, Constance gave a nod of
her head in response. I peeked into open doorways as we
passed by, catching glimpses of sparse but comfortable-
looking rooms: iron-framed beds with multi-pillows, bright
bedcovers, fresh flowers on small cabinets, a wardrobe here
and there, small, portable televisions on sideboards, all cosy
and well kept. Occasionally, an old face returned my curiosity, but mainly the residents I saw seemed preoccupied with

their newspapers, their little television sets, or the empty air in front of them. Some had tubes attached to their bodies, while others lay still in their beds as if already dead. Through the windows in the rooms to my left I could see fields and sparse woodlands, distant houses dotted here and there, yet on my right, from where the views of the River Thames and beyond would have been glorious, there were only blank walls.

I had no time to ponder this, for the nurse who had waved to Constance was strolling towards us.

''Lo, there. A new friend, is it, Constance?' There was a nice Irish lilt to the plump nurse's voice.

'Just someone to see Hildegarde, Theresa,' Constance replied, showing no strain at having to repeat the familiar line.

Theresa – pronounced Ther*a*isa – was a pleasant-faced girl, with a chubby, freckled face and an easy manner. 'Is that right, now?' she said. 'That's a good thing. Hildegarde will enjoy that.' She seemed genuinely unfazed by my appearance and I wondered if that was because of her daily contact with Constance. 'I've just left the poor old' – *auld* – 'thing an she's as quiet as a mouse. Not sleeping, though, so you won't be disturbin her.'

As the plump young nurse stepped aside to allow us by, she gave me a little wink, then grinned at Constance.

'There's a fine feller,' she said, and you know, I think she meant it.

When I peeked a sideways look at Constance, I was amazed to see she was blushing. I almost laughed.

'I'll be seein youse later, Constance,' Theresa called as she went on her way. 'An see youse both behave yerselves, mind.'

We heard her chuckle to herself and Constance gave me a sheepish glance.

'Don't mind Theresa,' she said. 'She's always jolly.'

Jolly? Oh yes, I loved the words Constance used. 'I bet

'she's a good worker, too,' I replied trying to help her out of her embarrassment.

'She certainly is.'

'How many medical staff or carers work here?' I asked, waiting for the redness in her cheeks to fade.

'Eight in this unit, five in our other section. Then there's Rachel Fletcher, our chief administrator-supervisor/senior nurse, and her secretary, and our main lobby receptionist, of course.'

'The guy with Nurse Fletcher – he's a nurse, too?'

'Bruce is a general orderly, but also a kind of assistant to Rachel.'

'What is this other section you mentioned?'

For some reason she seemed almost relieved that we had reached the doorway from where Theresa had waved. Was I asking too many questions? If so, I still didn't understand why that should make her uncomfortable. Then again, why was I asking so many questions anyway? Too many years as a professional snooper. I thought at the time it was my natural – some might say *un*natural – instinct, the one I relied on so much in my line of work, needling me, sending little vibes to pester me; little did I realize it was so much more than that.

'If you'll just wait a moment I'll check on Hildegarde first,' Constance said, ignoring my last question.

She disappeared into the room and I heard her say in a voice that was louder than normal: 'Hildegarde, your visitor is here. Remember I told you someone was coming to see you? Are you feeling well enough?'

There was a throaty sound that might have been assent or just a cough.

Constance returned to the doorway and dropped the pitch of her voice. 'She'll be fine. But please don't make your visit too long, will you? There's a buzzer by the bed should you need any assistance.'

With that, she looked directly into my eye again, as if

164

searching for something there. Perhaps it was the truth behind the lie.

'Th-thank you.' Yes, I actually stuttered and it was my turn to feel sheepish. There was a sudden warmth to her gaze, and then she was gone, moving awkwardly around me and heading back towards the main stairway. With one last look at her hunched back, I entered the room.

It was like all the others we had passed, the walls painted the same peaceful cream colour, the woodwork white. The large sash window overlooked the drive and lawns, the light from the north subdued. In one corner was a small sink, a rectangular mirror with a strip light over it. A free-standing screen stood close by, the edge of what looked like a commode just visible behind it. A picture of Christ hung on the wall opposite a narrow iron-framed bed, a deep red heart burning from His chest, golden rays bursting from it like brilliant shafts of sunlight. The compassionate eyes seemed to watch me as I crossed the room, and one of His hands was raised in benediction.

The thin, frail figure of Hildegarde Vogel, 'Sparrow', was raised by pillows at her back, a nebulizer and other apparatus close at hand on a bedside cabinet. Like the Christ image, she watched me as I drew near.

Her trembling, skeletal, blue-veined hands reached out to greet me.

In a voice so tearful and weary that the last word fell away in a moan, she uttered: 'My . . . poor . . . baby . . .'

15

Pale and watery though those aged eyes were, they seemed to burn with an inner fever. I was dismayed at the pity and deep sadness I saw in them.

'My ... poor ...' Hildegarde repeated, but this time the last word eluded her.

I flinched at the thin, claw-like hands that reached for me, somehow afraid to let them touch, fighting the revulsion I felt for this cadaverous old lady lying there propped up by pillows, her long dry white hair, the scrawny chicken's neck, the yellowish skin, with its deep creases and rampant liver-spots – and most of all the fetid smell that came from her, musty-sweet and tainted by the odour of degenerating flesh. I despised myself for giving in to the very emotion I reviled in others, those people who cast eyes upon my own shape for the first time and who, either because of surprise or ignorance, were unable to disguise their reactions. I quickly pulled myself together and managed to smile.

'Sparrow,' I said, and her expression changed as she remembered the nickname. Her mouth widened into a thin, toothless grin.

But as I drew even closer, her weak eyes narrowed and the grin shrivelled to a glower. She cocked her head to one side, eyeing me suspiciously.

'You're not one of my ...' Although the words she spoke were more crisp, the sentence trailed away again. Her hands dropped to the sheets covering her skinny old body and now there was consternation on her face. So cavernous were her cheeks that they were shadowed, and although she was slight, some of her flesh hung loose, as though the bone inside had shrunk. I hated to admit it, but the only bird she reminded me of was a vulture.

'Miss Vogel . . . er, Sparrow, I'm a friend,' I forced myself to say, angry at myself for giving into such prejudices. There was a hardbacked chair against the wall and I pulled it nearer to the bed. My hump pushed me forward when I sat and I rested my wrists on the edge of the narrow bed. Her head slumped back on the pillows and she watched me with distrustful eyes.

'You are not, you are not a friend.'

The German accent was still evident in her weary voice, although it was slight, an intonation rather than a pronunciation.

'George Wilkins told me about you.'

Her wizened face formed a thousand more wrinkles as she frowned in concentration. 'George?' It sounded like *Chorge*. 'I don't know anyone . . .'

'Sure, you remember. He and his wife used to run a shop opposite the hospital you worked in.' Shit, what was the wife's name? I'm supposed to be a pro, I should have made a note of it. 'The Dartford General. You were a good friend of George and his wife. You used their shop all the time.'

'Emma. Where is Emma? Has she come to see me?' She craned her neck to look at the open doorway as if expecting her old friend to enter. 'Where is . . . ?'

Her hand gripped my wrist on the bed.

'Yes, Emma. See, you do remember. Emma Wilkins.'

A toothless smile again. Heavy lids closed over her eyes as she recalled her friend. I hoped other memories would come back to her this afternoon.

'I worked in many hospitals,' she muttered and I could hear the wheezy rattle of her breath as it settled into her leaking lungs.

I had no idea that she had, but I prompted her. 'Yes, you did. But you remember Dartford General, don't you?'

Her breath now made a whistling sound as it left her mouth. 'Is . . . is Em . . .' the name almost escaped her '. . . Emma coming to see me today?'

'No, not today.' I didn't want to upset her, so I lied again. 'Emma's not very well, but she sends her love.'

Another thin smile and she opened her eyes once more. 'And tell me, why are you here? I'm sure . . . I'm sure I do not know you. Or are you just someone else I've forgotten? I do forget things these days. I do not mean to . . .' Her hand unclasped itself from my wrist and her eyes began to close once more.

Afraid she might fall asleep, I hastened my approach. 'Another friend sends her love, too. Shelly Teasdale. You do remember her, don't you?'

Hildegarde gave a feeble shake of her head. 'No, I do not . . .'

'You helped deliver her baby in Dartford General. It was a long time ago, eighteen years . . .'

'Baby? Oh, the poor babies.'

She lifted her head and began to look around, this way and that, searching for something. In frustration, she slumped back and turned to me. I saw a sharpness in her eyes then, a clarity that had not been there before. It was as if the wasting of brain cells had been held in check for a moment.

'Where are the babies?' she demanded to know.

I probed as gently as I could. 'What babies do you mean, Sparrow?'

'The poor little ones. The unfortunates. He said they would always be cared for.'

'Who said? Was it one of the doctors you worked with in Dartford?'

'All over. Other places. We always worked together. The Doctor has always been . . . good . . . to . . . me . . . to . . .

others...' She drew in a long quivering breath. 'Ever since...'

I was losing her and I gave her arm a gentle little shake. 'Ever since when, Hildegarde? Tell me what happened.'

Her eyelids sprang open and I saw an excitement there, as though the memories had suddenly become clear, pleasing her, giving her back some vigour. She looked up at the ceiling as though it were a screen on which those recollections were being played out.

'I was young then. Not like this, not old and useless.' A wheezy sigh, and then a short struggle to regain the breath she had lost. I waited impatiently, ready to grab the nebulizer mask should it be needed.

'Oh dear Heavenly Father, I remember that night so clearly.' She smiled and I couldn't tell if it was because of the visions she saw, or because of the sudden lucidity of her mind.

I leaned closer, ignoring the smell that had so stupidly offended me earlier. 'Tell me about it, Sparrow,' I whispered. I didn't know why, but I wanted to share in her reverie. Perhaps I thought she was referring to the time when she had been midwife to Shelly Ripstone *née* Teasdale.

'The hospital was in London. It was ... no, I can no longer remember its name.' Her voice was querulous, but it had an underlying strength to it now, the visions helping the telling. 'The hospital was in a bad part of the city, where the bombs had done so much harm.'

I guessed she was talking about London's East End, or the docklands, which had been so badly battered by German planes during the Second World War.

'Wilhelm was gone. Oh my darling Wilhelm ... killed by the enemies who were to become my friends. Seven years after the end of the war there was nothing for me in Berlin and our conquerors were begging skilled people to come to their shores. In Germany we were trying to rebuild, but there was nothing there for me, no close relations, not many companions, not enough food, and the money paid for labour was a pittance. It was little wonder I saw England as a land of opportunity.'

Although her eyes remained open, some of the fresh lustre had faded from them.

'Tell me about the hospital, Hildegarde,' I urged quietly.

'Ach, the hospital. So drab, so grey. Yet I thought it was wonderful, even though I was treated as an outcast. The people found it so hard to forgive and who could blame them for that? But I worked . . . my God, how I worked. Both night and day – it made no difference to me, I had nothing else to do . . .'

I was disappointed. Hildegarde was going back more than fifty years, long before the time I was interested in. Yet now, having urged her to remember, there was no diverting that train of thought.

'I was on night duty, very tired – I'd helped deliver three little ones that afternoon. I think it was midnight. Yes, I'm sure it was . . . I took my break about that time. I had no one to talk to – the people were still suspicious of us Germans even after all that time, and besides, my English was still very bad.'

A silence followed and I had to prompt her again. 'What happened that night, Hildegarde? In the hospital, it was around twelve o'clock at night . . . ?'

Her head slowly turned so that she could look into my eyes.

'*You* do not know?'

It sounded like an accusation.

She spoke in a harsh whisper. 'Are you not one of them? Is that not why you are here?'

'I'm not sure what you mean, Hildegarde. Why don't you just tell me about that night?' I was perplexed, but put her confusion down to the disease in her brain.

'That night . . . ? Oh yes, that night. I decided I would explore the hospital . . . *mein Gott*, what was it called . . . ?'

'It doesn't matter, Hildegarde. Just tell me your story.'

'Yes, my story. The one you already know. Are you trying to trick me, do you think I am insane? Is it that you wish to find out how much I still know, how much I have forgotten?'

'No, Sparrow.' I persisted in using both her Christian name and nickname in the hope it would make me sound more familiar to her. 'I'm interested, that's all. I'm not trying to trick you.'

'How do I know that? The doctor tells me I should forget. But I do not *want to forget!*'

Her voice had risen in pitch and I patted her hand reassuringly, afraid she might alert one of the staff. 'It's okay. Take your time. Don't upset yourself.'

'Are you a friend?'

'Yes, I'm a friend.'

'Like Emma?'

I nodded my head.

Tears formed in the corners of her eyes. 'The doctor isn't my friend any more.'

'I'm sure he is.' I wondered who this doctor was. Could she have meant the proprietor of the home himself, this Dr Leonard K. Wisbeech?

Her chest, which had began to rise and fall rapidly, became calmer.

'Nobody told me there were places in the hospital where I should not go. But I was young, and curious, and I had nothing else to do that night. I wandered through the wards and corridors, getting to know the place, introducing myself to the other duty nurses. I was a stranger and I wanted to be accepted, I wanted to know my way around. It was such a huge building, but eventually I found myself on the top floor.'

She started to cough, at first softly, but then the exertion sending spasms through her whole body. I became anxious, unsure of what I should do: help her use the nebulizer, or press the call button so that a trained nurse could deal with the situation? But even as I fretted, the spasms grew less

171

violent, the coughing less harsh, until eventually the seizure passed. Her cheeks were damp with forced tears and spittle drooled on to her chin.

I took tissues from a box on the bedside cabinet and gently wiped her face. She appeared not to notice.

'The corridors were dark up there,' she went on as though nothing had occurred, the rise and fall of her thin little chest assuming a regular rhythm once more, 'so very, very dark. I did not realize this was *verboten*, that I should not be there. I thought perhaps that this part of the hospital was unused and I wondered why. I found the doors to a ward that had no name, no markings or numbers, nothing at all. I was too nervous to go inside, afraid I would get into trouble.'

Her voice descended to a whisper and she leaned my way, as if to confide in me. 'I looked though. Oh yes, I peeked inside. And that was the beginning for me, you see, that was the moment it all started. That was when I became involved.'

I tensed. I didn't know why, but my body, my mind, became suddenly alert. I tried to control my impatience. 'What was in that ward, Hildegarde? What did you find?'

Those grey, watery eyes fixed on me. 'I found the infants,' she said. 'The poor little ones whose only offence was how they looked.'

A peculiar sensation ran through me, a kind of rush that heightened my senses and set my nerves on edge. I *knew* the answer even before I put the question.

'What was wrong with them, Hildegarde?'

She spoke as if from a distance, her eyes looking ceiling-wards, its whiteness a screen once more.

'They were like you,' she said. 'But worse. Harmless little babies born so hideous that they had to be locked away in darkness so that the world would never know its shame. Infants whose mothers did not know they were alive.'

Her eyelids closed like curtains to the ceiling's screen, shutting out the images, bringing an end to the spectacle. But it seemed that the pictures in her mind were far stronger than those conjured on the ceiling, for now she was closed in with them, the impressions bolder and more disconcerting because they were even more intimate. She began to twist her head from side to side.

'They . . . they are calling me . . .'

With horror, I realized that for her, the past had become the present. Her enfeebled brain had brought the memories to her, so that she was reliving the moments of many years before. I reached for her wrist and made soothing sounds in an attempt to bring her back to reality. It was no use though: her mind was in another place.

'The older ones . . . they are . . . their poor little stunted arms . . . they are reaching out towards me . . . "Mama", they call . . . "Mama" . . . and I take them in my arms . . . I comfort them . . . and they love me as I love them . . .'

She was thrashing around in the bed and I stood, my hands going to her shoulders, all the time trying to calm her, to soothe her with words I knew she could not hear.

'And he . . . and he finds me there . . . but it is too late . . . I know the secret . . .'

She was rambling, her words beginning to make no sense, her voice rising in pitch.

'Who found you, Sparrow?' I said close to her ear.

'God, help them . . . please help them . . . I cannot . . . any more . . .'

'What on earth is going on here?'

The harsh, new voice came from the doorway and I turned in surprise. The senior nurse and administrator, the one whose wrath Constance had incurred in the hallway earlier, was standing there, a look of pure rage blazing from her broad face. I hardly knew what to say. Shit, I hardly knew what to *do*.

Hildegarde was wriggling in the bed, the sheets becoming entangled with her stick-thin legs; she was making terrible sounds as she fought for breath, her desperate inhalations dry-raw, her wheezing alarming to hear. Her bony, blue-veined hands beat at the air and her lipless mouth was like a black hole at the centre of her face.

Nurse Fletcher hurried in, brushing me aside to get to her patient. 'It's all right, Hildegarde, please calm down,' she said as she tried to smooth the little woman's brow with the palm of her hand.

To me she shouted: 'Why have you been upsetting her? Just what do you think you're doing?' Ignoring my pleas of innocence she stabbed at the call button by the side of the bed. A red light above it blinked on.

'I really didn't do anything,' I tried to explain.

'I heard her shouts from the other end of the corridor,' the nurse said through gritted teeth. 'You must have done something.'

I have to admit, I found this woman daunting. There was too much icy fury in her, too much barely-restrained power in her stance. I backed towards the door.

Hurried footsteps pounded the corridor outside and then the male nurse, the big guy Constance had called Bruce, was in the doorway. His handsome-but-flawed face looked dumb in its incomprehension as he glanced from me to the action on the bed.

Nurse Fletcher yelled at him: 'Help me pin her down so I can get the mask on her!'

Again I was rudely pushed aside as he ran to help the nurse.

'Just push her down and hold her there for me. We'll use the nebulizer to help her breathe, then I'll give her something to sedate her.'

By now the old lady was screaming between gasps for air and, as the orderly placed his beefy hands on her scrawny little shoulders to press her down on to the bed, I decided to leave the room – I didn't want to witness any more of this. Outside, I leaned back against the wall and closed my eyes; still I could hear the struggles from inside, the torturous inhalations now muted by the nebulizer mask but heart-rending all the same.

'Oh shit,' I said to no one but myself.

I'd pushed the old lady too hard, and I regretted that, but unfortunately that was sometimes what a PI's job was all about: probing, delving, winkling out the truth even when it meant upsetting people. This time though, I wondered if I hadn't gone too far.

Time to leave, I told myself. No point in hanging round just to take another harangue from Head Nurse. Besides, I wasn't going to learn any more from Hildegarde Vogel that day. As I headed for the main stairs, pale, time-worn faces appeared in doorways, some shrinking away as I passed by, others bold in their curiosity, wondering what the fuss was all about. These latter residents either glared at me, annoyed by the interruption, or looked askance, perhaps hoping I would linger awhile to explain the disruption to their daily tedium. A bald-headed man with rheumy eyes and a complexion that was slightly less healthy than a cadaver's shook his walking-stick at me as I went by his room. He stepped into the corridor behind me, snarling and warning me to keep my distance. I not only kept it, I increased it also, hurrying to get away from there as fast as I could. More grey heads peered round doorways to disappear as soon as I drew close and I began to feel like some kind of pariah, an untouchable, spreading disease in my wake. I avoided their gazes, casting my own eye downwards so that all I glimpsed was slippered feet, the hems of dressing-gowns and nightdresses, the wheels of invalid chairs, and all I heard was mumblings and mutterings and the occasional intake of breath and the odd slamming of a door or two. My breathing had become laboured, my steps more lumbering, and I had broken out into a sweat, all because of the fear and hostility directed at me. It was funny, but the corridor seemed longer than before.

175

At last, I turned the corner into the main hallway and landing, and there was Constance Bell coming towards me, her own breathing a little ragged after her climb up the stairs.

'What is it?' she asked, her lovely face filled with concern. 'Hildegarde's call bell – '

'I'm sorry,' I blurted out. 'I really am sorry.' I was still walking, heading for the staircase.

She put one of her sticks across my path to stop me. 'What did you do, Mr Dismas?' There was no anger, only dismay in her voice.

'I didn't mean to upset her,' I replied, coming to a halt. 'I only asked her a few questions.'

'What kind of questions? I thought you were a friend of Hildegarde's.'

She frowned at my silence.

'You'd better come along with me,' she said abruptly, like a schoolteacher at the end of her tether with a disruptive pupil. She turned back to the stairs and began to descend. Meekly I followed.

Yet even though contrite and not a little embarrassed, my natural inclination as an investigator soon edged discomfort aside as we clumped our way down the broad staircase. I had remembered something the care-supervisor had mentioned earlier. 'Er, Ms Bell, you said that you already knew Hildegarde Vogel's nickname was Sparrow before she even came to PERFECT REST. Can I ask you how you knew?'

We had reached the small landing at the turn of the stairway and the care-supervisor wheeled round to face me.

'Just who are you, Mr Dismas?' she said, suspicion now causing her to frown. 'What is it that you want here?'

'You also implied that she had connections. Is someone paying for Hildegarde's stay here? She doesn't have any relations in this country, does she? And even if she gets a state pension, it could never cover the cost of care in this place.'

Constance stared back at me and in her silence I thought I could sense . . . well, it felt like fear. But why should she be afraid of my questions? Why should she be afraid of *me*? My God, that was the last thing I wanted.

She didn't answer. She turned away and resumed the descent. Again, I meekly followed.

Only when we reached the ground floor hall did she address me.

'I want you to leave immediately,' she said, and I noticed that her hands were trembling.

A conversation further down the hall between the receptionist and the young Irish nurse who had joked with us earlier came to a halt mid-flow as they both turned in our direction.

'Look, I really am sorry,' I said to Constance and it came out more like a plea than an apology. 'I want to be honest with you if you'll take a moment to listen.'

'So you admit you've been dishonest?' she came back.

'Well, yes. But only because I didn't know how you'd react if I played it straight.' I could tell by her expression that this hadn't helped my case much. 'Look, I'm a private investigator and I thought Hildegarde Vogel might be able to help me with some information.'

It was as if I had slapped her face.

'I thought it would make things easier for me, you see,' I added hurriedly. 'I thought I wouldn't be allowed to talk to her if I wasn't a relative or at least an acquaintance.'

'What kind of place do you think this is? Our residents have visitors all the time.'

I didn't think it was worth mentioning that the visitors' book at reception only had one other name on it that day. 'Hildegarde is old and unwell,' I said, 'and private investigators don't always have the best of reputations . . .'

'And you wonder why?'

'. . . so I thought you might be reluctant to grant me access.'

'I've already asked you to leave, Mr Dismas, so please do so before I call Security.'

Security, in an old folks' home? Well, I supposed it was necessary these days in most establishments. 'Look, if I could just see her once more, maybe when she's feeling better?'

'Please, Mr Dismas . . .' Her face was set and she had half-turned towards the desk as if about to issue instructions to the receptionist.

'Okay, okay.' I knew when to give up. 'Let me give you my card though, in case you change your mind. I'm just trying to trace a missing person for a client, that's all.' I reached inside my top pocket and presented my card.

It was with some reluctance that she took the card, and she did not even give it a glance before tucking it away in a pocket.

I half-raised both hands as if in mock surrender. 'Right. I'm leaving now.' Then I felt abashed once more – no, I felt low, I felt miserable, and I wished the ground would swallow me up. I'd played it all wrong and I was never going to forgive myself. I really didn't want this person to despise me.

'I, uh, I really am sorry,' I said in a quiet voice and walked towards the main entrance. I'd almost reached the reception desk when she called out.

'What has this missing person got to do with Hildegarde?'

I stopped, shuffled around. 'She was midwife to my client. It's the child that's missing.' Even as I spoke, I realized how ridiculous it sounded. But Constance Bell neither scoffed nor frowned. She merely said:

'You don't seriously believe Hildegarde can help you?'

I shrugged. 'Maybe not. It's kind of complicated anyway. But the midwife is all I've got.'

'Then I really am sorry, Mr Dismas,' Constance said, and I had the feeling she honestly meant it. 'But you must have seen for yourself that Hildegarde is in no condition to offer any information.'

I knew she was right.

'Good-day, Mr Dismas.'

At least some of her anger seemed to have dissipated. 'Ms Bell . . . ?' I began.

'Good-day.' It was a *firm* farewell this time.

'Yeah . . .' I said, and left.

16

With early evening rush hour traffic already stacking up on the motorways it took almost two hours to get back to the office, and I was in a low mood by the time I arrived. The thing that was bugging me even more than the pointless exercise of tracking down Hildegarde Vogel was my altercation with Constance Bell. I'd had plenty of time to mull it over during the long drive back to Brighton and I kept asking myself why I was so bothered. She was a stranger to me, yet I felt I knew her. Yes, I felt I knew her intimately. Crazy? Of course. But I thought I understood why. We were the same, Constance and I, two people saddened by our own Calvaries, the lifetime's purgatory to which we had been born. I had caught the loneliness in her lovely eyes, the disquiet that shadowed their gaze; and I had sensed the yearning that lay hidden in that same shadow, a constant longing which, on another occasion, in different circumstances, might have bonded us, for it was something else we both shared. Was I fooling myself, was it merely wishful thinking on my part, or had something intangible – a mutual reaching out, a fusion of emotions – passed between us as we had faced each other in the grand hallway at PERFECT REST?

But even if I were right, it no longer mattered anyway. I had blown it, my deceit had ruined whatever might have been.

The self-torture continued. Might have been? *What* might have been? Did I honestly think I stood a chance with the beautiful girl? Just because she had a crippled body like mine, did that make me a contender? I was kidding myself. She, at least, had a wonderful face and fine, delicate hands while I had no redeeming features at all. I was a freak: she was stunning. Stupid, stupid, stupid! Yes – I was stupid!

By the time I'd climbed the creaky stairs to the agency and lumbered through the door, my mood had changed from anger – anger at myself – to almost lachrymal self-pity.

Ida and Philo had left for the day, but Henry was still there, going over his precious books, looking as prim and self-satisfied as he always did. He peered over his bifocals at me as I slunk into my office.

'Any luck?' he enquired.

'Nothing useful,' I replied distractedly.

'Mrs Ripstone called while you were out. Wanted to know if there were any developments. You only saw her this morning, so I don't know what she was expecting.'

I groaned. 'I've got to tell her again, haven't I?'

'That it's still a no-go? Dis, we did our best for her. Some cases just don't work out, and we've plenty more to be cracking on with.'

How could I explain to him that this one was special, that something inside me – something *deep* inside me – was telling me not to let go, that something extraordinary was happening and I was part of it? How did you explain such a 'sensing' to someone like Henry who, despite his occasional flamboyance, was an accountant, a facts and figures man who relied on profit margins and balance sheets to steer him through life's little minefields? How the hell did I explain it to myself?

'Yeah, you're right, Henry. We're not exactly starved for work right now. I'd better call her back and tell her the bad news.'

'At least she's getting used to it.' He gave me a grin, still peering over his spectacles. Abruptly – and this was typical of Henry – he changed the subject. Maybe he could tell I

181

was a little bit down and wanted to cheer me up. 'Why don't you come over tonight, Dis, watch a film with mother and me?'

Henry's mother was the archetypal Jewish widow who doted on her 'boy', often sending him to work with chicken sandwiches and flasks of soup when the agency was on overload, aware that he would skip lunch altogether rather than leave his books for an hour. Evie Solomon had been a feisty little woman in her time – she looked as if she were made from three obese globes of unequal sizes, all balanced one on top of the other, a fat little head, a fatter little torso, and a very fat stomach and butt, these component parts balanced on two short legs and tiny feet – until failing health (which apparently no doctor had ever been able to diagnose, but which became extreme every time Henry made plans to leave home) had rendered her a little more temperate. Henry's father had walked out when Henry was a small boy and the stepfather who had taken his place had suffered a fatal heart attack years ago and that, I suspected, was when Evie's emotional blackmail had truly begun, her various maladies increasing in number and severity as the years progressed and her son's natural instinct for independence had come to the fore. We'd never discussed it, Henry and I, but we both knew he was irrevocably stuck with his situation – until, of course, Evie passed on (which, truth be told, would have a devastating effect on him).

'I don't think so, Henry,' I said in reply to his invitation.

'Hey, I've got a good vid. You'll like it. Gene Kelly and Cyd Charisse. Such legs! Cyd's, I mean. Up to her neck, those legs, the longest in showbiz in the Fifties. It's a musical.'

'I didn't think it'd be a Tarantino. What is it – *Brigadoon?*'

'Hah, gotcha! *It's Always Fair Weather*, actually.'

I turned away from his gloating: it could just as easily have been *Singin' in the Rain*, although the Charisse role was minor in that one. 'Yeah, you got me, Henry. But I'll pass on it tonight, if you don't mind.'

He must have caught the dejection in my voice. 'Are you okay, Dis?' he asked. 'This case got you down? You know, it's hardly make or break.'

I gave a huffing kind of sigh. He was right, of course. But then Henry wasn't aware of all the peculiar things that had happened since Shelly Ripstone had visited my office three days ago, nightmarish incidents that seemed to give the search for our client's allegedly missing son some special, although for the moment obscure, significance. I was tempted to confide in Henry right there and then, but I was sure he would only scoff at the idea of strange 'forces' at work and the ragging I'd take over the next week or two would be unbearable.

'I'm all right,' was all I said. 'Maybe I'm just tired of telling Shelly Ripstone that all bets are off again.'

I went into my office, slumped into the chair behind the desk, and reached for the phone.

The call from Constance Bell came through on my other line while I was talking on the phone to Louise Broomfield. I had already spoken to Shelly Ripstone and was now explaining to the clairvoyant just why there was little point in continuing with the case, that this time we really had reached a dead-end. Henry had lifted the receiver in the outer office and he had come to my door to let me know the call was for me.

'Someone by the name of Bell?' he said as I raised my eyebrows at him while covering the mouthpiece of the phone I was using. 'A lady. Sounds very nice. Needs to speak with you.'

I waved an okay and said to Louise: 'I've got to take another call and it might just be relevant to our discussion. Can I phone you later?'

The clairvoyant agreed and I replaced the receiver, immediately grabbing at the other phone on my desk.

'Ms Bell?' I said.

That sweet voice again. 'Mr Dismas? I hope you don't mind my calling you.'

Mind? My foolish heart was thumping. 'No problem,' I said. 'What can I do for you?'

'Our proprietor at PERFECT REST heard of your interest in Hildegarde Vogel today and he would like to see you. He thinks that perhaps he might be of some help.'

'Your proprietor . . . ?'

'Proprietor, director, senior doctor – he goes under all those titles. Dr Wisbeech.'

Ah. I remembered the name from the board outside the gates of the old people's home. Dr Leonard K. Wisbeech. 'Did he mention how he could help me?'

'I'm afraid not, Mr Dismas. He just asked me to get in touch with you.'

'Could I come over tomorrow?'

'Dr Wisbeech said some time in the morning.'

'Around 10.30? Would that be all right?'

'I'm sure it would.'

'And, er, will I see you again?'

There was a pause at the other end. You can read so much into a short pause, and probably all wrong.

'I'll be here,' she said.

'Um . . .' For some reason I needed to clear my throat. 'Uh, fine. Tomorrow, then.'

'Yes.' She said goodbye and I held the receiver to my ear even after I heard the distant *click*.

A night of dreams and constant awakenings.

Images of wings, white-feathered wings.

Which did not belong to birds; they belonged to angels.

Eyes snapping open, instant wakefulness, body in a sweat.

Sleep again. Disturbed, troubled sleep.

Dream: Cyd Charisse dancing with me, both of us naked, the top of my head only reaching the top of her legs, so that I looked at thick black pubic hair sprinkled with sequins. Those lovely long beautiful legs, leading me in the dance, the scent of her womanness strong in my nostrils. I weave with her rumba rhythm, but I'm not so happy: I *know* I'm taller than that, that my head should at least reach her shoulders. I begin to weep at the unfairness. And then she changes and I'm dancing with Constance, our bodies perfectly – *im*perfectly – matched, her arm over my crooked shoulder, my eye looking *down* into hers, her face upturned, her lips lifted towards mine, and the music is changed, it's slower, more dreamy, and we glide and we twirl and our lips draw even closer ... And Gene Kelly is tapping me on the shoulder, on my *crooked* shoulder, and as I turn at the interruption the great dancer shimmers and he fades and he morphs into someone else, someone whose face I recognize, because it's so familiar, so well-known, so famous ... A tall and elegantly handsome man whose name I can't recall ... his smile is a leer and I hate him, I fucking hate him ... But there's nothing I can do as he takes her away from me and although I protest, although I try to hold on to her, they are gliding away from me, so light on their feet, so heavenly graceful ... And he is holding Constance aloft like a beautiful prize and he winks at me ... so handsome, so diabolically handsome ... and they are fading into the night while the melody ... and his fucking laughter ... lingers on ...

Again I wake.

But I resist the drugs that I know will alter my mind-state, will help me slip back into a more happy slumber. I resist and already I regret the resistance ...

Because now the dream is *truly* horrible ...

I am in darkness, but I am not alone. I cannot see the others, but I can hear their tortured cries. Clumsy hands snatch at me, voices whisper pleas in my ears. I reach out and I touch someone . . . something . . . and I feel a form that is as twisted as mine. It pulls away, but another takes its place and this time I feel its face, as a blind man might feel the contours of a companion, fingertips substituting for eyes. But there is no face. Only a deep, glutinous hole where there should have been features, a great yawning, toothless mouth that seeps liquids and expels foul fumes. As I recoil, other, stronger hands grab at me and arms snake around my neck and my waist and squeeze and crush, so that I scream . . .

And my own scream wakes me for the third time.

I am already sitting up in bed, my neck stretched, my mouth open wide.

This time I am weak: I *have* to take something, anything that might soothe my nerves, something that would help me drift into sweet oblivion. But instead I think of Constance and it's her image, her voice, the precious touch of her hand in mine, that soothes me.

I wipe my brow with the bedsheet and sink back against the pillows, and my mind is calmer, my trembling beginning to settle. I am more tired than I know, for I am immediately sliding into troubled sleep again.

I find myself drawn into a phantasmagoria of shapes, sounds, and impressions, a soft-focus variegation of shifting images, all distantly calling to me, invocations that I cannot understand. Even *he* is there, so charming, so sublimely perfect, yet still imperceptible, ill-defined . . . until . . . until he begins to come towards me, freeing himself of the chaos around him, advancing and raising a hand . . . and I can see it's a well-manicured hand, for his shape is becoming sharp, focused . . . and I can *see* his face, discern his features, and I begin to recognize him, recognize him because I know him so well . . . and, like the others who have almost faded to invisibility, he is pleading with me. He tells me we are the same, he and I, and I can only return a bitter laugh as I look into his deep brown eyes . . . but he is adamant . . . asks me to find it in my heart – in my *soul* – to save him – to save us

both, for we really *are* the same – from eternal misery ...
and as he begs his face crumples and his spiritual tears flow
... and he is drawn away from me, paling into the
oblivion ...

And yet again I am conscious, this time awakened by the
dawn light stealing through the breach in the curtains.

I push myself up and look around me as if to make sure I
really am here in my gloomy bedroom, here where I should
be, and I'm relieved that morning has finally come. And in
that very instant, I forget all the dreams of the night.

17

Only snatches of those dreams came back to me (I was to remember them in their entirety eventually) during the long return trip to PERFECT REST, and because they presented themselves as short jumbled images, they made no sense to me at all.

When the spectre of the dark Adonis, the deity of good looks, appeared in my mind's eye I almost steered my car into the side of an overtaking XJS. The sharp and repeated tooting of the other driver's horn quickly brought me to my senses, and as I pulled back over into the proper lane, I waved an apology, while he held up a middle finger for my delectation. I slowed down to a speed that was accommodating to introspection.

You see, now I recognized this tuxedoed charmer and I began to understand the reason for those recurring visions and last night's dreams a little (at least, this was how daylight logic aspired to provide me with a rationale). With my knowledge of old movies I should have identified him before, because he was a famous matinée idol of the late Thirties and early Forties, a screen star famous the world over for his gay (in the *old* sense) repartee and rugged prowess, a celluloid adventurer who could play swashbuckler or sophisticate, hero or roguish charmer, priest or gunman. He was everything I yearned to be – tall, athletic, debonair, and devishly and devastatingly handsome – and this was where the first gleaning submitted itself for consideration. The images of him that I saw in mirrors were not *reflections* but were *projections*, mere, yet deep, wishful-thinking on my part, a fantasy stoked by drugs present but mainly past (as you know, I no longer did the hard stuff), those chemical residuals still floating around in my system – *and in my psyche*. For me, flashbacks had become drawbacks and I was becoming haunted by them.

I thought my illusions had ended with childhood, but now I realized they were only repressed. I still wanted to be something other than I was, and who could blame me for that? So when I looked into mirrors these days, I sometimes saw, aided by those chemical imbalances, that which I desired to be rather than what really was. The other hallucinations? Perhaps they were nothing more than psychological manifestations of my own tortured soul (and by now you'll know just how tortured my soul was).

And yet . . . and yet there was still one thing that bothered me: I could not remember this old-time film star's name. Every time I thought I had it, it eluded me. Every time it was on the tip of my tongue, it tripped off again. And I was supposed to be good at that sort of thing.

The XJS I'd almost side-whacked earlier was stuck in a long line of held-up traffic in the fast lane and I gave him a friendly toot and wave as I sailed by; he glared back, but there was no swivel-finger in evidence this time. I did notice, however, that a fantastic-looking blonde babe occupied the passenger seat and I wondered how obnoxious pigs like him managed to pull women like her. The shiny bright Jag provided my jealousy with an easy and probably quite erroneous answer, but it led my thoughts to Constance Bell. I realized I had become foolishly besotted with her and it was one of the reasons I was so eager to visit PERFECT REST again: I was fairly sure a meeting with the home's proprietor would not advance the search for Shelly's absent child one bit further, but the chance to meet Constance once more was too good to miss.

Why would I fall for her so rapidly and so easily? The

answer to this one was also easy – only this time there was nothing false about the judgement. You see, Constance Bell was like me: we both bore afflictions that made us unattractive to the majority of normal society (unfortunate, but it was an unpalatable truth that no amount of politically correct well-meaning propaganda would change). And because she was like me – except, of course, for her beautiful face and hands – she might just be attainable. Sad? Pathetic? You really wouldn't know.

The weather had been overcast since early morning and when I turned off the motorway, heading for Windsor, the heavens opened and it began to pour with rain. I switched on the Ford's sidelights and grumbled to myself about the usual changeable patterns of the English summer. By the time I turned into the rutted lane that would lead me to the Thames riverbank and PERFECT REST, the rain had ceased and the sun was making its first proper appearance of the day.

The car splashed through puddles and its suspension did little to prevent my body being jolted as it progressed through dips and over bumps, giving me further pause to wonder at the home's difficult location. Maybe death's waiting-room was meant to be isolated from worldly distractions. Even the jets passing overhead every few minutes scarcely intruded upon the calm. I took the bends in the lane carefully, occasionally taking time to peep through the gaps in the hedgerows on either side. I caught glimpses of flat grasslands where no animals seemed to graze, untidy clumps of woodland beyond. Here and there I spotted single houses, these almost as remote as the rest home itself. The square top of a pump station in the far distance, a church spire even further away. But I passed no other vehicle, nor any walkers, on this lonely track that purported to be a lane. I knew from the map book that the area was abundant with water reservoirs, some small, others as huge as lakes and even used by sailing clubs and water-skiers; there were also sewage works and sludge beds in the vicinity, as well as the remains of ancient monasteries and nunneries. Across the broad river was the very meadow in which the Magna Carta was allegedly signed. So it was a strange landscape, so close to the city itself and Heathrow airport, yet almost a hinterland whose pocket villages and hamlets appeared all the more forsaken because of the emptiness of the regions between them.

Not long after I'd passed the old abandoned house I'd noticed on my previous journey down the lane, with its boarded windows and overgrown frontage, I saw the rooftops and chimneys, then the gates of the home up ahead. I slowed the car almost to walking pace so that I could study my surrounds in more detail than before. If not for the sign declaring what lay beyond the gates and high walls, with high trees and foliage both before and behind the walls adding to the screening, a person this close (I was almost at the entrance now) might never guess that such an expansive dwelling lay just out of sight. The place was obviously visible from the other side of the Thames, the river itself providing a broad natural boundary. Through the bars of the iron gates I could see the tree-shadowed secondary drive, this much narrower than the one leading to the front of the house, and I assumed it was used by tradesmen and for deliveries, a route to the side or rear of the big building. It looked neglected and unfriendly, prohibited to the casual visitor.

I used the intercom on one of the stone pillars to announce my arrival and the gates duly swung open. I drove through and as soon as I rounded a gentle bend and cleared the trees, the great house that was PERFECT REST spread across my windscreen, quickly filling my view although I approached slowly, looming over me when I finally brought the car to a halt.

Out of habit I set the engine's isolation switch before climbing out of the car and making my way up the wheelchair ramp's slight incline. Maybe it was due to the long drive I'd just had, but if anything, my limbs and body were even more stiff than the previous day, the beating I'd taken on Brighton beach continuing to take its toll. I pushed through the vestibule doors and immediately saw Constance Bell standing by the reception desk as if waiting just for me.

There was a nervousness to her smile as I walked towards her, and I wondered why; then I realized I was nervous as well. Okay, don't misinterpret things here, I warned myself. The reason for her jitters was probably different from mine: maybe she just didn't like private investigators.

'Mr Dismas,' she greeted, using her elbow-crutches with practised ease as she moved forward.

'I'm a little early,' I apologized.

We shook hands, a mere touching of fingers, and I relished her softness. She stared at my face and I wanted her to examine my soul.

'That looks as if it's still very painful.' She indicated the bruised swelling on my cheek.

'Uh? Oh, it's not so bad now.'

'It must have been *some* door you walked into.'

I managed a sheepish grin and that did hurt.

'Let me show you to the visitors' room. Dr Wisbeech won't be long.' She broke away, moving back to the reception desk and pointing to the book on its shelf. 'If you'll just sign in.'

I followed the house rule, feeling like a schoolboy because of the height of the desk front. Hazel, the receptionist, barely gave me a glance before Constance led me towards the broad staircase leading to the upper floors, but we passed it by, heading towards the rear of the building. Along the way I studied yet more paintings on white walls, their style becoming increasingly bizarre the further we went.

Constance stopped at a large oak door on our left and paused with her hand on the doorknob. 'If you'll wait inside I'll let Dr Wisbeech know you're here.' She opened the door and stepped aside to allow me through.

'Miss Bell . . .' I began to say.

'Yes?' She looked at me expectantly.

'I . . . I just wanted you to know I'm grateful.' And that I think you're the loveliest creature I've ever met, I wanted to add.

'Grateful for what?' She gave a little, perplexed shake of her head.

'Uh, for getting Dr Wisbeech to see me.'

'But I didn't. I merely told him of your interest in Hildegarde and he decided he'd like to meet you himself.'

'Really? He didn't say why?'

'I can only assume he didn't want you to feel we were being uncooperative.'

I suppose I was disappointed that she hadn't engineered the meeting herself as a means of getting to see me again. Within the space of a few minutes I was left feeling like a schoolboy again, one who had a crush on the prettiest girl in the class and so mistakenly imagined motivations that were favourable to me. What a chump, I chided myself and the only excuse I allowed was that I was sure a *frisson* of excitement, pleasure – of *knowing*? – had passed between us at our first meeting. I couldn't believe it had all been in my own imagination.

'Mr Dismas?' She was still waiting for me to enter the room and as I went by her, she said: 'I hope we can. Help you, I mean.'

My spirits rose at that perfect smile and the warmth that emanated from it. Despite the faraway sadness that seemed perpetually to haunt her eyes – a sadness I understood only too well – I could *feel* there was a kind of union between us, that she could see beyond my physical shackles and she knew that I could see beyond hers. She closed the door and I listened to the sound of her irregular footsteps as they faded down the hallway.

I stood there for several long moments, gazing at the door, thinking only of this woman who had suddenly entered

193

my life. Don't expect too much, Dismas, I told myself. Don't expect too much and then you won't be disappointed. I had looked for and found no wedding ring on her finger, no rings of any kind, in fact; but that didn't mean she wasn't in a long-term relationship. With wonderful features like hers I would not have been surprised to learn she was romantically attached to some super-hunk, a tall, handsome guy with chiselled features and a kind disposition, all the things I didn't have. Oh Jesus, if that were true, I didn't stand a chance; no matter how much I might kid myself otherwise, I could never compete. My natural if cynical pragmatism brought me back to the real world and with an inward sigh, I studied the room around me.

Apart from two incongruities, it was strictly functional: two hard-looking couches, colour grey, a wooden coffee table between them, this one without magazines for visitors to browse through; an unhealthy palm planted in a terracotta pot in one corner and a tall hat and coat stand in another. The two incongruities? On one plain white wall was a large copy of Hieronymus Bosch's *The Garden of Earthly Delights*, the centre panel only and easily recognizable to me because one of Brighton's seedier private members' clubs I had cause to frequent (strictly in the line of business, you understand) had the same print behind its bar. The picture depicted a wild sexual orgy in a detailed landscape, bizarre beasts involved with distorted humans, its theme lust as the reason for mankind's downfall. I had to admit it was a fascinating piece of art and I might have taken time to study it more closely had I not taken an interest in the room's other inappropriate feature.

The horizontal mirror was on the wall opposite the door and it seemed too long for a room of this moderate size. It was black-framed and actually set into the wall itself, and if its purpose was to give visitors the opportunity to tidy themselves up before greeting whoever they had come to see, to me it seemed extravagant both in cost and dimensions. My natural suspicion was aroused.

Watching my own shambling reflection, I walked towards the glass and when I was only two feet away, I stopped. From my inside jacket pocket I drew out the pencil I always carried for rough sketches or diagrams, or for whenever my pen ran out of ink, and pointed it at the mirror. The lead tip touched the glass.

Now with normal mirrors there was always a double reflection, the stronger image at least an eighth of an inch away from the real pencil tip. This was because an ordinary mirror is always silvered at the back. In this case, the lead tips, original and reflection, actually touched, indicating that the glass was front-silvered. Which meant that this was a two-way mirror, the kind used for surveillance or voyeurism.

There had to be a darkened room next door, where someone could covertly observe the waiting visitors. Now why the hell would an old people's nursing home need such a set-up?

I moved away, wondering if someone was watching me from the other side at that very moment. Taking a seat and offering a profile to the mirror, I stared at the Hieronymus Bosch before me, relieved that I hadn't taken a closer interest in its nude figures before and now further wondering if this was not one of the reasons for its placement, the hidden observer watching the visitor's reaction to the picture. It might be just one of the ways a potential resident was judged suitable or otherwise, some kind of psychological test for the applicant. Maybe they were even questioned about the painting's subject matter afterwards, responses deemed unhealthy a negative consideration. Or perhaps it was a pre-interview test prospective staff unknowingly went through. Oh, come on! I was fantasizing. No establishment – particularly one of this nature – would use such a pointless procedure. But then, why the mirror? As I pondered, I heard the door open.

A tall trim man, over six feet in height, entered and raised a hand to bid me keep my seat. I was half-way up anyway, so I continued, proffering a hand towards him.

'Mr Dismas.'

His grip was firm rather than strong.

'Dr Wisbeech?'

I supposed I'd expected him to be wearing a white coat, stethoscope draped around his neck (or, as in the new fashion for young doctors, around his shoulders), but no, he wore a dark grey suit, finely-cut, mohair weaved into the material so that it seemed to have a subtle sheen to it.

He nodded to me. 'Won't you please be seated?'

His manner was extremely cordial, his light blue eyes keen with interest. He glanced at the bruising on my face, but made no comment; those eyes were taking in *all* of me.

The doctor was a handsome man and I judged him to be in his low sixties, possibly a bit younger. His well-groomed hair was dark grey, lighter-grey-to-white at the temples and over his ears, and he sported a neat beard, shot with white, not quite a goatee, but stylish all the same. He had a strong, almost patrician face, with a sharp, high-bridged nose that went well with his defined cheekbones. His pale blue tie and cream breast-pocket handkerchief were silk and the cuffs of his white shirt fell precisely three-quarters of an inch below the sleeves of his jacket. Even his black shoes had the right kind of dull shine and I was willing to bet his socks were black or matched the grey of his suit. I was trying to think of the movie star he resembled and it had come by the time he took the seat opposite. It was one of the old crowd, long since dead, but a major player in his time.

Michael Rennie. Remember him? Harry Lime in the black and white TV series, an alien in the film *The Day the Earth Stood Still*. Tall, gaunt, cold – and the perfect gentleman.

'I understand you are a private detective,' he said. (Incidentally, I'd have won my bet – his socks were charcoal grey.)

'Private investigator, actually,' I replied.

'I'm sorry, I didn't know there was a difference.'

He smiled as he spoke and I saw his teeth were something of a disappointment; not that they were unsightly, but they were yellowish, stained here and there by too much tea or coffee, a blemish on an otherwise impeccable presentation. It gave me some satisfaction.

'Well, an investigator is less glamorous,' I explained, immediately aware of the irony in my statement. 'Our work is usually pretty mundane,' I added.

'I see. And you are interested in one of our guests.'

Not 'patient', nor 'resident', but 'guest'.

'Hildegarde Vogel,' I said unnecessarily.

'Yes, so I believe. Can you tell me why?'

As we spoke, his eyes were constantly studying me as if interested in my misformed physique.

'She acted as midwife for a client of mine some eighteen years ago. My client claims the baby was taken away from her only seconds after the birth and she never saw it again.'

'Then presumably the baby died.'

'She says it didn't.'

'Was it a difficult birth, do you know?'

'She didn't say it was,' I lied.

'I merely wondered if she had been overwrought at the time. Sometimes the labour is a terrible ordeal for the woman, especially if it's a long-drawn-out experience. The mother might imagine all sorts of dreadful things, none of which have any basis in reality. Does she say the baby was healthy?'

'No. They told her that there was something wrong with the boy, that he died within minutes.'

'Then I really don't understand . . .'

'Neither birth nor death was registered.'

'You checked this for yourself. You went through the normal agencies?'

I nodded.

'And you contacted the hospital in question? I assume the infant was born in hospital and not at home.'

I nodded again. 'Unfortunately the hospital – it was the Dartford General – burned down some years ago.'

'And all records were destroyed?'

'Apparently so. That doesn't explain why the birth and death wasn't registered elsewhere, though.'

'Such things happen in any bureaucracy, especially one the size of the NHS. Incompetence, neglect, sheer laziness – it's rather common in the public services. I think we all know that the National Health Service is undermanned and under-funded, at least where medical matters are concerned. Mistakes and omissions happen all the time. And eighteen years ago, before computers were truly regarded as tools of the trade, the system was in an even worse state.' He still watched me keenly, now looking straight into my eye – or, I should say, the puckered hole where an eye had once been. 'I'm surprised you didn't relate this to your client,' he continued. 'Perhaps you needed the work?'

I ignored the implied sneer (his face was passive, not even the hint of a smile beneath that finely clipped moustache). I suppose I could have explained about the whispering voices, the mirror images, the illusion of thousands of wings, but I had sense enough to realize how utterly crazy it would all sound.

'I did try,' I said, 'but my client was adamant that the child was born and is still alive.'

'Your client's name?' It was a brisk question, demanding an answer.

'I'm not at liberty to say. Client confidentiality, and all that.'

'Very well. Yet you expect me to let you bother one of my clients.'

'Hildegarde Vogel might be of some help.'

His manner hadn't changed since he'd entered the room:

interested, detached, brusque, polite – yes, these were differences in tone, but his expression and attitude hardly varied.

'You witnessed Hildegarde's condition yesterday. Indeed, I've been told it deteriorated even further while you were with her. She is unwell, Mr Dismas, and very confused.'

'She was okay when I first spoke to her. Quite rational, in fact. It was only later, when she began to remember certain things, that she became upset.'

It was *then* that I noticed a change in him, a stiffening of body, an even greater sharpness in those cold, blue eyes. It was barely perceptible, but alterations in moods is another thing I'm good at recognizing – or *sensing*.

He scarcely missed a beat. 'And what was it that the poor woman remembered?'

'Deformed babies,' I replied.

It hung in the air between us, a statement so stark that we were both quiet for a moment or two.

Then the doctor said: 'I'm not sure what you want.'

'My client's intuition – a *mother's* intuition – tells her that her son is still alive. My guess is that the baby was so sick and malformed that they did not want to show him to her, and that he died soon after the birth. But my client will not accept that. Now if I were to bring her here to talk to Hildegarde herself, she might be convinced. Maybe the meeting might nudge something in the ex-midwife's memory, she might even recall my client – I understand that at the time Hildegarde was a great comfort to her. My client might listen to her and finally accept that her son is not alive.'

I was leaning towards him now, my one eye as intense as both of his, I'm sure, my humped back no doubt even more unsightly because of my crouched position, my gnarled hands clenched between my knees. He appraised me carefully, as glacial as ever, undisturbed by my proximity.

'What was your diagnosis in your infancy, Mr Dismas?'

'What?' I was taken aback. Indeed, reflexively, I even sat back a little.

'Cerebral palsy, spina bifida, osteogenis imperfecta – no, no sign of blue sclerotics in your eye. Marjous Syndrome, then? No, I doubt that's the cause of your deformities. Perhaps you had rheumatoid arthritis as a child? Poliomyelitis? Spondylitis? No, you seem active enough. So which was it, Mr Dismas? What did they tell your parents was wrong with you?'

'I've no idea and it isn't relevant.'

'Sometimes babies are born so badly deformed that not even their parents wish to keep them.'

'I didn't know my parents,' I told him, beginning to burn inside.

'Ah. Then not even your mother wanted you.'

'I don't see what –'

'Of course not. I don't expect you to. But I want you to understand. You see, even in this day and age, when treatment is so extensive and accessible, when the foetus can be studied in the womb and abortion is virtually on demand, malformed babies that are so grotesque that their mothers do not even wish to hold them are still being born. These poor unfortunates are taken away and left to die naturally. If there is pain involved, an injection might help them on their way. It's harsh, yes, I know, but the grief is soon over and the parents recover, perhaps to go on and have other normal, healthy children. Who knows what terrible tribulations they would have to endure if their disabled child had been allowed to live?'

'Everyone's entitled to a life,' I commented flatly.

'An anti-abortionist?'

'Just *for* life. Hardship and nuisance-value is no excuse for preventing life. It may be difficult, it might mean a lifetime of misery for the child, but he or she deserves the chance to live and experience things in their own way. It doesn't always have to be a bad existence. Consider your own care-supervisor.'

'Constance?'

'She's obviously devoted a large part of her life to caring for the sick and elderly. She's helped others just by her presence.'

The smile was in his eyes, but not on his lips. Was I so transparent? Could he sense my emotions towards her?

'And of course, your own time here on Earth has proved helpful to others,' he said, and I wasn't sure if the smile in his eyes was not mockery.

'Maybe it has. The point is, I was given the chance and so was Constance Bell. Think of all those others who weren't.'

'Well, there lies a huge moral dilemma: to give life and with it, great hardship, or to take it away as an ultimate kindness.'

I understood his meaning. There were many times in my own life when I wished I hadn't been born, and yes, I'd cursed the person who had allowed me to live after the moment of birth. Perhaps the one who had dumped me outside the convent in the dead of winter – I had always assumed that it had been my mother who had left me there – had taken the easy option, unable to smother me to death themself, so leaving me there in the cold to let fate play its own hand.

'As far as I'm concerned,' I said, 'it's every mother's own decision. I only wish some would give it more consideration. But I don't understand your interest in me. I'm here to discuss Hildegarde Vogel.'

'Life, in any form, has always been of concern to me. It's why I joined the medical profession in the first place.'

There was something about his eyes that was almost mesmeric. They made me feel uncomfortable yet, perversely, they seemed to draw me in. Purposely, I looked away.

Directly to the point, I asked: 'Will I be allowed to see Hildegarde again?'

He thought for a moment, then appeared to soften his stance (I say 'appeared' because I had no idea of what was going through his mind). 'Let's see how she is tomorrow, or perhaps the next day. I'm afraid the excitement yesterday affected her adversely: she really is quite unwell this morning.'

'You'll let me talk to her, though?' I was unable to conceal my surprise.

'If or when she's well enough. Why don't I get Constance to phone you tomorrow with a final decision?'

'That's fine by me.' It was more than I'd expected.

'Of course, if Hildegarde becomes upset again you must promise me you'll desist immediately. You will leave and not bother my patient again.'

'It's a deal. Believe me, I don't want to make her any worse than she is.'

He rose from the couch, a hand extended towards me, and I, too, got to my feet, gratefully taking that hand. As we shook he continued to observe me, his interest unconcealed. Dr Wisbeech towered over me and I could feel his power – not the kind that has to do with physical strength but the kind that has to do with the mind, the persona, stemming from an individual's very psyche, a faculty that enables them to intimidate/dominate others, sometimes without the other person even being aware. It was hard to ignore, but then I'd been fighting that sort of thing all my life – my stature (or status, if you like) made it a regular conflict. I grinned as I released my hand from his, and I think we both knew right then that an engagement (in the sense of battle) had been postponed. It occurred to me to wonder why I was thinking in these terms as I made my way towards the door, my grin fading to an inner wry smile. I had always been quite perceptive as far as the feelings of others were concerned, particularly if their feelings were directed towards myself, but the *animus* in this man, despite its suppression and his pleasant if condescending manner, could be felt as plainly as if he'd spat in my empty eye.

'Mr Dismas?'

I lingered in the doorway.

'Who are your friends? Are they others like yourself?' There was no apology in his question, no awkwardness.

'What do you mean by "others"?' I said stiffly.

Again, no awkwardness, no embarrassment. 'Others with similar disabilities,' he replied. 'Or have you managed to become accepted by normal people? Indeed, do you accept *yourself* as normal?'

My hand gripped the door frame. I wanted to throw myself at him, beat that handsome, patrician's face to a pulp.

'I hope I haven't offended you,' he said, but not as an afterthought: he knew exactly what he was doing.

What was his game? I asked myself. Was he deliberately riding me, playing for some kind of reaction? Or . . . was it possible? . . . was he genuinely interested in how I got by? No, nobody could be that insensitive. Or that wicked?

'I'll wait to hear how Miss Vogel is,' was all I said as I turned away and stomped off down the hall. If he uttered some response to that, I didn't catch it.

Bastard, I thought as I stomped, *absolute-bloody-bastard*. I could feel his eyes on me and I knew if I looked back he'd be there in the doorway, watching my departure with that peculiarly cool interest. *Bastard*.

Outside, I forced myself to take in some deep breaths, expelling the stale degenerative air of the home from my lungs and sucking in the purer stuff. The day had suddenly become overcast again, clouds with bulging, charcoal-grey bottoms milling low in the sky, each piled, cumulonimbus heap trying to gain elbow room, pushing against its neighbour and creating deep-growling rumbles, occasional flares of pure energy. The rain soon began, great heavy dollops of it, bursting, splatting, against the driveway, drumming an escalating beat on the roof and bonnet of my car. Turning up my coat collar, I made a clumsy dash for the Ford, my head and the hump of my back soaked before I could drag open the driver's door and bundle myself inside.

'Bastard!' I said aloud in the solitude of my metal capsule.

When you're as I am, you rarely completely forget your condition, your own oddity is always present in your mind (usually right at the front) and you never need reminding of how different you are to normals. You never ask to be reminded, either. You might have thought that Wisbeech, in light of his profession and lettered qualifications, would have understood that; as a learned and obviously civilized human being he might even have appreciated the insult his remarks might have dealt me. My guess was that he cared little about my sensitivities and nothing about the question itself: my belief was that he had been testing me. What that test meant, I had no idea; I just had the feeling that I'd failed.

Switching the isolation switch off and the engine on, I angrily shoved the gear stick into first, pulling away from the home's front entrance a little too fast, a little too powerfully, the tyres throwing up stones from the drive. I violently twisted the steering wheel to head towards the high gates, giving one last disgusted glance back at the building as I did so. My foot almost slipped from the accelerator in my surprise, for the dark upper windows of PERFECT REST were now filled with pallid faces.

It was as if most of the elderly residents had come to their windows to watch me leave. I only caught a glimpse, for the turn completed itself of its own accord and the car was set straight for the gates, but the image of those grey-white blobs against the glass, the rooms leaden behind them, stayed in my mind as I changed gear and controlled direction. A quick look in the rear-view mirror presented a receding reflection of the building itself and it seemed suddenly ominous in the sullen, rain-dulled light, a semi-Gothic mansion that was full of secrets rather than a restful haven. A raindrop had dripped into the crevice between my neck and shirt collar, running sideways around my hump and down my back, causing me to shiver. I gripped the wheel more tightly, straightening the car, and wondered at the home's sudden lack of charm. Now I could feel a hundred or more sets of eyes watching my retreat, every pair hostile. *Idiot*, I berated myself. *Imagination*, I tried to convince myself. They were just sick old people with nothing better to do, curious about strangers, bored inside death's waiting-room. There was no antagonism towards me on their minds; they probably watched every new coming and going in the same way. Visiting hours – if they had had set visiting hours – would have been a riot.

That's when I realized that on neither visit to PERFECT REST had I seen any other visitor. Nor anybody else who looked like an outsider, for that matter. This place really was private.

I kept the car in second all the way down the drive and when I entered the short, wooded area the gloom forced me to switch on my headlights. I passed through the gates that had already opened for me and pulled up outside. Taking out my small notepad and pen from my inside pocket, I leaned across the passenger seat, wound down the window on that side, and peered out at the sign on one of the stone pillars. I wrote down: MD, FRCS, FRCOG, FRCP, DCH. Then I drove on, quickly reaching third, sticking with it while the car splashed through instant puddles and lurched into existing dips. The landscape began to open up again and the rain pelted the windscreen with some force; the wipers struggled to keep vision clear, but I was soon forced to lean even closer than my usual position to the glass in order to see my way ahead. The turns seemed to come up too fast even though I was still only in third, and it was a while before I realized the engine was labouring, desperate for a shift upwards; unconsciously I had been trying to speed away from the home and the sinister – yes, I admitted to myself, that was the word, he *was* sinister – Dr Wisbeech. I eased off the accelerator, slowing to a more appropriate speed.

High and far ahead I noticed bright blue patches in the otherwise troubled skies that told me the storm would not last too long. In fact, the further south-east I went, the clearer it would become. But that was for later – right now it was cats and dogs out there.

I was approaching the now familiar abandoned house by the side of the lane when I saw the tiny figure sheltering hunched-up under a tree. Elbow-crutch resting against her hip, Constance Bell waved a hand at me to stop.

18

She was soaked, the tree she cowered under affording scant protection. As I drew up alongside her she took a couple of faltering steps towards the car.

'Get in before you drown,' I called out, pushing open the passenger door.

Constance put a hand on top of the door frame and peered in at me, her lovely eyes blinking away raindrops; she did not have to duck to see me. She looked like a child, a very troubled child.

'I can't,' she shouted over the pounding of the rain. 'I have to get back before they miss me.'

'You sound as if you've made a jailbreak.' I tried to ease her obvious tension with a grin.

'No, I mean it, I don't have long.'

'Then at least sit in the car so we can talk without hollering.'

She took a quick look around her, first back down the lane towards the home, then in the opposite direction. She pointed towards the abandoned house and the overgrown track that led towards the rear.

'If I do, will you drive us out of sight?'

I'm sure I registered disbelief, but I nodded anyway. 'Sure. Just get in out of the wet.'

She eased herself into the seat backwards, resting the elbow crutches against the door as she did so, then swivelled round so that her legs were also inside the car. Retrieving the crutches, she closed the door.

'Terrific,' I said and steered the Ford off the lane on to the bumpy track. Apart from the odd untidy heaps of timber and rubble, there was little else behind the house: a half-collapsed shed stood some distance away and beyond that there was only long grass and shrubbery, woodland their backdrop. I brought the car to a halt beside the building's battered rear door.

'What are you afraid of?' I asked my passenger as I switched off the engine and shifted round in my seat so that I could take her in more easily.

She was dabbing raindrops from her face with a tiny handkerchief, bedraggled locks of hair loosened from the tie at the nape of her neck to stick against her cheeks. I wanted to reach forward and brush the strands away, to push them gently behind her ears, an excuse to touch her, to feel her soft skin beneath my fingertips. Naturally, I sat there and did nothing.

'Why . . . why do you think I'm afraid?'

Her poor imperfect body rested awkwardly in the passenger seat; her gaze on me was intense.

'You obviously don't want to be seen talking to me,' I replied to her question.

'It's just that . . .' She gave a little shake of her head. 'Mr Dismas – '

'Please. People who know me call me Dis. Or Nick – my friends call me Nick.' (In fact, even my friends called me Dis, but I wanted Constance to use my proper Christian name.)

'I don't think you should come back to the home.'

'Hey, I'm not going to upset Hildegarde again. Besides, I only get to see her if your boss decides she's well enough. I promise I'll treat her gently.'

'You don't understand. It's the doctor I don't want you to upset.'

'Wisbeech? Why should I upset him? I only need the answers to a few questions, none of which have anything to do with him.'

'Please listen to me.' My hand was resting on the hand-brake between us and she touched the top of my fingers with her own. 'Dr Wisbeech is not someone you should anger. He's a very powerful person.'

I found it difficult to get my thoughts back on line despite the gravity of her tone. Her flesh against mine: dear God, was this how teenagers felt when first crush led to first touch? I wasn't experienced in these things, so I had no way of knowing (I guess that same lack of experience also accounted for my over-reaction right then).

'Did you hear me?' she asked, leaning a little closer, her puzzled eyes examining mine in the gloomy interior of the car. 'Mr – Nick, please understand what I'm trying to tell you.'

Her hand left mine and I managed to pull myself together enough to say: 'Why are you going to so much trouble to warn me?'

She seemed to withdraw into herself; certainly she moved away from me.

'I'm not going to any trouble. I nearly always take a walk along the lane some time during the day, usually in the late afternoon.'

'In the pouring rain?'

'It wasn't raining when I left.'

'But you are concerned.' I almost added 'about me', but that would have been foolish – and probably wishful thinking. 'What exactly do you think the doctor can do to me?'

'I have to go.' She began to turn, to reach for the door release.

'Wait a minute!' I caught her arm. 'Please. Talk to me a little while longer, okay?'

She was facing the door and I studied the long curve of her neck through the damp, loosened hair, a graceful line that led to her cruelly stunted body. Slowly her head came round and she rested back in the seat.

'I can't tell you any more than I already have,' she said quietly.

'You haven't told me anything.'

She remained silent.

'How could I anger Dr Wisbeech, Constance?' Just speaking her name for the first time sent a shiver through me. 'How is he powerful, in what way? He's only the manager of an old people's nursing home –'

'He *owns* PERFECT REST.'

'Okay, he owns it. How does that make him powerful? Are you telling me he has connections in high places and if so, why should my enquiries put any noses out of joint?'

'I used the wrong word. I simply meant he is very wealthy.'

'Wealthy enough to pay someone to discourage me?'

'You've got it all wrong . . .'

But I was on a roll, my PI instincts coming to the fore. 'Dr Wisbeech has an awful lot of letters behind his name. They look pretty fancy for someone who only runs an old folks' home. Why should he be paranoid about a few questions to one of his residents? And tell me this: why does he keep a two-way mirror in the visitors' room?'

That gave her a start.

'Those kind of mirrors are easy to spot,' I went on, pushing for an answer.

'Dr Wisbeech likes to study people before meeting them, particularly those applying for residency.'

'Odd way to vet future clients.'

'He prefers to see their real condition, not the one they put on for interviews. Dr Wisbeech is very selective of his guests.'

'But why should he want to observe me beforehand?'

'What makes you think he did? I told you, it's used when dealing with prospective guests.'

'Kind of weird though.'

'We have high standards.'

'So I noticed. I'm still wondering, by the way, how someone like Hildegarde Vogel could afford your services.'

'That isn't a mystery. Hildegarde is a very special guest of Dr Wisbeech. She worked with him many years ago when he was a consultant for several major hospitals.'

I allowed a moment or two for that to sink in. 'They worked together . . .' I said, more to myself than to Constance.

'Yes. The Doctor once told me that Hildegarde was invaluable to him during those years and because she's in such poor health now, with no friends or family to support her, he feels responsible himself for her wellbeing. I suppose it's his way of repaying Hildegarde for her loyal service.'

'He doesn't come across as the guardian angel type to me.'

'First impressions can be deceptive – as you, of all people, should know. Dr Wisbeech is a wonderful benefactor.'

'So why are you warning me against him?'

'To try and stop you becoming involved in something you don't understand. The Doctor doesn't tolerate disturbances to his work.'

'His work with old people? You know I'm still puzzled by his medical virtuosity. Isn't he a little over-qualified to be taking care of geriatrics, ailing or otherwise?'

'It's his choice. Perhaps he feels he can do so much more by dedicating himself to one area of medicine rather than many.'

'Yes, but *old* people?'

'What have you got against the elderly? Haven't they earned the right to live out the rest of their lives in some comfort? Haven't they paid their debt to society?'

'Some, maybe.'

'As I said, Dr Wisbeech is very discriminating. Now I really must get back.'

'Constance . . .'

It was too late: she had already pushed open the door and was sliding from the seat before I had a chance to question her further. We hadn't noticed, but the rain had lost its intensity to become a steady drizzle.

'Let me take you,' I pleaded as she braced herself with the crutches on the uneven ground.

'No. It's better that you just leave.'

As she lurched away I wondered why she didn't want to be seen with me. Was she that afraid of this wonderfully benevolent boss of hers?

'Can I phone you?' I called out.

'No!' But she paused. 'I don't know. I think it's probably better that you don't. Goodbye, Mr Dismas.'

'Dis. Call me Dis.' But she was gone. 'Or Nick,' I said to myself with a sigh.

19

When I got back to the office I sent Philo out for sandwiches and coffee while I went through paperwork that had accumulated throughout the morning. Working lunches were not unusual either for myself or for Henry – even when out on fieldwork a quick snack in a pub, or sandwiches scoffed in my car, were frequently the order of the day (the latter particularly when on surveillance). Lunchtime was also good for getting things done without being disturbed by phone calls from clients and contacts. I allowed Henry to get his daily fix with one movie question, mercifully an easy one: Which Marx Brother failed to appear in 1942's *Hellzapoppin*? Answer: All of them; the film was an Olson and Johnson starrer, who were serious rivals of the famous brothers at the time. After that, it was strictly down to catching up on boring but vital correspondence and office minutiae. There was one special phone call I wanted to make, but I had to consider the fact that others actually lunched out most days.

An hour or so later when I was readjusting a client fee that Philo had submitted for approval – he had a habit of forgetting to add ten per cent to all costs and expenses, including hours spent travelling on a case, so that the agency could realize a reasonable profit (standard practice in our business, my friend – pays for overheads, wear and tear, and all indirect costs), Etta Kaesbach appeared at my open office door.

'I thought I might catch you on my way back from lunch,' she said by way of announcing herself.

'Come in.' I laid my pen down and smiled, always pleased to see her.

She shook her dripping, half-closed umbrella out, making tiny puddles on the floor; I caught Henry's disapproving frown through the doorway.

'What a summer,' Etta complained as she took the seat on the other side of my desk. 'Glorious one minute, monsoon season the next.'

She laid the short umbrella on the floor beside her and removed the grip from her hair, pushing wayward strands back and regripping them once they were tidy. I watched, comparing her to the girl with whom I'd shared my car earlier in the day. Both had special qualities, but my feelings for them were different. Vastly different. And, of course, I thought I might stand a chance with Constance.

'My God, what's happened to your face?' Etta's own face was aghast.

Involuntarily, I touched the swelling below my absent eye. 'I took a tumble down the steps of my flat,' I lied, unwilling to revisit the humiliation of two nights ago.

'The wages of wine?' She was being lyrical, perfectly aware that I rarely touched the grape, beer and spirits my usual juice.

'Slippery stone. Sometimes the steps are tricky with this ol' leg of mine.' I tapped the offending limb under the desk, rapping on wood with my other hand at the same time.

Etta smiled as she shook her head, letting me know that she suspected booze was the cause of my 'downfall'. Then she got straight to the point: 'Why are you upsetting my client, Dis?'

Oh Lord, someone else I was upsetting today. 'Shelly Ripstone?' I asked.

The solicitor nodded. 'She called me yesterday, claiming you've dumped her twice. Shelly might be somewhat melo-dramatic on occasion, Dis, but she's a good client and her late husband was an even better one. Looking after her interests is a duty my firm takes very seriously. So please tell me what's going on. One minute you're on the case, albeit reluctantly, the next you're off it. Then you're back working for her again, only to give it up once more.'

I groaned wearily, resting my elbows on the desk and cupping my head in my hands. 'Would you believe me if I told you I was back on it yet again?' I said.

'Shelly doesn't appear to be aware of that.'

'I forgot to call her back when something else came up.'

'Something to do with her alleged missing son?'

'Possibly. I suppose at the back of my mind was the thought that it might be another wild goose chase – like the previous one of trying to find a record of birth and death. I didn't want to build up her hopes again.'

'Dis, I think you'd better tell me everything you've done so far, then perhaps I can pacify her.'

So I did. I went over the case from start to present moment – everything except hallucinations and visions of wings and birds and debonair men seen only in mirrors. I didn't mention whispering voices either and only spoke of Louise Broomfield in passing, implying that she was a friend of Shelly's rather than some clairvoyant mentor of mine now. But Etta was sharper than that.

'Who did you say this Broomfield woman was?' she asked, watching me suspiciously.

'She's a kind of, well, a kind of spiritualist. A clairvoyant, actually.'

'Oh Dis.' It was a reprimand.

'Hey, I didn't bring her in. That was our mutual client's idea.'

'I said Shelly was melodramatic. I hope you're not taking this Broomfield woman seriously, Dis.'

'You know me better.' Another deceit, but I really didn't want to get into all the psychic stuff right then. 'The point is, I'm hoping to see the old ex-midwife again tomorrow if she's well enough.'

'And you really think she might be helpful?'

'I seemed to hit a nerve the first time I spoke to her.'

'But she's sick and she's senile?'

I nodded. 'Yup.'

Etta rested back in her chair and shook her head despairingly. 'You should have let it go, Dis.'

'I thought you thought I had and that's why you were telling me off.'

'No. That was because you kept changing your mind so my client didn't know where she was. Now I think you should stick to your original decision. I'll explain it to Shelly, I'll tell her you've done your best but without further firm leads there's no point in going on with it. You'd only be wasting her money and your time.'

'I already mentioned that to her.'

'It'll come better from me. She might just see some sense.'

'And so lose control of a lot of money?'

'Sometimes that's the way it falls. She'll have to live with it.'

'Tough guy, huh?'

'Only when there's no alternative. It's best for all concerned.'

'I don't think she'll see it that way.'

Etta shrugged. 'That's too bad. One of my duties as her legal adviser is to make sure she doesn't throw away her money on lost causes.'

I surprised myself by pleading for a second time that day. 'Give me a little longer, another day or so. Let's see what happens tomorrow. If Hildegarde Vogel is well enough for me to visit, I may be able to wrap the whole thing up.'

'I doubt it, even if the poor lady is feeling better. There's no sense to it, Dis.'

'Only one more day then. Remember, it's Shelly Ripstone who's employing me, not your firm.'

'Tough guy, huh?' she countered.

'I won't even let Shelly know I'm back on the case and I won't charge her for my extra time if there's no result.'

'Is this the Nick Dismas I thought I knew? No charge? Come on, Dis, what's got into you? And what would Henry say?'

There was a mumbling from the outer office, but I didn't think Henry had caught the drift of our conversation, otherwise he would have been in like a shot. He must have just heard his own name mentioned.

'When I started this agency,' I said quietly to Etta across the desk, 'I promised myself I'd give every case one hundred and ten per cent's worth of effort and I've always stuck with that principle, even when the fee amounted to nothing more than the cash to buy a couple of rounds in the nearest and cheapest bar. We both know that attitude has served me well over the years, so I'm not about to break with tradition now, no matter how cynical and hard-faced I've become about the business. This extra day will just be that ten per cent over the odds.'

She held up her thin hands. 'All right, all right, you've convinced me. You're a noble person. In any case, as you've reminded me, Shelly's contract is with you, not my firm. It's up to you how far you go with it.'

'You know I wouldn't go against your wishes, Etta.'

At last she smiled. 'Yes, I do. Fine then, Dis, it's your baby.'

We both winced.

'You know what I mean.' She picked up her umbrella and rose from the chair. 'But promise me you won't give Shelly any more false hopes.'

'I didn't give her any in the first place.'

'No, but her expectations rose when you took up the case again.'

'This time she won't even know.'

'She's expecting me to call her, but I won't for a day or

two. And if she phones me in the meantime, I'll say I couldn't get hold of you, you were out every time I tried.'

'Thanks, Etta. I mean it.'

'I'm aware that you're crazy, but at least you're fairly harmless. Will you contact me if you discover anything that will help?'

'Of course. And if I do, shall we tell Shelly together?'

'Might be an idea. Then at least she'll know her solicitor is looking after her interests. Take care, Dis, and keep in touch.'

With an air-blown kiss, Etta left my office.

The rest of the afternoon was filled with more mundane agency work.

Mundane stuff, but vitally important to the business, because it meant a constant turnover of work and that was the difference between success and failure for an outfit like mine.

All the cases I entered into my day-to-day, week-to-week, month-to-month instructions book, the entries later to be filed on computer by Henry. Hard files would also be kept, these held in the current-work cabinets in my office, later, on completion, to be stored in cupboards in the outer office. Letters of acceptance would have to be typed for each new commission, fees for services included where necessary as well as requests for more information (usually unnecessary, for most of our professional clients knew the form). As neither Philo nor Ida could type, letters and reports were a task I shared with Henry, and it was part of the job I detested. I always promised myself that one day I'd hire a proper secretary.

Henry dealt with most of the incoming phone calls that afternoon, although one did come through to me when his line was busy. It was Ida and she was using an old ploy to obtain a certain telephone number (the one she was ringing from, in fact), which I'd used myself many times in the past. She was chasing down a divorced absconder who owed his ex-wife maintenance money for their kids; my instructing client, the woman's solicitor, needed the ex-husband's telephone number so that the man could be harassed for payment not just by letter, but also by verbal 'assault' (another old ploy greatly enjoyed by ex-partners). The absconder, who had gone to ground, naturally had gone ex-directory, so no BT operator was going to give out his number.

His new address was easy to find by the usual methods, and Ida, attired in her best granny clothes, had parked her car right outside his front door, claiming that it had broken down when she knocked and our target had appeared on the doorstep. He had taken pity on her (the ruse doesn't *always* work) and allowed her to use the phone inside the house to call her regular garage. While there she had done a swift and necessarily superficial inventory of the house's contents, peeking through open doorways, perhaps even asking to use the loo, so that she could sneak a look into the upstairs bedrooms. She would have already made notes on the building's exterior and surrounds, so that together with what she had learned from inside, she would be able to provide a reasonably comprehensive status report for our legal client (very handy should the ex plead poverty). However, the prime purpose was to obtain the covert telephone number, so instead of ringing a garage, Ida rang the agency using a special codeword we'd devised that indicated the phone she was calling from did not have its own number displayed. After a short dialogue with 'Harry the Mechanic' – 'Harry' being our codeword – she rang off, no doubt thanking the gullible householder profusely for the use of the line. The moment I heard the receiver replaced, I dialled 1471 and made a note of the number given by the automatic operator. Simple but effective; this runaway was going to get a lot of nasty phone calls from his ex-wife, her solicitor, and maybe even his abandoned kids. I had no sympathy for him.

Philo arrived back from a trip to Eastbourne further along the coast, where he had delivered a set of legal documents to a firm of solicitors for me, the papers too urgent to post and too important to risk a courier service; personal delivery was another of our minor but no less crucial services. I immediately sent him off to photograph a vehicle that had been involved in a road-rage incident, its headlights and windscreen not smashed in the accident itself, but by the driver of the other car wielding a tyre lever. The insurance company, who regularly used the agency when their own assessors were too busy, wanted the book thrown at the offender.

Nothing glamorous about our daily routine, rarely very exciting, and not often involving anything to fire the imagination. Despite my physical drawbacks, I was an ordinary guy conducting a fairly unexceptional line of work; flights of fancy were not the order of the day (night-time privacy was another matter). I guess I'm just trying to lay down a solid, even mundane base to emphasize just how extraordinary and unimaginable to me were the events that were to follow.

Anyway, it wasn't until towards the end of the working day that I got the chance to call the BMA, the British Medical Association.

20

Dreams again. Worse than ever. Bloody terrifying dreams.

At least, I *thought* they were dreams.

When I'd left the office that evening I'd warned Henry not to work too late; as much as I appreciated the effort, he was putting in *too* many hours, always complaining that it was the only way he could keep up with the paperwork when we were that busy. I reminded him that he had a dear old mum at home who relied on him for company, but he scoffed, saying it was good for her to get used to the idea that he had his own life to lead and working overtime was part of it. I left him to his accounts and time sheets, reluctant to tell him he was lucky to have someone to worry over him.

I went straight back to the flat without stopping for a drink on the way, and on my own that evening I smoked only straights, not even tempted to do Skunk or Rock, because I was mellowed out on something better. Constance Bell was my opiate that evening.

As cynical and streetwise that I thought myself to be – and I pretty much *was* both, life experience and my occupation seeing to that – I was still acting like a teenager in the throes of his first romantic crush. As I microwaved my frozen-pack lasagna dinner, I was even humming a medley of old love themes. Sure, I'd fallen in love before – I *thought* I had fallen in love before – and more than just once. There was a time my legs turned to jelly and my brain to mush at the mere sight of Etta, but this time it was different, this time I was on a level playing field. In my mind – and I had to

221

keep reminding myself it was in *my* mind – our disabilities cancelled each other's out; it didn't make them go away, but it kind of *absorbed* them. I felt that for the first time in my life I stood a chance with someone I could really care for, someone who stirred me in that perfectly normal way. Our relationship, if it had a chance to flourish – God, if it had a chance to *happen*! – could be that of equals and that some-how would make it ordinary – oh Lord, how I'd longed to be *ordinary*! It's hard to explain, but my world is a different world to yours, no matter how much the well-meaning and the politically correct might have it otherwise, and the thought that I could share in the normal emotional experi-ence made me feel like the luckiest man alive for a few hours. I was certain that something had passed between us, even on the first occasion we'd met. A mutual attraction, an understanding of each other's feelings and tribulations, a subliminal touching of senses? I had no idea what it was, but I was sure it was not one-sided on my part. I had also detected a strange trepidation in Constance's gaze, a distant haunting that I could not comprehend; its effect, though, was to make her seem even more vulnerable.

I wanted to phone her at PERFECT REST on the pretence of discussing the information I'd gleaned from the BMA earlier in the evening, the meaning of the list of credentials behind Dr Leonard K. Wisbeech's name, but in reality just to hear her voice once more, to imagine her lips so far away yet so close to mine. Common sense prevented me though: I realized she was probably off-duty by now and I didn't even know if she lived at the home itself or somewhere close by. It struck me that I knew nothing about her except that she was a care-supervisor and that life had played one of its cruel, dispassionate tricks on her.

Doubt insinuated its way into my happiness. Maybe Con-stance lived with a partner.

The thought froze me. She was lovely enough to gain the love and respect of anybody, regular or, like me, otherwise.

There were enough good people out there who had never worn the shackles of prejudice, who clearly could see another's inner self, their real worth, superficial physicality no barrier to true appreciation; and Constance, not *just* because of the almost mystical loveliness in those dark eyes, the beauty of her features, but because of the innate yet evident gentleness of her nature, the purity of her essence, would be easy to fall in love with.

My mood was spoilt; anxiety set me to brooding. Tormenting uncertainties accompanied me to my bed that night.

Voices screamed inside my head and wings, huge, powerful things, the wings of unseen unbirdlike behemoths, pounded my flesh. Amidst the cries were plaintive wails of despair and startled shrieks of terror, but I think it was the sound of my own protests that finally woke me.

I found myself raised from my pillow, bedsheets in disarray around me, tepid light from the hallway casting a wedge-shaped glow through the partially-open door on to the carpet. My skin was wet with perspiration and I was still yelling, my voice raspy, hoarse, as though I'd been at it for some time. My demands were for the creatures of my dreams to leave me alone, to get out of my head and my home, and there should have been some relief in waking, the nightmare should have ended, but they didn't: the screams, the anguished howls, the beating of gargantuan wings were still with me inside the room, as if joining me from my subconscious, invisible tormentors escaped from their dream base.

I thought I detected moving shadows in the darkest corners of the bedroom, but each time I endeavoured to focus upon them, they dissolved, becoming nothing once more, my eye catching movement elsewhere so that I looked away, only for the process to be repeated. I became aware of the seeping coolness of the air, a kind of icy cold that crept into the very meat of my body, slowing my blood, prickling my surface skin; yet I dripped with sweat and my head felt feverish. Even in the poor light, I could see the mists of my breath.

Pulling the sheet tangled about my legs up to my crooked chest, I retreated towards the wall behind my pillow, moving warily, cautiously, silent now with only my mind begging those persecutors to leave me; yet just as they had followed me from my nightmare they now inched after me along the bed, drawing close, sniggers and chuckles among the screams. Shadows seem to grow stronger, though still they could not be defined, and the light from the hallway seem to dim even more in their presence.

The hump of my back touched the unyielding wall and I turned to my side, drawing my legs up, hands clenching the bedsheet to my shoulder. No hero I, I began to whimper.

I would have fled, but my limbs had solidified and were of no use to me at all. Whimpers denigrated into sobs.

Horrifyingly, the shadows began to deepen, began to mass, so that they filled my vision, and I was too frightened to close my eye against them. The movements within took on forms and they seemed to convulse, to writhe, and even in that darkness I could see that they resembled no living creature that I have ever known. Unlike man and unlike beast, they squirmed before me, the light from outside fading pitifully under their weight.

I hadn't been aware, but my foot was exposed from the sheet and something intensely cold and slimy brushed against my toes. My own scream, the yowl of hysteria that so far had been locked deep within my constricted chest, finally erupted to fill the room and echo back from the four walls. It broke off, spasmed as the dark contorted shapes frenzied before me, and it re-emerged so piercingly shrill that even these amorphous night prowlers flinched.

I jerked my foot back under the sheet and pulled the thin cover over my head, the unsophisticated reaction of a child who was afraid of the boogeyman hiding in his bedroom closet, imagining that this insubstantial layer would be protection against the haunting. But cowering there, body quaking, I felt their weight through the material, felt their proddings and their jabs, tormenting nudges that sought to draw me out so that I would face their full horror. I resisted though, denied them their claim, and I prayed for reality to return, for part of me knew that this could not really be happening, that my mind must still be captive of my dreams, that somehow consciousness had not wholly escaped nightmare fantasy.

And so eventually, and in their own time, they went away, whispering and mumbling their discontent as they faded. Yet I still remained hidden and only the gradual dawn light filtering through my flimsy but shielding cloak finally drew me from cover. Only that and the sane, welcoming sound of the telephone ringing in the next room.

21

It had been Louise Broomfield who had called me in the early hours, rousing me from the chilling after-effects of the haunting, bringing me back to the natural world of cold hallway floor, stubbed toes, and insistent telephones, a conventional place uninhabited by ambiguous, shape-changing chimaeras. It had turned out that Louise had also been having a bad time of it, but her dream – her sleep-sensing, as she would have it – was about me and the nightmare *I* was going through. She had observed me cowering beneath a white shroud while shadowy, spectral demons had roamed the darkness around me, flailing me with ill-formed fists, screeching and berating me as they did so. Although the imagery was confused, she was acutely aware that I was in grave danger, for this was in her own dreamscape, one from which she herself could not escape. Louise had called my name, but I had not responded; she had chastised my tormentors, but they had not listened. All she could do, the clairvoyant told me, was to watch over me until the abuse ended. As had happened with me, the nightmare eventually had faded and early light had awakened her.

Her immediate thought had been to make contact with me, the idea that the dream was hers alone not even entering her head; the psychic link between us had been so strong, she said, and she was desperately afraid for my state of mind. I was both pleased and relieved to hear her voice when I answered the phone for, together with the pain in my stubbed toe, it helped vanquish the lingering remnants of the nightmare (yes, mentally I was already rationalizing the whole experience as a terrible and vivid dream, refusing to accept that for much of it I had been conscious. It's an example of how a frightened but pragmatic mind will alter perception to minimize the anguish). Louise had warned me that danger was hovering close by, that the dream was either a threat or a desperate message; ultimately, though, it was I who was trying to calm her. Although I was frightened and shaken, my natural cynicism offered a hubristic shield behind which I could take refuge, bravado my only weapon of defence.

Later, when I left the flat for the office, I saw that the skies were overcast, the sunlight grey, another dismal beginning to the day. So early in the morning the streets were quiet, with only a few shop assistants and office staff making their way to work. Seagulls swooped and circled overhead, searching for snacks, impatient for the first appearance of food-gobbling tourists with sandwiches to be snatched, crumbs to be beaked from the kerbsides. The alleyways and narrow passages I took as short cuts seemed particularly bleak and intimidatingly empty, and I hurried through them, the unfamiliar quietness increasing my unease. The broader thoroughfares were more comforting, but still not busy enough for me to feel totally safe. As much as I resisted the notion, the night had left me wasted and vulnerable.

When I finally slid the key into the agency's ground floor door, I almost stumbled inside. There in the gloom of the stairwell I wedged my hump into a corner and drew in exhausted breaths, my journey being more like a flight through suspect territories. I gave myself time to steady my breathing and for my trembling to settle, then began the climb up the creaky stairs to my office. I paused when a noise from the rooms above came to me.

After the night I'd just been through, I suppose I had the right to feel a little jumpy, even though I stubbornly (and perhaps necessarily) continued to dismiss the whole thing as a wild dream prompted by the worrisome events of the past few days. I peered up at the landing at the top of the stairs and debated with myself whether or not to carry on or turn around and head back outside into the living world again. Part of me was aware that I was being old-maidishly ridiculous, while the other part remembered another ascent to upstairs rooms, those in the repossessed house at the beginning of the week where a shattering mirror filled with agitated monstrosities (self-reflections, I'd later rationalized) had awaited me. I was reluctant to advance further, fearing yet another shock might be in store, and with that nervousness there came the acceptance of what had truly happened during the night. Those terrors that had invaded my bedroom, although perhaps instigated by a dream, had been real: they had materialized into something perhaps less solid than you or I, but nevertheless palpable, entities that could touch and use their weight, wraiths that could be heard and so feared as actual though unnatural beings. The pounding of giant wings, heard not just by myself, but by the clairvoyant and Shelly Ripstone too, had been no illusion, and neither were these night creatures. If I believed in one, then I had to believe in the other. And as I stood there on the stairway it came to me as a dawning recognition that the 'phantasms' had not been there to torment but were there to warn me. Louise had been partly right: their message was desperate. But somehow I knew – and God knows I was no psychic, but I *knew* – that their desperation was for me! And of course, this answer led to another question: Why? What *was* the message?

Another noise from above. The scraping of furniture. Then it hit me: Was the answer to the other question waiting for me up there?

The urge to turn and flee back downstairs was immense and, in fact, almost overpowering when I heard a door open on the landing above. I had turned, one foot already on the step below, when the voice came to me.

'Dis? That you?'

Henry. Bless his lovely Yiddisher heart, it was Henry! 'Uh . . .' was all I could reply.

He appeared at the top of the stairs, red braces brightening the gloom, his sky-blue shirt a little wrinkled, his gimlet eyes boring through thick, gold-framed spectacles.

'You gave me a fright,' he complained, shaking his head in irritation. 'I heard someone come half-way up, and then nothing. What happened – you run out of breath?'

'Jesus, Henry,' I managed to say.

'You all right, Dis?' He bent down, hands on knees, to get a better look. 'Bloody hell, you look awful.'

'What?'

'You look as if you've seen a ghost. What was it – a bad night?'

I hadn't realized the dread inside showed so plainly. 'I didn't expect anyone to be here at this hour, that's all. You took me by surprise.'

He cocked his head, still scrutinizing me. 'No, it's more than that. You really don't look at all well. Come on up, let me get you some coffee.'

I resumed the climb and he disappeared back through the door. When I entered the office, he was already by the filing cabinets, pouring boiling water into two mugs. 'I was making myself a cup when I heard you,' he said. Looking at my face, he shook his head again. 'You're as white as a sheet, Dis.'

'As it happens, I did have a pretty bad night.'

'Want to tell me about it?' He gave me a steaming mug, then took his own over to his desk. He sat and swivelled round to face me again. 'So. Talk to me.'

'Hmn?' I blew into the coffee before sipping. I scorched my lips, but it felt good; it felt real.

'Why are you looking so . . .' He searched for an adequate description. 'Well, so bloody grim and haggard. You look as if you've reached your first century and aren't looking forward to the second. Has someone upset you, Dis?'

James Herbert

Over the years, Henry and I had shared quite a few confidences over a few pints and gins and he had proved a good and comforting friend when my own burdens, those mostly to do with my stature and other people's attitude towards it – an odd remark in a bar that might have caught me off guard, chortled derision in the street that had been unexpected, the kind of slings and arrows that came with outrageous fortune, and stuff that as a rule I'd learned to cope with. Sometimes though, the word 'freak' got through to me and, as independent as I kidded myself to be, I needed some amicable words of compassion, someone to let me know that ignorance was a minority commodity and a sure sign of sickness of soul. He'd always matched me drink for drink, listening to my whining, always agreeing with me, but never trying to kid me that things were not as they seemed. He knew and *almost* understood the problems I faced, never ever suggesting they were in my own imagination, never once pretending I was anything other than I was: he was too shrewd and respected me too much for that. Henry was invariably sympathetic without ever becoming maudlin and because of that, and because of his honesty with me, I listened and accepted the point when he advised me I had to *be* what I was and never to imagine I could be anything else – that could only lead to further fantasy and further disappointment. His reasoning was that what I was was incredible enough: I had brains, I had determination, and I ran my own business, I had good friends, excellent associates, and I owned my own home; I was in relatively good health, despite my handicaps, and I was physically strong; I took shit from no one and anybody who knew me properly would never give it. In short, I had a whole lot more going for me than many people who had perfect physiques and good looks. That kind of sugared his words, although his initial advice was a little hard to take; but when I took time to think on it, to *really* think on it, I realized he made a lot of sense. My life was as it was and even among the harsh realities there was

230

a fair amount of good. I had much to enjoy and good people to enjoy it with. Because of Henry's pearls of wisdom, my expectations over the last few years had never risen too high; but then, neither had they been too limited. (What Henry wasn't aware of as yet was that a new light had entered my life in the person of Constance Bell, someone whose love would counterbalance every bad thing that had come my way. *If*, that is, she was free, and *if*, as my instincts told me, she was interested in me.)

The only regret I had as far as Henry was concerned was that although he'd confided in me about some things – the love-hate relationship he had with his mother and the frustrations of still living with her, the grief his hard-nosed father had given him when Henry was a young boy, this followed by further grief from a subsequent stepfather who had taken the place of his natural father when the latter had kneeled over and died from a heart attack at the age of forty-eight, the time he'd fled from the school playground because of bullying and had wandered the streets in the pouring rain so that he'd caught pneumonia and nearly died – he never once touched on his own homosexuality and the problems denial had caused him (I mean denial regarding his friends here, not self-denial: as far as we were concerned the closet was firmly padlocked and not even Ida, who freely admitted her lesbianism, had managed to find Henry's key). I found his reticence odd, especially in these enlightened times when homosexuality was accepted more and more as a life-choice (or, more accurately, a life-directive), and also because his preference was so obvious to those who knew him. Pocketbook Freud maybe, but I'd always surmised that the relationship with his mother and her old-school, die-hard, attitude towards what she considered deviant behaviour was the root of the problem: he hated to appear less than perfect in her bigoted old eyes. I also got the feeling that in keeping the true nature of his sexuality from his mother, he was in some way keeping it from himself; in refuting the reality, there was no reason to act upon it. Of course, this meant ignoring emotions and passions as well, so it was little wonder that beneath the exterior of prissy and acerbic coolness, Henry was pretty screwed up.

'Dis? I said has someone upset you?'

'Uh, no, Henry. Just a bad night.'

Who was holding back now? Should I let him in on the whole thing, perhaps allow a voice of sanity into the debate, or would my bookkeeper merely think I'd finally flipped? Wasn't I playing the same game as Henry, denial leading to self-denial? Whatever, I decided my friend and associate wasn't quite ready for this yet, and neither was I: I was too vulnerable at that time to risk his derision.

Henry's expression told me he wasn't convinced by my explanation, but he shrugged his shoulders. He swung back to face his desk and opened up an accounts book.

'No movie question this morning?' I asked to get the daily challenge over with and out of the way.

'I was too busy last night to give it any thought,' he replied distractedly, his brain already engaged in figures and balances.

'All work and no play, Henry,' I warned.

'You're a fine one to talk.' His voice was distant, because by now he was already in his other world where truth was in facts and nothing else. A clear world for clear thinkers. How lucky he was.

I left him to it, going into my office and closing the door behind me. I needed to think and now, before the daily grind began, was a good time. Later, when the working day for others had commenced, I would ring Dr Leonard K. Wisbeech, MD, FRCS, FRCOG, FRCP, DCH at PERFECT REST, for I was determined to visit Hildegarde Vogel again, no matter what her condition. My mind was going off on another track now, you see, wondering if the 'desperate message' contained in the nightmare (real or otherwise) was, in fact, a warning about the frail old ex-midwife. Was she the one that was really in danger?

The ringing of the phone startled me in the quietness of my office and I stared at the receiver for a few minutes before picking it up. I suspected Louise Broomfield was the caller, checking up on me again, and possibly with some outrageous new idea as to the relevance of last night's little episode. I was wrong though, it wasn't her.

'Mr Dismas?'

I drew in a breath. 'Constance?'

'Yes, it's Constance Bell . . . from PERFECT REST.'

You don't need to tell me that, Constance. I said: 'I was hoping to come over today.' Butterflies in my stomach? Well, something was fluttering around in there.

'I know. That's why I'm calling you.'

She sounded fraught and I suddenly had a cold, ominous feeling. 'What is it, Constance? Is it something to do with Hildegarde?'

'How . . . how did you know?'

I closed my good eye and allowed a slow breath to escape me. 'What's happened to her?'

'I'm afraid . . .' She seemed lost for words.

'Is she dead?'

There was a short silence before Constance replied. 'She died during the night.'

Why wasn't I surprised?

'Mr Dismas?'

'Please call me Dis. Or Nick. Call me Nick.'

'Nick.' Despite the gravity of her message, I felt a touch of warmth when I heard her say my name. 'Hildegarde passed away during the night,' Constance went on. 'We found her early this morning in one of the corridors.'

'She'd left her bed?'

'She often did. We often used to find her roaming the home until her illness worsened and incapacitated her almost entirely.'

'But not recently?'

'Not in the last couple of years.'

'Had she fallen, is that what killed her?'

'We're not sure at this stage. Dr Wisbeech thinks her heart just stopped beating.'

'A heart attack?'

'It seems likely. Inability to breathe correctly or confusion in unfamiliar surroundings may have induced a panic attack. In recent years her heart has been very weak.'

'I'm sorry, Constance. I know you liked the old lady.'

'I'm not sure that I did.'

Another surprise for me, but I let it go. 'How could she have left her room? Surely you have night staff to check on your patients from time to time?'

'Of course we do, but generally it's just one person, with others on standby. Unfortunately, the nurse can't be expected to be everywhere at once.'

It wasn't a rebuke, nor even a defence; it was more a deep regret over the situation. But a brittleness in her voice conveyed something even more to me: I sensed a slight anger and, inexplicably, a kind of dread also. It worried me.

'Look, I'd still like to come over there,' I said. 'Maybe I could see you, we could talk.'

'You mustn't!'

I was startled yet again, almost flinching from the telephone. It was the insistence rather than the shout that alarmed me. 'I need some questions answered,' I said, recovering quickly. 'If Hildegarde can no longer answer them, then perhaps you can. Or I could talk to Dr Wisbeech.'

'Nick, please don't.' The dread was more evident in her voice now. I felt her desperation when she said: 'Let me come and see you. Tonight, I could meet you tonight.'

'But I can easily get over there. It might be easier for you ...'

I hadn't meant to patronize, but she cut me short. 'I have my own specially adapted car and I'm an adequate driver.'

'I didn't mean – '

'I know you didn't. Please, let's do it my way, Nick.'

'What's wrong, Constance? What the hell is going on at PERFECT REST?'

'Nothing. Honestly, nothing.'

'Then why are you so afraid?'

'I don't understand. What makes you think I am?'

Intuition? Years of experience dealing with all kinds of folk, discerning all kinds of nuances? An unspoken *connection* between the two of us? 'It's just a feeling,' I said.

There was no reply.

'Constance?'

A further pause, and then: 'Yes?'

'Okay, look. Do you want to come here, to the office?'

'If you don't mind, I'd rather come to your home.'

Mind? Oh Lord, that sounded good to me even though I was mystified. 'I'd still like to talk to Dr Wisbeech again, though. There are questions that maybe only he can answer.'

'You can put them to me, Nick.'

'I'm really not sure you'll have the answers. Tell me something, how long have you known the Doctor?'

'Why do you ask?'

What was so difficult about the question? 'Just curious, Constance.'

'I've been employed at the home for many years.'

'But did you know him before that?'

She seemed uncomfortable. 'Leonard was a family friend. He knew my parents when they were alive.'

'They're both dead? God, I'm sorry, Constance, I didn't know.'

'Why should you have known? It happened a long time ago, so the worst of the grieving is over for me. They died in a motoring accident eleven years ago – the other driver was drunk. He paid the price though – a five hundred pounds fine and an eighteen months' driving ban. It seems he was not entirely to blame for the crash.' Her bitterness was apparent, but she didn't dwell on it now. 'Dr Wisbeech took me in. He was wonderful to me, Nick. He paid for my education as well as my upkeep, financed the operations I've had over the years and then for my training as a nurse and care-supervisor.'

'He sounds like a good man.'

She took my comment at face value. 'I have to go. Arrangements have to be made about poor Hildegarde, our other residents have to be reassured . . .'

'Wait, can't you talk to me a little longer?'

'I think I can hear Nurse Fletcher calling me.'

I couldn't understand her urgency to end the call. Was she worried she'd be overheard?

'You'll see me tonight?'

'I'll be there, but I only have your office address.'

I quickly gave her the location of my flat and rough directions on how to get there once she reached Brighton. I heard another muffled voice from the earpiece, one that I vaguely recognized as belonging to the senior nurse-cum-administrator I'd met during my first visit to PERFECT REST.

Without another word, Constance rang off, but it was another minute before I replaced my own receiver.

The next call actually was from Louise Broomfield. She was checking on me, anxious to know if I was all right, that I'd recovered from my nasty experience. I assured her I was fine, the shock had worn off, the memory already blunted, and she wondered what my intentions were now. I told her I wasn't sure.

'Dis,' she said, her voice taking on an even more serious tone if that were possible, so that I guessed I was in for another warning. 'You must be careful. I sense terrible danger and somehow it's all connected to Shelly's missing son.'

'You were wrong about last night.' I felt no satisfaction in correcting her. 'It wasn't me at risk, it was Hildegarde Vogel, our little sparrow. She died at the nursing home last night.'

I caught the small gasp.

'Look,' I added, 'she was old and infirm. I don't think you can read anything into her death.'

'Are you sure, Dis, are you really sure? You don't see these visions you've been having as premonitions?'

'They're too crazy for that. Surely I would have seen some sense to them if they were.'

'They led you to Hildegarde Vogel.'

I couldn't argue with that.

'Are you going to drop the case again?' the clairvoyant persisted.

'I told you, I don't know. Something tells me that this Dr Wisbeech and Shelly's missing baby are linked, so maybe I'll do some more digging.' For some reason, I felt disinclined to mention Constance Bell's forthcoming visit that evening.

'But you don't know why or how.'

'It's partly instinct. The other part – and I'll admit it's kind of flimsy – is that Wisbeech has a stack of qualifications behind him. One, an FRCOG, means that he's a qualified obstetrician and gynaecologist.'

'What does that tell you?'

'It tells me he used to have something to do with pregnancy and births. Yesterday I got information from the BMA regarding his other medical specialities. FRCS – Fellow Royal College of Surgeons; FRCP – Fellow Royal College of Physicians, which apparently encompasses treatment of geriatrics; DCH – Diploma in Child Health. Wisbeech is somewhat over-qualified to run an upmarket old folks' nursing home, wouldn't you say?'

'I don't understand what you're getting at,' was Louise's response.

'I'm not sure myself. But those capabilities are far-ranging and I'm wondering how they led his career in the direction of caring for the elderly. Maybe that's where the money is these days, with the majority of the population living longer that ever before. I'd like to find out where he got the money to finance such a Grade A establishment in the beginning even if the house itself belonged to his family.' Or maybe I just didn't like the man and it would give me great satisfaction to rake up some dirt on him. It was a mean and petty motive and I don't think I really believed in it myself; certainly it wasn't worth mentioning to the clairvoyant.

'Oh dear,' I heard Louise say, 'this seems to be becoming more than I expected.'

'Don't worry, it's routine stuff to me.' Routine? Broken mirrors, illusionary wings – well, you know the list, so no point in reiterating. There was nothing routine about this business.

'You will take care, won't you, Dis? I've told you this before, but from the moment we first met I sensed that there is something depleted about your aura . . .'

'Don't do this to me, Louise. I don't want to get into that kind of stuff.'

'Whether you do or don't, it doesn't change things. I've never met anyone like you before, I've never had such a feeling of . . . of . . .' She let out what I took to be an exasperated breath. 'I can't put a finger on it, it's something I've never before encountered.'

'I don't know if that's supposed to make me feel special or not.'

'Don't joke with me, Dis.'

'Who said I'm joking? I'm giving off bad vibes, is that it?'

'Not exactly. I told you, I can't explain.'

'All right, so I'll just have to live with it. Thanks a heap, Louise, you've really helped my mood.'

'I'm sorry, I didn't mean – '

'Yeah, yeah. I'll let you know if anything develops with this Wisbeech thing.'

'Dis – '

'Goodbye, Louise.'

I brooded for the next ten minutes after I rang off.

*

Next, I made a call. It was to the Prince Albert Hospital in Hackney.

I already knew that their employment records would not go further back than ten years, but I hoped to speak to someone who had worked there for much longer. And for once, I was in luck: the woman I spoke to was from the hospital's personnel office and she had been around the place for quite some time.

'Oh yes, nearly thirty years since I joined Prince Albert,' she told me, evidently with some satisfaction.

'Then you might remember Hildegarde Vogel. She was a midwife there, probably in the late Seventies.'

'Vogel?' There was a pause. 'Hildegarde . . . ? No, I'm afraid I don't recall. The name sounds familiar though. So many staff have come and gone in my time, as you might imagine. Vogel . . . Well, the name definitely rings a bell. Foreign, was she?'

'German.'

'Unfortunately, we don't keep records for more – '

'Yes, I know. It was just a chance you might remember.'

'Can you tell me what this is in regard to?'

I explained that I was a PI trying to trace a missing person whom Ms Vogel might know. I didn't say it was okay that she didn't remember Hildegarde, that I was more interested in someone else right then. 'You don't remember,' I ventured, 'a doctor by the name of Wisbeech being there around the same time, do you?'

'Wisbeech. Wisbeech, Wisbeech, Wisbeech. Oh yes, of course I do. What woman would forget such a distinguished and charming man. But no, he wasn't a resident doctor.'

'I don't understand.'

'Dr Wisbeech was a consultant. Oh, how the nurses used to fancy him. Had film-star looks, that man. I took a shine to him myself, as I remember. Of course, that was over twenty years ago. Is he still handsome? I hope you're not going to tell me he's died since.'

'No, he's still alive and well. Tell me, did he have a practice nearby?'

She gave a short laugh. 'In Hackney? Oh no. I think his rooms were in Harley Street or Wimpole Street, one or the other. No, Dr Wisbeech was more like a roving consultant – he used to visit hospitals all over the country as I understood it. Always brought in when a difficult birth was expected. I've never been on that side of things, so I don't know why precisely. He was a very well-respected man, I do remember that. But if you do need to contact him, I should contact the BMA, dear. They're bound to know where he is nowadays. Retired, I'd imagine. Has that been of any help to you? I do like to be helpful.'

'You've been terrific,' I assured her. And I meant it.

Most of the rest of the day was filled with the normal business of running an enquiry agency and we all shared the workload, although the heavy-duty paperwork and client contact was left to myself and Henry. It was around 4.30pm that I received the call from Dr Leonard K. Wisbeech.

'I'm afraid I have some rather sad news to tell you, Mr Dismas,' he said after announcing himself.

For a heart-stopping moment I thought something dreadful had happened to Constance, but it soon became apparent that the doctor wasn't aware that his care-supervisor had already been in touch with me earlier.

'I'm afraid our guest, Ms Vogel, passed away in her sleep last night.' He continued before I could put in a word. 'I'm so sorry that we cannot be of any help in your enquiries, but I doubt very much if Hildegarde would have remembered anything useful to you anyway. Of course, I'm not putting any blame on you, but I do believe the unfortunate circumstances on your first visit to her might somehow have precipitated her sudden demise. I'm afraid you did rather upset her.'

Whoa, wait a minute, I thought. 'I'm sure nothing I said or did would have caused her to leave her bed in the middle of the night to wander the corridors,' I said bluntly. I could almost sense his stiffening.

'How did you know she was found outside her room?'

There was a sharpness in his tone and I could have kicked myself for my stupidity. I recovered quickly. 'I didn't know. I just assumed she'd taken a fall and it must have happened when she was unsupervised.' It was pretty lame – she might just as easily fallen out of bed – and I don't think he was fooled. Wisbeech appeared to let it go, although I was certain he wasn't satisfied.

'Very well then, Mr Dismas. Again, I'm sorry that you were unable to find the information you were seeking. Your client, no doubt, will be disappointed.'

'The investigation isn't over yet.' I guess I wanted to rile him.

'But surely there's nothing more you can do?'

'Oh, there's plenty more. I can contact all the hospitals Hildegarde worked for as a midwife, for a start. You never know, I might strike lucky and dig up some long-termer who even worked with Hildegarde at Dartford. They might have some answers.' I wondered if he would fall for the bluff.

'Then I wish you luck.'

That was disappointing. 'It'll be interesting to discover if any other babies died under her supervision,' I said, almost in spite.

'I'm not sure I understand what you are implying by that.'

'I've just got an idea that quite a few babies failed to survive their birth when Hildegarde Vogel was in charge.' It was a hasty remark, but a deliberate insinuation. To my own surprise, wild though it was, the speculation was suddenly a suspicion in my mind.

'I would be extremely careful about making such preposterous accusations, if I were you,' Wisbeech said, rather severely, I thought. I couldn't help but smile.

'She's not going to sue me, is she?'

'Let me caution you again, Mr Dismas – be very careful with what you say and do.'

That was more like it. Civility had taken on a harder edge.

'I have to earn my fee,' I said amiably. 'And I've always believed in client satisfaction, you know what I mean? That's why I run a successful little business. We're not super-sleuths, but we're dogged; we don't give up easily. Incidentally, Dr Wisbeech, I'm very impressed by all those letters after your name. They must cover almost everything in the medical field, but I'm particularly interested in your work as an obstetrician.'

'I can't see that my career in medicine has anything to do with you. In fact, I believe that your own ... shall we say, shortcomings? ... are rather clouding your vision. Might I suggest that you stick to your own profession, Mr Dismas, and leave mine alone? Is that, at least, clear to you?'

I was too aroused by my own train of thought to take umbrage. 'Oh yes, that's very clear, Doctor. But you see – '

He didn't give me the chance to say anything more. The line went dead and to be honest, I was relieved, because I'd had no idea what I was going to say next anyway.

22

I was like a jittery kid on his very first hot date. I kept glancing at the clock to check the time and more than once I lingered over my stash, tempted to calm my nerves the illegal way. I resisted though and stuck to regular smokes, not because of noble resolve, but because I didn't want the distinctive odour of cannabis stinking up the place. I'd been on edge all day, not just because I was going to see Constance that evening, but because I was frustrated with the stop-go progress (or lack of it) of the Ripstone case; also I was still frazzled by the previous night's drama – in fact, just about *all* of my experiences over the past week! Life itself had never been particularly normal for me, but now it had turned positively *weird*. Everyone at the office was aware that something was up with me, but when their probing was constantly met with short, sharp responses, they soon gave up. There had been other times when I was just plain unapproachable, times I developed headaches so bad I wanted to scream, and I guess Henry, Ida and Philo assumed this was one of them. I was grateful when they left me alone.

I checked the clock again, then my wristwatch for corroboration. 8.15pm. She had said she would try to get here by 8pm after I'd given her directions. Had she got lost? Or had she changed her mind? Surely she would have phoned? Perhaps I should ring PERFECT REST, maybe she'd been told she had to work late at the last moment. Or maybe she'd forgotten our meeting – our date. No, I didn't think so for one moment: Constance wasn't the cavalier type.

243

I paced the sitting-room, the air blue with cigarette smoke. Had Wisbeech somehow found out about her plans and forbidden her to see me? Yeah, that wouldn't surprise me. He had that kind of arrogance. But wait, I was getting in a tizz for no reason at all. Maybe she couldn't find a parking space – Lord knows, the crescent was always filled with double-parked vehicles, so maybe she was touring the area, searching for somewhere to leave her car. Even parking spaces for the disabled were at a premium in Brighton. And if she had managed to find somewhere far away, it would take her a while to make it back to the crescent on crutches. Or it could be that she was circling the crescent right now, driving round and round until a parked vehicle gave up its space and she could nip into it. As I headed for the front door, the bell rang.

She was on the doorstep, petite and vulnerable, and I wanted to gather her up in my arms and tell her I was crazy about her.

'You found somewhere to park then?' I said.

'Yes, close by. It wasn't a problem.'

'I was anxious . . .'

'I'm sorry I'm late. I didn't allow enough time for the journey.'

'It's okay. I'm just glad you made it.'

Was that a flush on her cheeks? Light from the hallway wasn't too good.

'I've had a busy day,' she said by way, I thought, of saying something. 'There's always so much to do when one of our guests passes away.'

'I'm sure. Please, come in. Are you hungry? Have you eaten? I could rustle up something . . .'

'No, I'm fine. I managed to have something quick before I left.'

I stepped aside so that she could enter and I caught her perfume as she brushed by: Anais Anais, I guessed. The fragrance battled with cigarette smoke drifting along the hallway.

'Straight ahead, to the right,' I told her. 'Can I get you a drink?'

'Just coffee, please.'

Constance was wearing a pastel-green dress, its hem reaching her ankles, the skirt flowing gracefully despite the awkwardness of her steps. Over it she wore a simple beige jacket, a thin gold crucifix chain adorning her neck. Her make-up was minimal, practically non-existent, and she wore no other jewellery: no earrings, no rings on fingers. Her hair was tied back in its usual tail and I had to resist the urge to reach out and stroke it as I followed her into the sitting-room.

She stopped in the middle of the room and jokingly waved a hand in front of her face. 'You must enjoy bar-room atmospheres,' she said.

'Sorry,' I apologized sheepishly. 'I didn't realize it'd got so bad. Let me open a window.'

I rushed to the barred window, pulled it open, and began to flap at the smoky air with both hands. She gave a little laugh at my antics.

'It'll clear on its own, Nick. Please don't worry.'

I smiled, delighted again at the sound of my own name from her lips. 'Make yourself comfortable while I get that coffee. How d'you like it – milk and sugar? Cream? Only instant, I'm afraid.'

Constance returned my smile, but I could still detect a tenseness in her eyes, an apprehension that was scarcely veiled.

'White, one sugar, milk rather than cream,' she replied.

'Right. You're sure you wouldn't like something stronger?'

'No, but please don't let me stop you.'

Did I look as though I needed one? I had to admit, a good malt would have been welcome right then.

I left her settling into the lumpy sofa, going through to the kitchen and switching on the Morphy Richards, which I'd filled with water before she had arrived just for something to do.

'You sure I can't get you something to eat?' I called back through the doorway.

'No. I'm fine,' came the reply. 'Thanks anyway.'

While the water boiled I poured myself a large Dalmore, loading the tumbler with ice first so that the whisky didn't look excessive. It was a poor ploy – the dark brown liquid reached the brim of the glass and I had to gulp down some of it just so my guest wouldn't think I was an alcoholic. Then I realized I had swallowed too much and decided to top the drink up again to a decent level. By the time this rigmarole was over the plastic kettle had boiled, so I poured the water into the best mug I owned, only to remember I hadn't put in coffee grains beforehand. This remedied (and making sure I opened the *correct* coffee jar), I placed the mug on a tray with the sugar bowl and small jug of milk, added my whisky tumbler, and returned to the sitting-room.

Constance seemed to be taking an interest in the framed prints on the walls, but when I looked directly into her eyes, I realized she was distracted, that interest only superficial, her mind apparently on other matters.

'Coffee,' I announced needlessly, taking the mug from the tray and placing it on the low table by the sofa.

'Yes,' she replied, equally needlessly.

I couldn't make up my mind as to whether I should sit beside her or in the armchair opposite. The former might appear presumptuous, I reasoned, it might even make her more tense – nervous? – so I plumped for the armchair. It was growing dark outside by now and I switched on a standing lamp before I sat down. Its glow was soft, the shadows around us deep.

Constance lifted the mug and sipped. 'Hot,' she said.

'Sorry,' I replied.
'It's good,' she said. Then she began to weep.

I held her close to me, fingers lightly brushing the dampness from her cheeks. We had talked for a long time, Constance and I, and by now she was visibly growing weary, her emotions drained. She had spoken of her life, how disability had closed so many doors to her, but how she eventually had managed to overcome the worse aspects of other people's unthinking intolerance and carve out a decent and worthwhile career for herself. She had been sixteen years old, a time of psychological and hormonal changes that confused and frustrated even the most normal of adolescents, when her parents had been taken from her in the horrendous road accident, leaving her alone in the world, no siblings, no relatives there to offer support or comfort. Fortunately, Dr Leonard K. Wisbeech had been a close friend of her father's, who himself had also been a surgeon, and had for years taken an interest in Constance's progress, encouraging her in her resolve not to allow the spina bifida to ruin her life totally. Unmarried himself, with only one dependant, the doctor had brought her to PERFECT REST, where she had been trained to look after the sick and the elderly. It was obvious to me that Constance was deeply grateful to her guardian and mentor, but I sensed something more in her attitude towards him, something she did her best to hide. Again, the tell-tale signs were in her eyes, the shadowy veil that descended over them at each mention of his name. She was afraid of this man.

This did not account for her tears that evening, though, and I pressed her as gently as I could to discover what had upset her so. But she countered my probing with questions about myself, one leading to another, and her unselfish concern encouraged me to talk, her soft, searching gaze ripping through barriers maintained for longer than I could remember. I talked – perhaps I rambled – without rancour, following her example of truth without bitterness, recounting the hardships as facts, the difficulties as part of my history. And the good thing was, we were able to share the feelings of those moments, Constance knew, really *knew*, how certain things, certain slights, certain incapabilities, affected me. I was talking to someone who was *inside* my emotions, who had experienced *my* experiences, perhaps in different ways, but nevertheless with an understanding of the instances and the consequences. She knew how the tiniest indignities imposed by the oblivious few could make you want to hide away into the darkest recesses of your own space; she understood how the most trivial remark from the unwitting dimwit could resurrect barricades you thought you'd long since dismantled. Yet we spoke of funny incidents as well, those times our shortcomings had led to hilarity – not many, I grant you, but enough to share with humour and enough for us both to recognize mutual methods of coping. We both laughed, Constance through her tears, me through my top-ups of whisky, and we gradually broke down whatever safeguards there were between each other. We reached out and touched – or so I thought – each other's inner self.

I told her of how I had been found, a deformed swaddling discarded by an uncaring or frightened mother, how I had been reared in a home whose guardians were not unkind, but whose regime was not based on love. I explained how I had lost my eye, asking not for sympathy but for compassion. I related my early years as kitchen help, street market runaround, furniture shifter for the local council offices, all jobs I had while studying for a career as a private investigator, saving money week by week, month by month, year by year, until I'd learned enough and gathered enough to set up my own business. And why a private investigator? she had asked, and my reply had been that I really didn't know, but I enjoyed snooping, that my own curiosity had always been a driving force, that I always seemed to be searching for answers even when the questions were not themselves clear.

One important thing we discovered about each other was that neither one of us had experienced romance before. Constance had known what she had thought to be mutual love, but which had turned out to be pity on the other person's part, and once, when she had thought she had found someone she thought truly cared, it had turned out to be curiosity on his part, and both those relationships had been the cause of her own reservation, her resistance to anyone who might try to penetrate the emotional and, admittedly flimsy, shield she now hid behind. PERFECT REST had become her physical fortress and she rarely ventured far from its confines. The walk along the lane each evening was her own way of telling herself – *deceiving* herself – that she was free of such self-imposed constraint. I had begun to understand how difficult her decision to come to me had been. While not exactly a recluse – her job meant journeys in her car, various non-live-in staff to take backwards and forwards on occasions, errands to run, things to buy – Constance's whole life was based around PERFECT REST, and it was not just a place of work: it had become her home. She hated driving, she was timid (shy, I think) of people she didn't know. The journey to Brighton had been a challenge.

As we got to know each other and spoke of things never told to any other person before, it didn't seem quite right to sit so far away, and when Constance wept once more, I moved nearer, taking a seat at the opposite end of the sofa. Soon, both of us had edged even closer and gradually I held her in my arms. She hadn't resisted.

We fell silent for a while, both pondering each other's confidences and perhaps, she, like me, wondered at our own trust in a person hardly known before, at the mutual honesties disclosed, the private thoughts shared. Now she lifted her head from my shoulder and looked deep into my one good eye.

'You must never visit PERFECT REST again,' she said.

I was taken by surprise by the foreboding that was so apparent in her gaze. 'You have to tell me why, Constance. What are you so afraid of?'

She pulled away, turning her head aside. 'I can't tell you, Nick. It's better that you don't know.'

I spoke quietly and my anger was not directed at her. 'How bad can it be? It's a nursing home for wealthy old folk, for Christ's sake.'

'You don't understand.'

'So explain. Whatever is going on, I'm on your side, Constance. I'll do anything to help you. So tell me – is Dr Wisbeech running some kind of scam, is he getting his hands on their money before they die? Or working his way into their wills?'

'Of course not! Please, *please*, don't ask me any more questions.'

'Then why did you come all this way tonight? If you had no intention of saying anything about PERFECT REST and your precious doctor, why make the journey? I know it wasn't easy for you.'

'*Please*, Nick.'

'You came to warn me.'

'Yes.'

'But you won't tell me about what.'

'No. I can't.'

Another suspicion, a wild one, was beginning to form. I took a chance.

'Dr Wisbeech used to steal babies, didn't he? That's why he was so indebted to Hildegarde Vogel. As a midwife, she used to help him.'

Constance swung round to face me again, but I could not understand the look in her eyes: surprise, shock, anger. It could have been any or all of these.

I went on, not giving her the chance to speak. 'I contacted a London hospital earlier today, one where years ago Hilde-

garde was employed as a midwife. It seems that Dr Leonard
Wisbeech was a consultant in the same place, around the
same time. I know from the letters behind his name that just
two of his specialities are obstetrics and gynaecology and
that he was consultant to many hospitals around the country.
I'll bet that included the Dartford General Hospital until
it was razed to the ground by fire. I think both he and
Hildegarde were present at certain allegedly difficult births,
both in Hackney and Dartford, and for all I know, plenty of
others too. I also think that if I asked my client, whose newly-
born baby went missing eighteen years ago, she'd probably
remember the distinguished looking doctor who had
attended the birth. She'd probably remember his name too,
if I prompted her.'

Constance was shaking her head. 'What are you saying,
Nick?' She was also trembling. 'What are you implying?'

'New-born babies have always been in demand by infertile
couples. Even all those years ago they fetched a high price.
I'm just wondering, Constance, if that's how Wisbeech grew
rich. Setting up PERFECT REST must have cost a small
fortune.'

'The house belonged to his family,' she protested.

'But converting it to a nursing home must have been
costly.'

'Leonard has a wealthy brother who financed everything.'

That stopped me in my tracks. I recalled that Constance
had spoken of Wisbeech as having a dependant relative, but
I'd thought no more of it, assuming she meant someone
older, a parent or uncle or aunt. A brother hadn't come into
my thinking at all.

'So where is this brother?' I asked a little too belligerently.
I guess by then I had got carried away, not realizing how
much I was upsetting Constance. 'And who's to say they
weren't both in it together?'

'You've got it wrong, Nick. Leonard's brother is an invalid.
He hides himself away.'

'Where? At the home?'

She nodded. 'I haven't even seen him myself for three years. Only Nurse Fletcher is allowed to take care of him these days. Oh God, Nick, how could you suggest such a thing?'

She broke then. She threw herself away from me and buried her face in her hands against the arm of the sofa.

Already regretting my persistence, I reached out to her and she flinched when my fingers touched her misshapen back. I didn't pull away though: it would have made matters worse.

'Okay, Constance,' I said as gently as I could, my hand softly stroking, letting her get used to my touch. 'I just got carried away. It happens sometimes when I'm desperate for a result in a case. I won't do anything that could hurt you.'

She stirred from the sofa's arm. 'Do you mean that, Nick?'

She was weeping again and I felt like an all-time rat. 'I'll back off, if that's what you want. You're more important to me than any case I'm working on.' And I meant it. I didn't want to lose this woman, not after such a long search. Missing babies couldn't compete.

Constance came into my arms once more, her forehead snuggling into the space between my neck and shoulder. Her arm reached around me and for the first time in my life I was in someone else's embrace. Someone who might . . . eventually . . . learn to love me. My vision was blurred by welling tears and for a while I could not speak, too afraid my voice might break with a sob. I stroked her hair, her lovely neck, her arm, my hand finally falling to her waist so that I could pull her towards me. The pressure was soft and slow, because I feared she would resist, feared she might reject me. But she didn't, she came with my urging, she committed herself to me. She pressed against me, lifting her face, offering her lips. And then, sweet God, we kissed.

The bliss was perfect. My head felt alive with light and my senses reeled and soared so that I felt giddy with the happiness of it. For a moment I felt I might pass out, so exquisite was the sensation, so *rare* was the occasion; but no, this was a pleasure from which I had no wish to abscond. I maintained the pressure and went with the sensations.

We were equals: there could be no pity, and no condescension; our imperfections were a bond rather than a barrier.

Eventually, our lips parted, but not for long, only to give us time to draw in new breath; then our mouths brushed against each other's again, softly, searching, tasting the sweetness before developing into a second kiss. I relished the moistness there and almost gasped when her lips opened, inviting me to taste more, to explore with my tongue, the intimacy almost overwhelming to a novice like myself, the gentle probing that followed intoxicating to such a fledgling lover. When my tongue met with hers, every nerve seemed to tingle, every part of my body came alive, and when her hands moved over me, caressing, touching me in a way I'd never known before, I felt another part of me stirring. Although her touch was innocent and our kisses pure, the arousal was inevitable.

'Constance . . . ?' I said, pulling away a millimetre or so.

She murmured something as she kissed my cheek, my nose, my chin.

'Can we . . . ?'

'It's difficult for me, Nick.'

'I know, but . . .' It was just a 'but', nothing I could follow it with.

She took my hand and slid it over her body so that it lay upon her small breast. I breathed something, probably her name, this new intimacy sending me into rapture. My fingers – surprisingly not trembling – found buttons, undid them, lay material aside. I touched the wonderfully soft skin beneath the thin cotton of her underwear, felt the tiny mound that swiftly grew into a nipple, and heard Constance catch her breath. She gave a little moan.

'No, Nick, not yet.' She seemed close to tears once more.

'It's all right, Constance. There's nothing to be afraid of. I'm a learner too.'

But she had tensed and the glow had gone from her eyes to be replaced by that shadowy veil I had observed before. I understood her fear, but wanted her to know it was mutual, that I was just as afraid of exposing my twisted body to another, that a lifetime's shame could not be overcome in a moment. I wanted to tell her it was an experience we could go through together, our nervousness shared, and that would make it even more special; but instead I slipped my hand from her breast and drew her into my embrace once more, because I was just as scared that my body might offend. I dare not risk repulsing this woman I loved so dearly.

'I'm sorry,' she said, her voice muffled against my chest. 'I'm so sorry.'

'It's okay,' I soothed. 'Nothing's going to happen, nothing that you don't want to happen.'

'But I do.'

'Then . . .'

She huddled even closer.

'It's all right, Constance, it's all right.'

'Let's wait, Nick. Let's get to know each other first.'

Get to know each other . . . ? I soared, I wept, I smiled, I moaned (all inwardly, apart from the smile). The implication was that there was a future for us, we, together. Friends, lovers. I can't remember a time, a moment, when I was happier.

We stayed that way for a long time, holding each other, our pleasure coming from compassion rather than passion, our joy from whispered intimacies rather than sensual caresses. How long we would have remained that way, locked in sometimes tight, sometimes loose, embrace I've no idea, but it was that stark, interfering sound of the bloody telephone that shattered our peace.

23

The Ford's tyres squealed, burning rubber as I pulled to the right and jammed on the brakes, the car coming to a juddering halt by the kerbside. Strolling pedestrians turned in alarm to see what the emergency was, then continued on their way, shaking their heads and muttering something about idiot drivers who should never have been given a licence. A figure detached itself from the shadow of a door-way and hurried over to me.

Louise Broomfield peered into the open side window. 'I've only just arrived myself,' she said, taking in short breaths between words. 'Thank God you're all –' She noticed my companion.

'Louise, this is Constance Bell,' I said quickly, already beginning to open the car door and forcing the clairvoyant back on the pavement. 'Constance, this is Louise Broomfield. She's a friend of my client.'

Still crouched, Louise's gaze lingered on Constance a moment longer than necessary. She straightened as I emerged from the car.

'What the hell is up?' I almost barked at her, annoyed that my precious moments with Constance had been interrupted, but concerned with the urgency in her voice when she had phoned.

Louise grabbed my arm. 'I thought it was you! The voices weren't clear, but I was sure they meant you! It was only when I spoke to you on the phone that I realized the trouble was here.'

'You've never been to my office before.'

'I didn't need to. Once I heard you speak and you told me you were all right, I understood the message.'

I was rapidly losing patience. 'Come on, Louise, what's this all about? You didn't explain anything, you just said there was a problem at my agency.'

'You didn't hear them yourself? The voices, the whispering?'

'Maybe I was too preoccupied with other things.'

It was meant as a jibe, but I immediately wondered if it were true, that my thoughts had been directed solely on Constance to the exclusion of all else that night. Could everything else from outside sources, other thoughts, other *sensings*, be blocked by the sheer power of a person's emotions? In the light from a nearby café's windows I could see Louise's eyes were wide and staring, her trepidation genuine; even the fierce grip on my arm was an indication of her inner turmoil. Further along the street, people were spilling from the old Regency theatre's open doors and for a moment I thought I might be going crazy. Among the departing audience were odd figures, people so bizarrely garbed they might have escaped from one of my own weird dreams. They played and giggled amidst their ordinary companions, masked and painted faces grotesque in the streetlights. Fishnet stockings and sequined cloaks, humped backs and demented eyes – the exotic adornments of fools and funsters. With relief I remembered that the all-new, revised and improved *Rocky Horror Show* was back in town. Even so, even though I knew this was the audience's ritual pantomime of affinity with the show, I shuddered at the sight of all those grotesques mingling with the usual theatre-goers.

'The warning was linked to you,' Louise was saying insistently. 'I saw shadows and shapes moving among them and I sensed that they hid because they were ashamed to be seen. I couldn't understand, Dis, it was all so confusing. But there were no wings this time.'

My right leg felt weak, anxiety rather than fatigue taking its toll, and I leaned back against the car, one hand resting on its roof.

'I tried to see them more clearly,' the clairvoyant went on. 'I tried to see into those shadows, using all the power I possessed, but each time I focused on one it seemed to dissolve before me. It was as if they didn't want to be seen. I sensed fear and shame, but most of all I sensed that you were being threatened again.'

'But I wasn't. I was with Constance.'

'That's why I asked you to meet me here. It had to be connected to you somehow. This is the only other place . . .'

I was already looking up at the windows of my offices, two floors above the street. A dim light shone from one of them. Louise was still talking as I broke away and limped across the pavement towards the front door.

'Be careful, Dis. Please, I urge you to be careful. Let's call the police.'

I whirled on her. 'And tell them what? That you *think* there might be something wrong, that I'm being threatened by shadows in your own mind? Come on, Louise, get real here.'

I turned back to the street door, fumbling for the right key on my keyring. The buzz of conversations and music came from the cafés and the Colonnade Bar next to the theatre, and people strolled the pavement; vehicles were parked diagonally to the kerbside on the other side of the broad roadway, behind them the dark area that was the small park, gardens that led to the Royal Pavilion and museum. All appeared so normal on this warm summer's night, yet my hands shook as I found the right key. I could not be sure if I had been contaminated by the clairvoyant's panic, or whether my own inbuilt alarm system had been triggered by something else, a feeling that something was horribly amiss.

'Nick?'

Constance had followed from the car and was standing

behind me, a tiny figure relying on metal crutches for support.

'Stay here with Louise,' I told her and heard the shakiness in my own voice.

'Please tell me what's wrong.' Under the glow from street-lights and windows she looked delicate and appealing. I wanted to take her in my arms again.

'I don't know myself,' I said to her. 'Not yet, anyway.' She had insisted on accompanying me after the clairvoyant's phone call and for some reason I was glad she was there with me even though I didn't want her involved in anything unpleasant or dangerous. I guess she made me feel braver than I really was. 'Will you stay here with Louise while I go up and check out my offices?'

'No, I'd rather come with you.'

I had to resist embracing her and smothering her face with kisses. I'd never had someone to show that kind of concern for me before, not in this way.

'Constance, my agency is on the top floor and it's a long haul. I can do it more quickly on my own.'

I could tell she didn't like the condescension, but at least she saw the sense in it. She remained quiet as I turned back to the front door.

Even as I inserted the key into the lock, I realized it wasn't necessary: the door was already open, the latch off, the heavy wood only resting in the frame.

'Be careful.' It was Louise who gave me the warning as I pushed the door.

I entered and waited for a moment in the darkness of the short area before the stairs, a feeling of *déjà vu* coming over me. Hadn't I been through this that very morning, or had that merely been some kind of presage of what was to come? Was this now the real thing? Outside, I had noticed the dull light shining from the window of my office and I realized that the reason it was dull was because it came from next door, the outer office whose windows did not overlook the street. But I always closed my door each evening before leaving, so who had opened it again?

Reaching for the light-switch beside the door, I flicked it on. The bulb over my head had never been efficient, throwing more shadows than spreading light. The turn in the stairs above me was just a pitchy void which did not look welcoming. Unfortunately, the second light-switch was on the next landing.

Telling my two companions to remain outside until I called, I moved to the first step and began to climb. This was almost becoming tedious, I said silently to myself. These days I was climbing too many flights of stairs with dread in my heart and lead in my shoes. The unnatural events of the past few days had put the fear of God – well, the fear of *something* – into me, and tonight Louise Broomfield's over-reaction had reinforced it. Exacerbated it, in fact, because now as I climbed, I was twitching, my legs soft at the knees, a tic under my good eye, and my breathing kind of shivery. This is ridiculous, I informed myself, and so it was: I was a fully-grown – okay, *almost* fully-grown adult sneaking tremulously up a creaky staircase to my own office, expecting to find – *what*? That Henry had forgotten to turn off the light when he'd decided to work late just so he could get the books straight and please his boss? The VAT returns were due soon and Henry always got into a tizz about that. Some women suffered from pre-menstrual tension, Henry suffered from pre-VAT tension. VAT, the accountant's PMT.

My hand scrabbled over the wall in the darkness of the first-floor landing for the light-switch I knew was there. I found it, clicked it. Nothing happened, no light came on, and I remembered that the light-bulb had needed replacing for at least two months, the light summer evenings the reason for our tardiness. At least there was enough street-light coming through the window for me to see my way. The atmosphere wasn't improved though.

'Henry? Are you up there, Henry?'

I waited in silence. Deafening silence.

'Henry!'

I was forcing myself to get angry. Still nothing.

'Okay, I'm coming up!' It was meant to sound threatening, but my voice cracked on the last word so that 'up' had two syllables. Nevertheless, I hoped that if there was an intruder in the offices above, he realized he'd received fair warning. I rushed the next flight of stairs, boldness my friend, exclusion of further trepidation my ally. My limp slowed me a little, but I quickly reached the half-way mark, V1 to air pilots, the point of no return, full take-off an imperative. I couldn't go back, but when I saw the half-open office door, light from it brightening the way, I came to a breathless halt.

I supposed I was sick and tired of being a victim, fed up with being intimidated by things beyond my control, because I paused for only a second or two before rage boiled again, sending me clambering onwards, stomping stairboards to show I meant business. I barged through, slapping the door with the flat of my hand so that it banged against a filing cabinet behind, then bounced back. I blinked against the light's full blast.

I blinked against the horror that was laid out before me.

24

I'd smelled the blood even before I'd entered the office and it should have forewarned me, but my fear had made me reckless, had given impetus to my charge, knowing that to falter was to stop and that to stop was to turn around and scurry back down those stairs like a coward from confrontation, a rat from a wreck.

My feeble leg nearly gave way completely and I think I swooned as I grabbed the doorhandle for support. The sour, coppery stink of liberated gore was almost overwhelming and the sight before me was almost heart-stopping. I caught my breath and held it there somewhere between my lungs and my throat.

The half-naked body was lying across Henry's desk, one grey tartan-patterned sock hanging loose from the toes, the other covering a foot, but ruffled around the ankle. The legs were long and skinny. They were hairy around the calves and thighs. They hung over the desk, the toe of the loose sock touching the floor.

The body's head was out of sight over the other edge of the desk. The pink shirt was sopping with still-shiny blood and it was pulled back over a smoothly stretched belly, a belly so rounded it would have been a paunch in a standing position. The flamboyant shirt and socks should have been my clues, but I was still in the first stages of utter shock, where the mind is numbed and the senses insensible. Another clue was the charcoal-grey trousers neatly folded over the back of the visitor's chair, flashy red braces a tangle on the chair's seat, but, although I'd taken them in along with everything else in this newly-appointed charnel chamber, my attention now was concentrated on the blood-bubbles softly erupting from the well of pumping liquid trapped between the body's closed thighs. The groin's pubic hair appeared thickly gelled with red dye and more blood trickled over the fleshy walls to join with other flows, the main ones from below, from under the upper legs, forming a surging lake that expanded towards the desk's cliff edge, flowing around objects, making an island of a glass paper-weight, a jetty of the yellow pencil that jutted from the open crimson-soaked accounts book, one side of this squashed by the mutilated corpse's buttocks.

'Oh . . . dear . . . God . . .' I whispered, the words releasing the small breath I had left.

I held even more tightly to the doorhandle, at last forced to gulp in that bespoiled air.

Despite the evidence, I suppose that I did not want to acknowledge that it was Henry's poor body lying there like some unfortunate victim on the stone of a sacrificial altar, and the shock, disbelief, encouraged my beleaguered mind to play along with the game. No, this wasn't Henry, not my acerbic, bigoted, *caring*, mother-dominated, movie-interlocutor, *amusing*, identity-denying, *good friend* Henry. No, this was a stranger, someone who had wandered in from the street below. For what reason – who knows? Whodunnit – who cares? Just so long as it *wasn't* dear Henry. One way to make sure though, one way to eliminate Henry from the scene-of-crime. Take a look at the face. Walk around the desk, tilt your own head just to be sure, and observe the corpse's features. Then you'll see it isn't – couldn't be! – Henry. All you need is the courage.

So said the voice in my head, the voice that was my saner, wiser, softly-commanding, self. And I would do as it bid me. Because I had no other choice. I had to know.

Blood overflowed on to the floor, a slick stream that was

soon forming another swelling pool on the office's cheap lino floor, one border sliding towards another little crimson lake that I hadn't noticed before, this one seeping around the desk itself. Spilling, it seemed, from the body's head or throat. I forced myself – I *had* to force myself – towards the corner of the desk.

And it was Henry, all right. The hooked nose was the giveaway. It was Henry, except his glasses were missing and his eyes were gone.

Blood still flowed from those empty sockets, streaking his forehead and sparse hair red before falling to the floor to form the second radiating pool. Henry's mouth was still gaping as if in death-screams and I fancied I could still hear them, as if their echoes continued to bounce off the walls, suffusing the air itself. Hadn't anyone heard his cries? Had no one in the street below caught the sounds of his distress? I remembered the revelry outside, the bizarrely camp audience leaving the theatre, the almost carnival-like jollity, the voices from the next-door bar, music from restaurants and café, the footsteps and passing traffic – had they all conspired to smother the exclamation of mortal terror? Could life be so oblivious to the nearness of death?

I thought I could see the tip of his bloodied tongue resting against his upper lip, but I didn't want to look too closely. Dear God, dear Henry . . .

A noise from the room next door. From my office.

The door was ajar, enough light spilling in to throw a dim flush against the window – the glow I had observed from the street below.

A scuffling. Something dragging across the floor in my sanctum.

My first impulse was to flee and rejoin the rest of the world. But a whimper caused me to stay. At least, I thought it was a whimper.

I knew I should be hurtling down the stairs from whatever lurked in the gloom of my office, and perhaps I would have had not the clump of ungainly footsteps come to me from the stairway. I heard my name called. Not Dis but Nick, so I knew it was Constance's voice.

I stayed where I was, unable to move. I wanted to warn the two women to keep away, or at least to let them know of the terrible shock that awaited them; and I wanted to throw open my office door and face whatever whimpered in there, murderer or no. But I remained perfectly still, too traumatized to make the decision.

Louise came through first, Constance a few paces behind. Now I tried to shout the warning, but no sound came, I was voiceless. The two women stared first at me, and then at the bloody carcass on the desk.

I thought they would scream at the sight and they didn't. I thought at least one of them would faint away (as I nearly had) and neither one did that either. They just stared, their faces at first numbed with shock before creasing into rigid lines of revulsion. Before they, before I, could say a word, we all heard the muted sound from my darkened office.

Perhaps it was because I was no longer alone, perhaps I thought I had to be brave in front of Constance, but I jolted to my senses and quickly looked around for a weapon of some kind, anything I could use to protect us all. All I could find was a hard, wooden, straight-backed chair, the uncomfortable one reserved only for Philo and the VAT man on his yearly visit. I raised it high over my shoulder and turned back to face my office door.

'Nick, please, no!' Constance reached out for me but, like myself a few moments ago, seemed unable to move any more than that.

'Stay there,' I commanded with all the false authority I could muster.

I strode forward and kicked the door back with a foot, my bad leg almost collapsing under its burden – the chair plus me. Light flew in ahead of me and I stalled in the doorway, the chair quivering in my grip, my eye swiftly searching the shadows.

Something moved behind my desk, something low but with no discernible form, shuffling towards a far corner where the shadows were thickest.

For a moment, the whimpers stopped and I saw the white – greys – of two wide eyes watching me. My own one quickly adapted to the semi-darkness and I saw a skinny kid cowering there, a *naked* skinny kid, his shoulders and stick-arms trembling uncontrollably. He seemed to observe something in me that was terrifying, because now his whimpers graduated to screams.

Jesus Lord, I wanted to get out of there. The boy's screams were cutting through my head like aural daggers, reactivating my panic so that I wanted to back away – no, I wanted to turn and *rush* away, self-preservation my justification, cowardice my mentor – and only the figures of Constance and Louise Broomfield gathered behind me prevented me from so doing. Constance looked up at me questioningly, then back at the person huddled in the corner, his knees drawn up, naked arms over his head.

Even in the gloom he didn't look much, but I didn't know what kind of weapon he might have concealed behind him or somewhere close by. It would have had to be something horrifically vicious to have inflicted that kind of damage to Henry ... poor Henry. As was the way with me, anger helped me overcome the worst of the fear, and I snapped down the light-switch by the side of the door. I heard Louise gasp and felt Constance's hand on my arm.

He wasn't entirely naked, only from the waist up, torn baggy combat fatigues covering his legs, scuffed trainers on his sockless feet, the skinny ankles that were revealed almost the colour of bleached bone. And he wasn't really a kid, he was a youth, a teenager, his wavering arms occasionally exposing spiky blond hair, a young man's pallid face, a cheap metal earring studded through his ear. His frightened eyes protruded so much I thought they might easily pop from their sockets. Like Henry's. Although his had been ripped from their sockets . . .

I was still more than nervous, despite my growing rage but I took a step forward.

Wrong move. The intruder began gibbering and sobbing, sliding himself up the wall and towards the window. As he moved behind my desk he kicked out, sending it scudding a couple of feet across the floor, distracting my attention for a second or two. Before I could move around the desk to reach him, the youth had climbed on to the broad windowsill, clutching his trousers to his stomach with one hand (it seemed they were undone and threatening to drop) and pushing at the top of the lower window frame with the other. Fresh night air and noise from the street below rushed past his kneeling figure, invading like a hit squad sent in to break up a private party.

'*No, no, no, no!*' I yelled, staccato fashion, blindly rushing forward and half-sprawling over the desktop, knocking pens, pads and filing trays aside.

'*No!*' One last time as the boy scrambled through the black opening on to the window ledge outside.

I think all three of us must have stared in disbelief, listening to the sound of muted voices and a heavy bass beat now mingled with the intruder's – *out*truder's? – sobs and pitiful wails. Still half over the desk, I moved around it, heading for the window, praying I would not be too late to drag the boy back. And even as I did so, I heard shouts and calls from the pavements below as the figure on the window ledge was spotted.

My nerves were stretched to breaking point as I stood on tip-toe and stuck my head out the window, both my anger and my fear considerably diminished now that I knew the intruder, murderer, mutilator, was more afraid of me than I of him and that he was merely a skinny man-boy, with no weapon that I could detect. In fact, my emotions were somewhat mixed at that point: this creature had slaughtered my friend and yet what was he? A pathetic, scared-witless juvenile, is what he was, a miserable, shivering, punk perched on the end of my windowsill. One part of me wanted to push him off; the other part, which was just as sincere, wanted to calm him down and coax him back into the safety of my office. If he had shown aggression, then perhaps I might have acted differently; but I had spent a good deal of my life trying to convince others, especially but not exclusively children, that there was nothing to fear from me. I think that yet another part of me, the rational, logical side of my nature, told me this kid was too frail and sorry-looking to have inflicted the damage I'd just witnessed. I spoke soothingly as I reached a hand towards him.

'Take it,' I said to him, aware of the shouts and pointing fingers from below. 'Come on, just take my hand and let me help you back inside. Nobody's going to hurt you.'

'*Keep away!*' he shrieked. '*Keep away!*'

Putting a knee on the outside sill, I pushed my shoulder through the open window. I kept my voice low and soft, surprised by my own coolness. 'It's all right. I promise, no one's going to hurt you. Come back inside before you slip.'

But he edged further away and there really was nowhere to go. He stood erect, face to the wall, fingers digging into the cracks of the old brickwork for purchase. His combats began to slide over his bare buttocks and down his scrawny legs, and as he reached for them with one hand, he looked my way once more, his eyes still bulging and wide, but opening even wider when they took in my shape, the hunch of my back, the fall of my jutting forehead, the black, shrivelled hole where my own eye used to be. Even though it was night, I saw every dark-stained tooth in his head as he opened his mouth to scream, this scream louder than any that had gone before, its horror more intense than I thought could ever be possible. His fingers scrabbled at the wall as he lost his balance.

Then he was gone and I was looking at empty space.

His scream was cut off as if stolen by the rushing air even before his body reached the pavement. Instead, the unified cry of the watching crowd in the street came back up to me and I closed my eye, unwilling to look over the edge, disinclined to witness the inevitable, the *unavoidable*, consequences of a fall from that height.

But I couldn't close my ears against the short wet crunch of shattered bones and crushed flesh as the kid hit the ground.

25

No more Henry. It's the finality that gets to you. One day someone you know – even worse, someone you love – is there, the next they've vanished. That's the hardship. Not sorrow or pity, just the sudden and irrevocable emptiness. It's shocking and it's wretched. Nevertheless, it's something we all have to go/grow through at some stage in our lives, usually more than once. Unless you die young yourself, of course, which is the best way to avoid mourning others.

Curiously, you still worry about them, your departed ones. Where have they gone to? Who's looking after them? (If you've lost a child, that's the concern that can easily destroy you.) If there are destinations called Heaven and Hell, which train did your friend/relation/loved-one (not always in combination, these) catch? And if you do fear the worst, can your prayers help them change track mid-journey?

So how much better to believe that there is no life after death, that there can be no soul because there's no place for it to go once the body has withered to dust. Sure, you'd still grieve for the one you've lost, but you wouldn't have to *worry* about them any more, because that wouldn't make sense. All you'd have to do is remember them and miss them. Wouldn't that be easier?

Why then, do most of us cling to the idea that there is more to follow, that death truly isn't the end of the road? Because we can't stand the idea of nothingness? Because we won't tolerate the notion that all our life amounts to at the end of the day is a heap of dirt? Or does society itself realize that to live tolerably well together we must have higher resolutions that will be rewarded when the end comes? A kind of inbuilt subliminal stick and carrot. Can it be a misconception whose purpose is to encourage us to be civilized? Maybe. But maybe, also, everything around us speaks of regeneration, that things may appear to die, but they never quite cease to exist. Flesh corrupts to dust, which becomes particles, which becomes atoms, which become energy and energy is the magic that binds everything together, and energy is invisible ... just like the soul. Unconvincing, of course, unless you *want* to be convinced, and for that, you have to believe. Which leads us back to why we *should* want to believe. After all, oblivion means peace – of a kind – so why not yearn for oblivion? Because ultimately it isn't enough. We think we're yearning for peace – peace of mind, tranquillity of heart – but really we're yearning for something better (after all, if there is no mind and no heart, their peace is irrelevant). And by better we really mean something better than we have now, in this life. Despite times of great joy and even contentment, we know it's not finite, that it cannot last. It's a brief intermission between the bad parts. So we seek – perhaps even pray for – something better, which ultimately means something more than any of us really has, and oblivion isn't more, it's goddamn *less*. And who the hell wants something *less*, something that is actually nothing at all?

Catch my drift?

Anyway, here's the point: all my life I'd known – okay, I'd *believed* – there was a better existence waiting for me somewhere, although I'd never been particularly religious, never attended church much (I'd always been saddened, sometimes angered, at the way great causes and religions had been tempered, often distorted, by mankind itself, how even the noblest of intentions invariably had been tainted by mind-pygmies and politicians with their vain hierarchies, petty doctrines, and absolutist dogma); yet in my thoughts, and not necessarily way at the back of my mind, there was always the perception that this life was not the main event. Perhaps it was only self-comfort, and frequently self-pity, but somehow I could only make sense of myself, of what I was, by believing my state was for some, hopefully higher, purpose. It was never any more than a subconscious directive, something beyond logic or understanding, an oblique edict that could never be mentally focused upon, yet which somehow gave me resolve. Even in my deepest despair there had always been the tiniest flicker of . . . of what? Not hope, nothing so naïve. *Incentive* is the closest I can get, or maybe *aspiration*. And for *aspiration* you could substitute *higher resolution*, which was mentioned earlier and which relates to mankind's belief in something other than itself.

But it's only now that I understand that in all of us it's really an intuitive desire for *redemption*, and that we all have the means of finding it. You'll see.

And so, as they say, back to the plot . . .

I spent most of that night at the local police station, at first being interrogated by two (over-zealous) DCs, then by a hastily-appointed SIO – senior investigations officer. All constabularies nowadays adhere to a specially computerized package called HOLMES, an acronym for the deliberately laboured (to suit the said acronym) Home Office Large Major Enquiry System, which is based on designated roles and set procedures. It also helps the police to link up with any similar or simultaneous investigations taking place in any part of the country. Murder may seem commonplace these days, but every one is treated as a significant crime warranting a major incident room with an office manager, administrative officer, receiver, statement readers, action allocator, indexer and researcher, all set up usually in a suite of offices at the nearest copshop to the scene of the crime.

Naturally, I was cautioned, but not arrested, and because

271

I was well-known to the station's head of CID, Detective Chief Superintendent Oliver Macaroon (who left his bed to come and see me personally) I was given almost immediate access to my solicitor, Etta Kaesbach (who else would I choose?).

The problem for me was that I had been spotted by a large crowd of witnesses in the street outside my offices as I stuck my unforgettable, easily-identifiable, head out the upstairs window while the youth edged along the ledge away from me, screaming in terror as he did so. Also, the poor kid had not died as soon as he hit the concrete, and had been rushed to hospital where, after forty minutes of frantic surgery, he had expired on the operating table. It seemed, however, that in the ambulance taking him to hospital, the paramedics had heard him moan over and over again, 'Monster, monster, monster . . .' I guess you can see how my interrogators put two and two together and came up with the unholy number of five. Nor was there any embarrassment or apology in their manner when they pointed out the 'positive link' to me.

Thank God for Etta, who blew them out of the water with their victim's last statement and eye-witness accounts. How could I possibly have murdered my dear friend and colleague Henry Solomon when I'd spent the entire evening with one Constance Bell and had arrived at my offices that night with her, meeting Louise Broomfield on the actual doorstep (she'd met my two companions outside in the police station's waiting area and they had quickly filled in the sequence of events)? Did anyone actually see her client push the youth off the window ledge? Of course not, because he was trying to bring the poor boy back inside. And where was the murder weapon that had so cruelly mutilated Henry? Secreted away on Mr Dismas' person? Hidden somewhere in the office? Where *exactly* was it? Nevertheless, the last repeated words of the dying youth remained 'highly significant' to the detective constables.

They could have held on to me for twenty-four hours, longer in fact, if so disposed, but the arrival of my old chum DCS Macaroon, who knew I was no killer, put paid to that. He advised them of my worthiness, ran through the evidence (or lack of) with them, complimented them on their keenness, then further advised them to have me released. By 3am the following morning, Saturday, Etta and I were making our way out into the sea-chilled, empty streets of Brighton.

'They know who the boy was,' Etta said as she led me to her car, which was parked in a side street, the nearest free space she could find when she had arrived earlier. The little racing-green Monza MX-5 now stood alone at the kerbside, cool white lamplight reflecting off its sporty bonnet.

I lit a cigarette, yearning for something a little more soothing. I was totally drained, my limp exaggerated, my hump even more humpish. In the course of the previous night I had declared my love, lost a good friend in the most horrific circumstances possible, been scared near to death, and had witnessed the death of a kid who might well have been my friend's killer, or at least an accessory to the killing. And after this, I'd been grilled for several hours by the Law's finest and thickest. Yet despite my exhaustion and aching spirit, I was interested in what Etta had to say.

Etta unlocked the two-seater's doors, but instead of getting in, she leaned against the bodywork. 'He was a local rent boy, originally from London. He'd worked Brighton for two summers now.'

I drew in on the cigarette as I rested against the car's low bonnet. 'You think Henry . . . ?' I didn't have to say more.

'That would be my guess. Did he often work late at the office?'

'Yeah, now that you mention it, quite a lot lately. Shit, I didn't know.' Sadness, disappointment, often has a release in anger. 'You bloody fool, Henry!'

I could see why he'd done it, why he had brought the boy back to the agency yesterday evening. Where else would he take him? Henry's mother was always at home and she certainly wasn't the type of mother to understand her son's sexual predilection. I guessed it wasn't the first time Henry had used the office as a bedroom – it would account for all those early mornings he had put in, no doubt anxious to check out the place before anyone else turned up, making sure there was nothing amiss, no evidence of the previous night's activities, even though, no doubt, he'd already done so before he had left and locked up! Bloody hell, Henry! You didn't have to creep around like that, I'd have understood. And anyway, to use a rent boy when Brighton was the gay town of the South Coast! Safe sex was more than just using a condom, Henry! I thumped the metal behind me with the heel of my fist.

Etta put an arm around my shoulder. 'He couldn't help himself, Dis,' she said. 'I suppose he lived a lie so long he didn't know how to pull out of it. Perhaps he couldn't come to terms with his own sexuality himself, so revealing it to you was out of the question.'

'We already knew.' I was still seething.

'Yes, and you kept quiet about it. That isn't really acceptance, Dis, even though you meant it for the best.'

'It was up to him, don't you see? If only he'd opened up, confided in me ... Maybe I could have convinced him that everything was cool, that it didn't change him in our eyes in any way. Christ, things have moved on, we're talking new millennium.'

'From what you've told me before, Henry was terrified of upsetting his mother.'

'She's of another era, she wouldn't have understood.'

'He was her son. She would have accepted it eventually.'

'I guess he didn't want to take the chance.' I gave a small groan. 'I've just realized I should go and see her, let her know what's happened.'

'The police have already taken care of that. You can visit her later today at a more civilized hour.' Etta took in a deep breath, as if savouring the fresh sea breeze that shivered through the lonely streets. Then she said: 'Who was the girl, Dis? The crippled girl with the quite pretty face who was waiting for you at the police station?'

So much had happened that I'd completely forgotten about Constance. 'Her name's Constance Bell,' I said.

'I told her and the other woman – Louise Broomfield, the clairvoyant you told me about? – that it would be pointless for them to wait, the police might hold on to you for a long time. We had their statements, so there was no reason for them to stay.' She looked at me under the harsh streetlight in an interested way. 'Come on, Dis, you haven't mentioned this Constance Bell before, so what gives with you two?' There was a half-smile on her light-blanched face.

I tossed the remainder of the cigarette into the gutter and nudged myself off the car. Etta's arm was still around my shoulder and she made no attempt to take it away.

'I'd intended to walk back to the agency and pick up my car,' I said, 'but maybe you should run me home in yours. I'm beat and I'm sure you are too, but let me make you some coffee and tell you everything that's been going on. Despite all the gabbing I've been doing to the police, I need to talk some more.'

She just nodded and climbed into the Monza, while I took one last look round, wary of the street's shadows – and what they might conceal.

26

I noticed that my car, still parked on the double-yellow, had a parking ticket taped under the windscreen wiper. Great, all I needed on such a morning. The policeman stationed outside the agency's front door looked down his nose at me as I approached, his hard face expressionless. He must have watched as the traffic warden slapped on the ticket, but I guess it would have taken an ounce of humanity to explain the circumstances to the illegal parking and the constable's heart had no such measure.

'Where d'you think you're going?' he asked when I tried to slip past him.

'I'm Nick Dismas. It's my company up there.'

He seemed to enjoy towering over me. 'Yes, I know who you are and you're not going up those stairs. It's an SOC.'

'I thought I might be able to help.'

'It's off limits, mate, 'specially to you.'

'Is your lot up there?'

'SOCO and CID.'

Scenes of crime officers, who would be photographing the area as well as dusting for fingerprints and searching for telltale marks, loose hairs, or anything else that might be useful in solving the case, together with a couple of detectives no doubt going through desks, diaries and files, generally snooping around.

'Is Macaroon with them?' I asked.

'Detective Chief Superintendent Macaroon, yes.'

'Would you let him know I'm here?'

'It's my job to keep people out, not run up and down stairs all day.'

There's always one. In general, I got on pretty well with the local constabulary, most of whom, from CID to uniform, were a decent breed; but, as with any profession, you always seemed to come up against the mean-minded bastard of the bunch. Well, today I didn't need it.

In front of him, I took out my mobile and tapped in my office number. 'Is DCS Macaroon there?' I enquired when the phone upstairs was answered. 'Could I have a quick word with him? Tell him it's Nick Dismas.'

The policeman on the door watched me stone-faced.

'Mac? Yeah, it's Nick. Look, I'm down at the front door and the dickhead on duty won't let me come up and see you.' I winked my good eye at the dickhead.

The shout soon came down the stairs behind him. '*Let him up, Collins!*'

The policeman, who must have had ambitions to make it big-time as a nightclub bouncer, flushed red as he stood aside.

'Carry on,' I instructed him as I brushed by, the tiny venting of anger good for me: after the shock, sadness and depression of last night, I needed something to bite on.

He didn't respond, but I felt his eyes burning my back all the way up the first flight of stairs.

There was blue and white tape across the open office door and I ducked under it. Oliver Macaroon, who was talking to the two zealot detectives who had grilled me at the station, turned towards me.

'Nasty business, Dis,' he said, holding out a hand in greeting.

We shook and the other two officers, by now fairly certain I wasn't the villain of the piece, nodded in my direction. I nodded back and they went on about their business, rifling through open filing cabinets.

'Hey,' I said irritably. 'You know, those files are supposed to be confidential.'

'They should've had stronger locks then,' came the surprisingly mild reply from the one I remembered was called Headley.

It was frustrating, but already too late to do anything about it. He continued to thumb through the client tabs, looking for who knows what?

The forensic officer, dressed in all-in-one white overalls, was dusting Henry's desk with black powder, taking care to avoid the still-sticky blood and the drenched accounts book that had been half under the mutilated body, searching for 'latents', invisible deposits of natural skin secretions. Chalk outlined where my old friend and colleague had lain. I wondered if forensics had discovered any alien fingerprints yet – mine had been taken at the station and Ida's and Philo's would be taken later in the day for elimination purposes, if nothing else. The problem was that there would be scores of dabs, from the cleaning lady's to the many clients who had visited the offices, so how could they all be identified? I shuddered at the bloodstains that were not restricted to the desk and the immediate area of floor beneath it, but splattered around the room as if some crazy artist had waved a red paint-covered brush around.

'Anything yet?' I asked Macaroon to distract myself.

'Too early. Look, let's go into your office and chat.' The chief superintendent pointed the way, his words a command, not an invitation.

Macaroon was a tall beanpole of a man, six-two or more, his shoulders slightly stooped as if he were height-self-conscious. His huge ears stood at right angles to his head, like the open doors of a car, his nose strong, well-defined in a face that spoke of strength. His hair was a premature silver-grey and cut close to his scalp, a Grade Two at least. There wasn't much humour in Mac, but behind the rather austere veneer there lay a quietly compassionate man dedicated to righting the wrongs on his manor. We had known each other a long time, since, in fact, we were both comparative rookies in our respective careers, and we had helped each other on numerous occasions, feeding bits of information that often put either one of us on the right path towards solving or resolving our own individual investigations (reluctant to become known as a 'nark' in the town, though, I was always careful as to the kind of information I passed on, and never once had any of it ever led directly to anybody's arrest).

I went ahead and skirted my desk, which was still askew across the room. Mac followed me in, closing the door behind him.

'Here,' he said, placing his big hands on the edge of the desk, 'let's move this back to its original position. We've taken pics and video, and drawn a sketch, so we'll know where it was.'

He shoved and I guided, and soon I was sitting behind the desk as though everything were perfectly normal. A soft breeze caressed the back of my neck, the window behind me still open. Mac brought over a chair and sat facing me.

'Your men shouldn't have broken into my private files, Mac,' I complained.

'We have a search warrant.'

'That wouldn't cover access to confidential records.'

'We do what we deem necessary.'

That they certainly did, and whining about it would get me nowhere. I shook my head resignedly, an act rather than a reaction – I had to let him know my displeasure somehow. He took no notice though.

'What else can you tell me about all this, Dis?' he said, his scrutiny making me uncomfortable.

'Honestly, nothing more than I told you and your officers last night. I came up here and found Henry lying across his desk, half-naked, dead, and mutilated. I heard noises from this room and when I entered I found the kid crouched in the corner.'

'You told us he appeared to be frightened of you.'

'If he were the killer he might have been afraid of what I would do to him. Besides, he was already in shock.'

'We don't believe he was the murderer.'

I leaned forward on the desk, pressing my knuckles against my chin. 'How did you come to that conclusion? Apart from Henry, he was the only other person up here.'

'With those injuries to the victim there would have been blood on the perpetrator, and plenty of it. Also, we found no weapon on the premises that could have caused such damage. We've searched the yards at the back and the road below your window, even the roof over our heads in case the boy threw anything up there when he was outside on the ledge.'

'I didn't see any murder weapon on him when he climbed out.'

'We aren't actually talking about a murder weapon as such. The victim was dead before any knife or instrument was used on him.'

I felt a huge relief that Henry had not been alive when those cruel outrages had been inflicted upon his body. 'Then what did kill him?'

'The first officer on the scene noticed that the victim's tongue was protruding slightly from the mouth and on closer inspection he saw it was purplish, congested. Around the eyes – the parts not covered by blood, that is – there were numerous haemorrhaged capillary blood vessels. Your colleague was strangled, Dis.'

Once more, I felt relief that Henry had only endured strangulation. The thought of him being alive when his genitals had been cut away and his eyes torn out ... I reached inside my pocket for a cigarette, the tenth, or possibly the twentieth of the day so far.

'Our pathologist took an X-ray before carrying out the autopsy. He found damage to the thyroid and the cricoid cartilages, and most importantly the small bone just above the Adam's apple was broken. All indications of manual strangulation, Dis, and that suggests immense force was used. You saw for yourself how puny the boy was. I doubt very much that he could have killed Henry Solomon.'

I thought it over as I lit the cigarette. 'So who could have . . . ?'

'The boy's pimp, perhaps, if he had one. Another client, or even a jealous boyfriend. Or perhaps both Henry and the boy he'd picked up were followed here from the streets. This could have just been the work of some homophobic.'

'Then why didn't he finish off the rent boy as well?'

'It could be that whoever the perpetrator was, he thought it was the older man, the predator, who should be punished.'

I closed the lighter and drew in on the cigarette, almost feeling the pollution nestling in my lungs, the sensation perfidiously comforting. Macaroon could be right, it might well have been a random killing. But somehow I knew it wasn't. Some intuition – *again* – told me there was nothing at all random about Henry's murder. I blew smoke across the desk.

The DCS now leaned forward. 'What isn't clear, despite what you told us last night, is what made you return to the agency so late.'

I explained yet again.

'So you received a phone call from this Broomfield woman, who is supposed to be some kind of clairvoyant. You say she rang you and practically begged you to come here right away.' Mac frowned. 'I didn't know you believed in that sort of stuff, Dis. Psychic sensing, talking to the dead, predicting the Lottery numbers? I thought you were much too grounded.'

It was difficult to reply.

'And yet,' the policeman went on, 'at this woman's request, you came to your offices straight away. Is there something you're keeping from me, Dis? Has your company become involved with some dodgy customers, drug dealers, for instance?'

I almost laughed aloud. 'Mac, our work is delivering summonses or writs, tracing people, surveillance, debt collecting and catching out cheating love partners or insurance fraudsters. And that's just the "exciting" part of our job. Come on, you know how commonplace our work is.'

'Nothing out of the ordinary recently, then?'

I was tempted to let him in on the Ripstone case, but two things stopped me: one was client confidentiality, and two was that Mac would have thought I'd finally flipped if I'd told him about celestial wings, disembodied voices, images in mirrors and every other goddamn thing I'd been through since Shelly Ripstone had walked through my door. Ollie Macaroon had always known me as a pragmatist, someone as down to earth as he was himself, and I wasn't going to disappoint him now. What would be the point? Would it help him find the person or persons who killed Henry? I didn't think so.

'It's all been routine stuff, Mac,' I said.

'You can't think of a connection with any case past or present?'

I shook my head.

'Henry Solomon had no enemies that you know of?'

I shook my head again. 'None that I'm aware.'

'Has anyone called you a monster before?'

That hurt. Christ, coming from Mac that really hurt. 'No,' I said flatly, 'not directly to my face. You still think the kid was referring to me in the ambulance?'

Not even slightly uncomfortable, Mac relied: 'Who else could he have meant? I mean, do you, yourself, know anyone locally who might fit that description.'

'I wasn't aware that I did myself.'

Still not fazed, the DCS went on: 'You know precisely

what I'm getting at. Sorry if I'm being indelicate, but I don't
have time to spare anyone's feelings.'

He was right, of course. What's more, in his own way, he
was treating me as an equal, a sensible, objective equal.
Although I didn't consider myself a 'monster', I *was* different
from most of my fellow men, and Mac was straight enough
to treat it as a plain truth. I had to face it – I'd always had to
face it – I was unsightly, and although I knew Mac well
enough to be confident that *he* didn't think of me as a
'monster', we were both aware that there were plenty of
others out there who did. We were professional investigators,
even though there was a vast difference in the nature of our
individual work, and Mac respected me enough to know I
would understand his position. His question may have
sounded harsh, and sure, it stung at first, but in fact, it was
reasonable under the circumstances and, as I said, he was
treating me as an intelligent equal. Others might have mis-
understood, but I didn't.

'No, Mac,' I said, at last answering his question. 'I can't
think of anyone around town who might be described in that
way. We've got plenty of weirdos, our fair share of mental
cases, and even some pretty "monstrous" gangster types in
the neighbourhood. Nobody that you could describe physically as a monster, though. No one I've ever met, anyway.' I
stubbed the half-smoked cigarette out in the ashtray close to
my elbow. 'But tell me, Mac, d'you have any idea yet of how
it happened last night? I know the kid was scared out of his
mind when I reached him, but d'you think he was involved
in Henry's murder?'

The big policeman pondered awhile before answering. 'I
suspect that Henry Solomon had been using these offices as
a night-time trysting place for some time. The youth – we've
identified him as Jamie Kelly, by the way – was well known
to us as a rent boy and it's possible that it wasn't the first
occasion he'd been brought here. What we don't know yet,

and hopefully it'll only be a matter of time before we find out, is whether Solomon picked him up in a gay club or on the street, or whether they already had a prearranged meeting here. Until we've established either, we can't say if one or both were followed back to your offices. It could even be that some low-life passer-by discovered the front door downstairs was open and decided to have a look around.'

I began to notice the tiredness in Mac's face. He'd obviously worked through the night until he was satisfied that at least some progress had been made towards solving the crime.

'The other thing we can't know,' he continued, watching me – not suspiciously but in his usual intense way – across the desktop, 'is if the boy wasn't involved in the murder, then as a witness why was he not himself harmed?'

'Maybe the killer wasn't aware that the kid was here. For some reason he could have been in here, in my office, when the intruder arrived and then hid when he saw or heard what was happening to Henry.'

'It's a possibility, but we don't think so. We believe your colleague and the boy were engaged in sexual activity when they were disturbed. It would account for both victims – and we have to treat the boy Kelly as a victim even though it appears he caused his own death – being in a state of undress. Our pathologist, who worked through the night to feed us early results, found secretion in the boy's penis and trousers that suggest sexual arousal some time before he fell. Forensics are looking for similar secretions, if not even spilled semen, on the first victim's shirt, his desk, and the floor and chairs around it.'

'And Henry? I know that – '

Mac raised a hand to stop me. 'Not only have we been unable to find the instrument used to mutilate his body, but we still haven't been able to locate the missing body parts.'

I sat there stunned. For some reason it hadn't occurred to

me to wonder what had happened to Henry's severed geni-
talia and gouged eyes. I suppose my mind had refused to
think about it, my subconscious protecting me from further
shock.

'It's another reason you're no longer a suspect, Dis,' Mac
said, as if to reassure me. 'There's no way you could have
got rid of the cutting instrument and the removed organs
before the two women reached you, especially without even
a trace of blood on you. In fact, you wouldn't have had time
to commit the crime itself. We still have to investigate your
friend Louise Broomfield a little more, although she's not
under suspicion – no motive and she doesn't look strong
enough to mix it with two males. We're just puzzled as to
how she knew something had happened here.'

'She thought I was in danger.'

'So I understand. It doesn't really explain anything does
it?'

I reached in the pack for another cigarette, even though I
hadn't fully-smoked the last one. 'Not unless you believe in
clairvoyance,' I remarked.

'Well, I'm not sure that I do.' For the first time the DCS
looked uncomfortable in his chair. He cast his gaze away
from mine and pretended to examine objects and papers on
my desk.

'What is it, Mac?'

His eyes stopped their roving and fixed on me once more.
His voice was toneless when he told me. 'The attack on your
colleague was gruesome enough, Dis, but there was another
aspect to it.'

My already leaden heart seemed to take on more weight.
I didn't want to hear this, but I knew I had to: I had to learn
everything I could about Henry's murder.

'The wounds to Henry's face . . .' the policeman said, his
words now becoming slowed, yet still toneless. 'The bloody
holes where the eyes had been . . .'

My hand, lifting the cigarette to my lips, froze in mid-air.

'The pathologist,' said Mac, 'found semen inside one of them. Whoever strangled and mutilated your friend used the empty eye socket for his own sexual gratification.'

My hand dropped away, cigarette untouched.

27

When I left the agency after my conversation with Detective
Chief Superintendent Macaroon, I made for the nearest,
quietest bar I knew, somewhere I could sit in peace for a
while. I ordered a large brandy and took it to a table in a
secluded corner and there I sat for quite a while, ruminating
on life, death, and the sickness of mankind. It wasn't what
you'd call the Happy Hour.

Two brandies and a Löwenbrau later I made my first call
of the day. It was past noon by now and I wondered if Etta
might still be in bed, sleeping off our late night; we'd talked
long, hard and wearily till way past dawn, with me doing
most of the talking. It was Saturday, so no need for her to go
into work, even though she often did; I tried her at her flat
first. Etta was there and she was awake. When I invited her
to join me she agreed immediately.

During our conversation after leaving the police station, I
had told her *all* the details of the Ripstone case and the
events of the past five days, including the dreams I'd had,
the visions in mirrors, the crazy thing that had happened in
Shelly Ripstone's house. I spoke of my visit to the old
people's nursing home, PERFECT REST, with its oddly-chosen
paintings and inquisitive 'guests', and I mentioned the sudden death of Hildegarde Vogel, the long-retired midwife and
the only lead I had in tracing our mutual client's allegedly
missing offspring. I described the urbane yet somehow
sinister Michael Rennie *doppelgänger*, Dr Leonard K. Wisbeech MD, FRCS, WXY fucking Z, and his cold, autonomous

manner, as well as my suspicions regarding possible past misdeeds, namely newborn-baby abduction. Finally, I told her about Constance Bell.

All this got us nowhere, it didn't resolve anything but, as the phone company likes to tell us, it's good to talk, and at least I got everything off my misshapen chest, if not out of my mind. It also gave me the opportunity, while I was telling all, to put forward a suspicion that had been growing inside my head for a couple of hours, daft though it might sound. It was this: had Henry been killed as a warning to me? Worse – worse for Henry, that is – had I been the intended victim? I don't mean that Henry was mistaken for me, which was hardly possible considering our very different physiques, but that he was murdered because he happened to be at the agency instead of me?

Etta suggested I was being paranoid. If my suspicion was that this Dr Leonard K. Wisbeech was behind the dark deed (sometimes Etta could be too hardnosed), then why would a respectable and obviously eminent physician be involved in baby-snatching? Even if he had, even if he had stolen babies to sell on to infertile but wealthy couples – which, come on now, was hardly likely, was it? – why on earth would he resort to murder to cover his tracks? Especially if such an illicit trade would be so hard to prove anyway? If not para-noid, then I was being over-imaginative. Didn't these so-called visions – hallucinations, she would call them – didn't they indicate that my head was a little screwed up at the moment? Could it merely be payback time for all the drugs I'd experimented with over the years? I might be semi-reformed by now, but the damage was already done, the dregs of those chemicals were still floating around in my system. God knows what they were doing to my brain. Didn't I get frequent headaches, night sweats, the occasional lapse of memory, nothing serious, but hints that all was not quite right? I couldn't deny it, because I had mentioned the symptoms to her myself. But they were mild, just caused by stress, overwork. Perfectly normal, I swear, and nothing to do with debauched younger years. Besides, I had pointed out in our talk, Louise Broomfield had had similar visions – wings and voices, portents of danger, but Etta had argued that the clairvoyant tuned in to my feelings, picked up my vibes, experienced my distress. Get a grip, had been Etta's advice, start thinking rationally again.

And who could blame her for being so reasonable?

I had spoken to both Ida and Philo by phone, breaking the news of Henry's death as gently as I could and telling them to stay away from the office over the weekend. The police had their addresses and phone numbers and would probably be dropping by later in the day for statements from them. They might also be asked to go to the station for fingerprint elimination. They had understandably been upset and now I rang to ask them to join myself and Etta at the bar where we could mourn Henry over some stiff drinks. Both said they'd come at once.

After leaving the flat that morning, my first visit had been to Henry's mother. Unfortunately, she hadn't reacted too well to me. I don't know if she blamed me in some way for her son's horrendous and untimely death, assuming no doubt it was something to do with the business we were in, or if she merely had a thing about people like me. Henry had to have picked up some of his outrageous – and regretfully, some-times humorous – bigotry from somewhere (although I often thought it was superficial, part of his occasional flamboy-ance) and as his mother tearfully ranted at me, I began to suspect from where. She was in obvious shock, that shock no doubt compounded by the sordid circumstances of her son's death but, to be honest, it was a relief when she slammed the door in my face.

From Evie Solomon's house near the seafront, I had gone straight to the agency to be greeted by the parking ticket and surly copper.

Nursing my brandy now in the quiet corner of the bar I

tried to ring Constance for the second time that day (the first had been early morning, as soon as I'd dragged myself from bed after little more than two hours of restless sleep, and had been informed by PERFECT REST's receptionist that Ms Bell was unavailable). Holding the mobile close to my ear, I waited impatiently for the call to be answered.

Finally: 'PERFECT REST. How may I help you?'

In my mind I pictured the plump bespectacled receptionist, Hazel, sitting at her semi-screened desk in the nursing home's light, airy reception area with its long corridors leading off and doddery old folk in dressing-gowns shuffling by.

'Yes. I wanted to speak to Constance Bell, please.'

A pause. Somebody in a group at the bar laughed raucously and I cupped my hand over the cellphone's speaker protectively.

'And whom should I say is calling?' came the distant voice again.

I lifted my hand a fraction. 'Nicholas Dismas.'

Another pause.

'I'm afraid Ms Bell is not available.'

'You told me that earlier. Could you try her extension for me?'

'Ms Bell isn't here today.'

My turn to pause.

'D'you know where I can reach her?'

No hesitation at all this time.

'I'm afraid I don't. Good day.'

Click.

'Bitch!' The receptionist, I meant.

I tucked the phone away and lit another cigarette. My head was thumping, but it wasn't from a hangover. What was going on? I asked myself. Surely Constance wouldn't refuse to take my calls? Not after last night. We'd connected, I was sure of that. In a very intimate way, there was no doubt. And it might have developed into a physical intimacy, despite

Constance's initial reservations, if Louise Broomfield had not interrupted things with her call. And the hell that had followed shouldn't have distanced us: if anything, it should have drawn us closer together. I began to worry that Constance hadn't made it safely back to the rest home. But then, surely the receptionist would have mentioned the fact and not just told me the care-supervisor was unavailable?

As I fretted, dragging on the cigarette and sipping brandy and beer in turns, Etta Kaesbach walked into the saloon bar, closely followed by both Philo and Ida. We all hugged and exchanged commiserations, our shock, our sadness. My two colleagues plied me with questions and Etta wanted to hear of any new developments, but I refused them all until I had got in a round of drinks.

We toasted Henry – wherever he might be – before the remorse and weeping began. We celebrated his short life and we mourned its passing. We did what all good friends should do on such occasions – we shared funny stories about him, his sayings, his little foibles, his love of movies, especially musicals – and it was good for us, for it was the first step towards acceptance of this awful event in our lives. His faults – particularly his pseudo-racism – were ignored, his merits aggrandized. His over-fussy attention to detail, something that had irritated us all at some stage, was complimented upon and now admired as a great quality. We smiled and then, as the liquor-liquid flowed, giggled over his penchant for bright braces and colourful bow-ties and snazzy socks, all worn with deadly dull grey cheap business suits. We wept over his 'big secret' and regretted that he'd never felt comfortable enough with it and us to share the burden, a burden primarily of his own making. We worried over the fate of his ailing mother, on whom he had doted, and I didn't mention the slamming of the door in my face that morning, nor the harsh words with which she had scolded me. We brightened ourselves again by remembering Henry's acerbic but very funny humour, each of us relating a particular putdown from him, remarks we had had to laugh at even when we were the butt of the putdown. Henry had been complex, but he had been very real, an individual in a fast-becoming faceless society. We fêted him and we grieved for him.

I know our private wake did us all some good that day. There was a lot more sorrow ahead for us, but at least we had started the process of recovery. Henry would have enjoyed all aspects of the celebration.

As for myself though, I wish I had drunk even more. I wish I had drunk so much that I'd passed out until the following morning. Perhaps then I'd have been oblivious to the fresh horrors that were to visit me later that night.

28

Had I been dreaming? I can't remember. All I know is that I was suddenly wide awake without being aware of what had awakened me. Moonlight, that which had managed to filter through the canyons of tall buildings backing on to my premises, played through the partially parted curtains to create a long silver strip that ran across the floor and over my bed. A small mist curled in front of my face and I realized it was the vapours of my breath.

The room was ice cold.

I started when I heard a noise, perhaps a follow-up to the one that had aroused me from my booze-sodden slumber (yes, I'd indulged myself further after I'd left my inebriated friends and returned to the flat). The sound came yet again, a short, staccato rapping from somewhere along the hallway outside the bedroom. As if someone were knocking on the front door.

'No, they wouldn't . . .' I mumbled to myself.

Journalists had been waiting on my doorstep when I'd arrived home earlier in the evening, two from the local rags, another three from the national tabloids, and one, who was a little more restrained than his colleagues but not much so, from an upmarket broadsheet. How they had located my flat address I had no idea, although I suspected someone at the local copshop (all police stations are hives of information for journalists) had tipped them off. I wasn't in the phone book, so it had to be either that, or they'd looked me up on the electoral roll. They had bombarded me with questions as soon as I stepped out of my car (yes, I'd drunk and driven, and yes, I know it was stupid of me, but on that particular day I couldn't have cared less) and I'd had to force my way through them, then force the front door closed behind me once I was inside. Obviously they had got my description from the police or neighbours alongside the agency, because they had known who I was the moment my foot touched the kerbside. The journos had hung around outside for a couple of hours before giving up, ringing the bell and banging on wood every ten minutes or so, even tapping on the front-room window when that had no effect. I'd ignored them, drawing the curtains and going through to the kitchen for the hidden illegal palliative awaiting me there. Cocaine can sometimes help you cope with all kinds of pain, both physical and mental, and by then I was in desperate need of an analgesic, no matter how temporary its effect.

After the hit, and without eating anything – food was definitely out on that day – I'd gone straight to bed. Before reaching any kind of comforting high, I'd fallen asleep. And slept and slept, but not enough. The rapping had managed to disturb me.

I turned to the tiny alarm clock on the bedside cabinet and pressed the button that illuminated its face. 1.34am. No, they couldn't still be out there, not at this hour. Even the most determined reporters would have gone away to rest before their resumed onslaught the following morning.

The raps came again, harsh, resolute, in quick succession. I groaned, wondering whether if I downed what was left in the bottle of Dalmore, I'd finally find the oblivion I sought. My head was pounding, my mouth was an ashtray, and every move I made seemed to arouse little harpies of pain inside every part of my body.

'Oh God, please go away,' I moaned to the torture *and* the knocking on the door. Neither one paid any heed.

A thought rushed into my head and suddenly I was throwing off the bedsheet and scrabbling for the bathrobe –

for once I had gone to bed naked – lying across the end of the bed. It might be Constance out there.

I had tried to call her several more times throughout the afternoon, but the response had been exactly the same each time: 'Ms Bell is unavailable.' I'd even tried to speak to Dr Wisbeech, but wouldn't you know? – he was also unavailable. It had left me frustrated and tense.

I stumbled along the hallway, my shoulder bumping the wall. It had to be her! Constance would never have ignored me all day, not after what had happened last night.

'I'm coming.' It wasn't a shout to whoever was out there – *please, please, let it be Constance* – but more of a murmur to myself. Even though my attention was solely on the door at the end of the dark hallway, I was still conscious of the chill in the atmosphere, the robe offering little protection against it. It was as if winter had made a premature appearance.

'Hold on, I'm coming!' This time it *was* to whoever – *Constance, yes, yes* – was out there.

Although only a short hallway, it seemed to take me a long time to reach the door, which was now rattling in its frame.

'Yes, yes!' I yelled, as the rapping and the rattling became almost violent.

I was reaching for the catch when everything went silent.

I stood there, blinking in the gloom. The metal of the door-lock felt so frigid I feared my fingers might stick to it. Suddenly, I didn't want to open that door.

Someone had murdered Henry last night, mutilating his body in the most horrendous way. What if this same sick bastard was outside on my doorstep?

'Who's out there?' I yelled, managing to inflect a growl into my voice to imply fearlessness and even annoyance. 'I'm not opening up unless you tell me.'

The blow that hit the door shook it in its frame.

I staggered backwards, sliding against the wall, so startled I thought my legs might buckle under me.

'Who's there? What d'you want?'

A stillness followed my demand to know and it was full of – it was *drenched* with – foreboding. As if something were just waiting there out of sight on the doorstep. There was no sound at all from beyond the wood.

It came from behind me instead.

A light tapping.

Fingernails against glass.

I slowly turned my head to look back down the corridor.

Tap, tap . . .

Hump brushing wallpaper, I retreated from the front door, slowly inching my way towards the source of this new sound.

. . . tap, tap . . .

I peeked around the open door to the sitting-room opposite. The sound wasn't coming from there.

I moved on.

. . . tap, tap . . .

I swung round to face the kitchen. Listened. The sound wasn't coming from there either.

. . . tap . . . tap . . . tap . . . More evenly spaced now, but still deliberate, still insistent.

Not from the bathroom.

No, it was from the bedroom. The tapping was coming from my bedroom. As if whoever had been at the front door had raced around the apartment block to the back. But that would have been impossible. All the yards were enclosed.

I moved on again, treading warily, my dread adding lead weights to each foot. Someone, or something, was in my bedroom.

There was a second hall light-switch outside the bedroom door, the first being at the other end, beside the flat's entrance. I flicked it on and my eye was stung by the sudden brightness. I closed it briefly and still I heard the sound: it was even more ominous inside the darkness of my head.

. . . tap . . . tap . . . tap . . .

Someone was tapping on the bedroom window.

Then someone was *banging* on the front door.

My head swung this way and that, back towards the front door, back towards the open bedroom door.

The tapping on the window increased in volume, became a *rapping* that threatened to shatter the glass.

I rushed through the door, at least brave enough to confront whoever was out there – as long as they were *out* there. But all I saw was moonlight.

I hurried round the bed, making for the window, once there boldly throwing back the curtains even further so that the culprit would be exposed, the tormentor faced. But all I saw was my own small backyard and the buildings beyond, moonlight bleaching everything, while also creating shadows like deep black holes. Nobody was there. No one was looking back at me through the glass.

Yet still the tapping continued, softer once again, then building, returning to the *rapping*, becoming frantic so that the window rattled in its frame and even the curtains inside fluttered as if disturbed by a breeze or unseen hands.

And the sound from behind, from the front door down the hallway, was becoming even louder, the knocking on wood thunderous, the banging on glass deafening.

I clapped my hands to my ears and moaned, shaking my head from side to side.

Then it all ceased.

Abruptly. And it seemed, permanently.

It was the window I backed away from now, my footsteps light, as though I were afraid to rouse my tormentors again, and my eye watched the moonlight, waiting for the slightest shift in its shadows. I lowered my hands. The curtains settled.

I lingered in the doorway, the hall at my crooked back.

Something was impending. I could feel it in the very air itself, a rising tension so thick I could have wet my finger and felt its swell. Something was about to happen and I wanted to scream before it did. But my throat, my jaw, my voice, were paralysed. Almost mechanically, the movement so deliberately forced you might have heard cogs and wheels grinding, I looked over my shoulder.

Back towards the front door.

Which was bulging inwards, its wood beginning to creak, its metal lock and hinges beginning to squeal.

But it was the window that broke first, glass fragments exploding inwards and across the room like shrapnel from a cannon, tearing towards me to shower me with its glitter, stabbing me with its tiny shards.

It was fortunate that my face was turned towards the door at the end of the hallway, otherwise I might easily have been blinded in my single eye; and I think it was sheer gut-reaction that made me throw myself to the floor, thus avoiding the worst of the blast. The thick towelling of my bathrobe also served me well, for not too many of those glass daggers pierced its material, although even while falling I felt the sharp stings of those that did manage to penetrate. I curled into a tight ball when I hit the hallway floor, covering my head with my hands, too stunned even to cry out.

A loud crash and a fresh wind from the other end of the hallway. I looked up to see that the front door was open wide. Street litter and dust swept in with the storm, the air rushing at me with screaming force.

And with the wind there came the shapes, distortions, curling grotesques that might have blown from Hell itself. And I could hear their voices, although they made no sense, were incoherent murmurings and mutterings and screeches, the sound of chaos, the discord of bedlam.

The gale joined its sister from the shattered window, the gustings melding over my head, becoming a maelstrom around me, images swirling in the currents, strange, contorted limbs snatching at my hair, prodding my back, so that I was forced to move, forced to crawl along the floor towards the open doorway, the street beyond it seemed my only refuge. But even as I did so, the door at that far, far end of the short, brief hallway slammed shut once more.

Leaving me enclosed with these half-seen, half-realized hideosities.

A barely-formed face appeared before me, in place of its mouth a yawning gap, instead of its eyes two black pebbles with no expression, nothing beyond them. The cavern that was the mouth feebly opened and closed as though the formless creature were speaking, but no utterances came save for a high-pitched keening. It disassembled to be replaced by a thing so awful, so monstrous, I had to shield my eyes, the absent one too, against it.

Yet still I saw. With my eye closed and my hands across my face, I saw.

This thing was bloated and hairless, a pale blob whose veins seemed embossed beneath tightly-drawn skin. Its eyes were red, an albino's eyes, and when they blinked the pupils could still be seen through the fine layer of flesh.

Something touched one of the hands covering my face, the cold, liquid feel of it causing me to flinch, to jerk my hand away and open my eye. The bloated thing had moved away to be replaced by yet another face, one that grinned at me, that grin too wide, reaching too far across the barely formed face; and something interrupted that grin, a growth that extended down from what must have been a forehead, a horn, a tusk, that divided the expansive but human mouth, a feature that rendered the countenance an obscenity. This too, swirled away from me, other unsightly images taking its place.

I collapsed against the wall, swatting at those floating impressions with frantic hands, yet still they came, swimming before me in blurred profusion, different shapes, different distortions, all voicing disordered warnings or appeals, I couldn't tell which, their cries as varied as their forms, their agitation as frenzied as the silent breezes that swept around me.

A figure emerged from the darkness of the bedroom, forcing a cry from me.

As though in a mist, the figure came forward into the light of the hallway and I could just make out the golden, natural ringlets of her long hair, the clouded beauty of her face. Among this churning sea of grotesque perceptions, she came to me almost as a relief and in my desperation, I think I must have smiled, for tension left my jaw and I could feel my lips turn. She was the sanity amongst the lunacy. Or so I thought until I took in the rest of her.

Her image shimmered as if viewed through a heat haze rising from a hot road, her outline unclear, not quite in focus; and as she advanced and my eye took in the rest of her, I noticed that the legs were not beneath the torso, that they appeared almost to be walking below but alongside her upper body. It was as if she had been sliced in half, some magical process enabling both trunk and lower limbs to move independently yet as one.

Suddenly I didn't like the apparent beauty of that ill-defined face, the allure behind those blurred lips that seemed to smile down at me. I scrabbled away, rolling on to my hands and knees once more, scrambling towards the opening at the end of the hall ... stopping when my eye set on the thing that lay on the threshold.

It quivered and shook, a slug-like being, but too huge to be such. Stumps grew from it, placed like arms and legs but with no joints, no fingers, no toes, and at one end there was a protrusion, small, not in proportion to the rest of the body, that I realized was its head. The head turned towards me as if to see, but I observed that it had no eyes.

When something cold touched the hump of my back, iced fingers seeming to enter the material of the robe so that they felt my skin, slithered over the sac, I shrieked. I shrieked and clawed my way up the wall, rising to my feet and stumbling away, the shriek falling to a gibbering as I stag-

gered through the nearest doorway and slammed the door
behind me.

I fell to my knees and held my head in my hands, twisting
my shoulders, shaking myself as if to break free from this
. . . this . . . *nightmare*? It couldn't be, it was too real, my
mind was conscious. And dreams have that quality whereby
you know, even if you do not acknowledge, that they are
merely excursions in which you cannot be harmed. Tormented, maybe, but never physically harmed.

This was no dream. This was really happening to me. To
convince myself I slammed my hand against the floor and
felt the pain shoot up my arm. Oh yes, this was real enough.
These things were surely out there.

I heard their tappings on the door, fingernails scratching
wood, their muffled mumblings as though they were gathered in the hallway, entreating me to let them in. Haunting
me.

I straightened and looked back at the door.

If these, then, were ghosts, perhaps there was one person
who might rid me of them.

I lurched towards the telephone on the sideboard against
the wall, one unsteady hand lifting the receiver, the other
already rifling through the address book lying beside it.
Louise Broomfield. She would know what to do, she would
help me. The woman *talked* to ghosts, for Christ's sake! She
would tell me what to do, she would rush over to help me!
Where was her number? I knew I'd written it down; I always
noted the number of a new contact or acquaintance, you
never knew when it would be useful. Not enough light! Not
enough light coming through the basement window from the
lamps around the crescent! Had to get the light-switch . . .

But the receiver was tight against my ear and there were
voices already coming through, whispers, murmurings,
growing louder, gradually becoming audible, becoming
coherent.

'*Help us* . . .' they said. '*Help us* . . .'

The words were repeated over and over again so that they became a litany.

'. . . *help us* . . .'

And as they spoke, the receiver grew cold in my hand.

I stared at it, heard the voices, more distant now that the instrument was away from my ear, felt the seeping coldness creep into my own flesh to travel up my arm.

Then the voices altered, became a moaning, and then a wailing. As I listened closer again, I thought I heard sniggers among the wailing, and cries among it all. And the instrument grew even colder. Becoming so cold that I dropped it on to the sideboard, afraid it would stick to my skin. Yet it was burning that I could smell. Burning plastic.

Even in the dimness of the room I could see steam or smoke rising from the receiver, then from the curled cord itself. And the plastic was beginning to bubble as though the receiver were red hot – *red hot, even though I had felt it freezing*! The stench became stronger and through the tiny gaps of the ear- and mouthpieces, I could see a glow, as if the inner circuitries were overloading, the wires glowing. The bubbling of the casing became more liquid as the plastic began to melt. And the wailing diminished, grew fainter . . .

But began again from behind the sitting-room's closed door. And even then it began to grow fainter again, as if receding, moving down the hallway towards the front door, drifting off until there was silence save for the soft popping sound as the plastic bubbles exploded. Eventually, even that stopped and the telephone receiver was nothing more than a charred, misshapen mess. I squinted closer to the sideboard and although the light was poor, I could see that the wood beneath the receiver was unmarked.

I leaned heavily against the sideboard, hands clutching at its edge to prevent myself from sinking to the floor. I had to get out! I had to get away from there! They might come back, their haunting not complete!

I pushed myself away and hobbled to the door, afraid to open it and afraid not to. I listened and there were no sounds from outside. Had the sitting-room window not had bars to protect the flat from burglars, I would have climbed through and up to the street at ground level, not caring about my state of undress, only wanting to be far away from this place and the entities inside. But I had no choice other than to use the front door, and to do that, I had to go through the hallway.

Fresh adrenaline rushing through me, I yanked open the door and, without pause, ran into the hallway to charge towards the flat's entrance. I had been afraid that the slug-like thing would still be lying across the threshold, my intention being to leap over it and out into the night beyond. But it was gone. The hallway was empty. And the front door was shut.

I almost barged into it, so desperate was I to flee, but my hands took the impact. I reached for the latch, twisted it, and pulled the door towards me. My fingers slipped from the metal as the door remained where it was. I tried again, this time using both hands, twisting and pulling, trying to wrench the door open. Again, nothing happened, the door refused to budge. Next time, I lifted the letterbox flap, slid one hand through the opening to grip the iron-lipped wood, twisted the latch and tugged with all my strength. Still nothing happened; the door would not open.

Now I staggered back, away from the front door itself. It was as if it had its own will, its own volition. As if it did not *want* to open!

I slid away, another thought in my mind. The bedroom window. It was broken, I could climb out. I could stand in the yard and shout for help, or I could climb over the dividing wall, bang on my neighbour's back door. I didn't care what anybody thought of me standing there half-naked in my bathrobe, screaming blue murder about dreams and ghosts and murder and melted yet frozen telephones. I didn't care if they thought I was insane and men in white coats came to take me away. I didn't care about any of that. I . . . just . . . wanted . . . out . . .

My foot dragged as I hobbled back down the corridor and my hands slapped at the walls on either side as I passed. I ran straight into the moonlit bedroom.

But it was a mistake. It was a *huge* mistake.

For the things had gathered there and their unnatural forms preened in the silvery light. It was as if they had been waiting for me, knowing I would come to them, sure that I could not escape. And I saw now that the window was not broken at all.

The shapes moved in the moon's glare, but still shadows hid the worst of their malformations from me, although I caught glimpses, I saw partial deformities that seemed devised in Hell, for no true God would have inflicted them. Yet they appeared happy in their own monstrousness, for they revelled in themselves and each other, fondling and caressing their own and their neighbours' distortions, performing lewd acts that brought nausea to my throat. All in the moonlight of my bedroom.

Although nothing was specific, no shape could be discerned by me, the designs of some of these elusive creatures seemed perverse beyond imagination, so that their couplings were like those of beasts or demons.

I cried out against the sick, shadowy luridness of it all, but the sound merely drew them closer. Nebulous hands touched me, reaching beneath my robe to feel my flesh, defiling me with their contact, and I fell back against a wall, horrified then appalled, because my own body was responding to their touches, my senses aroused by the pawing.

'*No!*' I screeched, ashamed and repulsed by this dark lust, drawing myself away from those frigid, reaching fingers, from the sinister figures that slithered across the floor, pulling my robe tight around myself like some virgin afraid of rape. Still the orgy continued around me, these writhing creatures defying reason, their half-seen sexual deeds more perverse than anything that could be imagined. But it was only when I saw the familiar and beautiful face of Constance among them that the loathing overcame terror, and anger, once more, overruled my cowardice.

Like those around her, she was naked, her little body and wasted limbs like marble in the moonlight, and the creatures molested her, cupping her tiny breasts with scaly hands, reaching into the secret part of her that should have been forbidden to all except the one she loved and who loved and cherished her, pressing their mutant forms against her, engorged parts seeking orifices of any kind, any cavity between flesh . . .

I screamed and I ran at them, jumping into their midst, flailing their ethereal forms with clenched fists, swiping at these shifting inchoates, kicking at their orderless shapes, tears distorting my perception of them even more. I yelled and screamed and I beat at them furiously, and they bowed under my blows, even though I felt no contact, my fists smiting nothing more than vapour and shadows, my feet kicking only into floating chimaeras. They scurried away from me, these vague embryonic creatures, as if afraid of my wrath; yet still I heard their sniggers and chuckles, as if it were all a game, that my torment was their sole purpose.

I could no longer see the small wan figure of Constance among them and frustratedly, desperately, I continued to swipe at them, turning in the moonlight of my bedroom like some mad thing, whirling and striking, insane for the moment, gripped by hysteria, and almost broken by the pale image I had seen of the one I now loved above all else.

'*Constance!*' I shouted.

But I was alone.

The visions had dispersed, returned to whatever dark regions had spawned them, a few last curling vapours trailing in the air, slowly dissolving, becoming nothing, a deception of the mind relegated to a nightmare memory. Yet still I lashed out, the blows becoming feeble, my turning winding down, slowing further until finally I stopped. Exhausted, I bent double, resting my hands on my knees, my back arched. My chest spasmed with escaping sobs and I felt the nausea that had threatened before surging upwards. Clapping my hand over my mouth I staggered from the bedroom into the bathroom, vomit clogging my mouth and nostrils.

I let it go when I saw the dim whiteness of the toilet bowl beneath me, the discharge exploding from my mouth to splatter water and porcelain, its stink and the slimy feel of its rush causing me to gag again and again, to unload all the rottenness I had drunk and consumed that day, purging myself until all I could do was dry-retch, the sound disgusting and loud in the tiled confines of the bathroom. I hunched over the bowl, hands grasping its rim, the heaving and the retching continuing even though there was nothing left to expel.

Gradually, I was able to draw in deeper breaths and only a silky strand of spittle drooled from my mouth to the spoiled water below. Eventually, even this ceased and I was able to push myself away from the toilet. The room reeled around me and I clutched at the edge of the sink to prevent myself from falling. My stomach and throat felt raw and my head thumped, but mercifully I could see no more amorphous spectres sharing the darkness with me, no other movement at all save that caused by my own swaying. Lest those freakish things return using the dungeon gloom as their ally, I snatched at the hanging light-switch by the door, giving it a sharp tug, my breath now coming fast and hard.

Light filled the bathroom and I found myself looking directly into the mirror over the sink. It was misted by the vapours of my breath and I could only make out a dim reflection of myself.

The clouded glass began to clear, though, as my breathing became more controlled, less harsh. And my reflection began to appear within the mirror's counterfeit dimension.

And of course, it wasn't I who was standing there, staring back.

No. It was the handsome man. The sophisticate whose features, now that the fine haze on the glass was almost gone, were clearer than ever before. This time I recognized him, for I had seen that splendid face a *thousand* times in the past. I *knew* who he was, I could identify him, I could remember his name.

As I watched the reflection that was not me but a movie actor of old, a great star in his day, here attired in silk-lapelled dinner jacket and black tie, almost his trademark in that great golden Hollywood era when films were glamorous and their stars were 'luminous', he grinned at me.

And then he winked.

29

I hadn't thought it possible, but I did manage to sleep the rest of that night. I don't remember leaving the bathroom, nor climbing into bed, pulling the sheet tight around me, but that was where I found myself when daylight woke me next day. As always, I lay in foetal pose, face pressed into my hands, knees drawn up to my chest; like Joseph Carey Merrick, known as the Elephant Man, I longed to sleep on my back, but the curvature of my spine and its protruding sac prevented me from doing so. My eye twitched open, immediately closing again when the events of the night rushed into my head. And those thoughts forced my eye open once more so that I could see that the nightmare had ended and reality had arrived with the day.

Raising my head, I peeped over the hem of the sheet towards the window. The curtains were drawn open, but the glass was intact. Had it, then, been a dream?

I shuddered when I recalled some of those creatures that had crawled across the floor towards me, reaching for my flesh with appendages that could hardly be called hands; and I stifled a sob when I thought of Constance among them, her pallid body violated by their obscene overtures. *Oh dear God, it had to be a dream, a sick, vile dream!*

Tormented last night, now tortured by lurid memories, I kicked the sheet away and sat on the edge of the bed, fingers rubbing my temples as though the thoughts were physically painful. I still wore my bathrobe and it was open at the front; I quickly pulled it closed and noticed the tiny fresh cuts on my hands, little wounds that might have been inflicted by shattered glass. I looked at the window again and saw, as before, it was unbroken; nor were there glass shards on the floor or over the bed. Yet there were more cuts on my legs and when I lifted them I discovered there were still more gashes on the soles of my feet and dried blood smearing the skin. *How . . . ?*

It was a question I could not answer. There were so many questions I could not answer.

Another thought hit me and suddenly I was on my feet and limping into the sitting-room. The telephone – it had melted in my hands last night! Had that merely been in my imagination also? It had felt like ice, yet smoke had arisen from it and it had bubbled and turned liquid before my eyes. And there it was, still on the sideboard . . . a charred, ruined mess . . .

I stared at what was left of the receiver for a few moments before cautiously picking it up. The wood of the sideboard beneath was unmarked, undamaged, not even the faintest scorchmark to give evidence of what had occurred on its surface. Impossible, you might say. And impossible so it was. Nevertheless, all that remained of the telephone receiver was a melted shell over burnt-out wires. The curled cord leading from it was browned, but otherwise undamaged, and the instrument's base was unblemished. I stumbled over to the sofa and sank into its soft, worn cushions.

Visions of last night invaded my mind again, tumbling in like emptied litter, filling my head with grotesque images and obscene tableaux, leaving me trembling and whimpering. Had it been fantasy, or had it been real? The cuts in my flesh and the destroyed telephone told me one thing, the unbroken window and my own rational intellect told me another. I was confused and afraid, and when the memory of the face in the bathroom mirror came back to me, I felt sickened, for he was more monstrous than the monsters who had visited my home in the night, he was more loathsome than the graceless beings that had squirmed across my floor, because his imperfections were concealed beneath an exquisite exterior, the deviancy of his nature was disguised by a practised charm. The creatures were what they were – or what my mind made them to be: he was what he had made himself.

I knew of this man, this great star of the silver screen who had been dead for many decades. And I *knew* him, understood the cruelty of his narcissistic personality, for I had looked into those dark eyes and observed the very nature of his wretched soul. Here was a person so devoid of true compassion, so steeped in conceit and self-love, so oblivious to the love of others, that the Devil himself would be proud to make his acquaintance – if he hadn't already. I remembered reading just a few years ago of his untimely death in the late 1940s and how millions, most of them women, had mourned his passing. He had been adored and revered – even men had admired his roguish charm and athletic prowess – and subsequent rumours of his debauchery and miscreant behaviour put around by Hollywood scandal magazines had neither been proved nor sustained. To this day, his memory was cherished, yet last night I had truly looked through the glass darkly and recognized the blackness of his soul. I just didn't understand *how*. Nor *why*.

I forced myself to leave the sitting-room and go into the bathroom where, tentatively, expectantly, I looked into the mirror once more. The overhead light was still on, forgotten as I had stumbled back to my bed, and the reflection I saw in the glass was my own, my own imperfect features, my own crooked body. For the first time in my life it was a relief to see myself.

I sagged and gripped the sink for support. My head ached terribly and my spirit ... well, my spirit was as weary as my body. What delusions was I under? What chemical malfunction was still fucking with my brain? But the cuts, the telephone ...?

I lowered the toilet seat cover, sat down and began to think of what I was going to do.

30

Well, the first thing I did was to go out and buy a new telephone. How some kind of psychic force, manifestation, whatever it had been, could trash a machine, I had no idea, but the meltdown sat on my sideboard as evidence. I'd forgotten to plug my mobile phone in overnight – and who could blame me for that? – so the batteries were almost depleted. After eating a good breakfast (which was pretty amazing for me under any circumstances, but even more so because of my state of mind) I put the cellphone on charge and left the flat.

It was Sunday morning and most of the Brighton shops were closed, but I knew where I could pick up a new telephone easily enough and at half the price too. If I'd wanted a new camcorder, video machine, television, or even a dishwasher, all at low cost and never-been-used, then Theo the Thief (yes, even the police – *especially* the police – called him that) was the man to see. After telling me I didn't look so well, but without enquiring how I'd got that way (Theo neither liked asking questions nor answering them) he took me to one of his several lock-ups, a shabby-fronted garage on a nearby council estate that, when the up-and-over door was lifted, resembled a modern Aladdin's Cave, and allowed me to choose my own brand-new, still-in-the-box, telephone. It was the first time I'd ever knowingly bought stolen goods, but today I considered it an emergency: I needed to be on-line. Money changed hands and a leery Theo – he'd supplied me with information in the past for

James Herbert

small financial considerations, but never material goods – bade me good-day.

I drove home with the windows open wide, the salted breeze herding the remnants of fug from my head, almost clearing the ache there. It was a brilliantly sunny morning and as I turned into the crescent the whole panorama of sea and sky displayed itself to me. Sunlight coruscated off the waves, hurting my eye when I looked too intently, and distant sailing boats glided nonchalantly over the water's surface. People in shorts and T-shirts, in summer dresses and cut-away tops, made their weekend pilgrimage to the pebble beaches and broad lawns, the promenade and piers, and I was calmed by the sight. My anxiety became controlled, my stress governable; a sense of determination was rising within me.

There were no parking places outside my basement flat by now and I had to cruise around to the other side of the crescent's centre park before I found a free space. As small as it was, the park was full of gently undulating hillocks and I made my way through them on one of the concrete paths, filling my lungs with fresh air as I went, breathing in the very normality around me. My resolve strengthened: I wasn't sure of exactly what I was going to do, but I was determined to take command of what was happening, intent on discovering the reason for these visions. Were they warnings, portents, threats? I remembered the cries for help I had heard on the phone. None of it made sense. All I knew was that the last confrontation was with something quite evil.

'Hello, Dis.'

My gaze had been cast downwards, watching the path beneath my feet while not really seeing it at all. I raised my head at the sound of the greeting.

'Louise.'

She was sitting on a park bench, wearing a light green skirt and top, her large handbag balanced on her lap.

'I've been waiting for you,' she said. 'I tried to ring, but your phone seems to be out of order.'

I tapped the box I was carrying. 'New one,' I said. I wasn't sure whether I was glad to see her or not; all I truly cared about that morning was making contact with Constance and I wanted to get the new phone installed as quickly as possible in case she tried to ring me.

'Thank God you're all right.' She was studying me in her usual fashion, looking deep into my eye as though trying to read my inner thoughts.

I stood over her, curious, despite my haste. 'What makes you say that, Louise?'

'I had a terrible feeling about you.'

'Nothing new there, then.'

'This time it was far worse than ever before.'

'Even worse than the night Henry was killed?'

'Strangely, it was far worse. Last night I was overcome by an awful sense of dread and I knew it concerned you. I stayed awake just waiting for your call and when it didn't come, I decided I would phone you. Unfortunately, there's something wrong with your line and when I tried the operator I was told there was a fault and there was nothing they could do for the moment.'

'Did you ... did you see anything? I mean did you have any visions?'

'That was the other odd thing. I saw nothing at all, I just felt an overwhelming fear for you. Something blocked my thoughts towards you, Dis. I thought I might sense what was happening to you, but nothing came to me, only a terrible apprehension, and then, as I said, the dread. It was as if they were directing all their power towards you.'

'I've got to get home,' I said, disliking the effect she was having on me. I was beginning to feel debilitated again, my resolve waning.

She quickly stood. 'Let me come with you. You need me more than you know.'

I hesitated, but I didn't want to waste time arguing. 'Okay,' was all I said as I turned away and went loping off along the path towards the tenements on the other side of the road without checking to see if she was following.

One of my neighbours, a sprightly old cove whose apartment was directly above my own, was coming down the short flight of steps outside the big, ground floor entrance. His name was Sadler – I only knew him as *Mr* Sadler – a brisk but kindly septuagenarian who kept very much to himself and whose apparel was always as smart as his deportment. By his manner and his clipped tones I'd always assumed he had had a military background. Like I say, he kept very much to himself, but he never failed to bid me 'Good-day,' whenever we bumped into each other.

'Mr Dismas,' he hailed me. 'Good-day, sir.'

I was a little preoccupied, but I managed a wave.

'Everything all right, is it?' He stood on the second step, head slightly back so that he was looking down his nose at me, a quizzical expression on his clean-shaven face.

'Oh. Yeah,' I mumbled back. 'Fine.'

'Only, heard the rumpus last night. Bit of a party, was it?'

'Er, no. Bit of a nightmare, actually.'

Understanding dawned. 'Ah, that explains. Sleepwalk too, do you? Quite a bit of running about involved.'

'Yes. Sorry I disturbed you.'

'Quite all right, old boy. You can always knock on my door if you ever have upsets, you know. Better still, bang on the ceiling – be down like a shot.'

I stopped by the railings at the top of the basement steps. 'That's really kind of you, Mr Sadler. I'll remember next time I have a bad dream.'

'See that you do. S'what neighbours are for. Good-day again then.'

With that he stepped on to the pavement and marched towards the seafront for his daily constitutional.

By the time I was inserting the key into the front-door

lock below, I heard Louise's footsteps on the stone steps behind me. Earlier I had found the door locked as normal, no signs whatsoever of it having been forced open. The bedroom window hadn't been smashed, the front door hadn't been broken into, so what the hell had *really* happened last night? I led the way into the sitting-room, already tearing open the box I carried as I entered. Louise Broomfield took a seat and watched me as I ripped away the wrappings.

'What happened to your old one, Dis?' she asked.

'Take a look for yourself,' I replied, nodding towards the sideboard.

Her eyes widened when she saw the melted plastic.

The newly purchased machine was a sleek black job and I took it over to the telephone point and electric plug by the sideboard, quickly pulling out the old connections and replacing them with the new. 'I need to call someone, Louise, so will you give me a minute?'

She stood immediately, taking the hint. 'Of course. Let me make some tea for us both. Oh, it's coffee for you, isn't it?'

'Yeah. Jar's in the top cupboard, not in the lower one,' I emphasized, already tapping in the number to PERFECT REST. I wanted to be alone when I spoke to Constance.

The phone rang quite a few times before it was answered. The voice at the other end was unfamiliar at first.

'PERFECT REST, can I help you?'

'I'd like to speak to Constance Bell, please.' I kept my voice calm, even though I wanted to scream down the line.

Did I catch a hint of caution in the voice now? 'Who's calling, please?'

'Nick Dismas.' I gritted my teeth – I should have lied.

'If you'll just wait a moment.'

I should have faked a name, maybe even disguised my voice. I recognized the person at the other end now: it was the senior nurse and chief administrator, Rachel Fletcher, the tall, faded redhead who had been so terse with both myself and Constance on my first visit to the home. Obviously, Sunday was the normal receptionist's day off. I waited at least three minutes before the nurse came back to me.

'Ms Bell isn't here.' It was curt, the end of the matter.

'She wasn't there yesterday,' I pointed out.

'No, Mr Dismas. And nor is she today.'

'Can you tell me where she is?'

'I'm afraid I can't.' She didn't even bother to enquire what my business was with her care-supervisor. She'd been briefed, I knew it.

'So will she be there tomorrow?'

'Ms Bell will be away for some time.'

I *really* didn't like the sound of that. 'Then can I speak to Dr Wisbeech?'

'Dr Wisbeech is unavailable.'

'When will he *be* available?'

'I don't have that information. Would you like to leave a message?' Her voice was still flat, almost a monotone, but she couldn't hide the irritation.

Sure, like 'Fuck you,' I thought, but, 'No thanks,' I said. Before I rang off though, I decided on another tack. 'Wait, there is a message you can give the doctor.'

'Yes?' A cold, resigned response.

'You can tell him I'm coming over there and that I won't leave until I've spoken to Constance Bell.'

'But I've already told you, Ms Bell isn't here.'

'Just give your boss the message.'

'Would you hold the line, Mr Dismas?' The irritation was even more obvious and my name was said with just a little contempt.

There was silence for a while and I waited impatiently, my coldness easily matching that of the nurse's. Finally, I heard a couple of clicks as I was transferred, and then a new voice came on, this one cool, urbane, an indication of the person who spoke.

'What seems to be the problem, Mr Dismas?' Wisbeech said.

'The problem, Doctor, is that I want to speak to Constance Bell and all I'm getting from your people is the runaround.'

'I'm not sure I understand what you mean. Wasn't it explained to you that Constance isn't with us today?'

I bit on my lip to contain my anger. Condescending bastard. 'Yes, I was told, but I'd like to know where Constance is and why I can't be put in touch with her.'

'I'm afraid she has been rather unwell for the past two days. Ever since her visit to see you, in fact. Constance is a sensitive soul and obviously her health is delicate; what she witnessed at your offices would have traumatized the strongest of us.'

'She told you about the murder of my colleague?'

'Mr Dismas, it's all over the newspapers, particularly in today's more sensational Sundays.'

I hadn't seen the papers that day, nor did I want to: I was only too relieved that the Press now understood I wasn't a suspect and had left me alone.

'I had to read about it myself,' Wisbeech went on, 'on the day after it happened. Only at my insistence did she explain to me the circumstances of her absence the night before. Poor thing was extremely upset.' His voice had taken on an accusatory tone.

'I want to talk to her.'

'No, Mr Dismas, I don't think that would be at all appropriate. I've already mentioned Constance's frailty, both physically and mentally, and it seems to me that her association with you, as brief as it was . . .' I noted the *was*! . . . 'has led to a deterioration in her health. I am her guardian, Mr Dismas, and my considered opinion is that you should not see her again.'

'You can't blame me for what happened.' My anger was becoming harder to control.

'Perhaps not. But as I said, I am responsible for Constance and I will do my utmost to spare her any more anxiety than her condition forces her to bear. Surely you, of all people, must empathize with the unhappiness her disability causes. Why, indeed, should she have to cope with any more distress, particularly when it can so easily be avoided?'

'Because that's how life is. People like us want to be treated like everybody else, and when shit happens we can take it like anybody else.'

'I think that murder, mutilation, and boy prostitutes constitutes a trifle more than, as you so vulgarly put it, "shit" happening. And you see, I am not only duty-bound to take care of Constance because both her late parents were great friends of mine, but because she is my ward, I'm also legally bound. My role is to guide and protect her, to look after her interests. Forgive me for saying so, Mr Dismas, but you are not in her best interest.'

'And your brother? Is he some kind of father-figure to her, too?' I didn't know why I'd said it – anger, frustration, a need to rattle his cage? Or was it that natural instinct of mine, my old pal, the snooper's nose? Could be I just wanted to stir the waters.

'My brother?' I heard Wisbeech say, a new uncertainty in his voice. 'What has my brother got to do with this?'

'He shares the business with you, doesn't he?' I came back quickly, but with no idea of where it was going.

'That's hardly any concern of yours.' The iciness that came down the line should have frozen my ear. He became abrupt. 'I think I've spent enough time talking to you, Mr Dismas.' Funny how he now made the 'Mr' sound like an insult. 'I've plenty of important matters to deal with, so I will bid you goodbye.'

'Wait a minute. When can I see Constance again?'

'Haven't you been listening? You cannot, you will not. It's as simple as that.'

'But – '

It was pointless: the connection had been broken. I replaced the receiver to find Louise standing in the doorway holding a tray bearing two steaming mugs.

'Who was that, Dis?' she asked, remaining in the doorway.

I let out a weary breath. 'Dr Leonard K. Wisbeech, eminent physician, proprietor of a luxury nursing home, and God made incarnate.'

'He's upset you.'

I started to laugh. I couldn't help it. Perhaps some of last night's hysteria had returned, but I couldn't help but see the funny side of her remark. After all I'd been through that week, all the fear, pain, humiliation, and anxiety I'd suffered, and the clairvoyant thought I had been upset by a phone call. A tear rolled from my eye with the hilarity of it and Louise looked even more concerned than before.

The laughter didn't last long though. Thank *God* it didn't last long – Louise might have thought I'd finally flipped; in fact, *I* might have thought I'd finally flipped. No, I wiped my eye with the knuckle of my hand, drew in some deep breaths, and took one of the mugs from the tray. I sank into the sofa. It was time for more thought.

31

'Over there, look.'

I had brought the Ford to a halt along the busy, wide Windsor Road, drivers honking their horns as they manoeuvred around me, and was pointing across the great river that ran parallel to the road, towards the far bank.

Louise squinted her pale green eyes and followed the direction I had indicated. 'That white building?' she said. 'Is that the home?'

'I'm pretty sure it is,' I replied, engaging gear again and checking my side mirror. When there was a break in the traffic, I pulled out, heading west, towards the old town of Windsor itself. 'I'll turn round where I can and get us on the other side of the road. We'll get a better view over there if I can find a good vantage point.'

I had wanted to get a look at the rear of PERFECT REST and since I knew it backed on to the river, I figured the best place would be from the opposite bank. One of the golden rules regarding surveillance is to know your ground and I was applying it now.

Louise had stayed with me all day and although I'd slept some of that time, we had gone over every aspect of the last few days. I'd even told her about the man I kept seeing in the mirror, the Thirties/Forties film star whose reflection seemed to be taking great delight in haunting me. It rendered the clairvoyant more thoughtful, more enigmatic, than ever, but she provided me with no answers. After my short sleep that Sunday afternoon – it wasn't just last night that was catching up on me, but the events of the whole week – I told her of my surveillance plans for the evening, the one chance that might enable me to see Constance again (not for one moment did I believe the story that she had gone away – I was certain Constance would have contacted me first, or from wherever she had gone), and Louise had insisted upon accompanying me. These 'visions', 'hallucinations', whatever I cared to call them – *she* said they were 'messages' – were happening with more frequency and greater strength, and I needed her to be present next time; that way she could help me cope and perhaps even guide these apparently lost spirits towards their own peace. Besides, she too was concerned for Constance Bell for, during my incarceration at the police station a few nights ago, the two of them had comforted each other and, it seemed, formed an attachment. I could quite understand why the clairvoyant felt protective of Constance. Louise promised she would remain passive, wouldn't interfere in any way unless she felt I was under psychic attack, in which case she would bring all her powers as a 'sensitive' into play to help me. She was determined and hard to argue with, so reluctantly I had agreed. The deal was, though, that she was strictly an observer and if the surveillance that evening turned into something a little more – I did not expand on this – she was to remain in the car and take no part whatsoever.

Louise was silent in the passenger seat next to me as I drove on towards Windsor, and I sneaked a quick glance at her. Her eyes were closed and her brow was furrowed with concentration. I understood what she was trying to do.

'Anything?' I asked, no longer quite so doubtful of her abilities.

'We're too far away. Perhaps it is just a house, Dis.'

We soon reached a roundabout and I did the full circuit, heading back in the direction from which we had come. It wasn't long before the white building on the riverbank came into view again and I slowed the Ford to cruising speed. As we passed it, both of us craned our necks, peering across the broad, swift-flowing Thames to check out the nursing home with its red-slate roof and multitude of chimney stacks. It stood close to a sharp bend in the river, almost on the bank's apex at that point, with woodland and gardens around its other sides. It looked a perfect haven.

Here, the road we were on did not follow the river, but continued a straight course and I noticed a pleasure area filled the land space between the thoroughfare and the Thames itself. When we reached the entrance, I turned in, driving down to a parking area which took us even closer to the river bend. It afforded us with a better view of PERFECT REST, although much of it was obscured by trees, and now I observed there was something odd about its structure.

I reached across my companion and delved into the glove compartment, bringing out a compact pair of binoculars, one of the invaluable tools of my trade. I focused them on the bank opposite and let out a murmur of surprise.

'What is it, Dis?'

'Take a look for yourself.' I handed Louise the binoculars which, although small, were quite powerful.

'I can't see anything diff . . . oh yes, I see what you mean. It's very deceptive, isn't it?'

From the road directly opposite, the nursing home appeared to have a flat rear façade; however, from this angle, we could make out another wing projecting from the back of the building at a forty-five degree angle. So odd was the structure that it occurred to me that it had been added later. The additional wing was in perfect keeping with the main building itself, but it was angled like the broken stem of a T, and from a distance and face on, you would never have known it was there. The windows on the end facing us loomed directly over the river itself. The architecture was of such cunning design that I wondered if the wing was meant to go unnoticed from across the broad river.

'Didn't you see this part of the house when you visited

Hildegarde Vogel?' Louise asked, still watching the place through the binoculars.

'I didn't even know it was there. The old lady's room overlooked the front gardens and drive.'

'Do you think that perhaps it's the medical wing itself, for operations or intensive care?'

I shrugged. 'It could even be staff quarters, who knows? It might be where I'll find Constance.'

'You're still determined to get inside and look for her?'

'I can't shake it from my head that she's in trouble. That dream last night just seemed too real to be ignored. Okay, maybe it shouldn't have been taken literally, but there had to be a reason for it. Christ, you, yourself, convinced me of that.'

'How will you get inside? You can't just walk in.'

'No, I don't think our Dr Wisbeech would be prepared to give me a guided tour. I'll find a way, though.'

'I really don't like this, Dis. I can't rid myself of this feeling that you're in danger.' She became earnest, tugging at my arm. 'Why not just inform the police and let them deal with it?'

'We went through all this earlier. What exactly do I tell them? How would I convince them there's something going on inside that place when I can't even be sure myself?'

'But you *are* sure, aren't you?'

'That's irrelevant. The police would need evidence if they were to investigate the home and unfortunately, my word alone isn't enough. Can you imagine them applying for a search warrant just because a private investigator has been having bad dreams lately?'

'You could tell them you're concerned for Constance, that she's gone missing.'

'Come on, Louise, you know that still wouldn't be good enough. What proof do I have that she is missing? I've only known her a couple of days, so what the hell do I know of her way of life? Maybe she has gone away for a rest, maybe she needs a break after what she witnessed the other night. And Wisbeech *is* her guardian. He could tell the police he simply doesn't like my influence on her, so he won't allow her to see me.'

'I'm just so afraid.'

'You're not going anywhere near the place.'

'I'm not afraid for myself.'

'I'm only going to snoop around. It's my line of work, I've done it a thousand times. I probably won't even get inside.'

I turned the car around and we headed out of the pleasure ground, turning left into the main road. It took a little while to get to the northern side of the Thames and I passed by the unmarked lane leading to PERFECT REST, even though I'd found it twice before; I drove back when I realized we had gone too far, and finally spotted the lane on my left. By the time the Ford was bumping along the lonely, rutted track, evening was drawing in.

When we got as far as the old derelict house I pulled in, taking the car round to the rear where it would be concealed from any other passing vehicles and anyone out for a stroll. Louise looked questioningly at me.

'Constance told me she usually takes a walk along the lane, mostly in the evening,' I explained. 'Maybe she'll do the same now, *if* Wisbeech allows her out of the home.'

'You intend to watch from this house?'

I nodded. 'Might even be able to see PERFECT REST from the top windows.'

The clairvoyant scrutinized the decrepit building for a few moments, taking in the stained, worn brickwork, the ground-floor windows, so filthy with dust and grime they were impenetrable, the battered back door, upper half consisting of two dirty glass panels, and looking as though it hadn't been opened in years.

'How will you get in?' she said, bemused.

I smiled grimly. 'Trust me. I've broken into tighter places than this.'

As I made to leave the car, Louise stopped me with another question. 'If Constance is able to leave the home of her own free will, wouldn't she have found a phone box and rung you?'

I had been asking myself the same question since leaving the flat in Brighton after waiting in vain all afternoon for a call from Constance and frankly, it was a question to which I didn't *want* an answer. My dread was that she was physically being prevented from making contact with me; either that, or she, herself, no longer wanted anything to do with me, murder and police interrogation not the kind of thing she wanted to be involved in. Whatever, I was playing this by ear, hoping somehow it would all pan out. What else could I do?

'Maybe her guardian has persuaded her to have nothing more to do with me,' I ventured, hand resting on the door-lock. 'After all, what does she really know about me except that on our first date I introduced her to a mutilated corpse?'

'You gave me the impression that your feelings for each other went somewhat deeper.'

'Maybe I've been kidding myself.'

'I don't think so, Dis. In the brief time I had to get to know her, and under awful circumstances, I saw the way she looked at you and how frightened she was for you when you went up to your office alone. And remember, I had a lot of time to talk to her when you were being questioned by the police. She cares for you, Dis.'

It was what I wanted to hear, but this wasn't the moment. I stared blankly around the dilapidated yard with its piles of rubble and broken timber, grass growing between the cracks in the paving, moss on the stone itself, old flowerbeds completely overgrown with weeds. It looked as dispirited as I had felt in the early hours of that morning. My mood had changed though and it was because I had decided to act rather than *re*act. Now I was making my own agenda.

'I'm going to watch the lane from inside the house for a

while, take note of who goes in and who goes out of PERFECT REST. There's no other route, so whoever visits or leaves has to pass by. When I've done that for long enough, and if Constance still hasn't put in an appearance, I'm going down to the home itself. If she's there, I'll find her.'

Pushing the car door open, I stepped out into the yard and made my way over to the building's back door. I heard Louise following me.

The weather-battered and dirt-grimed door rattled in its frame when I tried the chipped, black-painted doorknob, but it held firm against my pressure. I tried to look inside through the glass panels, but they were too grubby and the interior was too dark. Then I attempted to lift the windows on either side, but they were stuck solid.

'How will you get in?' Louise was nervously glancing around like a novice burglar.

'No problem,' I replied.

I feared the lock would be rusted inside, making picking it difficult; worse, the door might be bolted on the inside. Breaking glass was a method I always tried to avoid, because it has a high-frequency sound, which meant it would travel a long way. Breaking glass also has a high-alarm factor – more people are alerted by its sharp resonance than by muted bangs and thumps. Although we were in an isolated area, I didn't want to take any chances that a passer-by or anyone living across the fields might hear. I gave the door a hefty kick just below the lock and it burst inwards immediately.

'Not exactly the high-tech approach,' I told Louise, 'but it usually works.'

Before entering, I returned to the car and opened the boot, taking out a canvas holdall. Inside was my basic OBS (observation) gear, which included thermos flask of hot coffee, binoculars (larger and more powerful that those I kept in the glove compartment), small cassette recorder, large torch, notepad, two cameras, and even a couple of chocolate bars. All or none of it might be useful, depending on how long the shift was and the activity I might observe, the exception being the torch, which always came in handy, sometimes even as a weapon of defence (it was a long black Mag-lite, as sturdy as a truncheon). I delved into the bag for the torch and went back to the open door, switching on and shining the light into the shadowy interior.

The back door opened into what appeared to be a near-gutted kitchen, only a dingy stainless steel sink remaining, the two taps over it rusted, cupboard doors of units around the walls missing. There was no cooker, washing machine, or anything at all to indicate that the place had been inhabited in recent years and I suspected that the building belonged to the owners of PERFECT REST. Why else would a largish detached dwelling which, because of its location close to the Thames and a half-hour's journey from the city, could easily be turned into a desirable property with a price tag to match be kept empty? Empty, of course, meant no one could observe the comings and goings along the rough lane.

'Louise, you'd be more comfortable waiting in the car,' I said before stepping over the doorstep.

'I'd rather stay with you,' she replied in a non-argument mode.

''S up to you.' I moved inside.

Our footsteps had a hollowness to them, the haunting kind you get in unoccupied buildings with no furnishing to absorb the sounds. Segments of faded wallpaper hung like rotting leaves in the hallway, while mould spread from floor to ceiling in some of the downstairs rooms. Ahead, the front door was bolted, the bolts themselves rusted through, and the windows of the rooms on either side were heavily boarded. The odour of damp and rot was everywhere and when we reached the stairs I warned the clairvoyant to mind how she trod in case the stairboards were weakened. Although they creaked and sagged alarmingly in places, we were able to reach the upper floor easily enough. I made straight for a room at the front, which I knew must overlook the lane, and although the curtainless windows there were grimy, they provided a good vantage point for surveillance. In fact, their dirt would make it more difficult for me to be seen from outside. There were no chairs, no furniture of any kind, and I advised Louise to sit on the floor.

'We could be in for a long wait,' I told her, using the binoculars to survey the area around the house. I scanned the lane, directing the glasses towards the big manor house at the end: disappointingly, I could see only the upper windows and rooftops of PERFECT REST above the trees. I wondered if Constance was there and now that I was so close, I was even more troubled.

For the moment though, while it was still fairly light, dusk only just beginning to settle in, there was nothing much I could do. I could only wait. And watch.

Nothing happened until at 8.46pm (out of habit I checked my watch) a large blue Transit van went by, the bumpy ruggedness of the lane's surface and the fact that the vehicle wasn't using its headlight restricting it to a low speed. I watched its progress until it disappeared round a bend, then wrote its registration number in my notebook. The Transit had been wide enough to take up most of the lane and I assumed it was carrying equipment or foodstuffs to the home; but there were no signs on its sides, nothing at all to indicate what it might contain. I thought that Sunday night was a strange time for a delivery, but I had no idea of how nursing homes operated; it might be standard practice, for all I knew.

It was twenty minutes or so later that Louise began to get agitated.

I'd been leaning against the dusty, paint-chipped window-frame, binoculars hanging against my chest, hands in my pockets, my gaze idly roaming the flat fields opposite and woodlands beyond, when I had heard the clairvoyant gasp.

I glanced towards her shadowy form sitting propped up against a wall on the other side of the room. 'You okay, Louise?'

She gave another short gasp and I hurried over to her, kneeling so that I could get a look at her face. Her head was raised upwards, as if she were watching the ceiling; but her eyes were closed. I placed a comforting hand on her shoulder.

'They're very close,' she said quietly. 'I can feel them . . . so close. They're upset . . . Oh dear God, they're afraid . . .'

I moved my face nearer to hers. 'Who, Louise? Who d'you mean?'

'You know who they are. They've come to us both before.'

I felt nothing. I heard no sounds, saw no visions.

Louise groaned. 'So afraid. We have to help them.'

In frustration, I said, 'Yeah, so tell me how.'

'They aren't far away, Dis. They're in that place, inside the home. Their presence is so strong, yet they're so confused. Oh . . . Dis . . . they're desperately afraid.' She turned her head from side to side and even in the dimness of the room I could see her anguish.

'Can you talk to them, Louise? With your mind, can you make contact with them, find out exactly where they are?'

'No. It has to come from them. They have to come to us.'

'Then why don't they? What's preventing them this time?' A week ago I would have figured that mental telepathy was merely an interesting concept, but now here I was fully expecting a psychic response. Was the stress getting to me, or was I finally waking up to the possibilities of other dimensions – other realities?

'I don't know,' Louise replied, still shaking her head as if suffering physical pain. 'It's all so . . . so uncertain, so vague. I don't think they are trying to make contact with us. No, I think I'm just picking up their distress.'

'Because we're so close?'

'Normally, distance wouldn't be a factor, but in this case, I think it is.'

'I don't sense anything, Louise. Not a thing.'

'It's because I am seeking them – they are not trying to reach us. You don't have the gift, but it's something I've lived with all my life.' She became still again and her eyes opened. 'I'm sure they sense me too, but they're unable to respond. They're suffering and I can't tell how.'

I heard her sniff and felt her shoulders trembling. 'It's all right, Louise, take it easy.' I moved my hand to her cheek and gently stroked it, talking softly in an attempt to calm her. 'Come on now, take some deep breaths and get control of your thoughts. Blank them out if you have to.'

She seemed to be doing as I asked. Her breathing became deeper, taking on an easier rhythm. The trembling began to subside. 'They're fading,' she said after a short while. 'The feeling . . . the fear . . . is leaving me.'

'Good. Try and relax.'

With a jerk that startled me, she grabbed my wrist. 'I thought the danger was to you.' There was dismay in her voice. 'Every time they came to us, I believed they were trying to warn you. But now I think they are in peril. Something terrible is happening to them, that's why they sought our . . . no, they sought *your* . . . help. I must go to them.'

The clairvoyant made as if to rise, but I forced her down again. 'You're not going anywhere, Louise. This is up to me.'

I couldn't explain it, but a feeling of urgency had swept over me. Perhaps it was because of what Louise had just told me, that the voices I had been hearing, *sensing*, were cries for help. It didn't explain last night, the warped creatures that had squirmed and writhed over my bedroom floor, indulging in depravities that had sickened me to the core, it didn't explain why I had observed Constance amongst them and had stood witness to her defilement; no, none of this could be explained by rational thought, but by now I was beyond logic.

When I stood, the clairvoyant held on to my hand. 'It's time I had a look around PERFECT REST,' I told her.

The pupils of her pale eyes were large and black in the bad light and I felt I could see into her very soul. There was both fear and concern there, but also a glimmer of hope.

'Find Constance,' Louise pleaded.

'I intend to,' I replied.

32

When I reached the tall entrance gates to PERFECT REST, they were shut tight as usual. I attempted to part them in the hope they would give enough for me to slip through. No joy though: they wouldn't budge.

By now the night skies had darkened considerably, although the bright moon did its best to compensate each time it escaped a cloud. I had been cautious as I'd made my way down the rough lane, ready to duck behind the cover of a tree or bush should I hear anything or spot approaching headlights. In the far distance, I could see a few house lights, as remote as stars and somehow emphasizing the loneliness of my surrounds; every so often an aircraft droned overhead, while higher and far away to the east even more circled air space nearer to the airport, their tiny lights, white and red, like cruising meteors. I pictured Louise Broomfield, left behind in the old forsaken house, watching the lane from the window and sending out thoughts of comfort to those she believed were under threat.

I examined the gates again, then held them like the bars of a cell as I peered through at the grounds. To the left was a great dark cavern, the track that branched off from the main drive, presumably for access to the side or rear of PERFECT REST. It was the way I had decided to go once inside.

The gates were high and would be difficult for me to climb; an alternative was to skirt the boundary wall and find a suitable way over, perhaps using a nearby tree's branches to clamber up. Then again, there might be an even easier way into the estate.

Walking to the gate-supporting pillar to the right of the entrance, I stuck my arm through the rails and ran my hand up and down the back of it. Finding nothing, I moved to the other side of the gates and repeated the manoeuvre, this time using my right hand and pressing my cheek against iron. I found what I was searching for set in the brick wall beside the back of the left-hand pillar. It always made me chuckle how certain security-conscious people used big, strong gates to protect their property, yet insisted on having a back-up opening switch or button out of sight, but within easy reach, in case the batteries of their remote control unit were depleted, or the unit itself lost or forgotten. I pressed the 'secret' button and stood away from the gates as they swivelled inwards.

As I slid through the widening gap, I prayed there was no alarm system from the entrance to the main building itself to warn of any unauthorized opening.

With high branches overlapping overhead it was pitch black inside the natural tunnel and I took my other torch, the slim pocket-sized Mag-lite, from my jacket. I kept the beam low, aiming it at the ground, ready to turn it off again the moment I heard anyone or anything coming. Very carefully, I made my way along the enclosed track, noting the ruts obviously caused by vehicles passing through and, as before, I guessed this was the discreet way to the tradesmen's entrance. It took a full five minutes to reach the end of the tunnel and I had switched off the torch well before I emerged. I hid behind a stout oak tree to survey the rest of the route.

The track had swept to the right under the cover of the trees and it journeyed on before me, sweeping around the side of the home as if making for the river beyond. I could see part of the river's bend, the waters deep and sullenly murky, glinting silver only when the moon made one of its now infrequent appearances; on the opposite bank car lights sped along the road that lay beyond the darkened pleasure ground where I had parked earlier, and it all seemed a long way off, not part of this world where I now loitered. A mass of starlings suddenly made their last flight before bedding down for the night, circling the estate with sharp cries and flurrying wings that reminded me of the visions. They soon settled back into the trees, leaving an unnerving stillness behind.

When a new light appeared at one of the home's upper windows, I jerked my head back out of sight, afraid of being seen despite covering shadows. A figure appeared briefly, then just as quickly vanished. Many other windows were lit up, casting their glows on the lawns below, and I imagined all the old and sick folk inside, making ready for bed, unaware there was an intruder in their gardens. Fortunately, the estate seemed to have no ground illuminations, making it easier for me to approach the building itself.

Directly opposite where I hid, an unlit conservatory, functional rather than elegant in design, projected from the end of the building. Its lower structure was of brickwork, which would give me cover if I could reach it unobserved.

Without further thought, I scooted towards it, my limp beginning to assert itself after the long walk from the derelict house. I was only half-way across the open space when the conservatory lit up in a blaze of light.

I dropped to the ground immediately and lay there, head and body pressed into the grass, waiting for the alarm to go up. But nothing happened. Warily, I raised my head and looked towards the long windows ahead. I was in the light's glare, but unless whoever was inside the conservatory walked over to the windows and looked out, I could not be seen because of the low, brick base. Raising my head a little higher I saw a woman dressed in the familiar pale blue uniform of the home's nursing staff inside; she appeared to be tidying cushions and folding newspapers, shifting chairs, all the while smoking a cigarette. I watched as a man in a blue, short-sleeved tunic entered behind her, recognizing him as the orderly I'd encountered on my first visit to PERFECT REST. He snatched the cigarette from the nurse's mouth, took a drag himself and exhaled smoke into her face. He then dropped the butt on the floor, and from his movement, I could tell he was stubbing it out with his foot. Sharp words were exchanged, but I couldn't make out what was said. The man – I remembered his name was Bruce – turned away and left the conservatory, still shouting over his shoulder at the nurse. She slyly gave his departing back the finger, then bent down out of sight, presumably picking up the squashed cigarette butt. She appeared again and walked to the door, picking up something else there – I saw a bin in her hand when she stood erect – dropped the butt into it, then left the conservatory, switching off the lights as she went.

I made use of the sudden darkness by scurrying over to the wall and squatting beneath it. There I caught my breath and planned my next move.

Which was simple enough. From across the river earlier and through the binoculars, I had noticed an outside fire escape tucked away between the broken-T annexe and the main part of the building, and such a staircase would have to have safety doors on each level. The older types of these exits generally had a pushbar to open them from the inside, and these were fairly easy to unlock from the outside with the help of thin wire that could be pushed between door and frame, looped around the iron bar, which was then jerked downwards. I began to crawl along the conservatory wall towards its corner.

When I reached it, I carefully peeked round and found myself looking into the curiously-shaped area between the main section and its angled wing. Outside a large ground-level double door was the blue, unmarked Transit van that had driven past the old abandoned house earlier. The drive,

I noticed, led directly to this extraneous wing rather than to the back of the main building. The van's rear doors were open, although there didn't appear to be anyone nearby. I squinted my eye, searching the gloomy space created between structures, looking for the fire escape.

There it was, on my side of the building, a black, metal stairway leading to the top floor. Although there were exit doors at ground level and first floor, I figured the highest would be the simplest one to break into without being discovered, particularly if the Transit opposite was in the process of being unloaded. Before I moved towards the fire escape, something else struck me as odd about the extra wing. The wall facing me had no windows; in fact, apart from the wide entrance where the Transit was parked, it was totally blank. From what I'd observed from across the river, the other side of the wing had a normal complement of windows for a structure of that size, so why none here? I could only guess that whatever went on in there was not meant to be seen by 'guests' whose rooms overlooked this section. Which, of course, begged another question: what the hell was it that was so covert?

Checking that all was clear, I eased myself around the corner of the building and limped towards the bottom of the fire escape, ducking below ground-floor windows, pausing only to try a door that I came across. It was locked and its position was too exposed for me to spend time opening it; better to stick to the original plan and use the exit door at the top of the metal staircase. I heard voices from inside the house as I moved on, other sounds from a radio or television played too loud – old people always had their sets too loud – and music coming from somewhere deeper inside the building. Just as I reached the staircase, I heard noises to my left, coming from the open entrance opposite.

Quickly I dodged into the gap between fire escape and wall, the cover not ideal, but the shadows helping. Crouching low, I stole a look between the iron stair-rails and saw a man in T-shirt and jeans emerge from the entrance and climb into the back of the Transit. Muffled scrapings, things being moved, followed before he stepped out again and turned to retrieve something he had shifted to the tail end of the big van. The object appeared to be a heavy box of some kind, which he carried back through the entrance; a pause inside to lay the box down and then he closed the double doors behind him, darkening the area between us even more. Immediately, I swung round on to the fire escape and began to climb, treading as quietly as I could but swiftly, afraid the doors might open once more, the light from inside exposing me.

Within moments I was on the first turn, testing the door there just in case it had been left open. As expected, it wouldn't budge, so I hurried onwards, climbing as swiftly and noiselessly as I could. I crawled over the top step, not from tiredness (although the weakened muscles in my right leg were complaining) but as a precaution, and rested on the small landing beside another exit door. Steadying my breathing, I peered over the edge and looked down into the odd-shaped courtyard below: all was quiet, apart from normal muted sounds of activity inside the home itself, and all was still. Satisfied, I turned to the fire escape door behind me.

It was painted black, like those on the first and ground floors, and I sighed when I noticed it was fitted with a conventional lock and handle rather than an interior pushbar. I moved closer to examine it, the moon coming to my aid by making a timely appearance. It was a mortice lever lock, probably only two levers, certainly no more than three. Easy enough to pick.

I removed a small pouch from my jacket pocket and selected a thin metal pick and a little sprung-metal tension wrench from inside. Kneeling before the door, I inserted the wrench into the keyhole and exerted pressure on the lock bolt, following this with the pick itself. Maintaining the pressure with the wrench, I *visualized* the levers and bolts inside the lock, *pictured* the tools working on them, and *felt* the strain of metal on metal. I was no student of Zen, but I think its proponents would have been proud of me.

In less than two minutes I had raised the levers and racked in the bolt. The door was open.

Returning the tools to the pouch, the pouch to my pocket, I gently pushed against the door until there was a gap wide enough to see through. I listened also, but all that came to me were the same muffled sounds I had heard earlier; those and that awful pervasive odour that seems always to linger in old people's homes. I eased my way in, carefully looking around, still listening, and closed the door behind me.

The long corridor I found myself in was quite dingy, its main source of light coming from two open doorways further along and a wall light where there was a turn, presumably towards a staircase. I guessed that this top floor was mainly staff quarters, for the décor and what pieces of furniture I could see were plainly functional. It disturbed me not to find hanging nearby, if not in the lock itself, any visible key to the exit I'd just broken through, and I wondered how the nurses and carers would cope if they became trapped up here by fire. Even if each staff member had their own personal key, the absence of one in or close to the door went against all safety regulations. Maybe Dr Wisbeech didn't like the idea of anyone casually wandering out on to the fire escape.

The sound of voices came to me from the turn at the end of the corridor and it was growing louder, coming closer. I realized I would have to move fast if I wasn't to be caught out in the open. I made off in the opposite direction to the voices and managed to duck into another corridor on the right just before figures appeared from around the corner. I leaned against the wall, heart thumping, wondering if I'd been seen.

The voices drew even closer, but there were no shouts of alarm or running footsteps. I quickly looked about me for a means of escape should it be necessary. Behind me was a staircase leading to the lower floor and possibly towards the home's main hallway; opposite were a couple of plain doors, probably to storage cupboards or bathrooms.

Fortunately, it wasn't a problem, for the footsteps stopped, although the conversation went on. It was two women talking, presumably nurses or care-supervisors, and they gabbled on for another few minutes until I heard a door close, then footsteps of one person continuing towards my hiding place. I slid back along the wall, ready to bolt down the staircase, not trusting the doors opposite to be unlocked. I was lucky again though: the footsteps stopped, a door opened and closed, and then there was silence apart from the usual faraway sounds in the nursing home.

I went back to the main corridor and checked it was clear in both directions. That was when I noticed for the first time the oddly-angled vestibule opposite the side corridor. Inside it was a cushioned chair and a long-legged wall-table beneath a framed picture, the kind of oddments you might find in the hall lobby of a slightly low-grade hotel. Its rear wall was diagonal rather than straight (which was why the space was odd-shaped), a large, flat double door set into it, and I realized this must be the entrance to the top floor of the annexe.

Making sure the coast was still clear, I crossed over to get a closer look at the doors. There were no handles on this side and one glance at the lock told me it was the cylinder type which, depending on the number of cylinders involved, can sometimes be the devil to bypass. Normally, I loved the challenge – I'd learned to pick locks many years ago, taught by one of Brighton's master burglars, aware it was a knack that could serve me well in my future years as a PI (and I'd been right), and it was an art at which I'd kept practised, purchasing all manner of locks, taking them apart and reassembling them so that I fully understood their workings, obtaining and even modifying the best tools for particular types, studying the surest techniques in manuals or taking advice from my pal the burglar, spending tedious hours on all varieties and variations, at first using strong rubber bands as tension grips until becoming fast enough to maintain my own pressure. Eventually, the obsession had become a hobby, but one, I'm proud to say, I was particularly good at.

I surmised by the appearance of the lock that there were only two cylinders inside, the inner one of which had to be turned to retract the bolt holding the door closed; to do that I had to raise the different-length spring-loaded pins that prevented rotation to a universal sheer level. I was hoping there were no more than five pins within, but knew that if this was a *serious* lock, then there might be as many as seven and all would have to be lifted twice.

As before, I inserted the small tension wrench into the keyhole and applied easy pressure against the first inner cylinder, turning it in the necessary direction. Holding the tension, I pushed in the pick itself and found the furthest pin; a little jiggle and it moved upwards. That achieved, I had to go all the way down the line, raising each pin until the bolt sprang back, a painstaking process that my nervousness did not help. I was on the third pin when I heard voices again.

They were some distance off, but growing louder with each moment, coming along the main corridor from the end stairway. I broke out into a sweat, aware that I could not dash back to my previous cover with its subsidiary staircase without being seen. I worked on the lock more quickly, praying that whoever was coming might turn off into one of the rooms along the way, forcing myself to remain calm, fingers beginning to tremble. I reached what I felt sure was the last pin – the *seventh* (it *was* a serious lock), and cursed when it stuck because I'd moved it too hastily.

Oh Christ. The voices were becoming louder, the footsteps closer, and I had to go through the whole process again! Taking a deep breath and steadying my hands, I went back to the first pin. Okay, pressure on the wrench again, tickle metal and raise that pin just a little. Done. Good. Next one. Quick. But easy, take it easy. Done. Good. Next.

And so I progressed down the line, moving determinedly, each new pin doing exactly what was required of it, the voices and footsteps drawing nearer all the while. I knew, I just *knew*, they were not going to turn away, that they were going to walk right by this niche in the corridor, but I couldn't work any faster. Without removing the implements, I ducked my head and wiped sweat that was threatening to trickle from my brow into my eye on my sleeve. I nearly lost it again on the last one and had to make myself ease the pressure. Slowly, smoothly, gently. *Feel* the metal against metal, *think* of the pin and pick as an extension of your own arm. The pin joined the sheer line and I left it there. Now back to the first one again – the whole process had to be repeated, the pins finely tuned. A soft touch, on to the next one.

The voices were almost upon me. A few more steps and I'd be in view. Jesus, this was painful. Next one. Got it. And now the last one, the trickiest of them all.

It was a man and woman approaching; I could hear their conversation plainly, something about a problem with one of the 'crusties' (a geriatric, I assumed), followed by a snigger. Oh shit. But I was there, the last pin, and gently, very, very gently, I lifted it. Slowly until . . . I was there, the pin was at sheer level with all the others. The lock sprung and I winced at the *click*.

Immediately, I pushed one side of the double door open, and slipped through. I didn't close it completely behind me – I couldn't risk the noise – but rested the very edge against the neighbouring door so that it would appear to be shut to the casual observer. Praying that the couple were not headed this way, I pressed my ear against the wood to listen. I heard the muffled voices pass by and I let out a deep sigh of relief. Returning the tools to their pouch and that to my pocket, I looked around me.

I was in a brightly-lit area, which had a bare wood floor

and partitioned rooms on either side. To my right was an open storeroom, a closed door behind which I assumed was the stairs to this level, and in the far corner the metal doors to a lift; on my left, the top half of the partitioning was framed glass, so I could see inside. It appeared to be an office of some kind, for there was a desk and filing cabinets, with stacked shelves making up the rear wall (I remembered there were no windows on that side). There was a sink, a dull-chrome electric kettle on its draining board. There was no typewriter or computer on the desk, but there was a large, open book – a desk diary, I thought – and a telephone; hanging on the wall behind were sets of keys and an intercom. Fortunately for me, it was empty of any persons.

At the far end, and directly opposite to where I stood, was another set of double doors, and it was only then that I noticed the smell coming from that direction.

As I've mentioned before, my sense of smell has always been acute – I can always distinguish different perfumes, even tell different blends of whisky purely by sniffing the glass – but I couldn't even imagine what this odour comprised. Yes, with it was the familiar mix of antiseptic and stale cooking, but there was also a kind of fetor about this stench that no amount of prophylactic measures could disguise. There was the scent of corruption. Corruption and something more.

I went towards the double doors, treading warily, alert for any new sounds. In fact, there was only silence here in this part of PERFECT REST, although I sensed it was an uneasy silence. Half-way across the floor I stopped, as if frozen. I listened, I breathed in the tainted air. I waited.

And as I waited, a terrible unidentifiable conflict raged within me. I felt that everything that had come to pass – and I don't mean just the phenomena of the past week – had led me to this point, as if *everything* that had ever happened to me was merely milestones in the journey towards this place and this moment. There was no rationale, no sense at all to it, just the overwhelming sensation that some kind of destiny awaited me here. My whole life seemed to present itself in one saturating but swift thought, the way it does, or so we're told, when death is close at hand, everything experienced again in a brief, encapsulating flashback. Yet all experienced objectively, the memories within the instant memory there to be considered and reviewed. It was inexplicable and unaccountable, irrational and profound – it was crazy. It stopped me dead and I shivered with its immensity.

Somehow I knew that an answer was waiting for me behind those doors. The problem was, I had no idea of the question.

An inner, more cautious voice begged me to get out of there, that whatever awaited beyond was not worth the fear and anxiety, that normalcy was better than any spiritual or intellectual revelation. The clairvoyant had warned that there was danger here for me, the sly voice of reason told me, and she was right, you *knew* she was right. But something drove me forward – an intense curiosity, a sense of what was right, that old standby, instinct? I had no idea what impelled me. I quickened my step as I drew nearer to the double doors, as if momentum would help defeat the doubts.

I arrived at this portal to God-knows-what in a rush, almost slamming against it. Unlike the door whose lock I had just picked, there were horizontal handles on each side here, and I pushed down on one. The door didn't budge.

As I reached for the leather pouch once again, another idea struck me. I went to the empty office on my left, its door already open wide, and examined the keys hanging on the board behind the desk. There were two sets, a whole group of keys on each, and one empty hook (I assumed whoever used the office had the absent set about his or her person). I snatched a ring and returned to the locked entrance.

One key belonged to a ward lock, the type used for cupboards or storage-rooms, and I disregarded it, choosing another that looked particularly suitable, and as I inserted it into the keyhole I thought I heard a noise on the other side of the door. Pressing my ear to the tight gap between doors, I listened for a few seconds, but heard nothing more. I tried to turn the key and nothing happened, so I withdrew it and pushed in the third one. I felt and heard the pins inside the lock move and the bolt snapped back. Before putting pressure on the handle to open the door, I listened.

Nothing. No sounds. Only that awful stench wafting through the narrowest of gaps between sides. I pushed open the door a fraction and the foul odour of rottenness swept over me, causing me momentarily to flinch away, almost to gag. Quickly I reached for my handkerchief and pressed it against my nose and mouth. Swallowing hard, I opened the door further and peeked in.

Inside was a long, dark room, its far end invisible in the gloom. There were a few nightlights scattered along its length, their glow too soft to illuminate much, but as my eye grew accustomed to the darkness, I was able to make out the nearest beds lined against both walls. Opening the door wide to allow in some light from behind, I saw shapes on those nearby beds, shadowy unmoving lumps. Even through the handkerchief mask, the smell was appalling.

My vision was rapidly adjusting and the extra light from outside enabled me to see that there were no windows in this room, although the wall to my right jutted inwards at regular intervals like blind, shallow chimney breasts. They puzzled me, because this wall was on the river side and I was sure I had seen windows from where I had stopped on the main road across the river. The wall on the opposite side of the long room, the one that overlooked the triangular courtyard, was also blank as would be expected, but this failed even to have projections to break up its plainness. With its cot-like beds, this place appeared to be a large dormitory; but one without windows and behind locked doors?

I stiffened when there was movement among the shadows. I could hear something shuffling from the blackness of the far end. Something moving in my direction.

I strained my eye, peering into the thick, inky gloom, even more afraid now that the unknown was about to be revealed. I was so scared that I could not even breathe.

The shuffling continued, a soft, scuffling approach, a disembodied sound until a shape began to emerge from the umbra. The dim glow from the nightlights began to give it some form and I wanted to reach for my torch so that I could throw my own light on to it, but I was mesmerized by the movement, immobilized by the fear. It appeared to be weaving slightly as it came.

Then I saw the figure was small and, as it advanced into the light cast by the open doorway behind me, I noticed it was wearing over-sized slippers. Finally, I let my breath go and stepped aside from the doorway so that I blocked none of the light coming through.

It was not only small, but frail also, unsteady as it moved, and I realized it was a child, a weak, unhealthy child. I almost smiled in both welcome and relief. But then I saw the face.

It wasn't a child's face, for it was wizened, deeply lined, the sickly pallid skin stained with brown liver spots that mottled its features and rose over the narrow, almost hairless skull. Whether male or female, it was too ancient and too ravaged to tell. The pale eyes that returned my gaze were watery and red-rimmed, yellowed around the pupils; and the flesh was so hollowed beneath the jutting cheekbones, the face seemed to be holed on either side of the lipless, wrinkled mouth.

The figure stopped a few feet away and the rheumy eyes studied me, seemingly without emotion. When that broken slit of a mouth opened to speak, the voice was high-pitched and raspy, and so querulous that it might have belonged to someone who was more than a hundred years old.

'You're here,' it said. 'At last, you're here.'

33

I was in shock, couldn't speak. And the figure just watched me.

In the periphery of my vision, other shapes stirred on the narrow beds. I heard murmurs, the rustlings of bedsheets, saw forms slowly disengaging themselves from the shadows. I took a step backwards, and the hump of my back shook the closed section of the double door.

'Who . . . who are you?' I finally managed to stammer.

'I don't know,' came the rasping reply. 'But I have a name and I have a number.'

The figure pulled at the sleeve of the loose robe it wore, a grey nightgown affair that reached to the ankles, and revealed a painfully skinny arm. I saw some blurred markings on the inner wrist and, curiosity overcoming other emotions, I took out my torch. The figure before me obliged by extending the arm towards the light.

I saw a smudged line drawn across the flesh of the wrist and as I peered closer, I realized it was a row of tiny, faded numbers. An old tattoo. A concentration camp identification tag. I felt sickened and now it was not just because of the room's foul stench.

'We have names for each other though,' the figure said. 'I'm called Joseph.'

There was more movement in the shadows behind the old man, but nothing came forward, whoever was there remained hidden.

'You are the one, aren't you?' the man called Joseph asked, and his voice was almost pitiful in its hope.

346

More murmurings came from the darkness, incoherent sounds that might have risen from – I felt faint at the thought – from lunatics.

'Please tell us,' the little man pleaded. 'You are the one?'

'I don't know,' I said, unsure of the question. 'I'm . . . I'm just not sure what you mean. What is this place?'

'This? This is our home.'

I thought of the door behind me that had been locked. 'Are you being kept here against your will?' I asked, concerned that I had broken into a dormitory full of disturbed people, perhaps patients whose senility had necessitated their confinement. I was becoming increasingly uneasy. This one, this Joseph, might appear aged and fragile, but what of the others . . . ? I began to slide towards the open section of the door.

'Please . . .' Without moving closer the old man reached out a hand towards me. His ancient face looked appealingly at me. 'Please . . .' he said again.

A sudden noise to my left caused me to shine the torch in that direction. Its beam lit up a bed tucked away in the corner and at first I couldn't make out the thing that lay on top. But when it moved I understood what it was and a wave of revulsion swept through me.

It was naked, naked and pale in the torchbeam. Naked and pale and huge, a great swelling from which emaciated arms and legs seemed to sprout. The woman – the long hair and pointed breasts resting atop of the mound told me it was a woman – was propped up by pillows so that she could see over the lump that at first I thought was her overblown belly, and I could see the terror in her eyes, a terror that perhaps was equal to my own. It occurred to me that she might be pregnant with some gross foetus, but I quickly realized this was no normal stretching of body flesh, for the lump was too massive and misshapen, the skin looked too hardened and was too rutted. No, this was a massive anomalous ovarian cyst, one that dominated its host body, rising from the rib cage and distending over the groin area almost to the knees. Its veins seemed to be embossed on the surface, a network of cannula-like tubes, some thick, others so fine they resembled massed cotton threads, and stiff, prickly hairs covered parts of it, springing from deep fissures in the flesh.

I stumbled back from the sight, almost falling.

'We won't harm you,' came the ancient's strangely distant voice again, but I was already heading for the open door. 'Please . . . !' he wailed.

And I faltered. Half-way through the door something – perhaps the heart-rending anguish in his frail voice – made me stop and turn my head.

'Please,' he said again, more quietly this time, but nonetheless in agonized entreaty. 'Don't leave us here.'

It was as if the moment for me to flee that place had come and had gone. I didn't know why – at the *time* I didn't know why – but I went back into the long dormitory. I turned the torch beam on the little old man called Joseph. His weary eyes blinked against the glare and I lowered the light.

'He doesn't allow lights,' he said. 'Not at night. They only switch them on from outside during the day. We're supposed to sleep.'

'Who d'you mean by he?' I asked him, nervously looking over his shoulder at shadows moving in the darkness. 'Is it Dr Wisbeech? Is he the one who keeps you here?'

'The Doctor. Yes, the Doctor.'

Although I must have been shadowed by the light at my back, he seemed to sense my apprehension.

'Don't be frightened of what you see here,' he said, but I could hear the nervousness in his own voice. 'After all,' he added, 'you are like us.'

I couldn't help but gape at this shrunken little man in his loose gown, at his almost-bald, wizened head set on narrow shoulders that sloped away from the scrawny neck, at those washed-out jaded eyes that so mournfully watched me in return.

Others

'I don't know what . . .' I began to say, but his thin, wavery smile interrupted me.

'We called to you,' he said, taking a step forward. 'Didn't you understand that it was us? We sent you wings. It was the only way we could hint at Momma's name.'

'Hildegarde Vogel?'

'Momma. She was good to us, she was always good to us.'

Someone moaned in the blackness behind him.

'Now she's gone,' Joseph said. He took another step and was no more than a yard away; yet when he spoke again, his voice sounded even closer, almost as if he were whispering into my ear. 'You know us. I can tell. The recognition is there in your mind, if not in your vision.'

He moved even closer and a cold, dry hand wrapped itself around my wrist. I almost dropped the torch.

'Please don't be afraid,' he begged quietly. 'Not of us, not of us.'

More whispers came from the moving shadows, and then murmurings. More vague shapes began to take on form as they drew closer.

Joseph spoke. 'You're here to help us. Now you must understand why.'

The first of those tenebrous forms emerged into the light.

'Learn to see with generous eyes,' the old man told me. 'Don't fear us. I promise you, there is nothing to fear.'

And so I looked and could barely conceal the revulsion, could scarcely hide the fear.

For although I had already witnessed the initial horror on the bed nearby, it had not prepared me for what was to come.

When I aimed the light at the young man who lurched from the dark, I saw only an innocent face with wide, child-like eyes, the hair long and matted, the jaw small and pointed; but as I let the beam fall on to the body I gasped

349

aloud and once more, nausea slewed around my stomach
and saliva moistened my mouth. At first glance I thought he
was carrying somebody, a smaller person whose head and
shoulders I could not see, a body whose twisted legs hung
just below its bearer's knees. One frail arm dangled by its
side.

Then I realized it had no head and there were no
shoulders, for the torso emerged – the torso *came* from –
the young man's chest. The man was host to the twisted
thing.

And it appeared to be alive, for it moved – it *flinched* – and
the carrier, whose hands were beneath the parasite's buttocks, hoisted the shape up as if into a more comfortable
position. He held it as a brother might hold a younger
sibling.

'Oh dear God . . .' I said it as a hushed breath.

'Please . . .' Joseph had stepped to my side and he
squeezed my arm as if to offer comfort – and to give me
strength.

Now a woman – no, it was just a girl, from the almost
dainty, light-footed way she walked I could tell she was a
young girl – loomed into the light. Her long dark hair hung
forward around her face and even beneath the loose robe I
could tell her figure was slim and, from the way she moved,
it was lithe. She watched me over her fingertips, for her fine
hands covered most of her face in the way young girls might
hide their shyness, and her blue eyes were beautifully large
and clear.

'Cecilia . . .' Joseph said to her in some secret command,
or perhaps, plea.

She glanced his way, and then back at me. She took
another step closer and I could not help but notice how
pretty her small feet were. She lowered her hands.

Nothing had prepared me for the shock that now gripped
me. I should have realized that this young girl with the slight
figure and lovely hair would be imperfect in some way, for

was she not kept here, apparently locked away in a covert section of the home, and hadn't her companions already given visual testament to their condition?

As her hands slipped from her face I shuddered, but did not avert my gaze. I forced myself to look, but I could not force my legs to stop their trembling, my heart to stop its pounding.

A hideous excrescence swept down from her lower brow, a sick travesty which replaced the nose for a tusk. It was long, hard, and its colour was grey, dividing her face to reach towards and almost touch her chin. And the mouth. Oh God, the mouth. Its thin lips stretched across her face, each corner almost touching her earlobes in a wretched, demonic grin, a Joker's grin.

Involuntarily, my hand cupped my own mouth, both in shock and to contain the rising sickness. I wanted to flee from there again and I think it was only shame that prevented me from so doing. It wasn't their fault, they could not be blamed for their aberrations just as I could not be blamed for mine.

And as the old man gripped my arm, the parade continued, each one of these unfortunates presenting themselves to me, some having to be coaxed, others gently led from the shadows into the light, but most willing to reveal themselves. I recognized some from my dreams, my visions, while others were a new shock, something more to be witnessed, and then accepted. And I did begin to accept, for the mind has a capacity to adapt, to learn and – albeit slowly – to acknowledge. Here, one horror led to another, one malformation led to something as bad or worse, and both my sensitivity and sensibility hardened a little more at each revelation. Still they came: the three-headed boy, two of those heads set close together on broad shoulders, the third on the edge of the collarbone, hanging limp and lifeless, as though ostracized by the others; a girl I remembered having seen among the hauntings of the previous night, a tall pretty young woman, whose face was innocent, but whose upper body did not align with her hips and legs, so that she seemed almost to be walking alongside herself; yet another young female, the legs of this one huge, elephantine, beneath her robe, calves and ankles swelling enormously like overflows of grey, clotted lava; the man who slid across the floor, propelling himself with his arms because his body ended just below his chest, his genitals – or whatever physical arrangement he had for his functions – presumably tucked out of sight beneath him; the man or woman, I couldn't tell which, whose arms sprouted other arms, whose legs sprouted other legs; the dark-skinned boy with the stunted body and a head so huge and soft it had to be held erect by a companion, the companion a woman whose face had another half-face melded into skull and flesh, so that she appeared to have three eyes, two noses, a small, twisted aperture whose lips denoted it as a mouth set askew on one cheek, while another, blistered mouth was positioned almost as normal above the jaw. They came to me like creatures from a nightmare – as, indeed, they had *first* come to me – although some still lingered in duskier parts as if afraid to let the light throw its full glow into their imperfect bodies; and I was relieved that these few last ones chose to remain hidden from me, for their shadowy outlines did not encourage closer inspection.

They stood in a semi-circle around me, these ... these *grotesques* – I could think of no other word for them ... and they swayed and moved in the half-light, whispering, holding on to each other for comfort. The stench from them – or was it from the room itself? – was almost as overpowering as their physical aspects, and I continued to fight the sickness that by now seemed to be welling in my chest. I watched them warily, my legs still shaking, the torch in my hand wavering, but I refused to let myself run from their presence. I don't think it was courage that kept me there; no, it was because I had a deep-seated empathy with these poor wretches. After all, was I so different from them? Wasn't my own appearance closer in form to theirs rather than my normal fellow man's? Wasn't I a freak among freaks?

In an act of bravado, defiance, or just plain curiosity, I raised the thin torch high and shone it over their heads, sweeping its narrow beam along the two rows of beds and cots behind them. It seemed that most were empty, although I could make out vague shapes here and there, which meant the majority of – inmates, internees, patients? – were standing here before me. I didn't count, but I guessed there were at least thirty of them. All kinds of questions sprang into my mind, but I could only look speechlessly at the little old man by my side.

However, Joseph had one more to show me. Arid skeletal fingers slipped into my hand and with gentle pressure, he led me through the ill-made crowd.

The cot was like all the other beds and cots, narrow in width, iron frames with rounded corners at each end. A single sheet and a flat pillow covered it. A tiny head lay on the pillow, the rest of the body on top of the sheet. I raised the torch to see better.

My mind reeled, the room about me weaved; I heard myself utter a small, startled cry. The hand holding my own became firmer, as if to steady me.

At first I could not be sure if the thing lying on the cot was human, so hairless and veined, so small and slug-like, was its appearance. The grip on my hand tightened even more and, though he did not speak, I thought I heard Joseph's soothing voice inside my head. *Be calm*, it said. *There is nothing to fear*. And somehow, I *was* calmed.

Even so, I had to will myself to look at the thing on the cot again.

To begin with, I could not distinguish any features that might refer to man, woman, or child; only when I made myself move closer to bend over the little creature did any such marks become apparent. Set in the white blob of a head were two, pink, pupilless eyes that stared sightlessly at the torchlight. The nose was of little consequence, a tiny bump of a thing with a single slit, presumably serving as a nostril, at its centre. The mouth – could it be called a mouth? – was no more than a toothless, lipless aperture that dilated and closed in an irregular rhythm as it took breaths. A shiny drool glistened around its edges. I was reminded of the creature that had lay across the threshold of my front door last night. This was smaller, but in essence the same. And this appeared to be blind, whereas in my vision it was without eyes.

My gaze travelled down from the head to the body, searching for limbs or anything that might give the creature human credibility, some normal definition, but I saw only protuberances at each corner, smooth stumps that occasionally twitched. One such stump near the head (there was no visible neck) had the same kind of tattoo that Joseph bore on his wrist, a blurred line of numbers, and I tried to discern them. 080581, I thought they read.

My search continued its grim journey over the pale swell that was its belly, a riot of veins visible beneath the thin skin, down to the brief appendages that were in place of its legs, to the flaccid hairless growth between them, a skinless penis that lay on a flat and empty scrotum.

At last my nausea refused to be contained: it erupted from me as I turned quickly from the cot, splattering the wood floor, soaking my shoes with slick saliva and vomit. I retched and retched as I had the night before, bringing up all the nastiness that had swilled in my stomach, expunging my body of its foulness. What kind of Hell had I stolen my way into? What other horrors dwelt here?

Fortunately for me at that time, I had no way of knowing.

34

Some sat on beds or cots, while others gathered around me, sitting on the floor, or just standing watching me. I rested on one of the few wooden chairs in the dormitory, far away from the mess I had made on the floor, even though its smell was nothing amidst the rancid odour of the room itself. The door was now closed and we talked in darkness save for the subdued glow of the nightlights. I preferred it that way.

Joseph, who had led me to the chair and had himself wiped the slime from my shoes with a rumpled rag, sat three feet away, his ankles crossed, thin, gnarled hands in his lap, his back surprisingly straight for one of his age.

'The Doctor refers to us as "exceptional departures from the ordinary",' he was saying, and I endeavoured to listen to his words, tried to ignore the stink and the creatures who shared the darkness with me. 'And that is all we are. You must believe me when I tell you that our outer shells govern neither our hearts nor our minds. Least of all do they taint our souls.'

Someone whimpered, another moaned softly, and I could feel, rather than see, movement in the gloom.

'We used to believe the Doctor was our creator, but Constance has told us this isn't so.'

'Constance . . . ?' I became even more alert at the sound of her name. I flicked on the torch so that I could see his face, and he blinked, raised a hand to protect his eyes. I lowered the beam, but didn't turn off the torch; a circle of light illuminated the floor between us and reflected a soft, limited radiance on both Joseph and myself. 'Does Constance take care of you?'

'She is our friend. Like Sparrow. Constance has told us that Sparrow has gone away for ever.'

Another quiet moan in the darkness.

'Sparrow was ill for a very long time,' I said gently.

'We know. But still we visited her.'

'You were allowed to go to her room?'

'Oh no, not that. No, we visited her in the same way we visited you. Her mind was always so confused, though, in later years.'

'You used mental telepathy? Is that how you got to me? But how? And why?'

'Michael showed us how. Ultimately, it was he who took us to you.'

'Which one is Michael?' I raised the torch, sweeping its beam around the room, lighting up the others there. A young man covered his face with enormous mutated hands, their fingers twisted and scaly, their colour black, but raw-reddened in parts, their size out of all proportion to his body; with horror I saw that his bare feet were the same, twisted and blackened and extended like the roots of a tree. The pretty girl, whose lower spine was so cruelly disjointed that her body was not above her pelvis and legs, clung to the stick she carried for support, the sudden brightness surprising her. A man or youth of obvious African origin looked at me in alarm, the huge flap of soft skin and flesh that covered his face lifted like a veil.

'There.' Joseph was pointing into the crowd, which parted to reveal the cot behind. I shone the light on the poor, stunted-limbed creature that lay there, the thing whose body resembled that of a giant, bloated slug, whose mouth was a mere aperture, its eyes pink, sightless orbs. A low keening noise came from it.

'Michael can only communicate by thought, a gift we have

only recognized in recent years, and in ourselves only some months ago.'

'But how did you find me? None of you could have known me, or even of me.'

'The clairvoyant helped us.'

'Louise?'

'Is that her name? Our collective mind journeyed to hers, whether by chance or by the force of wanting, we have no idea. We made ... a connection. We were then guided to you.'

I gave myself a few moments to let this sink in. Shelly Ripstone had contacted Louise before hiring my services and it was only then that I began to have the visions – those invasive *thoughts*. There seemed to be a weird kind of sense to it all, although it didn't explain the terror I'd been put through last night.

'I'm not sure I understand any of this,' I finally said in exasperation.

'Then let me tell you about us and of this place.'

And this, Joseph did.

PERFECT REST was the only home these unfortunates had ever known, and indeed, they referred to it as 'Home'. For a long time they had all believed that the Doctor – whom I assumed was Leonard K. Wisbeech, although they never called him by his name – was their creator, that somehow he was the father of them all. It was only through Constance Bell, who had come to them several years ago as carer and friend, that they learned they had come from different fathers and mothers, parents who were unable to cope with their offspring's disabilities and malformations. Constance had told them that they were here to be protected from the outside world, for out there normal people had a special hatred for those born unlike themselves.

Here, in this place – and it was purely for their own

357

benefit, carried out solely to help them – they underwent tests and experiments, were given strange liquids to drink, numerous tablets to swallow, their bodies examined and probed, their deformities studied. They were photographed and X-rayed (they didn't know the technical terms for these things, but it was easy for me to surmise), blood, tissue, and even cells taken from them. Sometimes, when certain experiments were performed on them, they suffered great pain; sometimes they underwent strange operations that left them in great distress and physically no better off. Sometimes their companions were taken away never to be seen again. Their abilities, both mental and physical, were constantly tested, and the only reward for their cooperation was the security of the Home.

Often they were returned to the dormitory heavily sedated and with no recollection whatsoever of where they had been, what they had done, what had been done to them. Always on these occasions, they were left distraught, parts of their bodies sore and bruised, frequently openly bleeding.

They remembered the one who had brought them treats, offered them comfort and told them wonderful stories of magic and families (many of them around me in the darkness now sighed and laughed at the memory, their apprehension momentarily allayed). This little woman had told them to call her 'Sparrow', but most of them preferred to call her 'Momma'. But she had grown old and frail, her visits less regular until they stopped altogether. That was when Constance had come to them and taken over Sparrow's role; Constance, who was not unlike themselves.

Hearing her name spoken with so much affection, even reverence, filled me with a longing to see her. It also filled me with fresh trepidation.

It seemed that others in this place had treated them far less kindly, regarding them as freaks rather than 'exceptional departures from the ordinary', some even beating them when displeased with their behaviour or slowness, while others were content merely to mock them (which, Joseph told me, was worse, far worse). They were never allowed to forget their imperfections, never allowed to think of themselves as anything other than oddities, strangers to the world beyond these walls, so it was easy for me to see how this room itself had become their home within the Home, their sanctuary from those who would despise them, the very darkness their retreat. Yet still they were curious about the outside world, lack of windows merely deepening the mystery of normal life (it became obvious to me that the projections along the dormitory's right-hand wall covered the fake windows built into the exterior wall so that the big house would appear normal to observers across the river or even passing boats).

Much of what these unfortunates knew of the world itself came from books, for they were encouraged by the Doctor, who was interested in their intelligence as much as in their physical capabilities, to read and learn. Constance had helped them, even bringing in books that were discouraged, literature that was not truth but not lies either, for they contained fiction that spoke of truth. When their thirst for this new kind of knowledge had grown into a passion, she had smuggled in a different sort of book, although it also contained many stories. She had told them it contained the Ultimate Truth.

From this they had learned that the Doctor was not their creator, that there was a Supreme Being who was Creator of All and It was known as God. Constance had helped them understand this God of all things, and those who could read had helped those who could not, until even those whose poor mental ability left them unable to cope with the simplest of tasks were able to grasp this new and wonderful message. And the message was that *all* were equal in the eyes of God and *all* were loved equally, even the aberrations of His own natural order, for they were – not *merely*, but *importantly* – a testing for *all* mankind.

(For someone like me, who had never forgiven God – if

there *was* such a Being, and the jury was still out on that one
as far as I was concerned – for creating me like this, their
belief was astonishing and, in a way, awesome, especially as
it came from nothing more than a book, the bestseller of all
time, admittedly, but still words on paper, a tome, a Holy
Writ that might be history or fantasy. It was odd, but I
felt both angry and humbled. Most of all, though, I felt
confused.)

It seemed that recently a great dread within them had
become almost overwhelming, an ominous and rising disquiet that had developed into a collective fear. That was
when the one called Michael had begun to take them on
mind-journeys.

At first, they had only visited Sparrow where she lay on
her sickbed within the Home itself, but her mind was too
clouded and muddled for mental dialogue, so they had
ventured further afield, wandering aimlessly for a while,
witnessing life as they had never before known it, but rapidly
becoming desperate as their inner trepidation increased. It
was Michael who had led them to the clairvoyant, the
clairvoyant who had led them to me. And in me, they had
recognized one of their own.

'Why now, Joseph?' I asked. 'You've lived here in these
conditions for so long, why is it only recently that you've
become afraid?'

'We've always been afraid, but at least we knew this place,
we felt some stability here, a kind of security. But now we
sense that something terrible is happening to us. With each
passing week we become fewer in number.'

'You mean when you're taken out of this room?'

'Yes.'

'And those who do return – they never remember what's
happened to them?'

He slowly shook his wizened head. 'But we dream,' he

said. 'We dream of horrible things, nightmares where . . .' He stopped speaking and his eyes closed. 'Even the dreams we cannot remember fully. Only snatches, scenes that frighten us. It's as if our inner minds know but refuse to tell our conscious selves.'

As I turned the torch on Joseph to study his face, a question that had lodged itself in my own mind came to the fore. 'Joseph, tell me why *you* are here. Unless your garment is hiding something you'd prefer not to be seen, you don't appear to have anything wrong with you. Yet you're kept in this place and you're much older than everyone else in here . . .'

I sat upright – as much as I was able – and stared at him. 'That's it, isn't it? I mean, you're older than the Doctor himself, so unless he is the successor to someone who first started all this . . .' I felt a sudden rush of excitement, an unexpected insight. 'Unless someone else other than Dr Leonard Wisbeech started snatching badly deformed children at, or soon after, their birth a long, long time ago . . .' I shook my head once in an effort to clear the thoughts that were bombarding it. Shelly Ripstone's illegitimate baby *had* been taken away from her eighteen years ago because it had been born like the others here, probably not expected to live anyway, but useful for study while it was still alive. The same thing had happened to many such malformed newborns, all thought to be terminal cases, or . . . or all thought to be useful as objects of research, exhibits to examine, for learning, for autopsies . . . And now, with genetics the new, fast-expanding science, their bodies – best of all, their living, breathing bodies – were invaluable as specimens for genetic research. Oh dear Lord . . .

As I looked at Joseph, thoughts still tumbling through my head, my original line of questioning came back to me. I leaned forward again in the chair, elbows resting on my knees, hands clasped together in front of me, one finger extended, pointing at the old man.

'You're not old at all, are you, Joseph? I mean, there isn't anyone in this room that's very old. You're all quite young and you, Joseph, are even younger than some, aren't you?'

It might have been a smile on that ancient, wrinkled face, or it might have been a frown of sadness, it was impossible to tell.

'We lose count of all time in the Home,' he said in that high, rasping, almost distant voice of his, 'but I know that not too many years have passed since I was brought here as an infant. Constance tells me it has only been twelve.'

It's called progeria, a rare disease that causes drastically premature ageing in children, even in babies. A twelve-year-old can look as if he were a hundred.

'Joseph . . .' I said. I wanted to weep. Right then and there I wanted to sink to my knees and weep for them all.

But I rose from the chair and took the few paces to stand before him. I knelt and put my arms around his frail little shoulders to hug him close.

Only then did I weep.

35

I took only two of them with me: the man-boy, Joseph, and the girl with the acute curvature of the lower spine, who was introduced to me as Mary, and whose hair hung in golden ringlets around her pretty face, and who possessed the most innocent eyes I'd ever seen. I remembered her too, from last night's visions, although her image had been unclear, shimmery. None of their friends who were able could be coaxed to join us, for they were terrified of being caught outside their dormitory unattended. Their fear was frightening in itself and I wondered if any government department had sanctioned such an establishment – after all, could babies just disappear from hospitals only moments after their birth without some collusion by the authorities? – or whether this whole operation was truly clandestine. Surely the health authorities had to have some involvement? Perhaps they did, but never bothered to monitor the conditions in which these poor misfits lived. Perhaps they had too much faith in the eminent Dr Leonard K. Wisbeech and all the fancy letters after his name. I prayed that that wasn't the truth of it.

There had been much whimpering and moaning as we three had sneaked through the double doors, but as soon as we were outside and the doors closed behind us, the sounds stopped. It was as if all those left inside the dormitory were holding their breath.

'Don't you have a warden of some kind on duty out here?' I asked Joseph, nodding towards the open doorway of the partitioned office.

'Usually there is one,' he replied, 'but Michael tells us there is something terrible happening here tonight, so perhaps our supervisor is being kept busy elsewhere.'

Michael. That poor blob of barely-human flesh whose only existence was acknowledged by a blurred number tattooed on to his skin. 'How does Michael know these things?' I said.

'He senses them. He travels beyond his own body. It's his only . . . gift.'

Nature compensates, right? Only what a sick joke in this case.

'And he communicates this to you?' I said, still in a whisper.

'He shares his thoughts with us. Not with words, but with feelings and emotions. It isn't always clear, but tonight he has shown us great terror and we are afraid.'

And Louise had felt it too. Back at the old abandoned house, she had sensed their panic.

'You're sure he knows where Constance is?'

Joseph gave a bow of his head. 'He will guide us.'

'Okay.' I wasn't reassured, but I knew when to follow my *own* instincts. I took the twelve-year-old by the hand and led him over to the elevator. Mary, hardly leaning on her walking stick, merely using it for balance, followed us.

We stopped in front of the shaft doors and even as I debated whether or not to push the call button, we were startled by a sudden clanking noise, followed by a low humming that grew louder.

'Quickly,' I said, now taking both my companions by the elbow and pushing them towards the closed door next to the elevator shaft. 'The lift's coming up.'

The girl hobbled awkwardly and the man-boy shuffled in his slippers, but it took very little time to reach the sturdy-looking door behind which I assumed was the staircase to this wing. Rather stupidly, I had also assumed the door would be unlocked.

The humming sound grew louder as I turned the door's

handle to no effect. The lock was a simple cylinder and on a good day I could have picked it within forty seconds; however, this was not a good day and nor did I have forty seconds. I whisked the keyring I had taken from the small office out of my pocket and chose the obvious key, the Yale. It turned the lock easily and just as the humming from the lift shaft sighed to a stop, I pushed my companions through the open door. I followed through smartly as the elevator doors began to clunk open and through the two-inch gap I'd left I caught sight of a blue-uniformed figure emerging from the lift to cross the landing, heading towards the office opposite. It was a squat, broad-shouldered man, the short sleeves of the uniform showing off his muscular arms. He whistled tunelessly, obviously happy in his work.

For a hair-raising moment, I thought he might test the dormitory doors that I had left shut but unlocked. Fortunately, he only paused before the entrance, seemed to listen for a while, then went on into his office. Inside, he took the newspaper that had been folded beneath his armpit and sat in the chair, leaning back to stretch his legs, resting his feet on the desk before him. With relief, I closed the stairway door all the way.

I found we were on a wooden, carpet-less and dimly-lit landing, to our left stairs, ascending, presumably to the roof or attic rooms, to our right, descending. Putting a straight finger against my lips, I warned my two newfound friends to remain silent, then immediately had to clap my hands over their mouths as they began to jabber. Obviously they were not used to that kind of sign language in this small, enclosed world of theirs and had no idea what I meant. The girl, Mary, who was slightly taller than I, jerked her head away from my hand, total panic in those innocent eyes, while Joseph clammed up instantly.

'I'm sorry, I'm sorry,' I whispered urgently, reaching for Mary's arm to reassure her. 'We must keep very quiet, okay? We don't want anybody to hear us.'

She blinked and Joseph nodded as vigorously as he could manage. The girl had raised a hand to her cheek, so that the sleeve of her robe had slid down to her elbow, exposing her lower arm, and I saw the markings there: 201079. Not a human to the people who ran this place, I reflected, only a number, a registration no doubt kept on file, somewhere.

'I'm s-s-s ... I'm s-sorry,' she stuttered so woefully it might have been an apology for her existence rather than the noise she had made and I had to rush my hand to her mouth again. This time she took a step backwards away from me, her spine hitting the landing's rail behind her.

'It's all right,' I hissed, remaining still in case I alarmed her further. 'I'm not going to hurt you. I'm a friend, remember?'

Joseph went to her and reached up for her wrists, taking them in his own hands and gently pulling them away from her face. 'He's the one we called to help us, Mary,' he said softly. 'He really is our friend.'

A thought occurred to me and I moved closer to them both. 'Joseph,' I said close to his ear. 'How did you get your names? Are they your real ones, the names you were born with?'

'Oh no.' He regarded me gravely. 'We only had the numbers to begin with. Momma Sparrow gave us our names. She could never remember the numbers.' He looked up at me with pale, weary eyes. 'Your name,' he said in a hushed voice. 'You haven't told us what you are called yet.'

'You don't know?' I was surprised. After all, they had been inside my head more than once now.

They both shook their heads and I was relieved to see that the girl appeared to have got over her fright.

'My name is Dismas,' I told them.

'The Good Thief?' Joseph said instantly with a kind of half-smile.

'That's right, the Good Thief, the bad-guy-turned-good, who died beside Christ on the Cross.' I'd forgotten that their favourite reading was the Bible. Joseph and Mary seemed pleased, despite their nervousness.

'Dismas . . . ?' Joseph said.

'Just call me Dis, okay?'

'Dis?'

'What is it, Joseph?'

'We are the same, aren't we?'

I was puzzled by the question. 'Of course, we're all the same. We're all human.'

'But you are more like us than others.'

'Yeah, I'm more like you. But there are *plenty* like us in the outside world.'

'I'm glad. Although I don't understand why only we are kept here, locked away.'

'Neither do I, Joseph, but we'll find out. I promise you, we'll find out.'

Another question that burned me was precisely what was Constance Bell's role in all this? She wasn't kept here under lock and key like these poor wretches and, from what Joseph had told me, she obviously cared for these people. It was impossible to believe that Constance was in league with her guardian, Leonard Wisbeech, but what other explanation was there? It was another question whose answer I intended to find out. I limped to the rail and stared into the stairwell. Mary did not try to back away from me.

There was the usual gloom from the floor below, as if the interior of the building was set in permanent twilight, and I heard no sounds, no other signs of life. Joseph joined me and stood on tip-toes to look over.

'D'you know what's down there on the other levels, Joseph?' I asked him.

His sad little face looked up at me and for the first time I saw the child behind the mask. There was a trusting in his eyes, even though there was apprehension too, and somehow it made me feel both inadequate and determined at the same time.

367

'The laboratory is on the next floor,' Joseph answered. 'The Doctor refers to it as his "museum of the anomalous and curious".'

I had to remind myself that Joseph was still a mere boy, even though he appeared otherwise and the words he spoke suggested a learning beyond the capabilities of a twelve-year-old. In normal society, he might even have been considered a child prodigy, and I wondered if Wisbeech treated him as such, feeding his intellect, encouraging him to extend his knowledge by reading from learned tomes. Maybe that was Joseph's true uniqueness, not his disease, but his intellectual powers. Something tugged at my sleeve and I turned to find Mary peering earnestly into my face.

'M-m-must go now.' She continued to pull at my jacket, demanding a response.

I straightened and managed to give her a smile, hoping it wouldn't frighten her. She, herself, managed a tentative smile in return and it made me feel a little better.

'I'll get you out of here,' I told her quietly. 'I'll get you all out of here. But we must find Constance first.'

Yes, I eventually would get them *all* out of this cruel, God-forsaken place, but I wouldn't take them to the authorities, not to the very people who had allowed this, either by negligence or plan, to happen. No, it would be the media first, a television station or an upmarket newspaper, not a tabloid but a broadsheet whose headlines would not feature the word 'FREAKS'. I'd make the story public first and only then would I involve the Law.

As skittish as a young deer, the girl hurried past me to the top step, where she grabbed the rail for balance and looked back at me for reassurance. Joseph's fingers curled around mine and this time he led me.

The three of us began the descent together.

*

We listened at the door on the next level, holding our breath, the tension between us almost palpable. I could feel Mary trembling beside me and Joseph had closed his eyes as if meditating. I guessed he was trying to pick up 'vibes' from Michael, our so-called 'guide', and mentally I shook my head in despair. We had to rely on ourselves, not this poor mute, helpless thing whose thoughts, they claimed, would assist us in our search for Constance. Despite all I'd learned, my natural scepticism was hard to overcome.

'You say there's a laboratory through here?' I whispered.

'Yes, but we must go on,' Joseph insisted.

'I want to see it.'

His eyes snapped open. 'No, no, please let's go before we are discovered. Michael is letting me know that Constance is not there.'

'I'm still curious. I'd like to know exactly what Wisbeech is up to before we leave this place. Look, why don't you two wait here while I sneak a quick look around.'

They both clutched my arm as if afraid to be left alone.

'It'll only take me a couple of minutes.'

They still clung to me.

'Okay. Then you'll both have to come with me. I promise it'll be quick.'

I could see the consternation on their faces, but nevertheless I tried the doorhandle. As expected, the door was locked and I reached for the keyring once more. The same key that had opened the landing door upstairs opened this one too.

There were pitch-black shadows inside, although moonlight flooded through from windows of the room's right-hand wall, apparently no ban on them at this level. Through them I saw that most of the clouds in the night sky had dispersed. The strong smell of formaldehyde wafted over us and it was almost a relief from the general stench that continued to cloy my sensitive nostrils. Cautiously, I pushed my head through the opening and was able to discern long bench tables running the length of the room, with cupboards, glass cabinets and shelving around the walls. Using the torch, I saw there were large glass cases and jars on the work benches, all of which contained floating things of no recognizable form – at least, not from where I stood. I felt the material of my jacket being pulled again.

'Please let's leave,' I heard Joseph implore from behind me.

'There's no one here,' I whispered back to him, my eye still drawn to those specimen jars and cases on the long tables. Although impossible to identify their contents from that distance, there was nevertheless something repugnant about them. The shapes suspended inside the clear liquid appeared to have no regular form and seemed almost like weird, modernist sculptures or the sick creations of HR Giger. I decided I wanted a closer look and so stepped into the laboratory, much to my companions' audible dismay.

Once inside, I was able to see work benches along the windowed wall, desk lights and computers on their surfaces. There was the usual scientific paraphernalia around on other worktops, from Bunsen burners to both ordinary and electron microscopes, from flat-bottomed and conical flasks to evaporating dishes and measuring cylinders, whose purpose I could only guess at. While Joseph and Mary waited by the door, I wandered further into the huge room.

I approached one of the long benches and shone the light on the closest glass cabinet there. With a small cry, I recoiled at the sight of the thing inside.

Again I felt sickened, yet I was also perversely fascinated with the huge, peculiar, unborn foetus floating in the preservative. The bulbous but only partly-formed head was tucked into tiny arms, a lizard's comb running from the scalp, over its arched back, to end in a pointed tail. Minute legs were bent and raised into its stomach, but I could see the fleshy webbing between its tiny, splayed toes. I would have assumed it was an animal or reptile of some kind had it not been for the pallid and soft-looking skin, the one visible eye, blue and very human, the growth that almost formed a natural ear. And if it were not for the glassy blankness in its stare, I might even have imagined it was alive. I prayed then that it had *never* lived.

Swiftly, as if for relief from this monstrosity, I turned the beam on a tall, thick jar standing next to the glass case and I groaned, for the specimen in this was as gross as its neighbour. Behind the curved glass there floated an infant's small head, its eyelids closed, its little pink lips parted. The face was not easy to look at, for it was squashed slightly and the cheeks protruded, as if it had been crushed between skull and jaw. It was attached to a trailing column of vertebrae and lengthy spinal cord; there was no body, no limbs, just a baby's flattened head drifting in pellucid liquid with a soft spine dangling from it.

The next jar held within it a large fibrous mass, a rough-shaped ball that looked like some terrible overgrown cyst, only embedded in its scabrous surface was an eye, and a few crooked teeth, and pieces of tufty black hair, all that remained of an embryo that had existed in some unfortunate woman's womb, sharing the space with, and finally absorbed into, this abnormal sac. I moved the light on, dreading what else I might find, but somehow powerless to stop myself, horribly gripped by these macabre exhibits, repulsed by them, yet curious to see more, as if I were under their morbid spell. Another large, glass case, suspended inside a tangled mass of limbs, intertwined arms and legs, two young bodies fused together in cursed embrace, heads melded by the faces, no spaces between their flesh. I thought I had seen the worst earlier that night, but nothing could match these fresh obscenities. Still I went on, my thoughts numbed, revulsion now strangely submissive; my sensitivities had detached themselves from the observations, my emotions self-protectively had hardened. This chamber of true horrors was too gruesomely awesome to remain shocking, for the normal mind cannot abide heinous repetition and will always

strive to shield itself for the sake of sanity. I'm not saying I
wasn't disturbed as I progressed along these rows of outrageous specimens, displayed here like bizarre trophies: all I
mean is that by now I was too stunned to be affected. The
mummified boy, who had another head growing from the
top of his own, the supernumerary head having grown upside
down and ending at the neck, meant nothing to me; the two
small skeletons lying flat inside a glass cabinet, both of them
joined together in longitudinal axis at the pelvis, so that
instead of legs each had the torso of the other – none of
them truly registered with me. The sights had all become
too overwhelming, and mercifully so; I passed between them
in a daze, the terrible afflictions at least muted by moonlight,
the torchlight never lingering on any one exhibit.

When I reached the end of the room and briefly swung
the torchbeam along the shelves bearing rows of various-
sized containers and jars, each one of these filled with fleshy
substances, I decided I had had enough and a glimpse of
disembodied eyeballs staring back at me from behind glass
reinforced the decision. I turned and almost dropped the
torch in surprise. Someone was standing right behind me.

'Jesus!' I said, almost jumping into the air. 'Joseph, don't
do that!'

He looked suitably abashed. 'I'm sorry. I didn't mean to
frighten you.'

''S all right. It isn't you, it's this bloody place.' I scythed
the light beam around the big room, not allowing it to loiter
on anything specific. 'Why? Why are all these things kept
here?'

'They are for the Doctor's researches,' Joseph replied,
'and for his pleasure.'

'He takes pleasure in all this?'

'He is obsessed by our forms.'

'He's told you this?'

'The Doctor likes to converse with me. I suppose he is
really testing my intelligence.'

'But what is he researching?'

'Our very nature. He talks very much of genetics and how tests on this thing he calls DNA eventually might lead to the eradication of the hereditary diseases that cause our mal-formations.'

I had to keep reminding myself that this was a twelve-year-old speaking, but it was almost impossible when I looked into that century-old face and listened to his words.

'And that's his sole purpose?' I asked. 'He's using you and your friends, he's studying you all, for the benefit of mankind?'

'Yes, or so I once believed. The Doctor has changed though; I think he has grown weary of us. I believe that he has other motives – perhaps he always had more than one. But we must go now, it isn't safe for us here.'

He began pulling at my arm, the way a child who hates a place might pull at a parent. I resisted though, because I had seen another door at the end of this room, a plastic double door without handles, the kind you might find leading to an operating theatre in a hospital.

'Come,' Joseph insisted. 'Mary is waiting for us and she's very frightened.'

'Wait, Joseph.' I indicated the plastic doorway. 'D'you know what's through there?'

I felt his shudder, and he continued to pull at me.

'I want to take a look inside,' I persisted.

'*No!*'

His cry startled me. 'Tell me why not, Joseph.'

'Michael is urging us to leave.'

'It'll only take a moment.'

'No, we cannot go in there. We *will* not.'

'Then tell me why.'

He stopped tugging and his voice was shaky when he answered me. 'Because,' he said, fearfully looking past me at the door, 'because that is the dissecting room.'

36

I could feel the beat of my heart as we stood beneath the dismal light of the ground-floor stairwell, me with my ear pressed against the locked door there, my companions holding on to each other like the two lost children they were. I listened for any signs of activity beyond the heavy wood, but either the door was too thick, or there was nothing going on on the other side.

Even I had not ventured into the dissecting room. I was scared. Yes, my senses had become numbed against all the distressing sights in this abominable place, but fear was something that could not be denied. I was afraid of the house itself, as if evil was seeping from its very walls, permeating the air with its corruptness, and creeping into me with malign intent. I wanted to get away from there, wanted to take deep, fresh untainted breaths again: with terrible guilt, I felt that I wanted to be among normal people once more. But I would not leave without Constance. Nothing could make me do that.

I stepped away from the door. 'What's through there?' I whispered to Joseph.

'I . . . I don't know.' He looked up at Mary, who shook her head. 'We're brought here sometimes, but none of us remember . . .'

'You're not telling the truth, are you?' There was something in his voice, the way he avoided my gaze.

He hung his head and I knelt in front of him. 'What is it, Joseph? I'm your friend, you know that.'

'We . . .' He took a breath. 'We have dreams. Michael tells us they are memories.'

'Of what? What happens in them?' Dreams were something I could no longer dismiss out of hand.

He kept his eyes downcast. 'Bad things,' was all he would say.

Before I could press him further, a noise started up behind the bare wall to our left. It was the familiar sound of the elevator moving. Almost at the same time we heard muffled voices approaching from the other side of the door. Then there came the scrape of a key being inserted into its lock.

I looked around wildly. I'd never get my two companions back up the stairs to the next floor in time – with my limp slowing me up, I probably wouldn't even make it myself. A narrow corridor ran alongside the staircase and in the dim light I thought I could make out a closed door at the end, one which undoubtedly led out to the riverbank behind the building.

'*Come on,*' I hissed, spinning Joseph and Mary round and pushing them in the direction of the back door.

Joseph shuffled and Mary hobbled, both moving as quickly as they could. I pushed past them, determined to have the door open before they reached it so that they could scoot outside without delay.

'Oh shit,' I groaned quietly when I saw it was bolted top and bottom. I guessed it would be locked as well, although now it was a moot point: by the time I'd unfastened the bolts, let alone tried one of the keys on the ring, the door at the other end would be open anyway and we would be in full view. The voices behind us grew louder as the door began to move.

It was as I looked back, ready to face whoever came through, that I noticed the pitchy hole underneath the stairway, more steps, these of stone, descending into it. Without a word, I grabbed the wrists of my companions, pulling them out of sight just as I glimpsed the door at the far end opening wide, two figures coming through. I expected to hear a shout, footsteps running after us, but the voices did not change their tone, nor did the footsteps quicken.

The girl almost stumbled as I urged them on, but I was able to steady her with my grip on her wrist. I wouldn't let either of them stop, because those sounds were advancing down the corridor, the people above us heading towards the rear door. I almost stumbled myself when I realized they might even be making for this stairway.

The stone staircase obviously led to the cellars or a basement area. I kept my companions moving, and I think the only reason that we were not heard was because the other people were making too much noise themselves, laughing and joking, one of them – there had to be three – even humming a tune. I might have been wrong – Lord knows I had more urgent things on my mind – but I thought I detected an edge to their laughter: it seemed too high-pitched, nervy, and their conversation was stilted, somehow forced.

It was even darker at the bottom of the stairs and I could only just make out the huge, black door that faced us. I listened for the sounds of bolts being drawn above, the click of a lock, but when I heard none of these and the footsteps suddenly grew heavier, I knew that the people behind us were descending the stairs. Even if the door in front of us was unlocked, there was no time to open it without being seen, so I did the only thing possible: I put my arms around Joseph's shoulders and Mary's wrist and hurried them round to the back of the stone stairway, quietly forcing them into the deeply shadowed and ever-diminishing gap between floor and angled ceiling. We huddled there, each of us holding our breath, listening to the loudening footsteps over our heads and the voices that approached with them. It was almost pitch black in our hideaway, and I was grateful for that. The air was musty-damp.

I could feel the two crouched bodies beside me trembling almost uncontrollably and I could only hope their nerve would hold, that neither of them would utter a sound in their fright. I squeezed them both, the only way I could think of calming them, but their ragged gasps for breath seemed inordinately loud to me.

The footsteps came to a shuffling halt and I heard the jangling of keys.

'Do we use sedation?' a man's voice said.

'A mild one,' came the reply from another man. 'Just for cooperation. He doesn't want it too dosed up.'

Metal scraping against metal, a key being pushed into a lock.

'It'll behave,' said a third voice. 'Always does when it knows it's in for a good time.'

More scraping, the big door being drawn back. Soft light brightened the corridor slightly and I pushed my companions further into our hiding place. A stench drifted through with the light, a reek that was far worse than the dormitory's.

'Who's the partner?'

The voices were becoming fainter.

'I think it's the little crippled girl again . . .'

As they moved further inside, their words became too soft to be understood, but I thought – God, I was sure! – a name was mentioned. It sounded like 'Bell'. Panic seized me. Had he said Constance's surname? Could I have been mistaken? What did it mean if he had? Dread upon dread had tormented me that night, yet none affected me as badly as this. Too many frightening visions rushed into my head, most of them obscene, triggered by the phenomena in my own bedroom the previous night, that sick, incorporeal, sexual orgy of which Constance had been part.

Joseph winced as I squeezed his shoulder too hard, but he did not let out a cry. I dropped my hand away immediately, but the thoughts, the cruel, taunting images, would not cease.

Why hadn't Constance told me the whole truth about PERFECT REST? Why hadn't she shared its awful secret with me? Had I been wrong to think there was something between us, a bonding that was all to do with love and not just mutual disabilities? Didn't she trust me enough to tell? Or was she ashamed? Did her involvement in what secretly went on at PERFECT REST shame her so deeply it was impossible for her to confide in me? Just what *was* her complicity in all this?

As the stench drifted out from the open doorway, almost choking us with its rancidness, the girl began to make soft mewling noises, the piteous sounds of an animal in distress. She crawled deeper into the corner created between sloping ceiling and floor, and I realized it wasn't the smell that was causing the reaction but its *source*. Beside me, Joseph was trembling as if with fever, but other sounds distracted me again, distant voices, a grating, something sliding across stone, then shouting, voices raised in excitement or anger, I couldn't tell which.

Quietness again. Shortly followed by a new disturbance.

It was a cumbersome dragging of feet, growing louder as it approached the doorway. Something grunted – I thought it might be an animal – and one of the men shouted. The dragging of heavy footsteps once more. Now all three of us in the sanctuary beneath the stairway pushed ourselves in further, trying to make ourselves as small as possible, using the darkness as a cloak as the sounds drew nearer.

I thought I could hear rough breathing, a guttural kind of sound, and it seemed very close, almost as if whatever was being escorted from that basement chamber was standing right over us. I realized it was the acoustics of the short, brick corridor, the concrete beneath us, and the angle of the stairway over our heads, a funnel effect that was deceptive. Nevertheless, we froze in the darkness, none of us daring to breathe lest we be heard, and even too tense to tremble.

The group of men and their charge was emerging from

378

the underground room and it was with relief that we heard the first footsteps over our heads. The scuffing-shuffling joined them and a tickling sensation on my cheek told me that dust was drifting down from our angled ceiling.

We waited there, still holding our breath, my knees hurting as they pressed into concrete, all of us too afraid to move for fear of giving ourselves away, until the footsteps and the scuffing died away and we were left nerve-racked and drained.

I slumped back against the wall and Mary finally let a shudder escape. There was just enough light in this little nook to see Joseph crouched on his knees, hands clenched to his chest as if he'd been praying. We remained alert for any more noises, the footsteps returning, the grunting of something less than human, but nothing came. Eventually, when we were able to control the shaking, calm our own breathing, I felt brave enough to speak, albeit in a low whisper.

'What the hell was *that*?'

Joseph leaned closer to speak into my ear. 'I think it's too late,' he whispered. 'I think we should leave now.'

'Without Constance? I'm sorry, Joseph, but that isn't an option.'

'You can't help her.'

'I can bloody well try.'

Mary twisted round to clutch at me. 'P-p-please . . .' she stammered.

'I'm not leaving without her,' I said firmly, even though my natural inclination was to get as far away from that place as possible. Forget the media, go straight to the police. These two alone would be enough to initiate an investigation and when I told the Law what I knew, they'd be applying for an immediate search warrant. It would still take time though, and who knew what would happen to Constance in the meanwhile? Images of her, vulnerable and naked, surrounded by creatures from some dark realm that knew no place on this earth, invaded my mind and I had the notion that the phantasmagoria last night, in my own home, was a portent of some kind, illusions based upon a terrible reality that was to come. No, I couldn't leave here without her, she was too precious to me. Even the fresh doubts as to her true involvement with PERFECT REST could not dissuade me.

'I have to go after them,' I said as I began to crawl from our hideaway.

'No, please,' I heard Joseph call after me.

But I was on my feet and swinging round on to the first step before he struggled out behind me, the girl following.

'Wait!' he cried, grabbing my hand on the rail.

'I can't, Joseph. I have to get to her.'

'There's another way!'

I hesitated on the second step. Their eyes were wide as they stared up at me from the gloomy corridor, and I saw that Mary had been weeping, probably through the whole ordeal.

'Michael says he knows where they are keeping her, but there's another way to get there, a safer way.' Joseph kept his dry old hand over mine on the stair-rail.

'But they took that thing up here.' I pointed at the way ahead with my other hand.

'There will be too many between us and Constance.'

'Michael is telling you this?' And in truth, I was having my own strange mind images – a long, dark chamber, doors on either side, a narrow stairway leading up – and something – not a voice, just a thought with these impressions – was urging me to follow Joseph.

'He's letting us know,' Joseph replied.

I peered up the stairs. 'But there isn't another way,' I said.

Joseph tapped my hand and when I turned, he was pointing in another direction. 'There is,' he said. 'Through there.'

I looked in the direction he was indicating, saw the black cavern of the open doorway behind us, felt weak at the thought of going in there. I really hadn't liked what I'd heard coming out just a few moments ago.

Slowly, I returned to the bottom of the stairs, reaching inside my jacket for the pocket torch as I did so. Joseph and Mary huddled together, watching me.

'Is that the way you two want to go?' I asked them.

They glanced at each other before Joseph replied. 'No, but Michael tells us it is the best way.'

I turned on the torch and shone it through the doorway. Its light barely penetrated the shadows.

'What else is in there, Joseph?' I asked. 'What does the Doctor keep down here?'

He seemed afraid to answer, and it was the girl who spoke.

'Others,' she said.

37

Others.

That's what Mary had said. Others. But what did she mean?

I thought I had seen everything in this God-forsaken hell-house, and now I was being told there was something more.

Others.

I felt my skin begin to crawl.

38

The light-switch was on the inside, beside the big iron door that had been left open, and I pushed it down to find that I still needed the torch, for even though at least six lights came on along both sides of the lengthy, low-ceilinged chamber, their glow came from behind thick, pearled glass and wire mesh. The stench prickled my nostrils and there was something deeply oppressing about the atmosphere itself.

My skin still crawled, as if tiny spider legs were scurrying over its surface.

I raised the torch, throwing its beam ahead. A wide, flagstone floor swept ahead of me, moss growing from its cracks, puddles of water pooling beneath the walls. I saw there were doorways all the way along on both sides, doorways set in shallow alcoves, rough-wood doorways with small barred windows in them.

Oh God, what next? I asked myself, and as I listened, I heard stirrings from the other side of those doors.

I went over to the nearest cell and its little barred window was just low enough for me to see through without stepping on tip-toe. I shone the light through the opening into the darkened, bare cell beyond.

The stone floor was slightly angled towards a round black hole in the far corner and I could only guess at the reason: somewhere in the grounds there was probably a huge covered cesspit, drains from these dungeon-like rooms running to it. On the opposite side to the hole, I could just make out a narrow cot, its iron legs bolted to the floor, its filthy, stained mattress without bedsheets of any kind. The smell was even worse here.

I jumped back with a start when a face suddenly appeared in front of me on the other side of the door. But the face had no eyes, not even indents in the skull where they should have been, and the two holes at its centre that presumably served as a nose dilated and closed in rapid succession, as if this featureless thing were sniffing the air. There was no aperture that could represent a mouth and as I continued to back away, I wondered how such a being could be fed. As if in reply, a long slit opened up in its jaw, a thin, lipless slash that had not been visible when closed. Uttering a high-pitched keening, this thing reached for me through the bars and I saw that its hand had only three fingers.

I reeled further away from it and crashed into another cell door behind me. At once something slid around my brow, something smooth and soft, like a tentacle. It pulled my head back against the bars of the cell door's window.

I could hear deep-throated gurglings close to my ear, and snufflings, the sound a rooting pig might make. Another tentacle-like thing slithered around my throat, tightening its grip as soon as it had hold, and I felt my flesh being crushed, my windpipe constricted. I pulled at this sleek, soft, noose with my free hand, but my fingers could not grasp it and suddenly I was struggling for air, my senses quickly beginning to swim.

In panic I looked around for my two companions, my head unable to move because of the vice-like grip around my throat and brow, only my single eye able to dart from side to side. Joseph and Mary were still in the underground chamber's doorway as if scared to venture further and, as the torchlight caught their faces, I could see they could not understand what was happening to me. I was in the shadow of the alcove, just a vague shape to them, and my torchlight in their eyes didn't help matters.

384

I tried to shout, perhaps even to scream, but the grip around my throat was too powerful and all that came out was a throttled-squawking that in any other circumstances would have been an embarrassment. I turned the light on myself, dazzling my eye as I pointed it at my own face, praying that now they would realize my predicament. I could feel myself beginning to swoon from lack of oxygen.

Fortunately my friends quickly realized what was happening and they both rushed forward as one, reaching for the fleshy cords that chained me there, pulling at them with all their strength. As my own fingers had, theirs also slid off every time they thought they had a grip and I could hear them both gasping with their efforts. My vision became tinged with redness.

Then something hard pushed by my cheek, scraping skin, but journeying on, striking into the black opening behind me. I heard a screech, felt the stick going in again, another screech, another blow, another screech. The coils around my head and neck loosened, only slightly, but enough for me to push my fingers between the lower one and my throat. Fingers joined with thumb, and I pulled, pulled as hard as I could, while Mary continued to pummel the thing that held me there, repeatedly smashing the end of her walking stick into it. I heard a squeal, and then a kind of yelp, and both cords loosened even more so that I was able to slip through them. I whirled around in time to glimpse a smooth, hairless head, its features minimal, all concentrated in a small area at its centre. Thick, lashless eyelids blinked at me just before Mary struck the thing with her stick again and it reeled away into the shadows, squawking like an injured crow as it went, the tentacles slithering back into the hole like limbs belonging to some exotic sea creature returning to their dark underwater cave. They ended in pointed, quivering tips and as they, too, disappeared from sight, I rushed back to the barred window and shone the torch through.

The light caught movement, something scudding across

the filthy floor to hide itself in the far shadows. I followed it with the beam, found it again, cowering in a corner, and I drew in a sharp breath at the sight. The creature hid its head beneath the tendril-like arms, so that all I could see was a pale, sleek, naked body that seemed to darken under the glare rather than lighten. It was as if a shadow were passing through its flesh, a grey blush that made the figure blend with the surrounding darkness. I realized this shading was some form of self-induced camouflage, a way of making the creature sink into its background. Within moments, it looked as if it were made of stone, yet still it pulsed, still it breathed, the tentacles wrapping themselves around the head and body, the 'knees' – although the legs appeared to be jointless and as bare and smooth as its 'arms' – tight into its chest. Soon, the whole thing became motionless and, seemingly, as solid as the floor and walls around it; only because I had kept the torchlight pointed directly at it could I tell it was still there. It had become a statue of sorts, only its shadowed contours admitting its presence by vaguely defining its shape.

I turned away and leaned against the damp wall beside the thick, wooden door, well clear of the barred window lest those tentacles return to seize me. My shoulder pressed into the hard, wet stone and I had to set my feet flat against the floor to keep myself standing. I'm not sure how long I stayed that way – minutes, seconds, I just don't know – but it was Joseph's voice that finally roused me.

'Dismas?'

I couldn't even look his way.

He tried again. 'Dis?'

I slowly craned my head in his direction, my shoulder still pressed into the wall, supporting me.

'Dis, we should leave this place now. Michael wants us to hurry.'

I pushed myself away from the wall. If I'd been in battle, then maybe you'd call me shell-shocked. But there were no cannons or exploding shells, nor were there the cries and screams of dying men: there was only the horror of the things I had discovered that night. Mary came forward and touched my face with her fingertips.

It was so strange, because in that touch, I could feel her pity for *me*, a compassion so sincere and so unselfish, I could have wept again. I took her hand in my own and kissed her fingertips.

Then I straightened. 'We'll move on,' I told them both, 'but first I'm going to see what else is here.'

I didn't feel courageous, nor did I feel curious, as I worked my way along the dim corridor, going from side to side to peer into each cell: no, I just felt resolute; and filled with a cold anger. I saw things there straight from my nightmare, and from many nightmares long past. A creature that lay watching me from the floor of its prison room, normal, if emaciated, in upper form and face (even if there was a little madness in its sullen eyes), but with just one limb descending from its hips, as though the legs had fused together to fashion a fish's tail of sorts. It rolled on to its stomach and pushed itself across the floor at alarming speed and I jumped back when I felt something scrabbling at my shoes. I shone the light down at the bottom of the door and saw another hole at ground level, one I hadn't noticed before and no doubt used to pass food through to these wretched inmates. A grimy hand had appeared there and it was this that was touching my feet.

My two companions mutely followed as I went from door to door, and I could feel their misery at what was exposed to me, an outsider, even if my own shape was not exactly of the ordained order. I also felt their dread of these other creatures, for although they were all of the 'anomalous and curious' kind, imperfections of nature that were beyond all bounds, there *was* something fearsome about them; why else would they be incarcerated in dungeons beneath the house? There seemed to be a malign intent about these creatures, an exudation of evil, as though their ill-formed configuration was representative of their inner singularity, a twisted psyche imagined by its physical shell. I, of all people, should have dismissed such an idea out of hand – book by its cover, and all that – but it was a feeling (not just a notion) that was too strong to reject.

I moved on, another cell, another monstrosity inside, although this time I thought that there had been some cruel mistake or that this person had been locked away for reasons other than physical abnormality. At first glance she was beautiful, with large, dark eyes and heavy lashes, raven-black hair that hung in long tresses around her elegant shoulders, small but perfect breasts, the nipples hard and pink against their pallid mounds, legs that were long and thighs that barely touched, the dark triangle of hair between them like a pointer to enticement. She *was* beautiful, but when my gaze returned to hers and I looked deeper into those appealing eyes I saw that same feeble-mindedness I had witnessed moments before in the other prisoner, an imbecile's gape now accompanied by an idiot's grin. And when, with a snicker muffled by her hand, she turned away, I saw the reason for her internment here.

There was no skin on her back, in fact, no flesh at all; neither was there much flesh behind her legs. It was as if the meat there had been cut away, leaving bones and muscle, gristle and tendons, organs and tubes, arteries and veins, all open to the fetid air, all displayed before my probing torch. I saw wires and dulled metal plates holding organs in place, tying blood vessels to her spinal column, gauze covering the most delicate areas, I saw tubing that was synthetic and of different colours, presumably there to aid bodily fluids and movement, replacements for parts that must have rotted or become dysfunctional. The cavities glistened with wetness and jutting just beneath the bands of muscle stretched over the bone of her shoulder blade I could see something throbbing in a regular rhythm; I realized it was part of her naked heart.

How one whose innards were so dangerously exposed could be kept from infection and disease, particularly in these foul conditions, I had no idea, but I guessed that her own immune system had adapted in some way to play its part, protecting her from invasive poisons and bacteria while medical application did the rest. Yes, I'd have thought it impossible, but I had observed too many impossibilities that night now to be astonished.

Still resolute, determined to view it all, I went on from cell to cell, peering in, dismayed but no longer shocked by the things I observed. A body so immense it made its prison seem tiny, a person, a non-person – a *freakish* entity – that appeared barely alive, tubes inserted into its orifices that, I presumed, flowed with life-preserving substances and liquids, an oxygen mask over its face to pump air into its weight-beleaguered lungs. In another, a figure so ulcerated and ridden with running sores it was impossible to identify gender, whose eyes gleamed with madness and pain, and whose screams under the glare of my light pierced my heart as well as my head. An empty cell I thought, until something scurried from one dark corner to the other. Each time I directed the beam on to it, it moved again, lightning fast, low to the ground, an odd shape with too many limbs. Finally I ensnared it in my small circle of light by moving ahead and waiting for it to end its run in the torch glow. Numbed though I was, a gasp still escaped me when it rested briefly and I was able to take it in.

Its body *was* low to the floor, for it moved on all fours, the arms and legs bent high over the body, hands and feet splayed outwards on the ground, its head watching me from between those spread arms as a spider might watch a fly. It was only momentarily frozen though, and once again, with incredible speed, it scurried away into the shadows. This time I had no desire to capture it in the light: I had seen enough.

Somehow I persisted in my determination to view them all, for these were the creatures of my last dream, visions made flesh, and they held a bizarre fascination for me. Maybe I wanted to confront my own nightmare, a perverse way of expunging it forever. Or perhaps – and I hated myself for the possibility – I wanted to feel superior (a rare experience for me), wanted to know that my own afflictions were nothing compared to those of these aberrants. Who could tell? Certainly not me, neither then, nor now.

As I went on I wondered how they had found me last night, wondered if somehow they had tapped into Michael's power, travelling with him along with the others to my home, to my mind. Perhaps the telepathy's very collectivity was so great that they were carried along with those directed thoughts despite themselves; or perhaps something deep within them, whether it was cunning or desperation, saw that mental power as a means of a brief escape for themselves. Again, there was no way of knowing for sure, then or now, but I'd always been aware that nature compensates – consider my own one-eyed but clear vision, as sharp as a hawk's, my hearing and sense of smell, as keen as any wolf's, the strength in my shoulders recompensing for the weakness of my leg – so maybe some of them had taken on this unique gift, the stronger carrying the weaker.

I filled my head with these ghastly depressing sights, some of which *defied* description, until I reached the end of the chamber. Only then did I press my forehead to the cold, wet wall to take stock, to absorb everything I had seen and somehow accept it. It wasn't easy, nor did I succeed entirely.

A hand touched my shoulder.

Without looking round, I said, 'Why, Joseph? Why would anyone keep them like this? Why would they be allowed to live?'

The hand withdrew.

'Life is a gift, whatever the circumstances,' Joseph said.

I whirled around. 'Like this? You think this is living?'

'It's all we know,' he replied.

'But –'

He raised a frail hand. 'Even for these others, it's all they know. It's the only life they have experienced and they know no better.'

'You do, though. Michael has shown you, you've read books. Constance has told you of other things.'

'Even so, we might have been content to remain here. Now everything is changing . . .'

I was still blind with fury. 'Wisbeech is going to pay for this, I promise you that.'

'Just help us be free,' Joseph said. 'That's all we ask.'

'You will be, Joseph.' I looked back at all the cell doors, six on either side of the long room. Oh yes, they would *all* be free. I'd help them.

And I'd begin now, before we left this dungeon of the damned.

39

At this far end of the chamber there was another door, this one set back in a recess in the wall and, like the main entrance, made of iron, but much narrower. The same key fitted its lock.

'You're sure this is the way?' I asked Joseph before pushing at the door.

Joseph merely nodded.

'Michael's telling you this?'

He nodded again. 'Michael goes on many journeys through his mind.'

'He's aware of this place, these ... people ... here?'

'We all are.'

'And can he tell you where this might lead?'

'I can only sense him urging us to use it. The weakness is with me.'

'Okay.' What else could I say? What else could I do? I shoved the door and it opened with a squealing of hinges.

Inside was a stone staircase leading upwards, the walls so close I could touch both sides just by raising my arms slightly. The brickwork was rough and unfinished, the atmosphere cold. There was a light-switch, but I decided not to use it; who knew what lay at the top of those stairs?

It was a relief to leave the dungeon and its unfortunate but frightening denizens behind, and I shone the torchlight ahead as we climbed, my limp pretty bad by now, fatigue and trauma playing their part. In this narrow space, it was difficult for the disjoined girl to climb too, and when I glanced around, she was moving sideways, one hand on the steps above, her right foot leading. Joseph was last and he waited patiently as Mary struggled.

There was a short landing at the top, another door at the end of it. This door was sturdy-looking, but I knew I'd have no trouble picking its lock if I couldn't find the right key on the ring. The third one I tried opened the door easily and cautiously, after turning off the torch I looked through.

There was some kind of storeroom on the other side, lit by two neon ceiling lights, sliding-door cupboards around three of its walls, a work bench and smaller cupboards running the length of the fourth. At its centre was a large square, multi-drawered desk. I listened for a while, scanning the room as I did so, ready to duck back out of sight should the need arise. But there was only silence. I crept in, beckoning Mary and Joseph to follow.

Going to the desk in the middle of the room I looked around me and was surprised at what had been hidden from my view behind the door. The whole section of wall, from floor to ceiling, was filled with banks of VTR machines, the kind of set-up used for the mass production of video cassette copies. I went to the cupboards and slid back one of the doors: the shelves inside were packed with film cans, their dulled metal and faded labels informing me they were old stock. Without bothering to read the labels I moved on to the next cupboard, sliding back its door to reveal stacks of vertically arranged video cassettes: I cocked my head to read their labels, but all they had on them were sets of six-digit numbers, each set separated by a dash. I realized these were dates, some of them going back to 1979. A quick reinspection of the film cans confirmed that the handwritten labels were also dates, some of these going as far back as the Sixties. Perhaps they were case studies of everyone kept at this place, I thought, recordings of their progress. It might explain the changeover from film to video tape, the latter a relatively new and far easier method of filming and storing.

Dates ... birth dates ... Wisbeech wasn't interested in names; figures were obviously more factual to him. I doubted he even considered his charges as persons: no, to him they were probably just specimens, freakish examples with which to experiment, to research. That was what this was all about: PERFECT REST's secret wing was a research centre, a covert laboratory specializing in the unique, atypical and bizarre, the 'exceptional departures from the ordinary', to coin Wisbeech's own phrase, with its own 'Black Museum' of human divergences. The findings, the results of these studies, no doubt were shared – no, *sold* – to other medical or scientific research units around the country, if not the world, and there had to be hundreds of malformed babies – *thousands* worldwide – born each year, infants so badly deformed there seemed little chance of survival (or so the anguished parents would be told), only to be secreted away to become valuable commodities of research. And now, with genetics the new wonder-science as far as humans and animals were concerned, their value must have increased tenfold.

My head was spinning. What kind of bastard would do this to his fellow but less fortunate men, hiding them from the outside world, confining them in conditions unfit for the lowest beast, using them merely as specimens of study? Wisbeech, it seemed, was that kind, but I was going to bust the whole sick business wide open! I grabbed one of the video cassettes from the shelf and pushed it as deep into my jacket pocket as it would go. The top of it stuck out, but that didn't matter, it was secure.

Another horrendous idea occurred to me. If this was big business – and something told me it was – it was highly profitable. It was also very hush-hush. So was it profitable enough for force to be used to keep it secret? Henry. I was thinking of the murder of Henry. Could it be connected with this? Had it been a warning to me? Was it meant to have *been* me? And the manner of my friend's death, the mutilation of his body. I remembered the look on the face of the boy hiding in my office, the terror in his eyes when he saw my misshapen figure, and I thought of the things living in the dungeon below. Could it be . . . ? Could it be that an abnormal person with a subnormal brain had been sent up to my agency, there to discover Henry instead of me? I tried not to think of the unnatural things that had been done to him, but an overwhelming guilt swept through me. It should have been me, not Henry . . .

'Dis?'

Joseph's voice brought me back.

'Are you all right?'

I looked down at this tiny man – *boy* – and my rage only grew. 'Yeah, I'm just dandy, Joseph.'

'Can we go, then? Please?'

I looked away from him, scanning the room again. The second door was at the end of the work bench, almost opposite the one by which we'd entered. Pointing, I said, 'D'you know where it leads?'

'No,' he replied.

'But we have to use it, right? There's no point in going back the way we came?'

He shook his wizened head. 'Michael is very afraid for us,' he said then.

'*Too* much information, Joseph. I don't think I wanted to know that.' I tried to give him a grin, but it didn't come off. He held out his hand to Mary and she hobbled over to him, her walking stick tapping on the bare floor. 'How about you, Mary?' I said to her. 'Do you know what's through that door?'

She, too, shook her head as she clutched Joseph's outstretched hand.

'Okay. There's only one way to find out.' But suddenly, I felt no enthusiasm for further discovery – I'd already learned more than I knew how to deal with about PERFECT REST and Dr Leonard K. Wisbeech. Sure, there were still plenty more questions, but my head – and my emotions – couldn't cope with any more. I wanted out, right there and then. I had evidence, I had two of the victims involved and their testimony: what else did I need?

Only Constance, I told myself. Just the person you've finally found to love and who could return those same feelings. I crept around the centre desk and over to the second door.

It was unlocked.

40

Amidst the intense umbra of the vast room beyond the door there was a bright oasis of light. And in the light there was a large bed draped with deep red velvet, the smooth material overflowing on to the floor and even running up the wall behind.

On the bed, naked skin contrasting with the rich colour of the fabric around it, lay a small figure with frail limbs and curved spine. Long loose brown hair splayed over the velvet beneath the head and shoulders. She was curled like a sleeping child, the knuckle of one hand touching her lips. Her soft lips. Lips that I adored.

Constance was so fragile and so vulnerable lying there that I moaned aloud before blindly stumbling forward, my attention on her alone, oblivious to whatever else lay in the room's oceanic darkness. My foot caught something on the floor and I almost fell, somehow managing to keep my balance, arms flailing before me, steps quickening.

I rushed into the ring of light, where concentrated luminance stifled anything beyond, and I knelt on the edge of the bed so that I could touch her shoulder. Constance stirred, but her eyes remained closed.

I shook her, gently at first, then a little harder, until her eyelids flickered. She opened them hesitantly and I saw that even under the harsh glare of the light her pupils did not contract. There was no recognition in her eyes when they fixed on me, just a dulled uncertainty.

I pulled her towards me and held her in my arms. In

397

panic, I studied her face and her body, looking, I suppose for signs of abuse. 'Constance, it's me. It's Nick.'

Her eyes closed again and a small groan escaped her.

'Constance. Please, try to wake up.'

A frown creased her forehead, but there was no comprehension in her eyes when they fluttered open again.

'Nick . . .' It was a soft, weary cry.

'You must try, Constance. I have to get you out of here.'

Desperately, I searched the area around us in vain for her clothes. Squinting my eye, I peered into the surrounding blackness and only then did I make out another pool of light some distance away, another red velvet-draped bed enclosed by dark borders, two figures on that bed, one of them small and naked, held by another who . . . who was not me.

At first I had thought I was looking at a reflection in a mirror on the far side of the room, but the person holding Constance looked nothing like me. It was someone I knew, though.

His shoulders were broad, his figure sleek, and he was handsome, oh so gloriously handsome. The shiny-lapelled dinner suit, the black bow-tie, the glossy slick-backed hair – oh yes, he was very familiar to me by now. And when I put my arm protectively around Constance's shoulders, he mimicked the movement, he matched me perfectly. And when I pointed a trembling finger at him, he did exactly the same to me. The only difference was that he was smiling and I was not.

That was when I finally began to understand that this person I was staring at – and yes, it was definitely a reflection in a mirror – *was* me. That I was, and had been, haunting myself.

But I had no time to dwell upon its significance, for suddenly the whole vast area was lit up in a shock of lights.

*

It came at me fast, a blur that was on me before I could make out what it was, an assailant that snarled and snuffled like an animal as it tore at me. As I fell backwards under its force, I caught a glimpse of a high-ceilinged room full of tall arc lights, light-reflectors, cameras mounted on tripods – and startled people, who watched this abrupt confrontation on the bed as if stunned.

I sprawled against the velvet as claw-like hands encircled my throat, losing my grip on Constance, unable to draw in breath, an odd pressure pushing against my eyeball from behind. As I fought for air the images that came into view all had soft edges, their focus shifting constantly, so that I couldn't tell if they were real or imaginary. I saw faces, Wisbeech's among them, and many more, strangers to me, then the nurse, the head one – *what was her name, what was her name?* – Fletcher! that was her name, and as they dimmed, became almost translucent, they were replaced by others, the faces of all those I had met that night in PERFECT REST, above and *below* stairs! and they too faded, returned, faded once more, and all had been grinning and laughing, as though sharing some huge joke, one that was on me! and then two more individuals appeared, both mocking me, their features shimmering as if viewed through a heat haze, the old midwife, Sparrow, and my own elegant former *self*! the person I once was, an *alter ego* that was not a wish but a past! and *they* were laughing at me too, enjoying the joke, for weren't they the ones who had lured me to this place . . . ?

My vision began to dull, even though my eyelid could not possibly close, because the eyeball had been pushed too far from its socket . . .

Yet still I could discern the face – the *face*? – of this demon-thing who was squeezing the life from me, the other images only superimposed over the reality; could see the great gaping mouth, a cavernous hole that almost took up the entire head, the lipless mouth ringed by thin, needle-like teeth, the gaps between giving each one its own deadly individuality, two longer ones – at least three inches long! – descending from the centre, their equally long counterparts below set wider to accommodate them. The eyes were severely slanted, located wide of each other on the long, angled brow, dark pupils against yellow backgrounds, like a cat's but even more sinister and *far* more malign, and there was no nose – Christ, there wasn't room for a nose! – and the brow canted back acutely to a tufty protuberance on top of its head, a topknot that might have been gristled skin or a reptilian crest. As if these demon's features were not enough for such comparison, the skin itself was reddish, as if it truly had been spawned in Hell, and even its ears were pointed and tufted like the top of its head.

This was no human, this could not possibly be of human origin. I refused to believe so. This *was* a demon, this *was* a BEAST! Nothing on Earth could have given birth to such a creature.

Its small head – *a head that was set in its chest rather than between its shoulders* – weaved about me, harsh, stinking hot breath poisoning precious air between us, black, pointed tongue quivering stiffly inside the huge hole of its mouth, those thin dagger-teeth only inches away from me, and I wondered if it would shred my face before or after it had choked me.

But something distracted it. Those terrifying, slanted eyes shifted their gaze, looking past me at the other person who had moved on the bed. The gleam in them seemed to change, to become lascivious.

I twisted my head, to follow its look, and I saw what *it* saw and I began to fight back, for it was Constance this thing was leering at, and she was lying naked, helplessly exposed to this creature. I understood its thoughts, the rapaciousness in its eyes.

I thought I might explode with the fury that swept through me

As I've said, my shoulders and arms have always been

strong, and now anger and desperation gave them power I had never known before. I grabbed the *beast's* hairy wrists, lifting my shoulders from the bed as I did so, the hump of my back providing leverage, and I forced those hands slowly, ever so slowly, away from my throat, the slender clawed fingers slowly unfurling, the *beast* returning its attention to me, bewilderment in its rabid eyes. My hands and its wrists shook with opposing pressure and I was aware that ulti-mately it was a battle I could not win, my attacker had a superior strength that would sustain him longer than my fierce but temporary outburst. So with one last effort, I lifted him away from me and then let go. And as I let go, I brought my own head up.

My forehead smashed into its shallow lower jaw, closing that gaping mouth, but while I cried out with the shock of pain, the *beast* merely grunted. I fell back on to the bed, all senses spinning, and once more the tenacious fingers with their curling nails found my throat. The pressure resumed as if there had never been an interruption, and this time I knew I was totally helpless, that my reserves of strength were all but used up in that last-ditch effort. At first I thought someone was using a dimmer switch on all the lights because everything began to grow dark, but I soon realized it was me, I was leaving it all behind. I tried – oh God, how I tried – to draw in breath, but soon it didn't matter: the pain had lost its bite, my panic had lost its relevance. I knew I was dying, that air would never squeeze through to my lungs to save me, yet somehow it no longer mattered.

I was dying and it wasn't so bad. Hell, it was relatively easy.

41

It was a voice that saved me. A voice from a very long way off. It had quite an effect though, for the pressure at my throat suddenly eased, and then all the pain and fear and helplessness came rushing back.

I slumped to the floor beside the bed, clutching at its soft material and gasping in great mouthfuls of life-giving air. The voice was still some distance away, but not as far as before.

'Take it away,' it was saying, and I realized it was the pounding in my own ears, blood rushing through them, that muted the words.

When I finally managed to look up, still gagging for air, body hunched over my knees, I saw the smiling face of Dr Leonard K. Wisbeech peering into mine.

'You took your time getting here, Mr Dismas,' I thought I heard him say.

'Wh . . . what?'

His voice became clearer as my heartbeat dropped to a more regular, though not yet quite normal, rhythm and the roaring in my ears softened.

'Did you think you weren't expected?' he said, the smile remaining, but the eyes as hard as steel. 'You were on camera the moment you showed yourself at the gate. Hidden cameras, of course, and fitted with night-sights. I was curious as to what you would get up to, you see, so I let you have the run of the place in the knowledge that you could easily be brought here when we were ready for you. It seems you've saved us the trouble though: here you are in the very place to which you would eventually have been brought.'

His face moved away from mine as he straightened and I could only watch silently as he towered over me. Behind him was the thing that had attacked me, the grotesque I could only think of as *beast*, and I shivered at the sight.

It – I could *not* refer to it as *he*, for this thing was part-animal, part-man, neither species, it seemed to me, dominating the other – was now under restraint, the male orderly I knew as Bruce holding one of its arms, another thickset orderly clinging to the other. Its reddish, mottled skin was mostly covered by short, wiry hair and its shoulders were massive against a slim waist and legs, even its forearms thinning beyond the elbow to the wrists, its hands long, slender fingers ending in curled nails, like claws.

And then I saw the most frightening thing of all about this mad-eyed creature, for events had happened too fast, my sight too restricted, when I had been attacked. Springing from the creature's naked loins like some lengthy erubescent rod, whose colour paled and surged, was a penis of the like I had never before witnessed. Although it was slender considering its stretch – a foot-and-a-half at least! – it was gorged with blood that set it rigid and quivering, the flow inside accounting for its fluctuating hues, and at its end was a split, bulbous head that glistened wetly under the harsh lights. Rather than a natural organ of procreation, this looked lethal, more like a weapon of destruction. I shuddered at the thought of the damage it could do if it entered someone as small and frail as Constance.

It all came to me then – the high-tech video cameras, the arc lights, the black cables that littered the floor like a vast nest of snakes; the people spread around here in this high-ceilinged studio, the man sitting by a box full of switches, a sound-man wearing earphones. Jesus Christ, this was Hollywood sleaze in the Home Counties, the kind of porno stuff that even the most hardcore fans might find hard to take. It struck me like a thunderbolt, although it still failed to make any kind of sense.

I had thought that at its very worst, PERFECT REST was some clandestine research centre involved in the nature of deformity, but now I had uncovered a far deeper, a far darker, secret: the inmates here were being exploited in much more grievous ways, their abnormalities used by the profiteers of celluloid voyeurism. Barriers had been breached, boundaries pushed back, in the last decades and public taste and acceptability had been redefined, the search for more and more outrage an ongoing quest; and here, at this so-called place of perfect rest, it was being provided for them. What could be more titillating to such degenerates than sordid sexual acts between ... there was no avoiding the term ... *freaks*? It was beyond all bounds and I could not understand what would make an eminent physician like Leonard Wisbeech turn to such abomination. Was it just for financial gain? Or was there another motivation? Had his own moral depravity led him to this? Was his smooth, sophisticated exterior, his obvious pre-eminence as a physician, merely the disguise of a corrupt soul?

'Cover him!' Wisbeech barked at the *beast's* 'handlers' as he walked away from me, as though suddenly offended by the brutal nakedness of this creature.

The senior nurse, Fletcher, appeared with a robe held out in front of her. She swiftly threw it around the shoulders of the agitated demon-like thing and, almost comically – only I wasn't laughing – the material fell around its jutting member. The *beast* snarled and tried to pull the robe off, but its guardians held firm.

'Shall I sedate him?' Fletcher asked Wisbeech, who by this time had turned about and was watching the proceedings.

'Only mildly,' the doctor replied. 'We'll be needing him soon.' He eyed me as I lay slumped against the bed. 'After I've had a little chat with our new guest,' he added.

I struggled to regain my feet. *'What the fuck is going on?'* I yelled at Wisbeech, even though I knew the answer in part.

Bruce, the orderly, quickly stepped forward and slapped me down again. I fell on to the bed and felt Constance move behind me. She gave out another small groan.

I looked from her to Wisbeech. 'What have you done to her?' I pleaded, voice cracking, mid-sentence.

'I've made her compliant,' Wisbeech answered and I wanted to tear the contemptuous smile off his face with my bare hands. 'Rohypnol, *Mr* Dismas.'

The *Mr* was exaggerated, all part of his contempt.

'It's a sedative, normally prescribed for sleeplessness, but sometimes used to induce an almost hypnotic state. It makes the subject not only more malleable, but forgetful also. Constance has never fully remembered what has happened to her in this state, although I'm afraid her subconscious is bothering her more and more nowadays. I believe she is building a resistance to the drug, but no matter, her usefulness has come to an end.'

'What are you talking about? What have you been doing to her?' I gathered Constance up in my arms again, trying to cover her nakedness with my own body, aware of the shame she would feel at having her crooked little body exposed to the eyes of others. To people like us, nakedness before strangers is more than just an embarrassment, it's a humiliation.

Wisbeech silently regarded me for several moments, as though engaged in private thoughts in which I figured prominently. When he spoke, his smile had returned. 'What do you say, Nurse Fletcher? Does this hunchback deserve an explanation? After all, there is no one he can tell.'

The senior nurse shifted agitatedly. 'It's getting late, Doctor. I think we should carry on as planned.'

Wisbeech's response was firm. 'No. I'd like to discuss matters with *Mr* Dismas. Can't you see the curiosity in that lonely eye of his? Oh, and just feel the anger emanating from him. I do believe he would like to render me harm. Isn't that so, *Mr* Dismas? You do see me as the villain of the piece, don't you? And you know, it's not *entirely* deserved.'

'I've seen the people you keep locked up in this place, I've seen what you've done to them.' I spat the words in his direction. 'You treat them worse than animals, far worse, when they should be under strict medical care.'

'But they are,' he protested only mildly. 'They're nurtured and they are examined regularly.'

'You keep a lot of them in filthy underground cells!'

'Unfortunately, some of these – oh, I know you'll object to the word, but apparently having observed them yourself, I'm sure the term "creatures" was not far from your own thoughts – some of these *creatures* are very dangerous. Witness the fate of your own colleague by the hands of one of them.'

'What?'

'What was his name? It was in the newspapers. Your agency accountant, I believe. Jewish sort of name . . .'

'Henry. You *did* kill Henry.'

'Henry Solomon. Yes, that was it. No, I didn't kill him, Mr Dismas, but this fellow did.'

He was pointing at the *beast* who was swaying between his two 'handlers', the nurse at that moment withdrawing a syringe needle from his arm. Although it was still making snuffling sounds and small grunts, it was already beginning to quieten, yellow eyes beginning to take on a marbled glare.

'A remarkable being, don't you think?' Wisbeech spoke with some satisfaction. 'Not from this country, of course.'

'Not from this fucking planet either,' I managed to say, clawing at my open shirt collar as if to relieve pressure that was no longer there. No, I wasn't feeling feisty – I was too much in shock for that – but instinctively I was already trying to pull myself together, starting with the brain. Sarcasm in the face of threat was one way of doing it; it was a kind of defence mechanism that misfits or weaklings often use, and right then I was both.

'Very good, Mr Dismas.' He had dropped the *Mr.* 'Very amusing. It's from the Hubei province of Central China, in fact, and cost me a small fortune to acquire, then another rather large amount to smuggle it back into the country. The drugs we used to keep it sedated in its sealed box nearly killed the thing in transit, but I'm pleased to say it's of a hardy breed – *whatever* that breed may be – and it survived to become the fine specimen you see before you now.'

'Wisbeech, you've either got to be crazy or mad.'

'Spare me any more of your wit, Dismas.' Not even Mr, now.

'Doctor, please . . .' The nurse, Fletcher, had come forward again, and her hand swept around the studio, indicating the others waiting there.

'Yes, I take your point, Rachel, but I feel a need to explain myself to this man. At this moment, he sees things only in black and white, and that isn't worthy of thirty years' diligent research on my part.'

'Does it matter, Leonard?'

'I'm afraid it does. To me. Besides, it's information he will never pass on.'

It was hardly unexpected, but still I didn't like the inference in that last remark.

'Now why don't you take everyone outside,' Wisbeech continued. 'It must nearly be time for a break anyway.'

A middle-aged man with long, thinning hair, dressed in sweatshirt and jeans, who was standing beside one of the tripod-mounted cameras, interjected. 'We haven't even started yet. A couple hours is all this would take, you said.'

'But things have changed,' Wisbeech told him placatingly. 'I promise you, tonight's work will be the best yet. Tonight we will go further than ever before.'

The cameraman considered this, then looked around at

what I assumed was his crew. The sound engineer shrugged, the lighting man grinned. I'd heard of shady film crews like this, involved in porn stuff, even snuff movies where people were killed on film for the delectation of perverse bastards whose sensory palates had been blunted by excess and this lot were obviously up for hire, no questions asked. In a sick world, these people were among the sickest.

This Cameron of filth turned back to Wisbeech and gave him the thumbs-up. 'Fifteen minutes,' he agreed. 'Coffee and fags, boys,' he said to his chums, indicating the large double doors across the room with a toss of his head.

The electrician made as if to switch off the glaring arc-light that lit up the velvet-draped bed, but Wisbeech stopped him.

'Leave it,' he ordered.

'Need to save the lights.' The 'sparks' addressed the cameraman rather than Wisbeech.

'I rather like the idea of Dismas being under the spotlight, so to speak,' the doctor said, his tone brooking no argument.

Just to make me feel more vulnerable? To intimidate me? Or so that he could observe every part of Constance's body? Who knew what ran through this degenerate's mind?

'Besides,' Wisbeech added more reasonably, 'this won't take long. You'll soon be able to resume filming.'

The director-cum-cameraman shrugged and turned towards the exit door. The electrician gave a resigned shake of his head and followed.

'See to them, Rachel,' Wisbeech ordered the nurse before waving a hand at the two orderlies, who still held the arms of his 'prize' specimen. 'Take it into the corner for now and keep it calm. Let me know immediately it begins to be a nuisance again.'

The film crew, and another orderly and nurse, left the studio, closing the double doors behind them. I heard Constance softly moaning again, but when I looked her way, her eyes were still closed. Her body twitched as though she were having a bad dream. Because of the added lights I now spotted a grey dressing-gown or robe draped over the back of a nearby chair and I guessed it might belong to her, because propped up next to it were her metal elbow crutches. I pushed myself to my feet and limped over to the chair, aware that the two orderlies had released the *beast* and were about to rush me. Wisbeech, realizing my intent, raised a hand to stop them and I returned to the velvet-draped bed to lean the sticks against it. I wrapped the robe around Constance's shoulders. She murmured something I didn't catch, but I could see she was beginning to revive. No doubt if it hadn't been for my unexpected interruption, filming would have been in full swing by now and I was pretty sure Wisbeech would have wanted her actively 'involved', whether fighting against what was happening, or meekly submitting to it, I couldn't bear to think; but her sedation would have been expertly administered and timed so that she would not merely be sleeping. I sat next to her on the edge of the bed.

Wisbeech had come forward once more, bringing with him a heavy-looking chair-stool, one made of chrome and leather and which, no doubt, made him feel superior to everyone else in the room when he sat on it. He placed it a few feet away from me and sat, one supremely polished shoe on the foot-rest near its base; he turned gently from side to side in its swivel seat.

'Would you like a cigarette?' He reached into the inside pocket of his suit jacket and proffered a silver cigarette case, its lid springing open with a press of a side tab.

A last cigarette? I wondered. It would be the only reason he'd offer me one. Leaning forward, I took it from the case. It was an expensive brand, long and slim, filter-tipped, the kind I wasn't used to. When Wisbeech lit it for me, the smoke felt cool in my throat.

'I haven't quite completed the story of my finest specimen, have I?' So pleasant and conversational was his tone, he might have been in a bar – or perhaps one of his gentlemen's clubs, the Garrick maybe.

'Wisbeech, I don't give a shit.'

'Ah. Well, perhaps you should, given that your fate is in its hands. As was your unfortunate friend's.'

I wanted to throw myself at him then, but the time wasn't right just yet. I was still weakened from the attack on me and still unnerved by unfolding events. The bright light was dazzling my eye.

'Are you really not curious, Dismas?' He seemed concerned.

Despite our plight, I realized I was. I wanted to know what made the man this way, I wanted to know everything that went on in this place, how he had got away with stealing malformed babies, how he managed to imprison these imperfect but very human beings here without the knowledge of local authorities, government bodies, the Department of Health – anyone who *should* have bloody well known what was going on. And I wanted to know *why*. Oh God, I really wanted to know *why*.

It was quiet in the huge studio room, only an occasional buzz of conversation coming from beyond the double doors, a raised voice now and again, laughter, as if the film crew and the PERFECT REST employees were getting on well, enjoying a normal 'tea-break' during the course of a normal night's work (which, no doubt, paid them an abnormal amount of money for both diligence and discretion). Sick, or what? Maybe they just had hardened mentalities, products of a hardened age where sensationalism was the norm, and moderation the humdrum.

Wisbeech stopped pivoting from side to side on his swivel chair and took a long draw from his cigarette. 'Now where was I?' he said with an exhalation of blue smoke. 'Ah yes, our friend in the corner.'

He allowed me time to glance nervously across the room at the semi-tranced monster there before continuing.

'It was discovered in a Quishang commune, born of – or so I was reliably informed – a peasant woman in 1971. Some claimed she was merely a barren wife who found the baby thing in the lower reaches of the mountains, while others said that, desperate for a child but married to a man who could not provide enough active sperm, she had copulated with one of the strange – some say mythical – beasts that on rare occasions were sighted roaming the region. The head of the commune, however, insisted it had been conceived naturally and was merely a freak of nature; I tend to believe him. From the direction of your rather dramatic entrance, I can only assume you found your way through the rooms below, so you must have observed for yourself the range of mutants possible to be born of mankind itself.'

I kept quiet, smoking the cigarette he had given me, waiting for some of my strength to return, not to mention my nerve.

'Word reached me of the find – you might be surprised to learn that there is a worldwide network of dealers in such "prodigiosa" – and I travelled to the Hubei province to see it for myself. It was three years old by then and, I can tell you, I was well pleased with the prize. Bidding was fierce, but our wealth was substantial in those days.'

'Bidding . . . ? You're saying others were trying to buy . . .' I shook my head in disbelief. 'There's a trade in these things?'

'Aren't you listening, Dismas? Didn't you hear me tell you just that? Usually it's legitimate but covert government-sanctioned research institutions that purchase them whenever they appear, but quite often independents such as myself manage to hear of them first and make our own private and more lucrative – for the seller, that is – arrangements.'

'You're saying that our own government is aware this was going on?' I was incredulous, but not that surprised.

'It was, and is – although much more discreetly these days.'

'Your –' I almost snorted the word '– *researches* are government-funded and authorized?'

'No longer. In the beginning yes; but then our noble ministers realized the political implications if such studies became generally known. They and, of course, the Health Authorities, gradually backed away from my work and finally washed their collective hands entirely of me. Fortunately, they could not undo what was already done, and I progressed in my own way.'

I wondered if the authorities had backed away from Wisbeech because they had begun to realize that his interest was more than just scientific.

'So tell me why, Doctor?' I said almost genially, glancing around as slyly as I could, looking for anything I could use as a weapon. 'How did you become involved in this kind of research in the first place? You know, it's kind of hard to imagine the fascination.' Or the perversion, I thought.

I don't think he was fooled one bit, he was too smart for that, but he knew he held all the cards.

'Oh, and by the way,' I added. 'You do keep them all on drugs, don't you? That's why you manage to control them, isn't it?'

'It isn't just a question of control. It's a way of commanding their respect, also.'

'As a supplier?' I kept the disgust out of my tone, and it wasn't easy.

'As a benefactor. They've learned to rely on my benevolence, you see? And they're only mildly drugged, otherwise the effects would interfere with our experiments, and while our own medical and scientific authorities are no longer so interested in the results, there are plenty of institutes in other countries that are.'

'But when they don't behave ...' or *perform*, I said to myself '... you cut off their supply.'

'It's a way of ensuring their cooperation.'

'So you profiteer not just from film-making, but from your researches too.'

'Profiteer is putting it harshly, but times have changed and finances have to be maintained. At one time, the money generated from those researches provided for everything.'

I wanted to ask him more about Henry's death, but I knew at that moment I would never be able to control myself when he provided the answers, so I encouraged his ego instead, biding my time.

'It must have been difficult to start. Didn't you meet with opposition from others in your profession?'

'You'd be surprised how little. Ever since the dawn of medicine itself, there has always been a fascination for curiosa, rara, monstruosa, selecta, exotica, lusibus naturae, occultis naturae, these exceptional deviations from the natural; my own interest, and that of my brother, has merely been stronger than most.'

The mention of this mysterious kinsman interested me, in spite of my predicament. 'Do I get to meet this brother of yours?' I asked, as if it would be an honour.

'I'm afraid not.'

'Why? Isn't he here?'

'He's watching us. I'm afraid he's very shy.'

'But that's his thing, isn't it? He likes to watch others.' I remembered my first meeting with Wisbeech, the long, horizontal mirror in the room where I had waited. I had sensed someone watching me from the other side of the treated glass, but had figured it was Leonard Wisbeech alone. Obviously the two-way mirror was there for the amusement of the doctor's reclusive brother.

I was too afraid to feel foolish when I said, 'Couldn't I meet him? Just to say hello? I mean, he's obviously a big part of all this, so it would be interesting to talk to him, if only for a couple of minutes.'

Wisbeech might have laughed at the absurdity, but

instead his face grew deadly serious. For the first time I
noticed the tiredness in those piercing blue eyes of his, the
lines in his face that had not been quite so evident before.

'Dominic was not born as well-blessed as I,' he said
gravely.

Was that remorse I now saw in his eyes; or could it be
cold anger? It was difficult to tell in a person as self-controlled
as Wisbeech.

'He was older than me by twenty minutes,' the doctor
went on, dropping his cigarette to the floor and stubbing it
out with his shoe.

Twins? There was another one like Wisbeech running
around? Wait a minute: he had said the brother was less
fortunate. A suspicion began to grow in my mind.

'My mother was in her early forties when she became
pregnant with us and whilst still in the womb my brother
and I were diagnosed as suffering from "twin-to-twin transfu-
sion syndrome". The blood vessels in the placenta were
delivering too much to one foetus and not enough to the
other. But it seemed that I had not only taken blood from
my twin, I took his strength also. In fact, I took everything
that would have made him normal, even space in the womb
itself.'

He brushed an imaginary fleck of dust from his knee, as
though in momentary need of a distraction. I detected a hint
of regret in his gaze when he returned it to me, but the
coldness was still there too.

'My brother should not have survived,' he said, reaching
into his suit pocket for the silver cigarette case again. He lit
up, noticing that my own cigarette was only half-smoked,
then tucked the case away again. 'But he did. And although
deformed and terribly debilitated, in some ways Dominic was
much stronger than I. Yes, I must grant him that: he certainly
knew how to survive almost from the day we were born. As
we grew older, he learned how to dominate.'

There was more movement next to me and I glanced

down to see that Constance's eyes were half-open. I gripped her arm and used gentle pressure to reassure her, hoping she would understand.

'Although our parents never mentioned it, I knew they blamed me for my brother's condition – they were a handsome, some would say perfect, couple in the physical sense, you see, and their vanity would never allow the notion that the fault could be theirs, or perhaps of one of them. No, they never had to voice their accusation, but a child knows, a child will always feel resentment directed towards it. Ironic, in its way, that the perfect couple should resent the son who exemplified their own united beauty whilst cherishing the one who might have been an embarrassment to them. Perhaps it was pity for Dominic. Perhaps their plan for me was part of my punishment. Perhaps they loved their less fortunate offspring so much they wished to make sure he would never lack material comforts.'

Constance tried to rise, but my grip tightened, holding her there. I think she was too confused or strung out to resist.

'It was they who decided I should devote my life to medicine, particularly to medical research dealing with genetic disability and abnormalism, their hope being, I suppose, that I would find ways of making Dominic's existence easier, perhaps even to cure some of his maladies. And part of my father's masterplan was to leave all his wealth to Dominic – he was the elder brother, after all – a means of tying me to my twin for as long as he lived. Of course, he was perfectly correct; my father knew my character only too well. What he failed to see, however, was that my own guilt, drummed into me, albeit subtly, from a very early age, irrevocably tied me to my twin in any case. Foolish, I know, but once it was explained to me just what had happened to us both whilst still in the womb, how I had appropriated Dominic's sustenance and life force for myself, I had always felt to blame for his tragedy. So it wasn't difficult for me to follow my parents' wishes, fear of poverty having very little to do with it.'

I wasn't sure how all this had led to the making of pornographic movies, but I was willing to listen – and learn. After all, there really wasn't anything else I could do right then.

'As it turned out,' Wisbeech went on without any prompting, 'I proved to be an apt pupil as far as medical matters were concerned and I made rapid progress. If I thought that would please my parents, I was right; but only in the sense that they approved of my achievements because they placed me in a better position to help their other son. Oh, he was an angel to them, despite his deformity; but they failed to see the other side of his nature, the side that was more fitting to his form. Only I glimpsed that, and Dominic was never too afraid to reveal it to me; he was too cunning to let others know, though, particularly our parents.'

I saw the reflection of Wisbeech's back in the long mirror across the studio, saw my own hunched figure too, sitting on the bed, huddled shape of Constance beside me, her legs drawn up, an arm across her breasts, as though she had become aware of her nakedness.

'Both our parents died when I was establishing myself as a medical researcher after having trained as a physician and then a surgeon, so I never quite had the full opportunity to make them proud of me. A silly regret for someone of my years, don't you think?'

No, I didn't think it was silly at all, but I didn't say so. This was a complex man before me, the veneer of cultured intelligence and physical attractiveness concealing inner depths of labyrinthine complexity, psychological intricacies I could only guess at. I'd always been aware that no one can be judged on appearance alone, that we're all taking part in some great masquerade and the human psyche is far too complicated, even too devious, for such superficial appraisement, and Leonard Wisbeech was no exception to the rule.

'Could I have another cigarette?' I asked, ignoring his question, which was probably rhetorical anyway. The butt I held in my curled palm was only two-thirds smoked, but I wanted a fresh one.

Wisbeech took out the cigarette case once more and we both stretched forward so that I could take one. He lit me and we both settled back.

'So you still haven't explained how or why you got into baby-snatching,' I said, deliberately provocative, feeling the anger burning deep inside, but managing to keep my cool.

'You sound as though you're accusing me of some wrong-doing,' he remarked, surprisingly unruffled.

'Taking infants away from their mothers isn't wrong?'

'Not if I can offer those infants something more than an early, agonizing death. And that's the point – at least, that *was* the point all those years ago – of my quest. Prevention and alleviation were my goals. Companionship for my brother was a by-product of my pursuits.'

'Company?'

'He wished to know others like himself. He demanded friends to whom he would not feel inferior. He wanted to indulge in activities without being unequal. As for me, I began to see the beauty in them all.'

As much as I should have welcomed that last remark, I knew only too well that the sentiment wasn't reasonable, no matter how hard these 'love-all-your-fellow persons, we're all beautiful inside', politically correct idiots might try to convince themselves and others (believe me, I've known many of these types myself and they've never convinced *me*, let alone normal people). Wisbeech wasn't looking at his charges through natural or honest eyes: their beauty to him was as experiments, as research specimens. Unless ... I took in the cameras, the arc lights ... I remembered the artworks around the home itself, the subtle change in beauty's definition the further you ventured into the build-ing ... unless he and his twin brother, both coming from

417

different directions obviously, had become so wrapped up in their arcane world that their own proclivities now leaned towards the unnatural ... Perhaps the film-making was, to use the doctor's own word, a profitable by-product of their own unhealthy interest. Perhaps the other twin was so disabled he could only watch, the films an extension of his own voyeurism ... I looked towards the mirror again. Complexity upon complexity. Jesus, now even *I* felt unclean.

I became aware that Wisbeech was still talking, still using me as ... as what? He *was* using me, of that I was sure. As a confessor? No, I don't think he felt any shame in what he did, what he had become. An arbiter of some kind, then, someone who might understand and even bless all his good works? Could it really matter to him? I think now that ultimately he was trying to justify himself *to* himself, that he had reached a point in his life, one that comes to us all eventually, usually at a certain age when something tells us that death is not that far away, when it was time to take stock and perhaps assess oneself *for* oneself. Complexity upon ... I've already said it. Suffice to add that it all made some kind of sense to me later.

'I had become quite established in my profession by the time I approached the relevant authorities to allow me custody of unfortunate babies born so disfigured that there was virtually no possibility of their survival. I'm sure that you're aware that the worst defects are allowed to expire shortly after death through their own unnatural causes. Without the knowledge or permission of the parents involved, of course. It's a practice that has been going on since both man and animal have roamed this earth – animals are merely less sentimental about it. Doctors have always informed parents that such newborns have died shortly after birth to spare them the shock of knowing they have given breath to a monster. Terribly sad but, I'm afraid, a fact of ... well, a fact of life itself. However, what is not generally known – certainly not by the public at large – is that some of these mutants do not always die immediately after birth. Some can live for years afterwards and these are hidden away and cared for until nature truly does take its course.'

'That's . . . that's wicked. Christ, it's obscene.'

'Is it? You think it's kinder to let a mother know she has just given birth to a grotesque?"

'At least it would be her decision whether or not to let the baby die.'

'You think so? Even though such offspring usually expire within moments of being born? You honestly believe the mother's grief should be added to in that way? Your emotions, if not your brain, should tell you otherwise.'

I suppose I was stunned into silence, even though I'd learned little more than I had suspected.

'So, after very little persuasion, I might tell you, my researches were authorized and funds were even granted provided I matched them with some of my own. Dominic was delighted to help me with that. The stipulations were very strict – I was only allowed to take away babies who had no hope of living beyond a very short time, those so en-feebled by their disfigurements that they would, indeed, be better off dead. However, the survival instinct of humans, no matter how tortured their bodies might be, is incredible. Not many, but at least some, lived beyond all expectation, and here I have nurtured them, raised them, cared for them.'

'You call what you've done in this place caring for them?' This time I couldn't hold back my contempt, my disgust.

'Would you have preferred them to die? Perhaps you would have had them aborted before they even left the womb? At least I have given them life.'

'What kind of life is it to be locked away in windowless rooms, or in underground cells, kept on drugs, used in ways . . .' I shook my head, spitting out the words. 'Shit, you call that *life*?'

'Your anger should be directed at those who would give them no life at all merely because they do not come up to normal expectations, abortionists who kill for money or their own prejudices, mothers who dispose of their unborn babies for the sake of convenience. Even *those* who deem it merciful to put less fortunates out of their misery. Look at you, Dismas. Would you rather have been murdered at birth? Has living given you no joy at all?'

'You can't compare my life to the lives of those you've hidden away here.'

'Why not?'

'Because I've always had my freedom.'

'But what kind of freedom? Haven't you always been imprisoned by your afflictions? And isn't it so-called ordinary people who have forced that upon you? Tell me what you think would have happened to those flawed children – and I regard them *all* as such, as my children – tell me what would have happened to them had they been left to exist in the outside world. If they had been allowed to survive after their birth, that is.'

'They would have been taken care of.'

'They would have been treated as freaks of nature.'

'Isn't that how you treat them here?'

'Have you no comprehension at all? They live among others like themselves. They are with friends, and here, no one is abnormal, because they are all abnormal, nonconformity is the conformity. They even form attachments. They are allowed to procreate, Dismas. Can you imagine that happening were they under the protection of the authorities, or in the care of their own parents?'

'Allowed, or coerced? Isn't that part of your experiment with them, encouraging them to produce offspring, just so you can monitor the results? Christ, I've seen some of the specimens in your laboratory upstairs.' I puffed on the cigarette, not too much, just enough to keep it alive. 'You're a sick son of a bitch, Wisbeech,' I told him mildly.

This time I got through to him. His patrician's face

darkened and a vein began to throb in his temple. Those keen blue eyes of his took on a glare.

I continued to taunt him. 'How did it come to this?' I waved a hand towards the cameras. 'How long did it take before your interest – and maybe it *was* an interest born out of duty towards your brother, who knows? – how long before it became a perversion? And then how long before you saw it as an opportunity to make even more money?'

I grinned meanly at him, enjoying the glare that had now become a blaze in his eyes. But then he surprised me by smiling back, a cold superior smile that maintained his original contempt. Cigarette held between his fingers, Wisbeech gave me a slow, soft handclap.

'Well done, *Mr* Dismas.' The *Mr* was back. 'You almost succeeded in annoying me again. You are quite perceptive, but not wholly correct.'

He folded his arms, one hand raising the cigarette to his lips. After exhaling a forceful stream of smoke, he said: 'Even though my brother had inherited considerable wealth, it could not last for ever. An establishment like PERFECT REST and its annexe is expensive to maintain, even if our older and ostensibly "normal" guests pay a high charge for the privilege of residing here; little do they realize that a large portion of the fees they pay goes towards this more important work of mine. I have to travel far and wide for rare exotica, from Brazil to India, from New Guinea to Cuba, their recognized value to collectors such as myself making them ever more expensive to purchase. The wealth we had – that Dominic had – was soon dwindling and I had to look for other means of finance. You would be amazed at the high price the films we produce command. They're unique, you see – '

'They're degrading filth!' I felt Constance start at my raised voice.

'They are exquisite,' Wisbeech insisted, unperturbed.

If I thought he might admit his own degenerate obsession

had led to the natural progression of turning sick propensities and private activity into celluloid entertainment for those with similar tastes, I was wrong; Wisbeech obviously could never be that self-accusatory.

'Twenty years ago,' the doctor continued as if enjoying his own lecture, '"snuff" movies were all the rage and, of course, freak shows have always been popular, with or without the sexual element. Imagine a combination of both. Have you any idea of the kind of money such explicit extravaganzas can fetch? I no longer sell my films to a secret élite of well-heeled enthusiasts, whose special tastes demand more and more extreme and taboo-breaking divertissement, I *auction* them.'

I wanted to leap on him, wanted to smash his past-its-prime-but-still-handsome fucking head with my fists, but I contained myself. All right, I *struggled* to contain myself, but I managed because there were still questions I wanted to ask before I made a move of any sort.

'You allowed Hildegarde Vogel to stay at PERFECT REST presumably at no cost,' I said, as a preamble to the first of those questions continuing to trouble me. 'Was she blackmailing you? Was she threatening to expose your whole operation because she'd worked for you in the past, helped you find and sneak away those deformed babies?'

He gave a short and quite unpleasant laugh. 'Hildegarde was a person who would not even conceive of the idea of blackmail. She was a kind little woman and she always thought she was doing the best for those poor creatures she helped bring into the world. As a midwife, Hildegarde knew what would happen to them unless she intervened; she had helplessly stood by too many times and watched those infants die. Hildegarde Vogel was invaluable to me for a great number of years; I might even say she was devoted to me, or at least to my cause.'

'She knew about your tests, your experiments with them.'

'Good God, no. She only saw them in the place in which

they were kept. I doubt Hildegarde even knew of the laboratory's existence, and she certainly wasn't aware of the chamber beneath us and the extreme cases kept there. But eventually her health failed her and, I'm afraid, so did her mind. She began to suffer from dementia, as well as the appalling emphysema, and I could no longer trust her to remain silent about our work. Unfortunately, her tongue had begun to ramble as much as her brain and so I brought her here, where I could keep a careful eye on her. She had no family and very few friends, so her visitors were almost nil.'

'Did you have her killed? After I came to see her, were you scared of what she might give away?' My stare was as blunt as my questions.

'I was concerned, but she came to no harm from me.'

'You didn't answer my question. Did you have her killed?'

'Her heart simply gave out. Admittedly, it was after a night visit from our friend over there in the corner.'

'You bastard.'

'Oh, her time had come, Dismas. As it comes to us all eventually. As it will come to you . . .'

I ignored the scarcely veiled threat. 'As it came to Henry Solomon?'

'Your agency colleague? I thought we would return to that matter sooner or later.'

'Why? Henry had nothing to do with any of this.'

'Wrong place, wrong time. How often does that happen in life? How often does it lead to death. It could have been you, Dismas.'

'You came to my office to kill me?'

'Not at all. I had no intention of killing anyone that evening. I merely wanted you frightened, a sort of warning to keep away from PERFECT REST. Your enquiries were becoming a nuisance. We had no idea it was your office address that you left in our visitors' book.'

'But you didn't have to kill Henry!'

'It wasn't my choice. I allowed our demon friend to go up

alone, aware that it would tear the place apart. Instead, it was your colleague who was torn apart. You know, I'd forgotten that Brighton is such a lively place – I thought the streets would be quiet at that time of evening, so at first I was a little worried that there were so many people about, wandering the streets, particularly along the street in which your office is located, with its restaurants and theatre.' He gave another short, humourless laugh. 'But the irony of it. Even though my – what shall I say? My protégé? – wore a voluminous cloak to disguise the worst aspects of his shape, I was concerned about the attention his appearance might still bring, so when I saw so many people dressed in bizarre costumes, wearing such extravagant and grotesque make-up, I could hardly believe our good fortune. At first I thought they were all on their way to some fancy dress event, but then I realized what the show was at the nearby theatre.'

Yes, I remembered too. *THE ALL-NEW ROCKY HORROR SHOW*. What a joke. I felt sick to my stomach.

'Although I let him go up on his own, Nurse Fletcher took him to the door first – which was open, by the way. Very careless of your late colleague, although one hefty push from our friend would have opened it anyway; but Solomon's carelessness was useful – not having to force the door saved us from gaining further attention. I had noticed a glow from a window that I assumed belonged to your office, and naturally I assumed you were working late. Thought you were a one-man band, Dismas, didn't realize you had an organization behind you. Your type of cheap investigator generally doesn't.'

I was becoming impatient, the cigarette I was occasionally drawing on burning low. I still wanted answers though, before making any kind of move, so I kept quiet, let Wisbeech enjoy himself.

'I wanted you to be badly frightened, even badly beaten. What's the phrase? Ah yes, – I wanted you put "out of the game" for a while. Obviously there could be no indication that I was involved, although it was all right for you to suspect so; as long as you had no evidence to take to the police, everything would be fine. Unfortunately, it wasn't fine for your friend. It was Nurse Fletcher who, after a suitable period of time, went up to your office to find our yellow-eyed monster sexually abusing your friend in a most horrible way.'

He was taunting me, enjoying my anguish, for he spoke as if the creature had been discovered engaged in nothing worse than picking its own teeth with the best silver dinner-set fork. I remembered that Henry's autopsy had revealed semen among the blood inside his empty eye socket.

Wisbeech waved a hand towards the red monster across the room, docile at the moment, but closely watched by his 'handlers'. 'It's an interesting creature, which can only be controlled by certain medicines. On that evening, he was on methamphetamines, the only thing that could arouse him from the drug-stupor we generally keep him under, and I'm afraid Nurse Fletcher may have been a little too liberal with the amount she administered. It has no fear, incidentally, and it's only in recent years that I discovered the physical reason.'

The doctor leaned forward, as though sharing a confidence. 'Fear is controlled inside our brains by the amygdalae, two tangles of neurons located just behind our ears. Investigative surgery has shown me that this creature does not possess any such neurons. I could go on, tell you of other discoveries I've made about these creatures by carefully opening their bodies and examining certain areas, but there isn't time.'

'I'm in no rush,' I said. 'I've got all night, if you like.' I could always cadge more cigarettes, keep one alight at all times.

'Oh, but you haven't. Nurse Fletcher is already throwing me impatient glances and my film unit is eager to get back to work. Besides, my protégé has only been minimally sedated; he will soon be barely containable, but perfect for what I have in mind.'

Another ominous little tidbit. Time was running out, but there was one more thing I had to know.

'Tell me what Constance has to do with all this, Wisbeech,' I said, feeling her move against me at the sound of her name. 'I can't believe she approves of what you do here, so why is it she never left?'

'Do I detect a note of affection in your voice?' His eyebrows were raised as if he really were surprised. 'Well, well. Like attracts like, I suppose.'

Again that almost oblivious contempt.

'Where do you think she would go, *Mr* Dismas? She has been with me since she was a child. She knows no other home and I'm afraid her condition has relieved her spirit of any boldness. Constance has wonderful beauty though, don't you think? On film she is very popular with my bidders.'

'You bastard!'

'I believe you've already expressed your opinion of me and, I can promise you, it will not be overlooked. You should be made aware though, that I have always cared for Constance.'

'Cared for her? You mean you've corrupted her, don't you?' No wonder that since I had first met her I had noticed a haunted look in Constance's eyes, shadows behind veils, secrets masked by the drugs she was forced to take (I wondered if Wisbeech kidded her that they were for health reasons) but never expunged completely, unfocused memories floating in the depths of her subconscious, tormenting her with elusive intimations, filling her with a bewildering dread. I felt sure that Constance was unaware of her involvement in her guardian's sick agenda, but I'd always believed that the human psyche cannot permanently be deceived, that self-hidden truths will eventually drift towards the conscious level. And, as if to confirm my own theory, Wisbeech said something that made me even more tense.

'The problem now with my beautiful but physically flawed ward is that recently she has begun to ask awkward questions, as if a certain awareness is stirring within. Her association with you seems to be leading towards an escalation of that awareness. I'm afraid it's a problem that has to be dealt with tonight. It's unfortunate, but ultimately it will be to my own advantage.'

That was the part that made me shudder. 'So you intend to issue yet another death certificate,' I said flatly while I screamed inside.

'Alas, a genuine one this time. I've always been very fond of Constance, but she cannot be allowed to jeopardize my whole operation.'

Well, well, as if I hadn't already suspected it, Wisbeech was a psychopath as well as a sociopath. If the spirit, the soul, whatever you might care to call it, was a visible thing, then this man's would have been uglier than anything he kept in the cells below.

'Such unfortunate people are meant to die at an early age, nobody questions it, least of all the officials who monitor such statistics. In fact, none of my charges here are known to be alive; as far as the authorities are concerned, each one died a long time ago. They *belong* to me, Dismas; every one of them *belongs* to me. And tonight, so do you.'

'You're going to have me killed?'

'Oh yes.'

'That won't be so easy to cover up. People know I've come here.'

'You are a very awkward man, Dismas. In the physical sense, I mean. A tumble down concrete steps, a fall from the fire-escape while trying to make an illegal entry. It won't be hard to arrange, nor to explain.'

What really made my blood run cold was that this arrogant bastard was right. Who would ever suspect such a reputable physician, one who had spent his career researching the problems of the infirm in body in an attempt to

understand and perhaps eventually alleviate the worst of
their suffering, and latterly devoting his time in care for the
elderly, of murder and kidnap? Dr Leonard K. Wisbeech was
a pillar of society with all the medical credentials behind his
name to prove it. Who the hell would doubt his word?

The robe slipped from Constance as I pulled her to a
sitting position. She quickly covered her breasts with her
arms again, her hands grasping her shoulders; her thin,
wasted legs drew themselves up and her eyes blurred with
tears of shame. I wanted to hold her close and tell her it
didn't matter, her body was wonderful to me; but this was
not the time. She looked at me imploringly, shaking her
head in confusion.

'It's okay, Constance.' I tried to be soothing, but there was
a tightness to my voice, a kind of sprung-wire action to my
movements. I pulled the robe back around her again and
said, 'Put it on. We're leaving.'

'Nick?' She still didn't understand what was happening.

'Just put it on, Constance.' I wondered how much she had
taken in over the last fifteen minutes or so. I faced Wisbeech
as he rose from his chair.

But it was the *beast* that I had to contend with as it
charged across the room at me.

42

I'd nurtured the second long cigarette Wisbeech had given me, drawing on it and the one before occasionally to keep it alive. It had burnt down close to the filter by now, but was still usable as a weapon and certainly the only one I had close at hand (literally). Many years ago I'd been taught the basic techniques of fending off an aggressor with the use of everyday objects such as a rolled magazine, a small stick, a spoon, a pencil, even a matchbox (you had a two-to-one chance of knocking someone out with a fist-clenched match-box), my teacher a nightclub bouncer who had spent some time with the SAS before one public brawl too many had brought about an abrupt end to his military career. He had shown me how a glowing cigarette could be lethal if applied correctly to the right area of a body.

As the *beast* rushed towards me I could hear Wisbeech yelling, '*Stop it, not yet, don't let it –*' but the orderlies were too slow and too clumsy as they tried to grab the thing, one tripping over cables snaking across the floor, while the other, Bruce (Rambo with bad eyesight), succeeded only in pulling off the loose robe his charge wore, the creature twisting its body as it ran and easily slipping free. I don't believe Wisbeech was in the least concerned for my well-being; no, if I was to be maimed and killed, then better that the cameras were rolling to capture the moment.

It came at me with a swift, rolling gait, an animal really, hardly human, and it was a scary sight, those bared needle-teeth in that huge gaping mouth, lipless edges joined by silky drool, those yellow, demon's eyes intense on me: the gross thing that quivered from its centre was raised more like a weapon than an aroused organ. I readied myself to meet the charge, slightly crouched, leaning forward, stronger left leg braced a little bit behind for stability, but immediately I took up the stance, I realized it was a mistake. The *beast* was coming too swiftly and with no caution at all: I knew I would never be able to withstand its rush. It was too reckless, too fearless, and it would be too overwhelming, no matter how fast I dodged.

So I took one step to the side and swiped a hand, cigarette between fingers, at the tall arc light that was there to illuminate the bed for the cameras. It came crashing down, the long stand angling itself between myself and the charging creature. The creature was either too dull-witted from the drugs, or was naturally stupid (a bit of both, I guessed), to avoid the sudden obstruction, for it ran straight into it, taking no evasive action whatsoever, tripping over the metal bar, a flailing claw-like hand smashing the powerful lightbulb. An incandescent shower of sparks shot from the high-powered exploding lightbulb as the whole thing crashed on to the velvet-covered section of floor beside the bed. More sparks flew out and wisps of smoke rose into the air as the material began to smoulder.

I didn't wait around. Even as the creature stumbled over the metal rod I was moving towards it, and when it fell to the floor I also went down, stabbing at one of its eyes with the remainder of the cigarette.

It yowled. Christ, then the *beast* screeched, an ejaculation of sound so fierce and piercing it stung my heart and I screeched too (after all, I knew the feeling). But I did not draw back. Avoiding those snapping teeth below me by holding its neck as hard as I could against the shiny floor (I told you my arms and shoulders are powerful), I pushed the cigarette butt further into the socket, with my other hand feeling the sclera, the white meat – in this case, the *yellow* –

of the eye, and the black pupil, melt beneath the steady pressure, ignoring the whispery sizzling and the steamy smoke rising from under my fingertips. And still I drove the tiny brand further in, knowing that I stood no chance against this *beast* otherwise, that I had to maim it as badly as I could, put it out of action before it destroyed me. It thrashed around beneath me, legs entangled in cables and the arc light rod, its clawed hands flailing my head and shoulders. I was vaguely aware of the double doors across the room crashing open, people rushing in, their shouts seemingly a long way off; and out of the corner of my eye I saw Wisbeech rise from his chair, the two orderlies rushing towards me, the nurse's mouth wide as she screamed something.

Then I was sailing back through the air, finally tossed aside by the creature who, by now, had gone quite berserk with agony. I landed heavily against the side of the bed and felt hands clutch at me. I glanced up into Constance's horror-stricken face and saw the sharpness in her eyes, her senses having at last returned, shock no doubt speeding the process. There was no time to say anything to her, for everything had gone crazy: more lights and reflector sheets were being knocked over by rushing bodies, most of these seeming to be rushing at me, everybody appeared to be shouting, the clamour adding to the confusion; and most terrifying of all, the creature, *beast*, was tearing to and fro, upsetting one of the tripod-mounted cameras, kicking aside chairs and anything or anyone else that got in its way, clutching at the ember embedded in its eye, and howling like some demented thing – which is exactly what it was.

I figured I had nothing to lose by joining in on the fun. Before doing so though, I hissed at Constance: *'Cover yourself and get ready to follow me.'* She looked down at the robe, which again lay ruffled around her waist, as if seeing it for the first time. As I pushed myself to my feet she began to struggle into it.

Bruce, probably wisely, had decided to let the *beast* run

amok for the time being and to concentrate on me, for he was cautiously making his way round the agonized creature, his eyes fearful, until he had a clear run at me. Then he came, tearing at me with all the elegance of an enraged bull.

Ignoring the rest of the chaos around us, concentrating just on the big guy, I moved slightly away from the bed and waited for his charge. It came fast and furious, less than a second's waiting time, and I turned my angled body away from him, sticking out my leg and grabbing the front of his tunic with one fist. His height and my lack helped the move, for he pivoted over my protruding hip, his rush and his own weight carrying him forward, the move upsetting his balance. It was a simple fulcrum manoeuvre, taught to me by my pal the bouncer and one which rarely failed when used on big men. Bruce flipped over on to his back but, although winded, he hadn't lost it completely: he grabbed my leg – my right, the weak one – and brought me down on top of him. Now there was no way I was going to mix it with him in a wrestling match – I wouldn't have had a chance – so I had to act before he had time to damage me seriously. When I'd fallen he had changed his grip so that his arms were around my lower back, just below the hump, and foolishly he thought a bear-hug might subdue me. He was doubly foolish because he had also allowed my arms to be free.

You might think that a few good punches from me would have earned my release, but you'd be wrong; when you're floor-wrestling it's almost impossible to get any bodyweight behind a fist-blow or jab, no matter how well-placed it might be. The answer is to maim or gouge and I chose the latter (I'd done enough maiming already that night and, even though it had been to save my own life – and ultimately, Constance's – I felt sickened by it). The first move I made was to stick my little finger straight up one of his nostrils, as hard and as deep as I could. Sounds mild enough, I know, but believe me, it isn't. Bruce probably thought I'd magically produced a Black and Decker from somewhere and was attempting to drill right into his brain.

He tried to lift his head back and away from me, but my little pinkie went with him (and wasn't I glad I hadn't had a chance to trim my fingernails that week). I could have carried on doing that and his grip on me would have soon broken; I wanted him stunned though, wanted to put him out of the way for a while. As his head reared further back and his neck stretched I went for one of the most gouge-sensitive areas on the human body. Pulling my finger free, I stiffened my thumb and drove it into the indent just below the ear and behind the jaw, where muscles, glands, and a cluster of nerves just beneath the skin make this place so vulnerable. He screamed when I dug into the stylohyoid and digastric muscles, separating them so that I could squash one of the spinal nerves no less. It hurt him, oh it fucking hurt him, and he let me go, trying to scrabble out from under me, his hands now grabbing my wrists, straining to pull them away. But I was relentless; I showed him about as much mercy as he would have shown me.

This all happened much faster than it takes to tell, a matter of seconds I would guess, and the action around us was still in full flow, the *beast* stumbling around, screeching, wrecking the place, claws still clutching at his injured – his *ruined* – eye, film crew and PERFECT REST employees still shouting and gawking and attempting to save toppled equipment, and Wisbeech, face like thunder and not quite so handsome any more, pointing my way and yelling, expecting someone to do something about me.

Maybe my luck so far had made me over-confident, maybe adrenaline charging around my body had got me high, but instead of grabbing Constance and getting the hell out of there, I rose to my feet yet again, leaving the orderly squirming on the floor, his big hands holding his neck, and advanced on Dr Leonard K. Wisbeech. And perhaps I was out for revenge as well, not just for the poor wretches that had been locked away in this place for so many years, used and abused, their unfortunate physiques merely a source of study, experimentation, and pornography, not just for Constance, whose frail little body had also been abused and who was meant to die that night for the ultimate erotic thrill and to ensure her silence, but for myself also, for all the crap I'd taken in the past six days, the nightmares, the intrusions, the loss of Henry, the police suspicion and interrogation, even the bloody beating I'd taken on Brighton beach, which had nothing to do with this but was something I'd had to endure anyway. I'm sure it was *all* these things, plus every humiliation and indignity I'd had to suffer throughout my miserable life, every jibe, every cruel remark and joke at my expense, every blatant stare – every fucking unfairness that had come my way. I had planned to emulate the *beast*, to join it as a dervish of destruction, anything to create havoc and confusion so that Constance and I could escape while the enemy was in disarray; but now my rage, my *resentment*, was directed at one person, this paragon of the medical world, this handsomely well-favoured physician whose fine exterior hid a soul as repellent as Satan's. Wisbeech understood my intent the moment he looked into my eye.

He began to back away and I followed.

I felt strong. God, I suddenly felt powerful. That's what an adrenaline rush will do for you and you had to use it while it was there, because it never lasts long, your system can't take too much. Those other people in the room, apart from the *beast* thing which was now on its knees, rocking backwards and forwards, head held in its clawed hands, and Bruce, who was just dragging himself up from the floor, one hand touching the tender spot behind his jaw, were watching me warily, no doubt impressed by the way I had dealt with both my attackers. Maybe they were equating me with other dangerously crazy monsters locked up in this place. There was something odd about the studio-room, a flickering reflected on its walls, but my attention was on Wisbeech alone. I advanced on the doctor and was satisfied that there was at least some fear in those bleak eyes of his; he moved away and I went with him, angry to the point of rashness, too set on exacting some kind of retribution when I should have been concerned only with escape. It was a cold anger rather than a passionate one, and unfortunately its single-mindedness overrode common sense for the moment. As I passed by, I picked up the heavy swivel chair on which Wisbeech had throned himself while boasting to me of his devotion to others less fortunate than himself, of his brilliance in combining care and medical research with profit, how he had allowed my friend and colleague to be murdered, and how both Constance and I were soon to meet with a similar fate, all spoken with a patronizing civility as he smoked his expensive cigarettes.

I brought the chair up to chest level, its construction and weight making it awkward to carry; he walked backwards, one hand raised as if to ward me off, and I stalked him. He nearly tripped over cables, but quickly recovered, moving back, his gaze never leaving my face, his pace steady and, almost admirably, without panic. Finally, he could back away no further: he had reached the other side of the room. Although that glimmer of fear remained in his eyes, his voice was calm – and a little weary, I thought – when he spoke.

'Will someone please stop him,' he said.

By now, I had raised the chrome and leather chair above my head, the three-pronged base pointing towards my quarry. I stood on tip-toe, my arms and legs quivering as I arched my back as much as my curved spine would allow. At last Wisbeech cowered, lifting his arms to protect himself, and I threw the chair.

But not at the doctor.

I threw it at the two-way mirror behind him.

43

The glass shattered inwards and light flooded through to the blacked-out room beyond. The hurled chair, its force absorbed by the impact, dropped out of sight.

I stared at the tiny, mummified creature strapped into the motorized invalid-chair on the other side of the broken mirror.

44

At first I thought it was a small, shrivelled ape, so incredibly wrinkled and leathery was its face. An ape dressed in a dwarf's suit. But then I looked closer and saw that its features were human. Just. The skin was brownish in colour, rough in texture and torn and pitted in places. Long wisps of grey hair hung over its mottled scalp, their ends resting against almost visible cheekbones; the cheeks themselves were so sunken they appeared as shadowed holes (perhaps they *were* holes; I couldn't tell from where I was standing). The eyes were little more than twisted scraps of gristle that hung loose in their sockets, the eyelids frozen half-open around them. There was not much flesh to the shrunken corpse's nose, cartilage visible through what spoiled meat remained, and the mouth below it was long-since gone, crooked, stained teeth exposed in a permanent rictus grin.

Dominic Wisbeech, Leonard's older-by-twenty-minutes twin brother, who in life must have been a deformed dwarf, was now nothing more than a poorly-embalmed carcass, its stunted figure attired awkwardly (not because of size or withering, but because of physical deformity) in a shirt and tie, and dusty suit, in grotesque parody of the doctor himself. From where I stood I was unable to see its feet, but I was willing to bet it was wearing an expensive pair of child's shoes.

I almost laughed, but it would have emerged as a frightened, hysterical cackle, so I stifled it.

The dwarf-corpse was bound tightly to the motorized

chair, skeletal hands resting in its lap, and the pieces of gristle-like matter that once were voyeur's eyes seemed even now to be watching us, awaiting the rest of the performance.

'You really are mad, aren't you?' I said to the doctor.

And it was Leonard Wisbeech, himself, who appeared suddenly shrunken. His noble face had paled and, beneath his carefully-trimmed beard, his lips quivered. The anguish in his eyes was almost pitiful.

'Fucking hell,' I heard someone, perhaps one of the film technicians, perhaps even one of Wisbeech's own nursing staff – by their shocked reaction I suspected none of them shared the doctor's secret – say behind me.

'What's the answer, Wisbeech?' Although goading him, I was genuinely curious. 'Some deep psychological desire to keep your brother alive, at least in your own mind, so that you can continue your sick games in the pretence they're for *his* amusement? Or are you so full of guilt because you couldn't prevent his death – you, the great researcher into physical aberrations, the distinguished doctor of so many letters you probably can't remember them all yourself – that your mind won't accept it? Christ, did your parents fill you with so much guilt-shit it warped your brain?' Even now I'm not sure what the truth with Wisbeech really was and I don't think he knew himself. Probably all aspects played their part, but I think the main factor was that Leonard K. Wisbeech was born of abnormal mind, just as his twin was born of abnormal physique. Right then, that night, in that crazy-house, I could only shake my head, not out of pity, but in disgust, and mutter: 'Yeah, you really are fucking mad.'

Nurse Fletcher suddenly appeared between us. 'You've done enough damage, you little freak!' she spat at me. Her hand snaked out and she raked my face with her fingernails.

I staggered backwards and my feet abruptly left the ground as someone grabbed me from behind. I smelled the irritating odour of his aftershave and knew it was Bruce who had sneaked up behind me and was holding me there in a bear-hug, my feet dangling at least six inches off the floor. He was cursing me, thick, Stallone lips close to my ear, mumbling something about what he was going to do to me for causing him pain and squeezing me so tightly I could feel my lungs being compressed and the muscles of my upper arms squashed against my own body. I tried to kick back at him with the heels of my shoes, but he was wise to that one and stood with his legs apart, crushing and cursing me all the while. Just to add to the joy of it all, the head nurse, who would have been at home in Kesey's Cuckoo's Nest, ran at me and started slapping my face, the slaps soon becoming punches.

She was a strong woman, and her blows had a lot of power: my senses began to spin yet again. Events of the night, including the many shocks, were taking their toll on me and I could only struggle weakly, the tricks I'd learned about defence and attack only vague and useless recollections: my arms were pinned to my sides, I was unable to draw in air, and my head was losing awareness because of the battering it was taking. I *was* dimly aware, though, of the smell of smoke fumes vying with the stink of Bruce's after-shave and I could see blurred, orange flames across the room, eating up the velvet drapes I hazily remembered had covered the bed and wall behind, the floor itself; and I could hear distant shouts and even screams, crashing sounds and running feet. But my brain could no longer cope: none of it made any sense at all to me.

That is, until the pressure around my chest was released and I fell to the floor. A body slumped beside me, its descent slower, and when I turned my head I saw it was Bruce, the end of a glass shard from the broken mirror/window protruding from a point between his shoulder blades, dark blood bubbling from its edges like red spume. He was screaming and trying to reach the looking-glass dagger with one hand, his fingers scrabbling against his fast-staining tunic.

Other hands pulled at my arms and I rolled over to find Constance on her knees, her lips moving as if shouting something at me, something I couldn't hear properly, not just because of the pandemonium around us, but because I was still confused, my faculties not yet quite together. I blinked at a prickling in my eye and realized it was smoke. That brought my senses tumbling over each other to get themselves organized.

Constance was wearing the grey robe and the metal walking-sticks lay next to her on the floor. Standing over me was Mary, supported by a terrified-looking Joseph, one of her hands clutching the other, blood streaming through her fingers. Her horrified gaze was on the injured orderly who writhed in agony beside me, and I realized that it was she who had rescued me by finding the glass dagger among the fragments and plunging it into Bruce's back. She was rigid, in shock, and despite his own terror, Joseph was doing his best to comfort her, stroking her upper arm and talking quietly to her, although I doubted she could hear his words over the clamour.

Helped by Constance, I struggled to my feet and only then was I properly able to take in the mayhem around us.

The creatures, those shocking beings from the nether-world below, whose cell doors I had deliberately unlocked before leaving, had done exactly as I had hoped: they had followed after us, climbing the narrow stone steps and finding their way into the studio. I learned later that Joseph and Mary, who had remained hidden inside the storeroom, too afraid to follow me, had fled before the creatures as they had emerged from the stairway.

As they had invaded my dream, the monsters now invaded my reality, running amok in the big room, screeching, wailing, making whatever noises came naturally to them, sights that almost defied the imagination – the thing whose every square-inch of body was plagued by dripping ulcers, the disjoined abhorrence that scuttled across the floor like a human spider, the creature that slithered, one limb like a fish's tail dragging behind it, eyes alight with madness and the reflections of flames, the girl, the *beautiful* girl with raven hair, whose open back bristled with metal clips and wires, implanted tubes, and who whirled around in some crazy dance of freedom – all those who could leave their cells unaided were here, and the nurses and orderlies and the members of the contemptible film crew backed warily away from them, just as they had backed away from me when they had become afraid of my strength, had suddenly regarded me not as a freak to be despised but as a freak to be afraid of. But the minds of these poor creatures were too far gone for them to revel even momentarily in this new sense of power: their joy – if they were capable of such emotion after years of dark and solitary confinement – was (I can only suppose) in being unleashed, no longer restrained, finally free to do what they wanted. And when their disturbed eyes fell upon Leonard Wisbeech, the person they must have known was responsible for their incarceration, was to blame for the pain they had endured all those years because of his experiments and tests, for the very misery of their wretched lives, well that was when their feeble minds began to focus as one.

As his conscienceless lackeys, grubby, debased mercenaries, ran from the chaos and spreading fire, the doctor became aware of all those crazy and hate-filled eyes upon him. He must have suddenly known exactly how Baron Frankenstein felt when his badly-stitched monster rebelled and cast his borrowed, resentful eyes about for his creator.

My eye was on him, too, and seemingly, so were those of the shrivelled husk that was his dead brother behind him. Light from the flames flickered over the little corpse, somehow giving it movement, life, lending its ghastly grin a luridness that had not been present before. It was an illusion, but still I shivered at the sight.

Wisbeech was backed up against the ridge of broken glass and as he tried to move towards the open double doors after his fast-defecting cohorts, a shape moved to block his way. Whether by accident, or perhaps these creatures were endowed with some cunning, the thing with arms like tentacles had cut off the doctor's exit, trapping him there. Its sleek, hairless body rippled with shifting hues, the flames not reflected against the skin, but seemingly absorbed by it so that it flickered and glowed. At any other time I suppose the sight would have been fascinating, but I was too jaded by everything else I had witnessed that night, too numbed to be impressed; besides, there were other things on my mind. The fire had almost taken complete hold and flames billowed across the ceiling like inverted, sunset rapids, another awesome sight that was too dangerous to be admired for long.

'Keep away from me!' No longer the cool-blooded sophisticate I had first met, but a very ordinary frightened man confronted by a nightmare some might say was of his own making, Wisbeech held both hands out towards the approaching escapees and shouted at – pleaded with? – them.

Some of them only grinned though, while others hastened their approach, shuffling, sliding, dragging themselves forward, their eyes – those with eyes – cruel with intent. But it seemed the doctor had one remaining ally, someone who had not bolted with the others. Nurse Fletcher, whom I'd completely forgotten in the confusion, even though she had been slapping and punching my face only moments before, suddenly appeared from nowhere. She stood protectively in front of Wisbeech, facing the oncomers with a fury that apparently no fear could subdue. Perhaps her contempt overcame any intimidation.

'Get back,' she ordered them in a raised, no-nonsense voice, pointing over their shoulders and talking to them as if they were children found out of their beds after lights-out. 'Turn around and go back to your rooms.'

It could have been comical if only they had obeyed, but I knew, just *knew*, what was going to happen. I briefly wondered, a lightning flash of thought, what kind of relationship she had with Wisbeech – surely it couldn't just be professional, not for her to lay herself on the line like this, with the room burning around us, creatures from Hell creeping forward and looking as if ready to tear someone – particularly Wisbeech, although anyone else who got in their way would be a bonus – to pieces. Well, maybe I was wrong, maybe they only looked menacing and Nurse Fletcher knew they were pussycats really, and a firm word from her would send them scuttling back to where they belonged. Maybe, but I didn't think so.

Neither did they.

A thing that had a beak for a nose and talons for hands rushed at her and she screamed as it slashed at her throat with one of those eagle-like claws, the sound ending in a spluttering-gurgling as blood erupted both from the wound and her mouth. She toppled backwards and the creature pounced on her, the others quickly joining it like predators upon a helpless prey. She became lost under a mêlée of misshapen, rummaging bodies and I started forward, knowing I couldn't let this happen, no matter how much I despised the nurse, I couldn't let her die in such a way.

'*No!*' Constance grabbed me and held me tight, her grip surprisingly strong. 'You can't help her! They'll kill you too!'

She was right, but still I struggled to free myself. I didn't have the strength to fight them all and by the savagery of their attack Fletcher was probably too badly injured already to be saved. Joseph joined us and began pushing me back.

'They're bad things,' he was saying in that high, faraway voice. 'They're not like us, Dis, that's why they're kept locked up. They aren't human, you must believe me!'

I gave in to common sense, and admittedly was relieved

to do so. 'Okay, okay. Let's try and get past them to the door. The fire's out of control.'

In a way I suppose we were lucky that the creatures were too busy with their screaming victim to notice us slinking by the open window that was, until a short while ago, a two-way mirror. Glass fragments stood like a miniature mountain range along its length, lethally sharp peaks that glowed orange as they reflected the raging fire, and I warned my companions to keep clear. Wisbeech was a few feet away from us, his lower back leaning against the glass-edged frame, either for support or in an unconscious effort to keep as far away from the affray as possible. It seemed Nurse Fletcher's loyalty didn't stretch both ways.

Gone was that patrician manner, the all-powerful, righteous master replaced in a few moments of threat and primitive violence by a tremulous coward who watched the attack on his senior nurse goggle-eyed and fearful. You had to wonder how flimsy was his disguise for it to fall away so swiftly, what dark pressures had lain hidden beneath the facade to burst through so easily. His finely buffed shoes scuffed against the polished floor as he tried to push himself even further away from the brutal slobbering mob, and when one of them looked up from its work, blood dripping from its jaw, self-preservation finally told Wisbeech he could not just melt through the wall itself, that it was not an obstacle that could be penetrated by will alone. He wheeled around and I winced when I saw him grab hold of the jagged window-frame and haul himself up; he cried out as glass cut into his knee and blood spurted from the palms of his hands, the sound attracting more attention from the frenzied horde. They left their victim – alive or dead, I couldn't tell, but her limp body was soaked in her own blood – and fell upon the doctor.

He was yanked back by his ankles so that his arms gave way and he collapsed on to the sill, his neck catching the broken glass, cutting deep into his throat. The wall beneath him was immediately drenched in a great wash of blood and he was caught there, the underneath of his jaw snagged by the embedded glass, his knees bent, toes against the floor. The mob had paused momentarily as though fascinated by the blood that was pumped from the wound in a regular cadence. Perhaps they had even become afraid, awed by what they had done to their master, this hated but venerated demi-god; perhaps, like Dr Moreau's wayward, island children, they had become overwhelmed by the realization of their own rebellion. From where I stood I had a view of Wisbeech's profile and I could see that he was gazing at the dried little husk that had once been his brother, a wrinkled cadaver strapped to an invalid chair from where, when alive and, it seemed, long after, Dominic Wisbeech had been entertained by acts of the worst depravities, perverted copulations that sometimes ended in the death of one of the participants, a private affair to begin with, but later a financial enterprise with high rewards; all arranged and, in a way, engineered, by his sibling, Leonard. What the doctor was thinking as his life's blood poured away and his eyes slowly glazed, can only be guessed at, but at least his dying muse did not last long.

His creatures, *his* mutants, had become emboldened by their master's helplessness and they plucked at him, touching his hair, his shoulders, immediately snatching their fingers away like nervous kids touching a dead animal; then, impatience getting the better of them, they hauled his body off the glass and threw it to the floor. I was glad I could not see what they did to him then – there were too many heaving backs and rearing heads and limbs – for the sounds of ripping and the breaking of bones were enough.

We backed away, Constance, Joseph and Mary gathered behind me, clutching each other, Mary out of her shock and whimpering uncontrollably. Our escape route was blocked by the mêlée between us and the double doors and I knew we had to skirt around it. But when I realized the extent of the conflagration, I wondered how.

45

Although the flames were still some distance away from us, they were spreading fast and their heat already seemed to be searing our flesh. It was becoming difficult to breathe too, great billows of black smoke filling the air, the inferno itself greedily consuming the oxygen we needed. Across the room, the bed that had been draped in red velvet was nothing but a funeral pyre, the wall behind it and ceiling above obliterated by fire. Great chunks of plasterboard that had covered the ceiling joinery were falling inwards, burning as they dropped; light reflectors blazed like burning bushes and the snake nest of cables on the floor was melting, the acrid fumes poisoning the atmosphere, causing us to clamp our hands over our mouths and noses. My eye stung and tears began to blur my vision; my throat felt scorched and each breath became successively more laboured. It was the same for the others and I knew I had to get us all out of there before we succumbed to the heat and smoke.

It took me less than two seconds to figure it out. If we couldn't skirt around that rabid mob hunched over its gory prize, then we'd go through it. All right, maybe not directly through it, but through the edge of it, as far away from the fire as possible.

'*Constance, give me your stick.*'

Her teared eyes looked at me uncomprehendingly.

'*One of your sticks,*' I repeated, pointing at it. '*I'm going to need it. Joseph, help them both and follow me. Stay close, but keep behind. If I run into trouble, keep going.'* My throat felt raspy, but not from shouting.

Taking Constance's metal elbow-crutch and holding it before me like a baseball bat, I began to make my way towards the blood-crazed creatures, flinching at the sight of a naked arm raised high into the air. It wasn't attached to its body and I knew it belonged to Wisbeech: they were literally tearing him apart.

'Oh my God!' I heard Constance cry and I knew she had caught sight of the dismembered limb too.

I glanced over my shoulder and saw that my companions had stopped. Despite the swift-approaching flames, the stifling heat, the choking smoke, they were frozen to the spot.

'Come on, keep moving!' I yelled at them, grabbing Constance and pulling her forward.

Unfortunately, either her cry or my yell had attracted the attention of one or two of the creatures. Two began to rise – the tentacle-armed man and the backless girl. I think the girl recognized me, for her lunatic smile widened and her arms reached forward as if to embrace. I noticed the running blood that covered her hands and wrists. The tentacle-man started coming towards me. The girl disengaged herself from the crowd and followed.

I was ready for them though. I felt no pity, no shame, as I rushed forward and brought the metal cane down hard on the naked, hairless thing's bald skull.

The impact ran up my arms, almost numbing them, and the man went down hard and fast, his skull caved in like a broken egg shell; I hadn't realized his bones were so fragile and I don't suppose I would have cared anyway. All I can say in my defence is that there are extremes and then there are *extreme* extremes. The fact is, these creatures were scarcely human and they appeared to be driven by something evil inside them. I'm sure some social workers would condemn me for my uncompromising stance, but then, what the fuck do *they* really know? Besides, these demented creatures were going to kill us, just as they had killed Nurse Fletcher and Leonard Wisbeech, just as they would kill anyone they came across that night. They were bad and they were mad, and that's the end of it.

Its tentacle-arms twitched and quivered and it was soon gone.

The girl with the lovely face and raven hair and madness in her stare, whose inner organs, bones and arteries were exposed inside her fleshless back and legs, was not at all deterred. She stepped around her companion on the floor and continued to approach, her arms still stretched towards me. I saw others behind her beginning to take notice.

Even when a burning ember flew into her hair, causing it to smoulder, she continued. It was hard – oh, it was goddamn hard – and I had to keep reminding myself she was too far gone to listen to reason and even if she meant me no harm (which I seriously doubted) the fire would take us both within minutes. I hit her, not as brutally as I had hit the man, but with enough force to stop her in her tracks.

I had struck her on the shoulder and she had staggered a little. Now she blinked and I thought she was about to cry. She didn't though. Her face turned into an expression of utter vileness, as though the insane gleam in her eyes had merely been seen through the holes in a mask. The mask had slipped, somehow knocked away by the blow to her shoulder, and here was the real face, no longer beautiful but ridden with malevolence. Her stretched-out hands slowly curled to become claws. But at the same time her smouldering hair flamed up to become a blazing halo around her head.

She started screaming, the harsh fact of being alight cutting to the core of her deluded mind, and wheeled around and around, metal inside her body catching the fire-glow, distracting the other creatures from their task.

'*Now!*' I shouted to Constance and the others. '*Run!*'

Although traumatized – Constance had her hands to her

mouth, Mary was sobbing helplessly, and Joseph's mouth was agape – they did as I bade them, scuttling past me while I brandished my weapon at the mob. There was a sudden *whoosh* behind me and something fell from above, sending showers of sparks and embers our way, a wave of fresh heat washing over us all like a dragon's breath. I felt my hair singe at the back, another blast of fiercely hot air engulf me, and then I, too, felt as if I were on fire.

The creatures fell back, not afraid of me, but of what lay behind me, and for a brief moment I saw what was left of Dr Leonard K. Wisbeech on the floor. One arm was missing, cleaved from his shoulder by God knows what, and his face, his once handsome, distinguished face, was a bloody pulp. His clothes were torn open and so was his body: it was as if they had dug into him with trowels, yanking his innards loose so that they glistened in piles around his inert form. It was just a glimpse, and quite enough; I turned my head away.

Then I moved fast, running after my friends towards the double doors, flames licking at the left side of my body, scorching my cheek. Half the room was an inferno, the bed vanished, the door by which we had entered behind a wall of fire (a fleeting thought of all those inflammable film cassettes in the storeroom, the flames reaching them . . .) the wood floor itself ablaze. At least some of the smoke had found an outlet, most of the ceiling covering gone, the fire licking at the exposed beams, already eating into the room above, timber crashing inwards. A figure appeared before me – I think it was the thing whose face was mostly covered by a huge hard beak, but my vision was too blurred by tears to see properly – and I swiped at it with the crutch without thinking, without even hesitating, concerned only with escaping the fire. Something else rose in front of me and I didn't even *try* to look, I just swatted at it with my sturdy weapon and it, too, disappeared – disappeared with a shriek. I stumbled over something lying on the floor and I think it was the creature whose lower limbs were transmuted into what resembled a fish's tail. Its bloodied hands snatched at my ankles, just as they had in the dungeons below when they had reached through the aperture at the foot of the cell door, but I kicked them away. Ahead of me, a black-skinned man had his arms wrapped in Mary's long, tangled hair and was pulling her backwards, away from the door and back into the throng where some of his fellow fugitives cowered before the advancing fire, while others continued their work on Wisbeech's mutilated corpse, too retarded to appreciate the terrible danger they were in. I was only momentarily distracted by the growth at the centre of Mary's attacker's naked back, for nothing else could shock me that night. It was a superfluous head hanging there just below the man's shoulder-blades, its dead, white-eyed gaze on me, the eyelids drooped, its features slack: this was merely a growth like the membrane sac on my own shoulder, an addition of no merit and absolutely no use. I reached over to grab its host's wild, coarse hair, and, pulling the legitimate head backwards just as he pulled Mary's, I brought his forehead within reach of my weapon. I brought the iron rod down hard, once, twice, and a third time, after which he released Mary and staggered away. I bundled the sobbing girl towards the door where Constance and Joseph anxiously waited, both of them almost doubled up with the pain of coughing smoke from their lungs.

There was a mighty roar behind us, another explosion of heat, but I didn't turn back, I just kept going, dragging the tall girl with me, helping her keep upright, my own limp unnoticed. Joseph was on his knees when we reached him, his slight body wracked with pain, and I mentally chided both him and Constance for not getting out of there while they had the chance, for waiting for us when the blaze was about to consume everything in the room.

Thrusting Mary and the metal crutch at Constance, I picked up Joseph in my arms, his weight hardly slowing me at all. Together we fled the inferno, bursting through the double doors leaving behind the sounds of screams and crashing timbers, the blistering, destructive heat.

Leaving behind the creatures who didn't stand a chance of surviving. And who never had.

Smoke gushed through the double doors after us as we all but fell into the hallway beyond. Choking and spluttering, I dropped to my knees, hastily laying Joseph on the floor and pounding his back as he tried to draw in great gulps of purer air. His aged lungs wheezed with the effort and I kept thumping him with a flattened hand between the shoulder-blades until he began to gain some control and his breathing steadied. Constance and Mary clung to each other, tears running down their dusty faces, they, too wheezing as they gasped for air. There was movement around us in the smoke-filled hallway and I assumed, although it surprised me, that those who had fled the fire before us still lingered. When I hauled myself to my feet I saw that I was wrong.

Milling around us, while some still descended the stairs, were the others from the dormitory at the top of the annex. They were crowding around Constance and Mary, calling their names like excited children, clutching at them, trying to gain their attention. There were no nurses or supervisors among them – as far as I could tell in that short time and hazy atmosphere – those who had been inside the studio with Wisbeech, including the film crew, had vanished into the night. Maybe one or two staff members had run to the main part of the building to warn of the fire outbreak, but I heard no alarms. I did hear someone calling my name though.

It was difficult at first to detect where it came from over the hubbub of other shouts and agitated voices, but then I noticed someone waving at me from the stairway.

'*Louise!*'

She and two others from the dormitory were helping the

woman whose stomach bloated massively beneath the bed-sheets that had been wrapped around her, the gigantic ovarian cyst hidden under the material impossible for her to carry alone; while Louise supported her on one side, the girl with the excrescent tusk held her on the other, the young man, whose face was only partially concealed now by a great tagged-back flap of skin and flesh, was on the lower steps beneath the swelling, bearing most of the growth's weight on his shoulders. Louise awkwardly waved at me again.

'Dis, thank God you're all right,' I thought I heard her say.

I pushed my way through the crowd to reach her, yelling back to Constance to keep everyone away from the studio entrance, one side of its double doors now closed, probably by the rush of scorched air from inside, flames seeming to fill the opening completely. I turned my attention back to Louise, disengaging myself from the woman whose arms clung to me and whose double-face, another's melded into her own, was only inches from mine. She was frightened, pleading for me to help her, to help them all, and as gently as I could I directed her towards the open door at the end of the hallway, pushing her towards it, reassuring her with words spoken close to her ear so that she could hear them over the clamour. Louise and her ungainly little troupe were almost at the bottom of the stairway by the time I got to her and she managed an anxious smile.

'Dis, I was so worried about you,' she said breathlessly.

'What are you doing here?' I said as I helped the young man who had literally been taking most of the load on his shoulders. He twisted as he rose, his arms continuing to take the woman's weight. 'How did you get in here, Louise?'

'Let's get everyone outside first, Dis,' she said, and I saw the soundness of her advice. The fire was going to spread rapidly, the ceiling above the studio-room already eaten through.

I squeezed her upper arm and looked behind her as more figures appeared above at the turn of the stairs. The three-headed boy, the third head lolling uselessly from his shoulder, was making his way carefully down the steps, beside him the youth who carried the extra half body that sprouted from his own chest through a large hole in his gown, holding it before him as though it were a younger sibling who had fallen asleep. They looked petrified and I pushed past Louise to get to them.

'You're going to be okay,' I told them, trying to smile in the hope it would calm them a little. 'The door's open at the end of the hallway and you'll be safe once you're outside.'

Something caught my eye behind them, something very small scuttling down the stairs. I saw it was the one whose body ended just below his chest and I waved him forward when he stopped to survey the scene below, his eyes fearful and his arms trembling.

'Come on,' I encouraged him. 'You're all getting out of this place right now.'

A different fear came into his eyes and I realized that even though they hated it here, it was the only home they had ever known. Of course the idea of leaving was intimidating to them.

'Constance is waiting for you,' I said hopefully and it worked, the sound of her name, the thought of her waiting for him, did the trick. He came down the stairs fast, like an infant shuffling on its bottom, squeezing past the others and disappearing into the crowd below.

'Dis!'

It was Louise's voice. She looked up at me, then pointed along the hallway.

'They're afraid of the fire,' she called out. 'They won't go past the doorway. We'll have to close it.'

I saw what she meant. Along with billows of dusty smoke, flames were licking out from the studio-room, lapping around the edges of the door frame. The closed half of the double doors was alight from the inside, its white paintwork blistering, the raw wood beneath turning a dark, scorched brown. I

453

thought I could hear screams from inside, but the noise from those in the hallway and the roaring of the fire itself was too loud to be sure. Constance was urging those in the packed hallway to hurry past the opening, but they cowered back, some even turning towards the stairs.

I hobbled down to meet them, waving my arms and shouting. *'Not this way! The quickest way out is through the front door! Come on, please, go back!'*

They hesitated, but were not convinced. I pushed through them until I was beside Constance. She stood close to Mary, who clung to her like a frightened child, while holding the hand of a small man – he might have been just a kid, but what I could see of his face was so lined and wearied, probably from the misery of his burden, that it was impossible to tell. A huge tumour grew from the side of his head, the hardened flesh so rutted and bulbous it seemed to be cascading from him; so large was it that its base rested against his shoulder, its heaviness causing him to lean to one side.

'Nick, they're too afraid,' Constance said, her voice raised so that I could hear over the general din.

'Yeah, I know. Don't worry, I'm going to try to get that door shut.' Their hesitancy was strange, for the hallway was wide and they could easily have kept to the far wall, well away from the room that was on fire. Yet I could understand their fear: it wasn't just the flames licking through that open doorway that they were scared of, it was the whole thing of leaving their hated but safe haven, the idea of stepping out into a world that none of them knew; I think the fire represented an obstacle, even a hurdle, that had to be overcome if they were to break from the life they had always known; or maybe it was just an excuse not to venture further, a reason for not hurrying down that hallway and out into an alien world. I could not let them linger here any longer though – the smoke was dangerously thick by now, many around me finding it difficult to breathe, their hands clasped to their mouths or holding their throats as they choked.

I edged along the wall towards the door, an arm raised to my face against the heat that spilled out, trying not to inhale too much smoke, my chest and throat already painfully restricted. When I was beside the open door, still protected by the wall, I whipped off my jacket and held it up before me with one arm, using it as a flimsy shield against the worst of the heat. I ducked around the door frame, the sheer intensity of that heat almost throwing me backwards. I cried out, but forced myself to reach forward with a scrabbling hand, trying to find the doorhandle so that I could pull the door towards me. I screamed when my fingers touched red-hot metal, snatching my hand away again. I spun back against the protecting wall, its hot bricks burning bare flesh. Oh God, why not just rush past and make for the main door? Surely they'd all follow? I could call back to them, they'd see I had made it safely. They'd be bound to follow. I looked around and saw Constance – Constance and all the others – watching me, eyes red and tear-stained from the smoke. I wondered if she could see my desperation.

'Be careful, Nick!' she called to me.

I groaned. Holding the jacket before me again, I whirled around to face the inferno, this time dropping my arm just enough to see. My eyeball immediately felt roasted, tears caused by smoke instantly evaporating, and I closed my eyelids to a sliver. In the second it took for me to hook my hand around the edge of the door and pull it towards me, I thought I caught something moving inside just beyond the conflagration; then the door slammed shut before me and I wheeled away, sticking my burnt fingers into my mouth, hoping the juices there (what juices? My mouth and throat were as dry as parchment laid out in a desert) would soothe the stinging. Ignoring the pain, I limped back to Constance.

'Okay, let's get them moving,' I croaked and she managed a smile for her friends, drawing them forward, encouraging them with soothing words. They began moving as one towards the big entrance doors at the end of the hallway.

46

I waited until they were all out, helping those who were struggling, lifting those light enough to be carried and depositing them outside on the step, galvanizing the slowest ones with encouraging words, giving them no more time to think or to be afraid. And Constance helped me, taking them through the wide, open doorway, leaving them gasping in fresh air, and returning to help me. We found a brief moment to look at each other and that did more to strengthen me than a couple of hours' rest.

Before running out into the night, I quickly checked the hallway to make sure nobody had been left behind in the confusion, or had collapsed unnoticed, overcome by smoke. It was almost impossible to see the stairs next to the lift at the far end and I ducked low to get a better view beneath the swirling haze. All was clear as far as stragglers were concerned, but I noticed flames coming from the crack beneath the studio entrance, as well as the tiny gap between the doors themselves. The paint that hadn't peeled or blistered was actually melting, running to the floor in gooey rivulets. Time to leave for good and I didn't pause a moment longer.

Outside, the others were gathered near the centre of the triangular courtyard and I heard them gasping and coughing, some of them sobbing loudly, while a few more were content just to gaze around bewildered by what they saw. I noticed that the big Transit had gone, the film crew obviously having had no intention of hanging around to see if they could help anyone still trapped inside. Again I wondered if the staff involved in this sordid sideline of Leonard Wisbeech's had fled also, or had gone to the main part of the home to raise the alert. I took a moment to listen, but heard no sound of fire alarms, so assumed they had made off to pastures new, unwilling to face the consequences now that the secret of PERFECT REST was about to be exposed. I was puzzled only briefly by the lack of alarms inside the burning annexe itself, quickly realizing that the sound of fire-bells attracting the rescue services to his hidden dungeons and dormitory was the last thing Wisbeech would have wanted.

The moon was behind a cloud and all I could see ahead of me were dark shapes, lying on the ground, others sitting, and still more milling around, quiet apart from their coughing and weeping.

'*Constance,*' I called softly as I moved among them.

'Here, Nick. I'm here.'

A shadowy figure detached itself from others and came towards me. I took Constance in my arms and held her so tightly I felt her wince. My cheek brushed her cheek and suddenly I was kissing her, finding her lips, her brow, even her closed eyes, finding any part of her face that was accessible, which was just about all of it as far as I was concerned.

'You're okay?' I asked between kisses.

'I think so, Nick. My head's a bit fuzzy, but I think I'm all right. You, Nick? You're all right? They didn't hurt you?'

I just found her lips again and kissed them deeply, kissed them with a passion that had nothing to do with lust, but a lot to do with wanting.

'How did you know where I was?' She was finding it difficult to catch her breath and I eased off a little.

'Your friends helped me.'

The moon resurfaced and the scene around us was bathed in its cold glow. Constance's eyes were wide as she looked up into my face and I could see the anxiety there, perhaps even the remnants of fear.

'We've a lot to talk about, Constance,' I said softly to her, holding her tight so that she would not get the wrong message.

'I know.' It was barely a whisper. She buried her head into my chest and her hold on me was as tight as mine on her.

'Dis.'

I raised my head to spot Louise coming towards me, carefully stepping around prone and sitting bodies. I felt a flush of relief, stored up since we had found each other in the hallway.

'Louise. How the hell did you get inside the house?' Still clutching each other, Constance and I turned towards the clairvoyant.

'I could hear them calling, Dis, stronger than ever before. As I waited for you in that old house, their thoughts came to me, so powerfully, so desperately. I knew they urgently needed help.'

She touched my shoulder, resting heavily against me, the breaths she drew long and ratchety.

'I knew they were coming from this place,' she went on, determined to explain as quickly as possible. 'I drove up to the gates and demanded to be let in, told them I was a distant cousin of Hildegarde Vogel.'

'They believed you? You're not even German.'

'They weren't to know that and the sound over the gate's intercom was so bad they probably couldn't tell I didn't have an accent. I insisted that I had to see Dr Wisbeech and they told me he wasn't available, it was too late. I persisted though and threatened them with all kinds of things, including going to the police over my "cousin's" death and the fact that I hadn't been informed. Oh, whoever I was speaking to claimed that no one even knew that Hildegarde had any living relatives to inform, but I blustered on and finally they allowed me inside. I think their intention was to see me quickly just to ascertain my nuisance value.'

Lights were coming on in the windows of the main building opposite us, and I could see faces looking down from them. The added glows lit up the courtyard, making us even more visible. Windows started to open.

'But I never made it to the main house,' Louise was saying. 'As I drove in I noticed a narrow lane by the side of the main drive.'

I nodded my head to let her know I was aware of it.

'The voices, those thoughts inside my head – they were calling me from that direction. I don't know how, direction isn't normally a part of the sensing, but somehow I knew they wanted me to come to them through that lane. So I turned into it and it led me here, this courtyard. The door over there was unlocked, so I went inside.'

I remembered I hadn't tried the annexe door after the man taking in equipment from the Transit had closed it behind him. I'd had no reason to – it was the main building that I had wanted to explore. We heard voices coming from above, the old residents, alerted by the disturbance below, crowding round the upstairs windows and jabbering to each other. We would have to warn them to get out before the fire spread, but first I wanted the clairvoyant to finish her story; a few more moments wouldn't put the old people in any more danger, the annexe almost totally sealed off from the main house, the heavy doors between them the only connection as far as I knew.

'There was a lift in the hallway and I used it to take me up. There was no one about, but I was sure I was being called from a room there. The voices were far stronger than they had ever been. And there was one among them whose ability is so powerful, it was as if he'd taken my hand . . . Oh my God!' She clasped her hands to her mouth.

Constance reached out to touch them. 'What is it, Louise?'

'The voice ... the boy. He's still up there. He told me to get all the others out first – he *insisted* that I take them – and to come back for him. He was aware of the fire, you see? He knew they were all in great danger.'

'Michael?' In panic, Constance was looking around us, searching for the limbless boy among the others.

'Michael? Is that his name?' Louise looked from Constance to me. 'His thoughts were so clear when he told me about this place and his friends here. He told me of the Doctor's work, the terrible things he did to them. He told me about *you*, Dis. He told me about you.'

In the moonlight, I recognized that same odd look she had given me when first we'd met.

'*You left him there, Louise.*' Constance's tone was not accusatory; it was distressed.

'I'm ... I'm sorry. But he urged me to get the others out first. We must go back!'

'No.' I was firm. The smoke rolling from the open doorway was full and black. And even as I made the decision, we heard a loud *thwoomp* from inside, the dark churning clouds immediately fused with a bright orange. The door to the studio had burst open, pushed by an explosion behind, and flames were pouring into the hallway. We all flinched, but then Constance made as if to dash towards the entrance. I grabbed her and held her fast.

'*We can't just leave him!*' she screamed at me.

'We're not going to!' I yelled back as she struggled to get away.

A hand tugged at my shirtsleeve – I'd lost my jacket somewhere back there in the hallway. I glanced down at Joseph, my head busy with thoughts of how I could reach the dormitory again.

'Michael's calling,' Joseph said, and his lips were quivering as if he were about to cry. For a moment, in that bleaching moonlight, he almost looked like the child he truly was. 'He's afraid, Dis. He's calling you, he wants you to go to him.'

'My God,' said Louise, 'I can hear him too, but this time it really is like a voice and not just a thought. He's calling your name, Dis.'

Terrific, I thought. Even if I'd had a choice a moment ago – and I *had* decided to go back for him – I had no choice now. Not with Constance watching me. Not with Joseph's ancient-child's eyes on me. Not with Louise on the point of passing out with anxiety. Not with them *all* seeing the good side of me, the side they all imagined they saw. I was no saviour, no matter what they felt about me. I was a coward. And it was the coward in me that was going to force me back inside that burning building, because I was too scared to let them down! Shit.

'Louise,' I said without giving myself further time to think, 'have you got my cellphone with you?'

She nodded her head, hastily reaching into the deep pocket of her summer dress.

'Good. Call the emergency services from here. We want all of them – fire, police, and ambulances. Do that before you warn the staff in the main building – it'll save time if they haven't already called them.' Because the windowless annexe was so cut off from the home itself, I suspected the staff were still not aware of the fire, unless somebody at the windows above had seen the smoke. 'I'm going to use the fire escape to get back up to the dormitory – it's how I reached it in the first place.'

'I'm coming with you, Nick.'

I turned on Constance. 'Oh no you're not!'

'I'm coming with you,' she persisted, her jaw set tight.

'You can't. You'll slow me down.'

It was the blunt truth, but she merely shook her head.

'I can help you.'

I held her away from me. 'I don't have time to argue.

461

Please, just stick with your friends here – *they* need your help.'

With that, I was off, limping towards the fire-escape, my leg dragging. People were shouting down to us from the windows, but I ignored them, too busy just getting to the metal stairway and cursing myself for ever getting into a situation like this. Now that Wisbeech was dead, killed in a most horrible way, my anger had dissipated somewhat, revenge, justice, already exacted (though not by me) in brutal fashion. I started to climb, but felt the metal rail judder behind me.

'*Constance,*' I yelled, '*please go back!*'

'Michael is in my care!' she shouted back. 'I have to help him.'

It was pointless to argue: Constance was going to follow me whatever I said. Although exasperated, I think my love for her reached a new high at that moment. I understood her compassion for these others, others like her, others like me, and I also understood the guilt – mistaken though it was – she felt. Perhaps she thought she could have done more for them, that she should have exposed her guardian and the 'researches' he indulged in here; she didn't understand that she was also a victim of Dr Leonard K. Wisbeech, that she had been manipulated and used by someone she thought cared for her. Someone who would have had her killed that very night. What else had this so-called physician done to her over the years, what other abuses had she suffered? How far had he gone with the drugs he had used on her? I shut the last screaming thoughts from my mind.

I went on, aware that even in my worn condition she'd have trouble keeping up with me. Smoke swelled across the courtyard from the ground-floor door opposite, curling around the iron stairway like a drifting fog. More shouts came from windows, the old folk beginning to get agitated. I was on the last flight of steps when a light came on above me. I stopped as a figure stepped out on to the fire-escape's top landing.

'Who's there? What d'you want here?'

It was a female voice and I thought I recognized the accent. She was dressed in a kimono-type dressing-gown, her hair in large rollers, and in her hand she held a key that I assumed was to the fire-escape door. I knew I had seen her before and I couldn't remember where or when. It was only when she peered over the railing – perhaps to locate the smoke's source, perhaps curious about the noise from below – that it came to me. It was the rollers that had put me off, maybe the kimono too, for the last time I had seen her she was wearing a nurse's uniform and her ginger-blonde hair was tied back in a bun at the nape of her neck.

'Lord save us, what's going on?'

It was the Irish accent that made something in my brain click. 'Theresa . . .' I said. Then I remembered the correct pronunciation: 'Ther*ai*sa, it's me, Nick Dismas. We met the – '

'Ah, I know you. You were with Constance, weren't you?'

It was then that Constance caught up with me.

'Constance, d'you think you'd be tellin me what's happenin here?'

In the light from the doorway I could see her chubby face was set in a frown. She cocked her head to look around me at Constance.

'There's a fire in the annexe, Theresa,' Constance said breathlessly. 'You have to get everyone out before it spreads.'

'Oh Mother Mary, I'd better get on to the fire services.'

'Already done.' I scurried up the last few steps to the landing. 'You just sound the alarm and concentrate on getting people out.'

'But how did it start, who – ?'

I shut her up by pushing past her and entering the building. As I made for the alcove further along the corridor,

I heard Constance's voice behind me ordering the plump young nurse to arouse everyone on that floor before going down to alert the patients and residents. Mercifully, I had left one half of the double doors in the alcove slightly open, resting against the edge of its partner, afraid of the noise it would make if I pushed it shut completely. (I thanked God that the nurse, Theresa, had come out on to the fire-escape to see what all the ruckus was about, because I was no longer wearing the jacket with my lock-picking tools in its pocket.) I went through into the annexe and found myself back inside the large area at the end of which lay the dormitory.

It was filled with smoke coming through the door to the staircase next to the lift which was wide open, no doubt left that way after Louise had shepherded the 'others' through, and I knew it wouldn't take long for the fire to follow the smoke. I quickly looked into the office on my left, not expecting to find anyone there, but taking no chances. It was empty and I assumed the orderly, who had almost discovered us earlier, had returned to the activities below before Louise's arrival. A noise behind me made me whirl round.

Constance was coming towards me through the smoke, the rubber tips of her elbow crutches clumping against the floor, her anxious face smeared with smoke-grime, tear-streaks creating white rivers down her cheeks.

'Go back!' I told her roughly. 'I can manage on my own.'

She came on and was in my arms before I could raise another protest.

'I'm . . . I'm so sorry,' I heard her say.

'You don't have to be, Constance,' I said close to her ear. 'None of this is your fault. You couldn't know the full story.'

'I should have done something about it. I've had suspicions for a long time. I shouldn't have cooperated in the way Hildegarde did. When I talked to Leonard about it, he said that nobody could do as well for them as he. Outside this home they would all be treated as freaks. He told me that only he knew how to keep them alive. His researches had taught him how. He knew the treatment, the best drugs to use – Leonard *believed* he was the only physician who could help them properly and I wanted to believe him. I *made* myself believe him.'

'Maybe he was right in a sense. How many like them are out on the streets, how many do we see outside? I find it hard to believe they all die at birth, so where are those who survive? In places similar to this? In the test laboratories somewhere? Or are they quietly terminated when nothing more can be done for them? I despised Wisbeech, but in the beginning, and in a weird way, he was trying to do something for them as well as his own brother. I guess the ideal just got corrupted along the way.'

I could feel the heat coming through the soles of my shoes as we stood there and smoke was seeping from the cracks between floorboards.

'Jesus!' I exclaimed. 'We don't have much time, Constance. Let's find Michael and get out of here!'

I started to move away, but she clung to me.

'Nick. Downstairs . . . what was . . .'

She was finding it hard to say the words, so I made it easier for her.

'You were tranked. You didn't know what was going on. Your caring guardian had spiked something you drank with Rohypnol and God knows what else. He's . . . he *was* . . . a skilful doctor and he knew the correct dosages to give you. Hell, he knew all about drugs and their effects.'

I squeezed my eye shut but the thoughts only became sharper, the pictures more focused. Oh Lord, what had Constance been forced to do when she was under . . . ?

'I love you, Nick.'

I hugged her close. She had said something I'd waited all my life to hear, just someone saying they loved me; but only in the wildest of my dreams did I imagine it would come from someone as wonderful as Constance. You might think I was compromising, taking the love of a crippled girl because I couldn't do better. You might think that, but you'd be wrong. Constance was no compromise, despite her disability: she was a prize, a wonderful, unexpected prize.

I was shaking my head in wonder as I began to say, 'You've no idea – '

A soft hand on my lips stopped me. 'I do,' she said simply. 'I felt it the very moment you arrived in my life. I know how you feel, Nick, because it's the same for me. I hope I haven't let you down . . .'

Something crashed on the level beneath us. Something in the laboratory. The floor seemed to tremble for a second or two.

'Let's hurry,' Constance said and sprang away from me, turning around with the aid of her crutches and making for the entrance to the dormitory.

I should have held on to her for a moment longer, should have squeezed her tightly, should have crushed her to my chest. Right then, I should have kissed her. But there was no chance – she was gone.

I hurried after her.

Light from the open doorway helped us find Michael as we made our way along the cot beds. The heat was stifling in the dormitory and the smoke was like a drifting haze before us and I offered my handkerchief to Constance so that she could use it as a mask. She declined, telling me she could not hold it and use the crutches at the same time, so I reluctantly stuffed it back into my trouser pocket: I'd use it myself only when absolutely necessary – which wouldn't be long by the look of things, for as we had passed the stairway in the area outside the dormitory, I had noticed the red glow on the far wall, reflections of the fire raging on the lower floor.

Michael was squirming helplessly on his cot and I could

hear that peculiar keening sound coming from him as he rocked his tiny head from side to side. I still found it hard to look at him, despite everything else I'd seen that night, but I reminded myself that this was a human being – a *young* human being – with a soul like everybody else. And if there was no such thing as a soul, well, he had a goodness inside him that had won him the affection of his fellow-inmates, and he had used his special telepathic gift to help them all. He had also insisted that Louise help the others before attending to him.

He stopped moving as I leaned over him, only that lipless mouth continuing to pulsate. His pink, blind eyes seemed to seek me out.

'Everything's fine, Michael,' I said as soothingly as I could. 'Constance is with me and we're going to get you out of here.'

'He knows,' Constance said.

'Uh?'

'Michael is aware I'm here. He always knows.'

'Will he hear me if I speak to him?'

'He'll hear you if you only think.'

When I reached down and touched his silky skin, an odd sensation swept through me, travelling up my arm and settling in my chest. It was a feeling of prodigious warmth – warmth that had nothing to do with the raging fire threatening us, for it was of the emotional kind. It might sound trite, but it was a feeling of immense love and I almost staggered back with the impact. Michael was showing me his gratitude; his gratitude and his *trust*. It was as if he had physically embraced me.

I began to understand his power then, this sensory gift that had enabled Michael *and* the others to reach out collectively with their minds to find me, Louise Broomfield the bridge between us, her own psychic skills the necessary link, for I had no such powers. What Michael could not foretell, though, was that the minds of the creatures kept in the underground cells, these other 'others', had also linked with his mind and it was their malign nature that had changed it into a nightmare for me. They had usurped the message so that it had become an abomination.

Almost tenderly, I wrapped the bedsheet around him and lifted him from the cot. All sense of revulsion immediately left me and I held him to my chest as you might hold an infant.

Constance tucked in the edges of the bedsheet around him before softly placing two fingers against his undefined cheek. Smoke was pouring between the floorboards as we headed back towards the door. Constance saw it first and gave out a small, shrill cry. I groaned when I looked.

In the wide, open entrance to the dormitory there now lurked the thing that had murdered and mutilated Henry, the monster that Wisbeech had wanted to film copulating with Constance. The creature I thought had died in the fire below.

It swayed in the doorway, naked once more, the fire behind silhouetting its figure so that it really did resemble a demon from Hell. I could not see the shadowed face, the damaged eye, those terrible needle-sharp teeth.

But I knew it was watching me. I could feel its hatred.

It was then that flames began to leap upwards from the dormitory's crackling floor.

47

We could hear its snuffling as it suddenly loped towards us, waving those wicked-looking claws before it as it came, as though trying to smote the smoke-filled air away.

'*Nick!*'

Constance's scream was directed at me, as if she, too, understood the creature's intention, that I was the one it was coming for.

The robe it had been forced to wear had probably been burned away by the fire in the studio-room and I briefly – *very* briefly, for the distance between us was rapidly diminishing – wondered how the hell it had escaped the conflagration. It seemed impossible that it could have got to the burning door and opened it while others inside were burnt alive. I remembered that this thing was lacking in fear so maybe it had just run right through the fire; or maybe it had found its way back to the dungeon, using the same route we'd taken earlier to reach the studio, past the cells, then up the staircase, all the way to this level, because the other floors and hallways were burning. Maybe its mind had tuned into Michael's – these creatures had done so before – and so it knew where to find me.

As it came towards me I saw that its black, wiry body-hair had been completely burned away, its skin horribly blistered and scorched, its flesh seared to a deeper red than before; its big hands were raw, its clawed fingers glistening with seepages, catching the light from individual fires around the room. Its long penis hung down between its legs, still peculiarly menacing even in its flaccid state. I wanted to run as fast as I could in the opposite direction (*my* brain wasn't missing any special neurons), but there was nowhere *to* run. The dormitory ended in a blank, windowless wall. I knew I had to stand and fight for the sake of Constance and Michael alone; I also knew that, as before, I didn't stand a chance against it.

'*Take him!*' I yelled at Constance, thrusting my burden towards her.

She immediately dropped her crutches, and took Michael from me. I didn't even bother to see if she could bear his weight: I twisted round and picked up a narrow cot by its metal frame, tilting it so that the mattress slid off; then, holding it like a battering ram, the springy wire base against my chest and shoulder, one hand at the end, the other holding the lower side of the frame, I charged towards the rushing *beast*, yelling a hoarse war cry as I did so.

We met midway and, using all the considerable power of my arms and shoulders, I smashed the metal headrail straight into the creature's face. It hadn't even had the sense to try and avoid the makeshift ram and it staggered back, too stupid to be surprised. It gave a kind of animal grunt and I followed up with another hard blow, aiming for the chest-centred head again. The *beast* lost balance and I ran at it again, this time knocking it down, opening up a wound in its skull. It crouched over its knees on the floor, head turned so that its yellow eyes could watch me, those deadly needle teeth gnashing at the air.

As I raised the cot-frame yet again, hoping to knock the creature senseless, its hand shot out and caught the end rail. It tried to pull the cot from my grasp, but I hung on and went with the momentum, adding my own force to push the *beast* backwards. It toppled and I pushed even harder, trying to keep it pinned to the smouldering floor.

'*Constance!*' I yelled. '*Get out, quickly! I can't hold it for long!*'

She hesitated and I wasn't sure if it was because she was afraid to get past the thing struggling on the floor, or because she didn't want to leave me.

'*Constance!*' I shouted her name as a command and this time she obeyed.

With Michael in her arms, she cautiously edged round the floundering figure, her wasted legs moving awkwardly, while I fought the *beast*, constantly shoving the end of the cot into its face, knocking it back each time it tried to rise. The demon-thing grabbed the end rail again and pulled, bringing me with it. I let go and swiftly reached for another cot nearby, dragging it towards me, its metal legs scraping against the floorboards. With strength I hadn't known I had left, I lifted the cot and threw it on top of the *beast*. Immediately, I grabbed another, sliding it over the floor, lifting and hurling it on top of the *beast*, who was frantically grappling with the two already bearing down on it, kicking out with its legs so that they became caught up in the metal frames. It yowled in frustration as it tried to get clear, but I kept them coming, burying it beneath more and more cots and beds, using mattresses and chairs too, anything I could find to build a tangled pile over the feral creature. As I hauled yet another bed towards the growing stack, the mattress fell to the floor, its cheap plastic cover instantly melting as it brushed one of the many fires springing up through the floorboards, the material inside – a foam block, I think – flaring up, rapidly becoming a blaze. I dropped the bed-frame and picked up the burning mattress by its corner, tossing it on to the heap. Fiery pieces of melting plastic dripped on to other mattresses in the heaving pile and these, too, caught alight.

I didn't hang around: I circled what was fast-becoming a funeral pyre, stooping to pick up one of Constance's discarded elbow crutches, which I'd almost tripped over, and hobbled towards the double doors, ignoring the screeches of the trapped *beast*, who had had a taste of fire and its consequences earlier so understood the trouble it was in even if there was no fear involved. I avoided the spreading fires that were quickly joining forces to become one massive conflagration, the heat intense, the atmosphere poisoned with black, boiling smoke. I found Constance on her knees in the doorway, the burden of Michael too much for her; she was dragging him along the floor, her thin arms trembling with the effort. She looked at me in weepy surprise when I hauled her to her feet and handed her the metal crutch. I scooped Michael up and held him against my shoulder with one arm; the other arm I used to take Constance's elbow and lead her through the doorway.

We stopped, aghast. Constance almost collapsed against me.

Fire had spread from the open door to the stairway across the whole area between us and the door to the main building, creating a raging wall of flame that completely cut off our escape. We realized that the whole top floor would soon be an inferno.

I searched around desperately, looking for a way out, aware that we had but a few minutes left before we were either choked to death by the smoke and lack of oxygen, or were burnt alive. The lift was close by to our left, its metal doors closed, flames belching out from the stairway door next to it. That was no good though – even if it were still operating it would only take us down to a worse hellfire below.

Constance brushed her cheek against my upper arm and I thought I heard her say my name. When I glanced down at her she looked so helpless, so defeated. I cursed my own uselessness, angry at myself for failing her, and I swore at the cruel irony of it all, that having finally found someone to love, someone who could truly love me in return *and* on equal terms, that joy, that fulfilment, was now to be snatched away, and in the grimmest way possible. The anger swelled inside me and I turned back to the dormitory behind us, still hoping to find a way out.

I had felt deep despair in my miserable little life on more than one occasion (several hundred occasions, I figured), but when I saw the *beast* emerging from the burning heap I'd tried to bury him under, I think I felt the deepest, blackest despair of all. It was as if God, Himself, were playing some wicked joke on me, setting me up for one fall after another. *Cannons to the left, cannons to the right* ... Those stupid fucking lines ran through my head as if my own mind had decided to join in the mocking game.

The *beast* thing, a man-demon from another culture, hurled a cot from its path and staggered towards me.

'*Nick, we must get to the top!*' Constance was tugging at me again and shouting over the roar and crackle of the fire.

'*We can't!*' I yelled back. '*The stairway's an inferno, we'd never make it!*'

'*The lift! We can use the lift! The attic is used as a storeroom and they take heavy stuff up in the lift all the time!*'

There was the light of hope in her eyes and it was a pity it wasn't infectious. I knew we didn't have time, even if the lift was still working. The *beast* would be on us before those metal doors even had a chance to open. And if the *beast* didn't take us, then the all-consuming fire would. It was hopeless, but how could I tell her that?

Once again, I passed Michael over to her. '*Get to the lift. Press the button and if it comes, don't wait for me.*'

'*No!*'

'*There's no choice. Just do as I say.*'

I pushed her roughly towards the metal doors, but she steadied herself, looking at me beseechingly.

'*Do it!*' I screamed. '*Think of Michael!*'

I didn't wait to see if she would do as I told her – there was no time. I turned back to the dormitory to face the approaching monster. *Shit*, I told myself. *Shit, shit, shit.*

And then, aloud, my own defiant war cry: *'Fuckiiiit!'* At least I'd give Constance and Michael a chance.

I expected to die right then and there, but curiously, I no longer cared. Life itself was taking the piss and I'd had enough. I rushed to meet the foe.

But the whole building rocked when something exploded in the laboratory below – a gas pipe, chemicals, who knows? Maybe, just maybe, it was the hand of God, the combustible hand of God – and the floor between the creature and myself split open, a jet of fire blasting through. I was thrown backwards out of the room, a shower of debris and burning wood landing on and around me. I curled up into a tight ball, covering my face with my arms, deafened by the roar, my head reeling. When shrapnel no longer rained down on me, I risked looking back into the dormitory, but all I could see were great billows of smoke pouring out, the wooden frame of the doorway itself on fire. One side of the double doors lay burning a couple of feet away from me; where the other side had gone I had no idea.

I felt fierce heat at my back and realized I had landed dangerously close to the fire that had spread from the stairway. I rolled away, coming to one knee, but not quite ready to rise to my feet: my head was so dizzy I knew I wouldn't be able to keep my balance.

Constance was huddled by the lift doors, Michael, like an infant in swaddling, held in her arms. Her eyes seemed even larger against the black grime that covered her face and her lips, those dear, lovely lips, were moving as though she were trying to tell me something. I crawled over to her, the heat almost overwhelming me, the eerie silence all around making everything seem unreal. I wondered why they were huddled there, why Constance's mouth was opening and closing, and why she was pointing at my head. And when I reached them, I wondered why she was attacking me, slapping my head with the flat of her hand. Sounds began to return, as though her slaps were beating my ears into obedience; I heard her excited voice, but it was still a long way off and I couldn't understand what she was trying to tell me. But when the numbness finally went and the pain set in, I realized my hair was on fire. I yelped, striking at my own head, but Constance was smarter: she unravelled some of the sheet covering Michael and pulled it tight over my head, pressing it down and smothering any flames that had survived our beating hands. Not just my scalp, but my face and hands felt singed, eyebrows just stubble, and there were brown patches on my shirt and trousers where flying embers had landed to be instantly dislodged by my own movement. Still confused, but my hearing swiftly returning to normal, I covered both Constance and Michael with my own body, shielding them from the overpowering heat that was now coming from all directions. I struggled to draw in breath, not quite sure why we were all huddled against this warm metal wall, when something clanked behind it and it split in two, opening up in the middle so that all three of us toppled through.

We lay there gasping on the floor, the air inside only slightly easier to breathe, smoke soon billowing in after us. My full senses came back in a rush and I hauled myself to my feet, a shaking hand reaching for the lift buttons. I was almost tempted to press the G button in the hope that the ground level fire had almost burned itself out, giving us a chance to get out of the building through the hallway: common sense prevailed though and my trembling finger stabbed at the top button.

It took at least two seconds, which felt like a lifetime, for anything to happen; then the door slowly, oh so slowly, began to come together.

Smoke continued to billow through the narrowing gap as I helped Constance, who still clutched Michael to her breast, to her feet. We pressed together against the back wall of the lift to escape the worst of the heat outside and Michael's little limbless body convulsed as though he were having trouble breathing, a wheezing sound coming from the aperture that was his mouth. Constance and I glanced anxiously at each other, wondering if he could take much more. I looked back at the lift doors, willing them to close faster, the smoke beyond them glowing orange. I stiffened when I thought I saw something move amidst those swirling, coloured clouds. It was gone in an instant, but still I watched the ever-narrowing breach with a puzzled – and concerned – eye.

There were perhaps three inches of the gap left when the dark form smashed against the door, clawed fingers reaching round each side to pull them apart again. Constance screamed and I think I yelled – okay, maybe I screamed too – as an arm, burnt raw, the skin of it puckered and blistered, reached through, the clawed hand, with its open, weeping sores scrabbling at the smoky air between us. The gap had widened again and I saw a yellow eye – *a demon's eye* – seeking me out. I pushed Constance aside, into a corner, and prayed – prayed yet again – that the lift doors were not the kind that sprung back when they met an obstacle. Fortunately, these were not of the sophisticated variety, and they continued in trying to close, the arm and the fingers of the other arm trying to push through, long fingernails, blackened by fire, almost scratching my face.

Ducking beneath its grasp, I picked up the metal crutch that had tumbled into the lift with us and brought it down hard on the intruding arm, smashing it against the wrist in an effort to break it, then against the fingers, the knuckles, again and again, my rage equalling that of the *beast*. I could hear Constance's screams, but I felt, rather than heard, bones shatter beneath my blows, and I didn't let up, I kept pounding that fucking demon's hand, wrist, and arms until it began to draw back like a withering weed, returning to where it belonged, where it could do no more harm. And still I kept on, roaring my anger, my anger *and* my fear, beating at the thing as though it represented every pointing finger I had learned to loathe over the years, every jibe, everything that stood between me and a contented existence.

It was gone and the lift doors closed on the burnt-raw fingers of its other hand, and I beat at those too, smashing then to pulp, until they released their grip. But just before that gap closed completely, a great tongue of flame belched through sending us screaming to our knees. Worse than our own screams though, were the muffled screeches from beyond the closed doors and we knew that the creature had finally been taken by the fire. Yet even as the lift lurched and began to rise, we could still hear pounding on the doors below us.

Those sounds continued but became weaker, not just because of the distance between us, but because the blows were becoming more feeble, the *beast* dying, burnt alive. Soon we heard only the roar of the fire itself.

The lift juddered to a halt and the doors clumsily rumbled open. I helped Constance to her feet and we stumbled out into the smoke-filled room beyond, both of us retching as we breathed in the polluted air. The sweltering heat was not quite as bad as in the rooms below, but it was nevertheless oppressive enough to draw our strength – what strength we had left, that is. I felt Constance beginning to sag and I held her more tightly, one arm round her back, beneath her shoulder, the other still gripping her bloodied elbow-crutch. She continued to clasp the sheet-wrapped bundle that was Michael to her breast.

Orange light came from the burning open stairway next to the lift shaft and in its flickering glow I could make out the lift's operating machinery above the shaft itself, this accommodated by a box-like structure built into the angled roof. An iron-runged maintenance ladder rising up the rough brick wall beside the closing lift door led to the machinery.

Opposite the lift shaft was a huge water tank, pipes running from it into a nearby wall, and piled beside it were tins of paint, cartons and boxes, lengths of material that might have been old curtains or background drapes used for filming, discarded pieces of laboratory equipment, and large empty jars. Most of the smoke came from the stairway and it curled around hefty support beams over our heads, the worst of it mercifully gathering under the roof's apex. A short distance away to our left was a blank brick wall which reached to the very top of the inverted V-shaped ceiling, obviously built to seal off the annexe roof space from the main building, and to our right was a broad doorway presumably leading to the storage area itself.

The floorboards beneath our feet were already smouldering and I knew it wouldn't be long before the fire broke through. Loud cracks, like gunshots, came from the wooden boards as they contracted with the heat, and my vision kept blurring, my eye aggravated by the smoke. Now what? I asked myself. So far my only plan had been to keep ahead of the fire, but now we had come as far as we could. Well, maybe not. There was always the roof itself. If we could climb out onto it and the rescue services reached us in time . . . I knew it was the only chance we had.

'*Are there any windows in the storeroom?*' I had to raise my voice again over the din.

'*Just one!*' she shouted back. Despite the grime that blackened her face, I could see from her expression she was in pain, her frail body not meant for the kind of exertion it had been put through tonight. '*It's at the far end of the storeroom.*' She pointed a waving hand at the wide door on our right.

'*Can we get onto the roof from there?*'

'*I – I don't know. I'm not even sure if the window can be opened.*'

'*It's our only option, Constance.*'

She nodded and once again I took Michael from her, handing her the metal crutch as I did so. I pulled back the part of the sheet that covered his face and winced at what I saw in the flickering light. His sightless eyes were closed and the strange aperture that was his mouth barely moved now. I put my ear close to it and thought I heard a very faint wheezing sound. It was hard to tell over the noise of the fire itself though, and if it hadn't been for the slightest movement of his mouth, I might have thought that Michael was dead. I covered his face again, loosely, giving him enough space to breathe, but protecting him from the worst of the smoke and heat.

'*Hang on to me!*' I shouted at Constance. '*Hang on to me and for God's sake, don't let go!*' For my sake too, Constance, especially for my sake.

She nodded again and her eyes told me she was placing all her trust in me. Together we headed for the storeroom.

The broad, sturdy door was the kind that ran on a rail and opened by pulling it sideways, and when I did so, heaving so hard it crashed against the rails' stoppers, bouncing back a little, I almost wept genuine, not smoke-induced, tears of despair. The inferno inside the storeroom seemed absolute.

The explosion in the laboratory had sent flames shooting up into the dormitory, which had lapped at the ceiling there, quickly burning through to the room above, the storeroom. A fierce wave of heat hit us instantly, sending us reeling back, and we cowered behind the rough wall, choking on the smoke, our throats seared by the broiling air we had inhaled. I felt Constance's arms go round me from behind, her weight dragging me down.

'Oh, Nick...' her lips seemed to say when I turned to her.

I pulled her close, Michael between us, and I wondered if this was where it was all to end. Having found each other was this our destiny – to die together? I almost gave in to it, almost accepted our fate, but my old friend and ally, anger, prodded me in the ribs once more. It's too bloody good to give up, I told myself. You've fought all your life, against hardship, against prejudice, against pain. You've been mocked, you've been taunted, you've been abused, and you've overcome it all. So are you really going to lie down and go out with a whimper? Are you going to let Constance down? Are you going to let Michael die too, just when you've won his freedom? What are you – a man, or just a . . . just a . . . *freak*?

'*What the fuck can I do?*' I screamed, the sound coming out like a raspy whisper, but vehemently enough for Constance to jerk away from me. Her teary eyes looked at me in bewilderment and at first, foolishly, I thought it was because she could not understand why I'd let her down; her hand touched my face though, a tender, fingertip caress, and I knew she would never think that of me. She had just been surprised at my outburst and had not been able to catch the words. Now her expression changed and she mouthed something that I couldn't hear, but could understand. She was telling me she loved me again.

I laid Michael in her lap and spun away so that my face was against the wall at the edge of the door. More cautiously this time, I peeked into the storeroom.

I must have noticed it before when I had slid back the door, the intense burst of concentrated heat pushing me away before it had a chance to register. I shielded my face with my arm and forced myself to survey the burning room. I spotted it straight away, then wheeled back to face Constance.

I tried to force saliva into my throat so that I could speak clearly, but it was impossible. Everything was too dry; my tongue felt like a wad of sandpaper, the roof of my mouth like old parchment. I had to make do with a raspy croak.

'*There's a chance,*' I said close to her ear. '*There's a line of boxes on the right-hand side. It's two rows high and the top edge of them touches the slanted ceiling. Their fronts are burning, but the flames haven't reached the back yet. Constance, I saw a*

*gap behind them and I think it runs along the whole length of
the room. We can make it to the end. I'm sure we can!'*

She found it difficult to speak too, but after two attempts
she managed to say: *'The heat, we won't be able to stand the
heat. We won't even get through the door.'*

'Wait there.'

Pushing myself up, I staggered over to the junk piled next
to the water tank and dragged out the folded lengths of
material. Quickly I sifted through and found two pieces of
thick curtaining. I pulled them clear, then found a box to
stand on so that I could easily reach the top of the steel
water tank. Dragging the curtains up with me, I tossed them
over the edge of the open tank, first one and then the other,
keeping a firm grip on a corner of material, immersing the
rest in water. When both were thoroughly soaked, I swallowed a cupped-palm of water, then hauled the wet curtains
back to Constance and Michael. The top step of the stairway
was now on fire, the flames spreading up the angled roof.

I wasn't sure if Michael was still alive when I took him
from Constance and briefly uncovered his face – his eyes
remained closed and his mouth was motionless now – but I
wasn't going to abandon him. As Constance painfully pulled
herself off the floor, one hand on the wall, the other on her
stick, I wrapped the first length of water-soaked material
around her head and shoulders with my free hand. She
tugged it tight at the front so that it resembled a huge shawl
and I began to do the same to myself with the other one. We
were forced to dodge flames that were springing up between
the floorboards and we knew we had less than seconds to
get out of that part of the roof space before it joined the
inferno.

Tucking the wet material around Michael while I held
him against my chest with one arm, I led Constance to the
doorway.

'Stay close behind me!' I instructed her, the drink I'd

snatched from the tank lubricating my mouth and throat just enough to improve my speech. *'Keep your face against my back, don't even try to see for yourself. Just follow me, right?'*

She gave me an exhausted nod and moved around me. I felt her weight against my curved spine and for the first time in my life I did not resent being touched there.

Although we were thoroughly drenched, the heat hit us again like a blast from a furnace and I felt Constance stagger against me, even though my body had shielded her from the worst. The temptation to get out of there was almost irresistible, but I knew there was nowhere else to go and forced myself onwards. Unbelievably, the curtain material was already becoming dry and soon it would be burning too; I tried to move faster, but it was so difficult to see, for now it wasn't the smoke that was blinding me, but the flames themselves. I found my way mostly by instinct, praying I wouldn't stumble over anything lying on the floor – if I went down, then that would be it, I would never be able to get up again – and remembering the layout from my second glimpse into the storeroom.

I lifted my head for another peep, aware that we should be near the boxes, and at first I thought they were now completely ablaze, the flames were so fierce. I kept going though, Michael an inert bundle against my chest, Constance heavy against my back as her frail legs became weaker by the moment, and soon my bowed head bumped something. With relief, I realized it was the sloping ceiling itself and I risked another peek at the burning line of boxes.

The relief increased when I saw the dark hole behind them. It took only a couple of steps to reach the opening and I took them hastily, almost losing Constance in the process. She hurried to keep up and knocked into me when I stopped. The nearest boxes, those I could see, were smouldering at the back, but were not yet alight. Moving even closer, I bent down a little to peer deeper into the dark passage created between boxes and slanted ceiling.

It was filled with unsteady shadows, fire reflecting through gaps between boxes, but the tunnel stretched a long way, almost to the end of the room itself, and I blessed the person who liked to store things tidily. There was a red glow at the far end, but I could see no flames. With luck – and dear God, we really needed that luck – the conflagration had not yet spread to the whole of the attic/storeroom area.

Without wasting any time, I ducked into the opening, quickly realizing it would be better to crawl its length because smoke filled the upper section. Constance, still right behind, understood my intention and dropped to her knees too. It was awkward holding Michael with one arm, the other against the floor, and I was wearying fast, but just the idea that we had a feasible goal kept me going. Half-way along, flames licked through a gap, but they had not quite gained a hold, and I was able to get by using the curtain as a shield. I waited for Constance and watched as she used the same tactic, but as she passed the narrow opening, flames shot through more strongly and the curtain she held caught fire. She quickly dropped it and scuttled on, joining me in the orange gloom. I couldn't see her face properly, but I could hear the raw grating of her breaths, each inhalation urgent and pained; my own gasps for breath did not sound much better.

'*Not much further,*' I managed to rasp.

She was too overcome to respond, so I moved on, the only thing I could do, hoping she would revive a little when we got to the window.

Both of us were dragging ourselves along the floor by the time we reached the end of the angled passageway, the heat and the smoke torturing our bodies. I was on my side holding Michael against my right rib cage as I emerged, sliding my body by pushing my feet and right arm against the floorboards. I snatched a look back to see if Constance was okay and saw that half the passageway was now in flames. I knelt and reached for her, pulling her out with one hand, before we both collapsed again and lay side by side, struggling for air, our chests heaving with the effort. But there was the window before us, the precious window, with feeble moonlight shining through. I would have wept if my ducts had had any fluid left; all I could give was a dry sob.

I figured we had maybe a couple of minutes left to get out, probably less. It was pointless even attempting to speak now, so I rose to my feet, my legs unsteady, the right one almost buckling beneath me, and reached down for Constance. She extended a shaking arm and I took hold of her wrist, pulling her upwards, but needing her to help if she were to stand. Unfortunately, she was unable to summon up the strength, so I dragged her by the wrist towards the moonlit window, too desperate to worry about hurting her, and too much in love with her to admit defeat.

I managed to pull her the short distance and she slumped against the wall, a frightened, depleted little thing, her flesh and robe blackened, her hair falling to her shoulders in matted, singed tresses. The warmth I felt had nothing to do with the fire at our backs, for it was within. I think at that stage it was the only thing that kept me going. I placed Michael by her side.

Straightening, and leaning one hand against the heated brick wall, I examined the window. And I almost broke when I saw it was solid, the kind that was never meant to open.

It was made up of many frames, the glass inside them thick with dirt, the moon outside a blurred, dim ball. But although it was wide and fairly deep, there were no sections that could be opened, no catches to unlock. I might have howled, but I didn't have the strength, nor did I have the spit.

It couldn't be. We couldn't have got this far to be trapped inside the roof itself.

A sudden crash – the floor caving in, something stored here toppling – made me flinch. Sparks and burning pieces flew towards me. Another crash followed the first and flames fanned out spreading around the triangled ceiling, washing towards our end of the room. The sudden shock jolted my senses.

What the fuck was I thinking? This was just glass and wood in front of me, the frames strong maybe, but not so strong that they couldn't be broken. I looked back into the room, shielding my eye from the blinding glare with a grubby, bloodied hand, and spotted the heavy metal drum almost immediately.

It was only yards away, but almost obscured by swirling smoke, and as I limped towards it, dodging around the separate fires springing up from the floor, I prayed it would be heavy, but not too heavy for me to lift. It was and it wasn't – it was heavy, but not too heavy for me to lift. I had no idea of what it had once contained – probably chemicals of some kind – nor did I care: I tipped it over and began rolling it back towards the window.

I could feel the heat from the floorboards through the soles of my shoes and I knew it wouldn't be long before the fire burst through to this end of the room, or the floor itself fell inwards. There were more flare-ups behind me, chemicals inside containers or flammable material caught by the heat, and glass bottles or jars shattered with sharp, explosive sounds, fragments hurtling through the air as deadly missiles. I felt one skim past my shoulder, tearing my shirt and grazing the skin; there was no pain though. Another smashed into the wall ahead of me, while yet another burst through one of the small panes in the window without breaking the glass completely, leaving a hole the size of a walnut, a corona of moon-silvered cracks around it. The top of my head was stinging and for a moment I thought my hair was on fire again, but when I clamped a hand to it, still rolling the drum towards the window with my other hand, I felt only singed, prickly tufts. Either the pain was just coming through, aggravated by the boiling heat, or I'd been too preoccupied, mind too busy on our survival, for me to notice until now. I ignored it – I was *still* too busy.

I saw that Constance had picked up Michael and was cradling him in her arms, holding the sheet around his face in a vain attempt to protect him from the worst of the heat. Her gaze was on me, watching my efforts with the drum, which kept rolling into obstacles on the floor, diverting it from a straight course, so that I had to keep correcting its direction; I could tell from her eyes that Constance expected to die.

If anything, the hopelessness in her expression made me even more determined – she had put her trust in me and I wasn't going to let her down. With a roar that was dry and painful, I lifted the metal drum, holding it by both ends, fingers wrapped round the rims, and raised it high over my head. Without pause I rushed at the window and hurled the drum at it with every last reserve of strength I had left.

The window broke spectacularly and glass fragments and wood splinters flew with the metal drum out into the moonlit night. Beautiful, fresh, reviving air swept in and I choked a cry of triumph as I rushed to the sill. I drew in great gasps of it, filling my scorched throat and lungs, drawing life back into myself, not even noticing the remaining glass fragments cutting into my hands. Unfortunately, the fresh air sweeping into the room also had a downside – it was fanning the flames behind me, giving them more power, helping them surge forward to claim us.

In desperation – *further* desperation – I poked my head through and twisted so that I could look upwards, towards the roof itself. I moaned – no, I think I wailed – when I saw there was no way we could reach it. I changed direction, looked down, hoping that the fire service might have arrived by now and that they had a ladder long enough to reach the top floor. But all I could see below was a broad expanse of black water, moonlight dappling on its surface, a kinetic pattern whose movement was caused by the flow of currents. Traffic moved swiftly along the road on the opposite bank, too far away to be alerted, headlights searching only into the darkness ahead. There were other lights in the distance, some alone, solitary houses in the blackness, others in clusters, villages whose gathered lights threw their glow into the sky. The lights of an aircraft drifted by high over my head and far in the distance was the great hazy glow over the city. All so normal, all so oblivious.

Only the river directly below seemed aware of the drama being played out, for it curved around PERFECT REST, almost touching the end of the queerly angled annexe, so close and so deep, its smooth gently rippling surface so soft, that it was almost calling me to jump.

It was a call I had to heed, an invitation I could not refuse. To stay would mean being burned alive. I ducked back inside the attic-room and once again the searing heat took my breath.

48

I'm not sure if we jumped from that window ledge, or if a blast or flare-up from behind threw us, I only remember being in terrifying freefall, our clothes on fire, Michael wrapped tight in my arms, Constance falling beside me. I know I yelled all the way down, but I don't recall hearing anything from Constance. Maybe I was yelling too loudly myself.

We dropped for a very long time, it seemed to me, before hitting the river with an almighty splash, and plunging into its depths. The shock and the terrible chill of the water caused my mouth to snap open, so that air I had tried to suck in after the yell bubbled from me and then the Thames poured in. I managed to keep my arms around Michael's little body as I kicked out for the surface. There was a great milky ceiling above, but it took a long time to reach it and I feared my lungs would burst before I did so.

I made it though, breaking through to pure moonlight with a lot of splashing and a great deal of heaving for breath. You might have thought that the cold and the shock would have revived me, but I really was running on empty by now, the last dregs of energy totally gone. I immediately sank again with my burden.

Everything was a dark murky grey around me, vignetting to a deep black the further I went down. For one brief moment, I thought I saw Constance floating nearby, her small, pale body slowly revolving in the water, arms outstretched. I tried to grab one of those arms, but it eluded me and she drifted away, stolen by a current, becoming smaller and smaller until swallowed up by the murk. I panicked, thrashing around, using up strength I didn't think I had. I sank even further into the depths and wondered why I had so foolishly worried whether the river was deep enough to take our fall. I could have laughed, because drowning didn't necessarily mean you lost your sense of humour.

I sank deeper and deeper and began to fancy that we had leapt into an ocean (I didn't realize that I was being pushed by the currents and my descent was not straight down; nor did I realize that all sense of time was gone anyway). Michael had become more than an encumbrance: he was now a deadweight in my arms. If I let go I might just be able to make it, might just be able to thrash my way to the riverbank. He was probably dead by now anyway – how would his little body take such punishment? A short while ago, he appeared to have stopped breathing altogether and there had been no movement from him for some time. God, it was tempting. I wanted to live, my life had not all been misery; I had good friends, a good business – and despite adversity, I had *learned* to enjoy most of my time in this world. I didn't want to give it all up, it was too precious; despite the hard parts, life was good. How many times had I had to make this kind of decision that day? I'd lost count. But how many times could a person be tested in this way? Hadn't I earned the right by now to consider myself, my own self-preservation? My head was becoming light. The need for air was becoming less.

I clung to Michael.

It seemed to be just the muted sound of rushing water at first, but as it drew closer, became more distinct, I knew it was the familiar flapping of hundreds of wings, but *angels'* wings, not that of birds, and I was very, very pleased to hear them. So this is what it's like when your time comes. Not bad, not bad at all. Kind of peaceful, in fact. No pain. It was like that delicious moment just between consciousness and sleep, the bad things of the day dissolving, the mind entering its rest period, where dreams were merely the recreation and gone within seconds, or minutes, brain cells shutting down for a while. I waited to see the bright lights they talk about, the long dark tunnel, that radiance waiting for you at its end. But I didn't get that – not yet, at any rate. No, I got the review, the flashbacks, the retrospection – perhaps re-evaluation – people who have nearly died talk about. Only it wasn't my life that played out before me, it belonged to the movie star, the Hollywood screen idol of the Thirties and Forties, the golden age of film, whose charm and magnificent looks had earned him fame and fortune, the bastard who was making his comeback as a reflection in a mirror with me as the one-man audience. He grinned at me and it was a wonderful grin on a wonderful face: deep, lustrous eyes, classically straight nose, cleft chin. He was all the things I was not, his figure tall, body powerful, his movement grace-ful, and his charm seductive; but he was a man with terrible, dark secrets and, as his life played out before me – oddly in monochrome, black and white, the celluloid medium of his era – these secrets were revealed. I sank and settled in for the performance.

In the early days of his career, friends and even associates had lent him money, helped him survive those first gruelling years most actors have to go through before success (though not necessarily acclaim) comes their way, and those same friends and associates were soon forgotten after he had begun to make headway in Tinseltown. Yet he put his name to numerous good causes and charities, anything in fact that wouldn't take money from his own pocket. He despised any actor who had achieved more than he – Grant, Bogart, Flynn, Gable, Cooper, the two Jimmys, Cagney and Stewart – although, naturally, he fawned on them in their presence, and he hated anybody that had achieved as much as he. Hated them, loathed them, and was always ready with a juicy snippet of gossip whenever the showbiz columnists and broadcasters, Hopper and Parsons, gave him a call, provided his own name wasn't mentioned as the source.

Yet he wasn't all bad. His work for charities was impressive, even if he did not donate financially (but then, his time could be considered donation enough) and he often steered young actors and actresses (particularly the latter) in the right direction as far as their careers were concerned (although often in the *wrong* direction as far as their private lives were concerned), more than once having a word in a studio boss's ear regarding casting for his own movies, commending the talents of a new young starlet. When he was in his movie-making prime, a major star for a major studio, and the Japanese had invaded Pearl Harbor, he was one of the first Hollywood legends to volunteer for military service. Unfortunately, turned down for active duty because of a mysterious ear ailment (all right, it was discovered by the studio doctor the day before their star was due his army medical), he nevertheless had worked ceaselessly making personal appearances to promote the sale of War Bonds and had even flown into dangerous territories to entertain the troops and boost their morale. While on location in Brazil he had met an eleven-year-old native boy who was in danger of losing his eyesight permanently because of a dangerous but not incurable condition; at his own expense the star had the boy flown to New York where one of the city's finest surgeons had performed a successful operation to correct the problem (again, wonderful publicity for the benefactor, but no less of a good deed for that). So he was complex, this legendary actor, but not entirely bad.

However, there were few greys or whites when it came to his sexual activities: they were mostly all black.

When it seemed likely that he would be indicted for having unlawful sex with two minors, a couple of under-aged teenage girls who had followed him from the studio one afternoon, money had changed hands so that the girls' parents, the investigating detective, and a certain elderly

District Attorney, who was busy building his own nest for imminent retirement, were satisfied that nothing truly grievous had taken place – a silly piece of childish horseplay was all that was involved – and the charge of statutory rape was dropped. When only a few months later he *was* charged with proper rape, the character of the other party, a young would-be actress who managed to survive the aspiring actors' system by waitressing in a cheap but 'fashionable' diner six days a week, was so besmirched by the star's legal team, that the case was thrown out of court. (And the would-be actress never did get a job in the movies after that. Eventually, disillusioned, she moved back to the little town of Hope – there's irony for you – in Arkansas, married her high-school sweetheart, and together they raised the money to open up their own less-'fashionable' diner in the larger, nearby town of Little Rock. At the age of forty-two – I saw all this, and other such episodes, as a kind of subtextual subplot to the actor's story, by the way – she blew her brains out with her husband's .357 Magnum – a sledge hammer to crack a nut, you might say – while he was out carousing with yet another later-edition sweetheart.) There were countless similar incidents in the screen idol's life that never reached court and, amazingly, I had a view of them all. They were sickening, amoral at best, immoral at worst, vile and vicious at their basest, but far too many to recount here.

He had made it his business to delve into the skeleton cupboards of those equally famous – actors, directors, producers, writers, even plastic surgeons, whose newly discovered skills were the marvel of Hollywood, most of whom had a dark secret or two hidden away somewhere – garnering any misdeed or offence they might have committed during their lifetime, no matter how petty or grand the misdemeanour, anything he could use for blackmail when it might be advantageous to himself.

It was horrible, but kind of cosy too. I felt comfortably warm and the feeling was not unpleasant. Strangely, I did not judge this man and his actions – I don't think that was the idea – but I was beginning to pity him.

He was wicked, but not completely, for he had helped others. Unfortunately, he had betrayed many more. He had loved many, but never as much as he had loved himself; and never enough to remain true to them. He had done terrible things, but he had also inspired and made millions of ordinary men and women happy for a little while. He had caused deaths, but never intentionally and certainly not by his own hand.

I saw the first woman he had married – actually 'witnessed' the ceremony – a pretty young starlet, who cherished and adored him, a girl who had joined in his excesses merely to please him, who was nervous of those who flocked around him, both male and female, all vying with each other in giving him the attention he craved and, of course, felt entitled to. And 'attention' often meant 'sex'. She concluded that if she joined him in *all* recreation, then she would always be part of every aspect of his life. With him, she indulged in, and sometimes was even a catalyst to, activities she once would have abhorred and been shamed by: the wild parties, the drugs, the alcohol, even the gambling – was part of it all. More than once, when his lecherous eye fell upon yet another pretty girl, she would be part of the seduction. And always part of the outcome, the lovemaking itself. She did everything to keep him happy and content with her, and their marriage lasted beyond all expectation – beyond the expectation of the Hollywood crowd that is, of those who knew him. But naturally, there was a price to pay, for eventually she, herself, became corrupted. She began to enjoy the extremes, the deviation, the threesomes, the foursomes, the *orgies*, and then back to the twosomes, but not with him or another male (although that sometimes sufficed), but with her and another her, secret liaisons that he did not know of. She loved the parties and the drugs and liquor, she adored the thrill of winning or even losing at the track – there were always plenty more bucks to throw away. But most importantly, she loved him, she still loved him.

Such excesses, however, have the constant and inevitable consequence of jading the appetite: the habit becomes stronger, the desire more demanding and eventually less satiable (and I'm not referring *only* to drugs here). She was no exception to the rule (and nor was he, for that matter, only he was more enduring). She started to drink *too* much, she took *too* many drugs (that already-nifty dragon always becomes more fleet of foot, so the chase becomes harder and harder), she lost *too* much money at the racetrack. And worst of all for her, because its effect was on *him*, she began to lose her looks, her vivacity began to fade, her sparkle to dim. But good fortune never entirely leaves a person's life, even if at times that seems to be the case: she fell pregnant.

She had prayed day and night for just this event, for she felt a child would affirm their relationship, perhaps be a fresh start for them both, a chance to reappraise their own lives, the marriage itself, and to turn it into something better. To her surprise and delight, her husband loved the idea of becoming a father, a brand new role for him that could only enhance his image for his millions of fans. He would be able to play the doting father and the public would see the tender side of his nature: he would be the ideal parent of an ideal moppet in an ideal marriage to an ideal woman. It was perfect, precisely the right time for such a career move, for the new breed of scandal magazines were beginning to publish stories on the shenanigans of movie stars, politicians and other prominent socialites, and his own dubious activities increasingly were catching their attention. Long gone were the indulgent publications whose purpose was mainly to follow the public relations line dictated by the big studios themselves: the public wanted more for its money these days, and more meant *interesting* stories, the kind at which they could shake their heads and tut-tut. Being the father of a little boy or girl, either one would do, would suit the more mature roles he was aiming for and the ageing process, itself, was demanding, so no wonder he was jubilant.

Only it didn't go as planned. It was a difficult, prolonged birth and the baby boy who was born was not quite right. In fact, he was considerably not right, a misshapen little thing with an abnormally large head and eyes that seemed pressured from behind, for they bulged alarmingly. The couple were informed by one of LA's finest and most highly-paid obstetricians that the boy would never be normal and that as he grew, the malformations would become ever more exaggerated: his intelligence would never become more than that of a five- or six-year-old's. The mother was devastated, the father mortified and shamed. How could he beget something like *that*? What would the millions of fans worldwide think of him? How would they ever accept that their screen idol, who was once voted the world's most beautiful male, could father a monster? His emotions swiftly turned to rage, which he took out on his wife, blaming her for giving birth to a mongoloid, that nothing so imperfect could be a product of his seed. He blamed her entirely, citing the drugs and alcohol abuse as accessories to the crime (never admitting, especially to himself, the hypocrisy of the accusation). The baby was never to be shown to the public – my God, what would the sight of it do for *his* image? The baby would have to be put into care – discreetly, of course. There were institutions who knew how to cope with children and infants with such disabilities. Never – *never* – was it (he called the child 'it' from the first moment) to bear his name. It was an abomination to him, a freak best put on one side and forgotten. Better yet, he had suggested, it might be preferable, and even more humane, for the boy to meet with an accident. Perhaps a fall on its head, a mishap in the bathtub . . . These things were never meant to live long anyway. If it died of asphyxiation one night, choked in its sleep, then who would know it wasn't a natural result of its condition ... ? After all, what were a few moments' suffering against a lifetime's?

She pleaded with him, she begged, for no matter how the baby looked, no matter how feeble his brain, he was theirs, he belonged to them, he was their flesh and blood. The 'flesh and blood' declaration incensed the actor even more and he informed her that if she did not get rid of the baby herself, then he would do so, and she would be abandoned along with it.

That was why, in a bewildered, drunken and drugged state, she had smothered her baby with a silk pillow. And even though she had done this for her husband and so that she might remain his wife, the actor had informed the police. Rather than be tried for infanticide, more strings were pulled and more money changed hands, and she was presented to the judge at the closed hearing as a repentant murderess, whose mind had been unbalanced by years of drug and alcohol abuse, and who had finally succumbed to total madness when her longed-for child had been born mentally deficient and physically abnormal. The judge was sympathetic and ordered her to be committed to a mental institution (as he had been bribed to do) where her addictions could be dealt with and, hopefully, her madness cured. She had been in the asylum only five days when she managed to hang herself by tying the belt of her robe around the wall fitting of a shower-head, the other end around her neck, and deliberately bending her knees so that her feet were off the porcelain floor-basin. It must have taken extraordinary willpower to slowly choke herself in that way but, such was her despair and self-hatred, she managed.

The actor publicly grieved for his lost son and now for his dearly beloved lost wife (some would say, those who knew him only too well, that he grieved magnificently), whose remorse over the killing of her own son had led to the suicide, and the world grieved with him. If there had been

Oscars for insincerity, then he would have had a mantelshelf full of them. He blamed himself, he told the world. If only he had known the extent of her sorrow, then perhaps he might have saved her. He still loved her, you see, even though she had been responsible for the tragedy of his beautifully perfect baby son's death. Women wept for him, men cleared their throats as if to waylay a sob.

There were many other grave and even mortal sins on the screen idol's life, although none quite as grievous. Blackmailing business associates over their supposedly secret transgressions, sexual or fiscal (embezzlement was *so* common among the film fraternity, where money was power and power tended to corrupt), threatening to inform the police, media, shareholders or wife, whatever was appropriate (sometimes all of them jointly), was par for the course for him; promising the latest paramour the earth and leaving them only with bitter regrets was a way of life; stealing of important roles in major movies already won by fellow actors – often good friends – by sly, underhand, behind-the-scenes dealings was merely part of the Hollywood game; having certain people 'reprimanded' by two hulking bruisers he kept on permanent retainer for having the effrontery to insult or slight him was normal practice as far as he was concerned. And then there was the business of the two nuns from the order of the Poor Sisters of Nazareth, but you don't need to know about that; suffice to say that one went to jail, while the other was sent by her Church to a remote mission in the Congo where she eventually died of severe blackwater fever. Our actor's name was never even mentioned in connection with the scandal.

I watched it all and I was horrified and contrary to the politically correct edict of the era we live in, I was *very* judgemental. Because I was judging *myself*.

I understood it all now. I knew why I was here, why I had been born so deformed. And I understood what had driven me to liberate these others, these other people who had been cursed (or tested?) with afflictions far worse than mine. I understood the tests I had been put through, most particularly in these last few days, was suddenly aware of their meaning and their value. I had a vague recollection of that other-world place, the one we call Hell for want of a better name. I even recalled the 'conversation' I'd had with the entities I called Angel 1 and Angel 2, and their God-sent (literally) proposition. I now knew of my previous life, because it had just been replayed to me almost as if I were sitting in some watery but comfortable viewing theatre, the screen itself inside my own head, inside my mind.

I had been that screen idol, the toast of Tinseltown, perfect in physique, countenance and manner, but oh so imperfect in spirit and conscience. The actor was me and I was he. I had been reborn the very antithesis of what I once was: unsightly, malformed, a *freak*. But it was a new opportunity, a chance to redeem myself, the person I had been. I suffered so that others would no longer have to, and now I was to die for them.

I was glad, I was exhilarated, because the hard part of dying, the painful part, the bit where you resisted, was over for me, and my only hope was that I'd done enough to redeem myself.

Yet another thing I understood was that I'd been guided all along, and I don't mean by the clairvoyant, nor by the dreams and the whispers of the others themselves. My guide had been of a much higher order; the highest Order of all, I guess you might say. Intuitions, motivations, those little 'insights' – all had stemmed from that one source – sorry, Source. As I continued to sink deeper into those murky waters, my heart, my spirit, soared.

There were just two things wrong, though. First, I still carried Michael in my arms and even though I could not be sure he was alive – and the odds seemed against it – if he were, then he had the right to experience a better existence that he'd had before. I was aware that the experience could only ever be limited, but who could tell the joy someone with such harsh disability might feel under more benevolent circumstances and environment? And who of us could ever know the purpose of his confined but sentient life?

Second, I had found Constance and she meant more to me than any spiritual afterlife. A kind of blasphemy, I know, but that's the God's honest truth of it. You have to remember, this was the reciprocal love I'd been denied all my life.

I started to kick for the surface again and all pain and fear and suffocation returned with a 'how-dare-you-resist-the-inevitable?' kind of vengeance. It wasn't easy with Michael clutched to my chest, but I was able to use one arm, and my legs – even the gimpy one – did their bit. Fresh panic had something to do with it, I'm sure, the idea of never seeing Constance again unbearable, and I broke through to the surface sooner than I'd thought possible. I vomited water, then sucked air, then vomited more water, repeating the process, until I gained more control. I saw the riverbank, surprisingly close, figures running alongside of it, keeping pace and pointing to me, calling my name. Beyond them, further back upriver I saw the burning building that was PERFECT REST, blue flashing lights, dark figures milling about, running around, great jets of water lit by moonlight rearing up the higher reaches of the building. I heard distant sirens, growing louder as more fire engines, ambulances and police cars arrived; I heard raised voices, shouts, occasional cries. I felt a new uncomfortable coldness after the cosy kind I just left and I felt pain, in my arms, my legs, and especially around my scalp so that I wondered if my hair was still on fire. Life itself hit me, and it was harsh and unpleasant and confusing. As they say – it was a bitch.

Someone jumped in the water near me, quickly joined by another. Then hands were grabbing me, hauling me towards the riverbank, and I realized it was my friends, my *new* friends – those 'others' who had never seen a river before, at least, not in the *wet*, as it were – who had formed a chain in the shallows so that they could pull me to the grassy bank. Someone strong relieved me of my burden and I was dragged from the water. I lay on my front and coughed river, feeling fists thumping my back, the blows avoiding my hump. Among all the voices and the distant clamour, I heard a surprised curse and saw someone kneeling next to Michael. Whoever it was – and I now know it was a paramedic – started pushing at the little, limbless body's chest and I prayed he or she would not be too squeamish to give the kiss-of-life. Then legs and kneeling bodies obscured my view and I thought I heard Louise's voice calling to me. I could only distinguish one word though. It was a name and it came back again and again.

'. . . Constance . . . Constance . . .'

My mind drifted away and my body followed willingly.

49

They found Constance's naked body a couple of miles down-stream the following day and my first thought, when they told me, was how she would have hated being exposed to strangers like that, her robe torn away by the currents, her little crooked figure and limbs revealed to all, her dignity gone along with her life. Then the shock kicked in and I thought I'd lose my mind.

The grief was unbearable, but I refused their sedatives and their counselling; I refused their meaningless condolences and their compassion. In fact, I refused contact with anyone for a while and it was left to Ida and Philo to carry on the business until another shock kicked my butt into gear again. Etta was terrific throughout my black time of mourning, keeping an eye on my employees and helping them out when things got tricky. Louise became a good friend, but it was a stretch before I could accept her comfort; and she never bothered me with all that psychic stuff although, truth be told, I was more receptive to it after everything that had happened.

Anyway, it's all okay now. Sure, the heartache is still there, but I've learned to accept everything – and I mean *everything*, even the cruel irony of refusing to die in those dirty waters because I wanted to be with Constance – that's been thrown at me during my lifetime and anything yet to come. You see, for me it's only a little while longer anyway.

Those headaches I'd been getting more and more frequently were not the result of too much drink or drugs (both of which I've given up completely nowadays because life itself is fun enough without either false-enhancement or desensitization – trust me on this), but from something even more sinister. I'd not only burnt my scalp during my adventures at PERFECT REST, but somewhere along the way I'd taken a knock to the head which had left a sizeable bump and when they had taken me to hospital to get my various cuts, bruises, and burns attended to, not to mention an overnight observation period because of the near-drowning, they had X-rayed my skull to check for fractures. Well, there weren't any, but what they did find was a tumour eating into my brain.

It's pretty big and it's inoperable (at least, if they did try to remove it and I survived the process, there's a ninety-eight per cent chance I'd be left in a vegetative state, odds I'm none too happy about). The doctors tell me I've got two or three months left to live, and I couldn't be more pleased.

I understand, you see, that I'd only been given this second go at life to redeem myself for those misdemeanours first time round and now that I've done so, my time is up. Why couldn't I have just drowned after leaping from that high window? Well, Michael's life was still in my hands (or in my arms), wasn't it? And in a way, so was the fate of my river rescuers and new-found friends – someone had to make sure they were not hidden away again by the authorities. It's okay though: a deal is a deal and now it's been done properly. Besides, I want to see Constance again, and the sooner the better.

At present, my friends, the 'others', are residing in a lovely manor house, in a remote, and equally lovely, part of the country. This time they are being well taken care of by the authorities – the public, ably kept informed by the media, make sure of that. People do care, you know, even though at times it appears the opposite is true. None of the other 'others', incidentally, survived the fire, which is probably just as well, for no amount of care and attention could have made their lives tolerable. Like me, Michael hasn't long for this world either. He knows this, even if the medics don't, and he told me – I've become quite adept at picking up his thoughts when I go for visits. And by the way, Michael is Shelly Ripstone's long-lost son. The tattoos were the clues, you see: Leonard Wisbeech registered each 'specimen' with their birth dates, and Michael's was 080581 – 8 May 1981, the precise date that Shelly gave birth. They were both DNA tested and the match was perfect. Even yet another cruel irony though, is that my ex-client wants nothing to do with her son. In fact, on the one occasion she was taken to see him, she was physically sick. Michael repulsed her and no amount of money left by her late husband would make her accept him. She said she never wanted to see 'it' again, and I think she'll stick to her word. Michael's got over it, but it took a while.

Me? I'm enjoying the short time I have left. When the pain eventually gets too bad, then that's when I'll use drugs again, but only those prescribed by the medics. I'll still nervous of death, of course, but I'm no longer afraid. I've glimpsed it, remember?

Besides, I've got someone waiting.

Metaphorically speaking, of course.

END NOTE

This story is based on a true incident that occurred in a certain London children's hospital some years ago and was related to me by the now elderly person involved. At least two of the main protagonists are known to me personally (one, alas, now deceased) and, lest I be accused of possessing an inordinately warped imagination, I should point out that most of the 'others' described herein are taken from actual medical case histories. I sincerely hope you have been disturbed.

JAMES HERBERT
London, 1999